twice the

Temptation

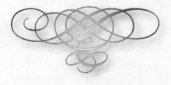

twice the

Temptation

Francis Ray

ST. MARTIN'S GRIFFIN
New York

TWICE THE TEMPTATION.

The Awakening. Copyright © 1999 by Francis Ray.
A Matter of Trust. Copyright © 2000 by Francis Ray.
Sweet Temptation. Copyright © 2000 by Francis Ray.
Southern Comfort. Copyright © 2001 by Francis Ray.
The Blind Date. Copyright © 2004 by Francis Ray.

All rights reserved. Printed in the United States of America. For information, address St. Martin's Press, 175 Fifth Avenue, New York, N.Y. 10010.

www.stmartins.com

ISBN 978-0-312-61430-0

First Edition: June 2011

10 9 8 7 6 5 4 3 2 1

AUTHOR'S NOTE

I'm very excited and thankful that for the first time St. Martin's Press is putting five of my previously published novellas into one beautiful collection. Revisiting the stories brought back lots of great memories. In each I wanted to create a heroine who readers could admire and root for, and a hero to fall in love with. I hope I've done my job, and that you'll enjoy reading each as much as I enjoyed writing them for very special readers just like you.

All the best,
Francis Ray

To my extraordinary and innovative editor,
Monique Patterson

ACKNOWLEDGMENTS

William H. Ray and McClinton Radford Jr., for their wide range of knowledge and unwavering support. You never failed to come up with the right answers. I love you and will miss you always.

CONTENTS

the

Awakening

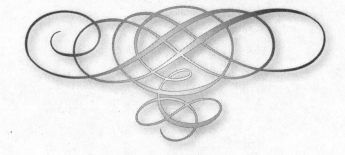

ONE

Gabe Jackson didn't like rushing and he didn't like being late. Thanks to the message he'd listened to an hour ago on his answering machine from Shelton, his younger brother, Gabe was both. And in one of the worst possible places—the crowded concourse of Newark Airport. Hurrying around a slow-moving family, Gabe passed Gate 17. Gate 23 was his destination.

A glance at his Rolex told him Flight 675 from Atlanta, Georgia, had landed ten minutes ago. There was no guarantee that Jessica Ames would still be waiting at the gate despite Shelton's instructions to meet her there.

Gabe blew out a disgusted sigh. Although he hadn't dated in months, it had been his experience that women generally did what they wanted, and although they could keep you waiting for hours, if the man were a single minute late, he'd have hell to pay. He was now eleven and counting.

He hurried past Gate 20, thinking it was a good thing he kept in shape by jogging every morning. The things he did for his only sibling.

Gabe certainly could have thought of a more pleasant way to meet his future sister-in-law for the first time. He hoped she wasn't snooty. More than a few of the rich young women he had met thought the world should bow at their well-shod feet.

Whatever the outcome of their meeting, he'd have more of a handle on why Shelton had given him that strange answer when Gabe asked when he had found time to fall in love or court a woman with his busy schedule.

Gate 23. Gabe quickly scanned the waiting area and saw only one woman alone. Her slim arms were wrapped tightly around her waist, and her eyes searched the crowd as anxiously as his did. His gaze skimmed past her, dismissing her completely.

Shelton liked his women sexy, elegant, and vibrant. The drab-looking woman had on a mud-brown suit that did nothing for her smooth, almond complexion. In fact, if she hadn't been standing where the sunlight poured through the windows on an unusually sunny October day in New Jersey, or hadn't looked so tense, he might not have noticed her at all. Talk about someone blending into the wall.

As seconds passed, Gabe's hope that Jessica Ames had patiently waited plummeted. Muttering under his breath, he turned to leave.

For some odd reason his gaze went back to the nondescript woman in brown. She was watching him, her lower lip tucked between her teeth. The moment he met her gaze, she glanced away in obvious embarrassment.

It had been so long since Gabe had encountered a shy woman that he simply stared. From the Louis Vuitton case at her feet, her handbag by the same designer, the long, brown cashmere coat slung carelessly on the back of a seat, it appeared she wasn't hurting for money.

Although someone should have told her that brown wasn't her color. Not even his mother wore deep pleated skirts to mid-calf. And her French roll-styled hair was definitely for a much older woman.

Poor thing, he thought. She must be waiting for someone to pick her up. She had apparently stayed put, whereas Jessica Ames had taken off to God knows where. He wasn't looking forward to tracking her down. Knowing he didn't have a choice, he went to find a phone to have her paged.

A short distance away, his steps slowed, then stopped completely as he recalled Shelton's answer to his question. "Some women don't require as much to woo and win, especially when there are other considerations and compensations to be considered."

Whirling, Gabe rushed back to Gate 23. The woman in brown hadn't moved. She waited, just as Shelton had said she would.

Gabe's certainty that she was Jessica Ames grew with each heartbeat, and so did his apprehension. He didn't like to think his brother was so cruel or so callous as to hurt any woman, but particularly one who seemed so vulnerable or ill-equipped to bounce back.

Gabe was a realist and he knew some people, unlike his devoted parents, married for reasons other than love, but he couldn't help wondering if she knew how Shelton felt or if he had pulled a fast one. It wasn't difficult to imagine his handsome, smooth-talking brother getting one over on this lusterless woman.

Although she wasn't Shelton's type, she had something else to attract his ambitious brother. If this was Jessica Ames, her father was senior partner of the prestigious Ames & Koch law firm based in Atlanta that he worked for. And Shelton wanted to become a full partner.

Although he loved his brother, who was five years younger, Gabe wasn't blind to his many faults. He was a climber, in society and business. He wanted to succeed and he was well on his way to doing so by being in charge of opening a new branch of the firm in New York. If Gabe didn't miss his guess, the woman standing several feet away was an integral part of Shelton's plan in obtaining that partnership.

Besides, Gabe thought, if Shelton really loved her, he'd have been there to meet her after six weeks' absence. He'd kiss her breathless, then whisk her off someplace where they could be alone. He wouldn't have been so thoughtless as to leave a message on Gabe's answering machine, then be out of his office and unavailable. It was almost as if she were an afterthought.

Same old Shelton. Always thinking what he had to do or say

was more important than what anyone else did. He couldn't have chosen a better career than corporate law. He'd do well swimming with the sharks. Gabe had once swum the same dangerous waters until he took a hard look at his life and hadn't liked what he saw.

Pushing away the memory, he walked up to the woman. All he could hope for was that she knew what she was letting herself in for. "Excuse me, are you Jessica Ames?"

She jerked her head toward him, her eyes widening. He was surprised at how beautiful they were despite being rimmed by the ugliest brown frames he had ever seen. Obviously she had noticed him watching her before and she took a hesitant step back.

Belatedly Gabe remembered the aviator shades he had forgotten to remove, and slipped them on top of his head.

There wasn't much else he could do to reassure her. The closely cropped beard and mustache, his mother was fond of telling him, made him look like a hoodlum.

He smiled in reassurance. "Sorry, I didn't mean to startle you. I'm Gabe Jackson, Shelton's brother. He couldn't make it."

Jessica glanced from the large, blunt-tipped fingers on the hand extended toward her, then back to the broad-shouldered mocha-skinned man in front of her. He wore a gently worn black leather bomber jacket, paint-splattered jeans, and a smile that probably let him get away with anything he wanted.

He looked wholly dangerous in a way only a woman could understand. It didn't take much imagination on her part to see him astride a big motorcycle, his hands gripping the handlebars as he revved the motor, daring fate, daring a woman to climb on behind him.

He frowned, deepening the grooves in his forehead. "You are Jessica Ames, aren't you?"

Hastily she extended her hand. It wasn't like her to be so whimsical. "Yes. I'm sorry. It's just that I was expecting Shelton, and you don't look anything like him."

The grin returned. White teeth flashed in his darkly handsome face. "So he likes to point out." He reached for her train case. "I know this isn't all you brought for two weeks in New York."

Picking up her long coat, she tried to smile, hoping he didn't remember her staring at him. At least he couldn't possibly know she had been speculating on the color of his eyes. Black, deep and velvet and as lethal as the rest of him. "The rest of my luggage is at baggage claim."

"For a while I thought you might be there, too, or wandering around the airport."

She shook her head. "No matter how much I travel, airports tend to make me nervous. That's why I wanted to meet Shelton at Newark Airport, since passengers coming into LaGuardia or Kennedy can only be met by the public at the baggage claim area."

"Smart thinking." Gabe's hand closed lightly over her elbow. "Let's go get the rest of your luggage."

She fell into step beside him, noting he was several inches taller than Shelton and broader, but moved with an easy strength in paint-splattered athletic shoes. Shelton favored Bally as his footwear of choice. "Is Shelton meeting me at my aunt's apartment?"

Gabe assisted her onto the gliding steps before answering. "Afraid not. He'll be tied up until late tonight."

"Oh," she answered and looked away.

Gabe glanced down at the slender woman by his side. She had to be unhappy that Shelton wasn't anxious to see her. "He's pretty busy opening the new office."

"I know. My father is quite proud of him."

"How about you?"

Her head came up, surprise clearly evident on her face, as if she hadn't expected the question. "Of course."

Gabe nodded. "You just wish it didn't keep him away from you so much."

She focused ahead. "Shelton's work is very important to him."

It was on the tip of Gabe's tongue to ask if she was important to Shelton when they reached the end of the walkway. Continuing to the baggage claim area, it occurred to him that Jessica didn't act like a woman anxious to see her man. From the stiffness of her body next to his he knew she was still tense, and for some reason he didn't think it was totally due to the busy airport.

With every piece of Louis Vuitton luggage Gabe pulled off the conveyor, Jessica's irritation and embarrassment grew. She had tried to tell her mother that she didn't need that much, but Henrietta Ames had been insistent. She even had the maid include Jessica's makeup case, which she hadn't opened in months.

Her mother wanted to make sure she was prepared when Shelton took her out. Jessica had tried to tell her that wasn't likely to happen.

She knew Shelton's priority was opening the new branch of the law firm in New York. His interest in Jessica had been fleeting at best. He had been kind enough to take her out several times during the two months he was in Atlanta, but it hadn't even begun to get serious.

Her parents believed differently. All they thought she had to do was accept Shelton's invitation to come to New York, and she'd have a big diamond engagement ring on her finger when she returned home.

Shelton might be "fond" of her, as he often told her parents, but his heart belonged to the law office. She knew that. Most of what he talked about when they were together was the law firm and how much he admired her father. It was embarrassing the way her parents started throwing hints about what a fine catch he was. As if he were the last chance for their dull only child to snag a man.

Jessica was aware she wasn't attractive or athletic, and no matter what she wore, she tended to look dowdy. She had reconciled herself to that long ago. She didn't mind being nondescript or being by herself. She was used to both.

She valued her work at the women's shelter, and in January she was returning to graduate school to work on her Master's in Education with an emphasis on counseling. She knew where she was going and it didn't include marrying someone who was "fond" of her, no matter what pressure her parents put on her.

Reminding her mother that Shelton's calls had been infrequent and hurried since he returned to New York hadn't dimmed her hopes of an engagement. She had simply had the maid take more clothes out of the closet. The wife of a corporate lawyer had to understand that business sometimes had to come first, but that in no way meant he didn't love his wife and family.

Jessica hadn't said another word. To do so would have shown her own doubts about how much her father loved his family. If that was how love was shown, she wanted no part of it. Only no one was listening.

"Five pieces. I'd say you came prepared," Gabe told her.

Jessica came out of her musing and flushed. If anyone knew how little Shelton thought of her or how unnecessary the mountain of baggage was, it was the man standing easily in front of her, his hands on his trim waist, a teasing smile on his mobile lips. She moistened her own.

There was no reason for her to notice his mouth. "You've been very kind. I can get a skycap and take care of things from here. Thank you."

Gabe stared at the small hand extended toward his, noted the unpolished oval nails, then lifted his gaze to Jessica's plain face. The smile was forced. "I hope you aren't going to insult me by suggesting I leave you."

Her hand wavered. "You must be busy."

"Not that busy." The moment the words were out of his mouth, hers tightened. "I'm self-employed. I make my own schedule," he quickly explained.

"Need any help with those bags?" asked a hopeful skycap, his hand wrapped around the handle of a luggage carrier.

"Thanks," Gabe said, grateful for the intervention, and he took

Jessica's extended hand. He accepted the slight leap in his pulse rate due to nerves, and the slight jerk in her hand due to the same thing.

She lifted those large, solemn brown eyes to him. "I don't want to be a nuisance. I don't mind renting a car or grabbing a cab to Manhattan."

"I do. Driving in New York takes skill, nerve, and practice. A weekday is no time to start developing any of those. And taking a cab unless necessary is sheer lunacy," Gabe said, leading her toward the exit, wondering where the crazy urge to hug her to him and reassure her that she wasn't a bother had come from.

"I may have been wrong about something," Jessica said, following him out the door.

"What?"

"You and Shelton are alike in some ways."

Gabe felt annoyance sweep through him, and without slowing his stride, glanced down at her. There was no way he'd stoop to what his baby brother was planning to do, or treat a woman the way he had. "How?"

"Once you make up your mind about something, nothing else matters."

Gabe simply kept walking. He didn't think she had given him a compliment.

TWO

Jessica hadn't meant to anger Gabe. But one look at the tight set of his mouth and she knew she had.

She was almost certain it wasn't because he had forgotten his trunk was full and he and the skycap were having a difficult time putting her luggage in the backseat of his Mercedes. She thought it more likely had something to do with her comparison of him to Shelton.

At the time she had thought she was stating the truth. Now, watching him help the skycap instead of standing back and deeming the task menial and beneath him as her father or his associates would have done, she wasn't so sure. In any case, she absolutely hated people being upset with her and she usually bent over backward to avoid it from happening. That particular attribute had gotten her into her present situation.

The back door of the car slammed. "What's bothering you now?"

She frowned. "What are you talking about?"

He nodded toward her purse. "You're clutching it."

Surprised that he had paid that much attention to her, she felt even more miserable. All he had been was kind to her and she had hurt his feelings. "You're very astute."

"A man in my business has to be," he said, and opened the passenger door.

"What business is that?" she asked, hoping they could start over.

"Shelton didn't tell you?"

She shrugged slim shoulders. "He talked mostly about the law firm."

"Figures." Closing the door, Gabe walked back to the trunk and opened it. "Please come here."

Curious, she watched his head disappear behind the raised trunk and did as he instructed. She was still looking at him when he gestured toward the open trunk.

"That is what I do."

Jessica turned. A soft gasp of wonder slipped unnoticed past her lips. Without conscious thought, she moved closer to the oil painting of a black woman in a blue silk robe, her slender body bent over that of a smiling chubby baby in a wooden cradle. The baby's fingers were curled around one of the woman's. The picture was one of complete love.

"You did this?" she asked, her finger gently touching the clasped hand of mother and child on the canvas.

Many people had admired Gabe's work before, but no one's reaction had affected him more deeply. "Yes."

She glanced back up at him, her eyes shining with moisture, her face soft. "How does it feel to create something so beautiful, to know that a part of you will live on long after you're gone, and give pleasure to everyone who sees your work?"

The question caught Gabe off guard as much as the desire he suddenly felt to touch her face, to hold her in his arms. Until now, no one else had understood his desire to leave something tangible behind. His hands clenched instead. "Humble, scared, grateful."

Her attention refocused on the painting. "Is this for sale?"

"No. It's a surprise gift to the woman's husband. They're friends of mine," Gabe explained. "I'm supposed to deliver it tonight."

Jessica straightened and pushed her glasses back in place. "I'm glad the portrait is going to someone who will appreciate and cherish it. A lot of things in life aren't. Thanks for taking the time to share your work with me."

"My pleasure," he said, meaning it. "Maybe you can come by my studio before you leave."

The idea was so intriguing that Jessica almost said yes before realizing he was probably just being nice again. Men, especially ones as sexy and handsome as Gabe, never had time for her unless there was an ulterior motive. Somehow she didn't want to chance finding out Gabe was like all the other men before him.

Smothering her disappointment, she said, "I'd like that if I have time. Shall we go?"

Gabe had never been around a woman who confused him more. On the slow, bumper-to-bumper drive back on the George Washington Bridge after delivering the portrait to his friends in New Jersey, he wasn't able to get Jessica out of his mind.

One moment she had tears in her eyes looking at his painting, the next she was stiff and unapproachable. But he couldn't erase the image of the careful way she had touched the clasped hand and fingers of mother and child.

Or the brief flash of hurt that crossed her expressive features when the maid at her aunt's apartment told her that her Aunt Irene had gone skiing with some friends. The maid wasn't sure when she would be back. Jessica was to make herself at home and her aunt would call later.

The thoughtlessness of her aunt and that of Shelton coming so close together had to bother her. Yet she had discounted both as if she had expected no less. Gabe's fingers flexed on the steering wheel as the black luxury car broke free of the bridge.

He'd attempted several times without success to reach Shelton after leaving Jessica earlier in the day. His secretary, then later his answering service, kept repeating he was unavailable. Gabe knew he wasn't with a woman unless it was business-related. Shelton might be a louse, but he was a loyal louse. Even so, sometimes Gabe could shake him.

Up ahead was the familiar turn to his brownstone on Striver's Row. If he continued, he could take 96th Street and be on the East Side with Jessica in twenty-five minutes. He rolled tired shoulders. Since dawn he'd been up painting. She wasn't his problem. Clearly she had wanted to get rid of him. He looked at the digital clock in the dash. Eight-forty-one.

The car passed his turn and kept going. It wouldn't hurt to check on her.

No one should spend their first night in New York alone.

Jessica couldn't have been more surprised to see Gabe through the peephole than if it had been Denzel Washington. Frowning, she unlatched and opened the door. "Did you forget something?"

One hand dug into the front pocket of his tailored slacks, but his gaze never faltered. "No. I thought I'd drop by and see if you were all right."

She stared at him a long moment, unsure if she had heard him correctly. People tended to forget her even when she was still in the room with them, but especially if she was out of sight. Her aunt and Shelton were perfect examples. "I beg your pardon?"

His hand zipped out of his pocket. "No one should spend their first night in New York alone."

Pleasure, slow as a sunrise, began to spread through her and reflect itself in her growing smile. "Actually I've been to New York several times."

"Oh." His gaze and feet shifted. "In that case, I guess I better let you get back to doing whatever it was you were doing."

He actually appeared embarrassed. The thought of her having such an effect on such a commanding figure was so incongruent that her smile burst into laughter. His shoulders stiffened beneath his leaf-green herringbone jacket. Nodding brusquely, he whirled and started down the wide, carpeted hallway at a fast clip.

He was several feet away before she realized he probably thought she had been laughing at him. She ran to catch up with him. "Wait. Please wait."

He did, but he didn't appear overjoyed by the prospect. "Yes?"

"I think you misunderstood me," she told him, searching his eyes for some softening. "I'd like it very much if you'd come back inside and have dinner with me. I've never had to eat dinner alone in New York and I'd like not to start."

Her hands were clasped to her chest, her eyes behind her glasses were bright with expectation. The tightness in his stomach eased. "Sure."

Her smile blossomed. "I'll get another place setting."

By the time he was inside the apartment and had closed the door, she was rushing out of the kitchen with silverware, china, and a wineglass. He went to help.

"Slow down." Relieving her of everything, he quickly arranged the elegant place setting atop a white banana-silk place mat with a matching silk organza napkin.

Looking up from placing the stemware etched in twenty-two-karat gold on the table, he found her staring at him. "Did I do it wrong?"

"I was just trying to imagine my father or one of his friends helping set the table, and I couldn't."

"Maybe they aren't as hungry as I am."

"I think it's more man that. Please have a seat."

He did, and in a matter of moments he was eating freshly grilled salmon. "My compliments to the chef."

She dipped her head in acknowledgment. "Thank you."

"You cooked this?"

She laughed, a low, sweet sound that made her expressive face come alive. Despite the lack of makeup, she was almost pretty. Large brown eyes sparkled in the light from the glass candelabrum.

Gabe found himself laughing easily with her and thinking models would kill for her cheekbones.

"Since you picked me up from the airport and carried all my luggage up here, I'll consider your outburst a backhanded compliment," she said easily.

"Please do." He took another bite. "How did you learn to cook this well?"

"My mother." The smile slowly slid from her face. "It's part of my training, but I'm afraid she's doomed to disappointment."

"Training for what?"

Her head came up sharply, as if she had unintentionally revealed too much. Her head dipped briefly as she pushed her salmon around on the richly colored china featuring exotic butterflies and delicate gold blossoms. "It's too boring to talk about. I'd rather hear about you and your painting. You seem to have done well for yourself."

He decided to let her change the subject. Maybe if she knew him better, he could help her with whatever it was that caused her to look so down and retreat from him. "What you see is from my other life a little over two years ago as a stockbroker when I was pulling down six figures a year plus bonuses."

He placed his fork on his plate and gave her his full attention. "I've bought relatively few things since I decided to paint full time. Frankly, my art is not supporting itself yet."

"You gave all that up to paint? Why?"

Gabe had seen the same astonishment in the faces of other people, but this time he didn't see the derision. Somehow he had known he wouldn't. "Because I lost two close friends in less than six months. One to a car accident, the other to a massive coronary." His hand tightened around the stem of the wineglass.

"The three of us had big plans and dreams for the future. For them, that day never came. I decided I didn't want that to happen to me."

Her hand lightly touched his jacketed arm. "Walking away took more courage than staying."

"Most people think it was a cop-out."

"Not to anyone who has seen your work. You obviously did well as a stockbroker, but people were probably waiting in line to take your place once you left." Her fingers tightened. "Your paintings come from the heart and they can come only from *your* heart. Therein lies the difference."

His large hand covered hers. "Thanks."

Awkwardly she pulled her hand free and picked up her wineglass and took a sip. It didn't help to steady her nerves or to stop the strange sensation quivering through her.

Somehow she still felt the lingering touch of his hand on hers, of her hand on him. She had been right. Gabe made a woman want to risk everything and tempt fate.

Too bad she hadn't the foggiest notion of how to do either.

THREE

The next morning Gabe repeatedly rang Shelton's apartment doorbell, then pounded on the door when there was no response. It was half past seven and Shelton seldom left for his office until after eight. His baby brother had some explaining to do.

The door abruptly opened. Shelton stood with a towel wrapped around his narrow waist, water beaded on his well-conditioned brown body. "What's all the rush?"

Stepping past him, Gabe entered the immaculate apartment, done completely in stark white with splashes of black for accent. Glass and chrome gleamed everywhere. The apartment always reminded Gabe of a showroom, not a home.

"Where were you all day yesterday and last night?" Gabe fired.

Shelton swung the door closed. "Taking care of business. What do you think?"

"You couldn't have found one minute to call the woman you claim you're going to marry?" Gabe asked, the anger that had been simmering all night coming to a boil.

The frown on Shelton's boyishly handsome face cleared. "You always were a sucker for the lost ones. You dragged home so many stray animals and people, Mom always said she sometimes hated to see you come home."

Gabe planted his hands on his hips. "Jessica is not lost. She's a grown woman who you should show some consideration and attention."

"I got it covered, Gabe," Shelton said dismissively, turning toward his bedroom. "Jessica understands. She knows business comes first."

"Did she tell you this or is it your assumption?" Gabe asked, following Shelton into the luxurious bathroom. Greenery cascaded from high arches, and mirrors reflected the men's images and that of the immense sunken whirlpool tub and glass-enclosed shower.

Shelton picked up the electric shaver from the marble countertop. "Look, Gabe, I know since you left the corporate world you tend to think less of those of us who stayed. Jessica has been trained to be the wife of a corporate executive."

"She's not a puppy," Gabe snapped.

"Gee. I should have known not to ask you to meet her, but I needed someone to look after her while I was busy. I still do."

"You mean you're not going to see her today either?" Gabe asked, wondering how his brother could be so callous. "Then why in the hell did you invite her to New York?"

Looking as exasperated as his brother, Shelton laid the shaver aside. "I thought I'd have it together, but there are a few glitches that I need to straighten out before the office opens in thirteen days." His face hardened with resolve. "But it will open on schedule."

Gabe didn't doubt it for a minute. Nothing stood in Shelton's way when he wanted something. That was the reason he was so worried. "In the meantime, you expect Jessica to spend her time alone in her aunt's apartment?"

"Irene is there with her," he returned easily.

"Irene went skiing and she left a message with the maid saying she didn't know when she was returning. Seems she had something better to do, too," Gabe said, not even trying to hide his annoyance at the absent aunt and Shelton.

"What!" Shelton exclaimed. "How could she do this to me?"

Gabe shook his head. Did Shelton ever think of anyone besides himself? "How indeed?"

Shelton's eyes narrowed on his brother. "I need you now more than ever with Irene gone. You have to help me on this, big brother. Keep Jessica occupied until I have time to ask her to marry me. Her parents have secretly given me their blessing."

Something tightened in Gabe's gut. "How does Jessica feel about this?"

"She'll be grateful. She's no raving beauty," Shelton scoffed.

Although Gabe had thought the same thing, hearing the words out loud made him want to shake his egotistical brother until his capped teeth rattled.

Apparently taking Gabe's silence for agreement, Shelton continued, "I know personally she hasn't had a real date in years. Her male cousins were her escorts to her prom, her debutante parties, and her sorority functions. I'm her last chance for a marriage and she knows it. Her parents know it also, and they approve of my intentions."

Gabe needed to know one thing. "Do you care anything about her or is she a means to an end?"

"I wouldn't condemn myself to live with someone I didn't care anything about. She's reserved, intelligent, and manageable. I haven't even tried to make a move on her," Shelton related. "I don't want my future wife to have even a hint of gossip linked to her name. After we're married, I promise I'll take care of her and respect her."

"In exchange for an eventual partnership in her father's law firm," Gabe stated, certain of the answer.

Shelton winked and smiled. "Senior partnership. Her old man can't live forever."

Gabe looked down at the black marble floor, then back up at the man he had carried on his back as a child when he was too tired to walk, had given the tire off his own bike until his could be repaired, had fought bullies to keep him safe. "I don't know you anymore."

"Gabe, don't get sanctimonious on me," Shelton pleaded, his

hand gripping his brother's upper forearm. "You know I always keep my word. I won't be a bad husband to Jessica. Just help me out and keep her entertained for a few days."

"On one condition."

Suspicion narrowed Shelton's black eyes. "What?"

"That you're up front with her and you let her make the decision; no coercion from you or her parents," he said, flatly ignoring something twisting inside him. "The choice has to be hers."

Shelton laughed his relief. "Whew. You had me worried. No sweat. Jessica knows what a catch I am."

Gabe shook his dark head in derision. "No wonder you've never liked wearing a hat. It would be impossible to find one to fit over that big ego of yours."

Grinning, Shelton playfully punched his older brother on his wide shoulder. "It's a good thing I love you."

"Likewise," Gabe said, then his eyes narrowed, his voice carrying a hint of steel. "Don't hurt her, Shelton."

"Why would I want to hurt the woman I'm going to marry?" he asked. "To show you, I'll send her some flowers."

Gabe nodded. It was a start. "A phone call and a visit would be better."

Shelton picked up the shaver and flicked it on. "I'll try to call, but I'm booked solid. Tell Jessica hello for me and I'll see her as soon as I can."

"I may help, but I'm not your messenger boy." Turning, Gabe left the room, feeling his brother's stare all the way.

Jessica awoke the next morning without much enthusiasm for getting out of bed. As she had told Gabe, she had been to New York before and although she thought the city fascinating, she didn't particularly enjoy the prospect of seeing it again by herself.

It was a sure bet that Shelton wouldn't be around to go with her. Not that she wanted him to, she thought, throwing back the goose-down comforter and getting out of bed. Now, his brother was a different matter and also entirely unlikely.

Pulling off her flannel nightgown, she adjusted the water in the shower and stepped beneath the tepid stream. Gabe was only being nice and she'd probably never see him again. The thought saddened her and the feeling stayed with her through getting dressed and eating breakfast.

Two hours later she still hadn't shaken her melancholy and was seriously considering booking the next flight home to Atlanta. Her parents would have to accept the fact sooner or later that she and Shelton weren't getting married. She had wanted to ignore Shelton's invitation, and had only accepted because her parents had insisted that she do so.

Sighing, she picked up a magazine. There was something to be said for moving out of your parents' home once you completed college. At least they couldn't nag you all the time.

She tossed the fashion magazine aside seconds later. It hurt to think that her parents thought so little of her ability to get a man on her own that they thought they had to practically throw her at Shelton. All right, she admitted, she hadn't been doing so hot in that area, but her parents were supposed to believe in her when no one else did.

Restless, Jessica pushed to her feet and stared at the New York skyline from her aunt's windows. She had known from childhood that her father had wanted a son to carry on the firm after he retired, and no matter what she thought of Shelton, he was reported to be a good lawyer.

The fact that he was in charge of opening the branch in New York was a clear indication and testimony of her father's faith in him. If George Ames couldn't have a son, a son-in-law was the next best thing.

He and her mother were both doomed to disappointment. Love was the only reason she was getting married and when she did, the man she chose wouldn't treat her as an afterthought. He wouldn't forget she existed unless he wanted something from her the way Shelton did.

The chime of the doorbell interrupted her thoughts. Waving away the maid, who had come from the study, Jessica went to the door. She had met many of Irene's friends. Her mother's older sister had quite a few colorful acquaintances. Hopefully it was someone Jessica knew and they wouldn't mind staying a little while to help her stave off boredom.

The idea was dismissed two steps later. She and Irene's female friends, cultivated during her aunt's twenty years in New York, during which she had gone through three wealthy husbands, didn't have much in common. Most of them were into fashion, men, seeing and being seen, and remaining on the A-list. Things Jessica had little use for.

Her spirits taking a nosedive, she slowly opened the door. "Gabe!"

"Good morning, Jessica," he said easily, trying not to be delighted by the quick pleasure he saw radiating in her big chocolate-brown eyes. He couldn't quite manage it.

"Come in. Have you had breakfast?" she asked, taking his arm and pulling him inside.

"Unfortunately, yes, if you were going to cook for me," he told her lightly, thinking the lilac-colored sweater she wore suited her complexion better, although it was two sizes too big and hung past her hips.

She folded her arms across her chest. "Cheese and ham soufflé."

"You really know how to wound a bachelor," he told her, enjoying the light of humor dancing in her eyes.

Her arms slowly came to her sides. "Maybe another time?"

"Count on it." There was no mistaking the wish in her soft voice. She was lonely and it was Shelton's fault. Gabe wasn't about to let her spend the remaining days of her visit waiting for his brother to call or drop by. She deserved better. "In the meantime I stopped by to see if you wanted to ride with me to the Hudson Valley. I have to deliver a portrait."

She didn't have to think. "I'd love to. I'll get my coat." Jessica dashed for the bedroom in an undignified manner that would have horrified her mother. She didn't care. She wanted to go with Gabe and she wasn't giving him a chance to change his mind.

"Get a scarf and gloves. The temperature is dropping outside," he told her retreating back, then shook his head. He didn't know if she'd heard him or not.

However, on returning, she was struggling to find the other sleeve opening on her long cashmere coat while continuing toward him. Brown leather gloves dangled from her coat pocket. An oversized paisley scarf hung around her neck.

Enjoying her enthusiasm, Gabe helped her with her coat. "You didn't give me a chance to tell you we'll be gone most of the day. Is that all right?"

"That's fine." With her coat on, she draped the scarf over her head and fingered her glasses back in place. "I have nothing scheduled. Is it another portrait?"

"In a way. Since you're from the South, you probably know that many old Southern churches deep in the rural country have a yearly homecoming celebration where all the old members return from wherever life has taken them. After service they eat dinner on the grounds because the churches are too small to hold everyone," he explained, following her to the door.

"Nathan Page, my client, is a retired minister who grew up going to homecomings in Louisiana. He commissioned me to paint such a scene using old family photographs."

She stopped pulling on her glove. "You re-created history. Can I see it?" she asked, then rushed on before he could answer. "No, I'll wait. I want to see his expression when he sees what a great job you've done."

He was touched. "You have that much confidence in me?"

"I've seen your work." Opening the door, she called over her shoulder to the maid. "Marla, I'll be gone all day."

"Yes, Miss Ames," answered the servant as she came across the living room. "Good morning, sir."

"Good morning," Gabe answered the elderly woman and followed a fast-retreating Jessica out the door.

Deep in thought, Gabe scratched his short-cropped beard as he followed her to the elevator. He couldn't help wondering how his brother could think her dull or reserved. Or how it was possible that he didn't want to be with a woman who obviously enjoyed life, if only someone took the time to show her how.

FOUR

The big luxury car ate up the road like a hungry cat slurps milk—
with finesse and pleasure. The heavily wooded and rolling countryside was postcard-pretty. Stately Colonial redbrick homes sat behind
white wooden fences. Horses, their tails high, their shiny coats
glistening in the noonday sun, ran for the sheer joy of being alive.

Gabe knew the feeling.

He'd never felt freer than he did these days. His checking account might not have as many digits as it had two years ago, but he
wouldn't go back for three times the money.

Some things were worth taking a chance for and came without
a price tag.

For some reason, he glanced at his silent passenger. Instinct and
observation told him that Shelton was so caught up in what he saw,
he hadn't taken time to look any further. Jessica was quiet, as she
was now, and people probably tended to dismiss her. That was a
mistake.

She was intelligent, sensitive, and compassionate. Which meant
she had two more qualities than his baby brother possessed. She
also had a smile that was pure sunshine. There was definitely more
to her than was initially apparent.

For the past thirty minutes she had been silent, her gaze lingering first here, then there, her enjoyment evident by the slight upward curve of her unpainted lips. Delicate fingers occasionally tapped on her knee in perfect sync to the jazz music flowing from the CD.

A gust of wind sent a swirl of leaves across the road. The myriad colors ranged from deep golds to smoldering reds. Nature had outdone herself and the endless battle to keep the leaves raked from yards would last for months.

Two preteens, judging from their size and height, were already finding that out in the immense yard up ahead. Even as they worked, the brisk wind sent more leaves drifting to the ground.

Jessica nodded toward them as the car drew closer. "I wonder how long before they start playing?"

The words had barely left her mouth, when the smallest of the two did a back flip into the middle of a pile that came to his waist. The other somersaulted into his pile.

Gabe glanced into his rearview mirror and chuckled. "You called it. Sounds like you spoke from personal experience. Have you pulled some leaf-raking duties yourself?"

"A time or two."

"You can't make a statement like that and leave a guy hanging. How about some details?" Gabe asked, genuinely interested, wanting to know the woman behind the quiet, composed exterior.

Jessica looked at him in that strange way she had sometimes, as if she were trying to figure him out. "The countryside is beautiful. Why spoil it with details about my boring life?"

"Everybody's life is boring to them."

"Well, mine actu—Don't hit Rocky!" she shouted, sitting up straight in her seat.

Gabe had already seen the squirrel dart out onto the highway and gently braked. "Rocky? Don't tell me you're a fan of Rocky and Bullwinkle."

"Don't forget Boris and Natasha, and the Fractured Fairytales," she admitted with a wry twist of her mouth. "I think my tolerance of cartoons is the main reason the children like having me around."

"Children?"

"I teach preschool to the three- and four-year-olds at the women's shelter where I volunteer," she said.

"There is no way you can tell me that's boring." Gabe looked at her. "Some of my friends have children that age and the only time they stop moving is when they're asleep."

"No, *they're* never boring, but working with them is the best and worst part of my job," she admitted slowly.

"How so?"

She sent him that strange look again, but continued, "A few women who come to the shelter are homeless, but the majority are there because of abusive relationships. The women have gone through a horrific amount of physical and emotional pain and suffering." Her hands clenched in her lap as she continued speaking.

"They have difficulty understanding why the man who says he loves them treats them so cruelly. It's so much worse for the children I work with. Their young world is in chaos. They want to go home, sleep in their own bed, and not be surrounded by strange people and unfamiliar surroundings. They can't."

Anger crept into her tightly controlled voice. "So many of them think being there or the situation at home is their fault. They shouldn't have to suffer because their mother chose the wrong man to fall in love with."

His hand closed around her clenched fist. "So you watch cartoons with them and let them know they're safe, and for that moment in time at least, they have control over some aspect of their lives."

"I want to do so much more," she said fiercely. "I'm enrolling in graduate school in January to begin work on my Master's in Education with an emphasis on guidance counseling."

Something wasn't right here. Shelton would want a wife at his beck and call. Slowly Gabe removed his hand. "In Atlanta?"

She nodded. "That way I can still work at the shelter. Mrs. Lewis, a retired schoolteacher, is taking my place while I'm here."

"I suppose you've discussed this with your parents?" he asked, delicately probing further as he pulled into the Pages' driveway.

"I'm not sure 'discussed' is the correct word," she told him, slipping her scarf over her head.

Gabe slowed down to a crawl and hoped the effusive, elderly couple wouldn't see him drive up and come out to greet him. "Would you care to explain that?"

"I told them and, as usual, they completely ignored my plans and kept talking about what they wanted me to do." She dug in her coat pocket and pulled on her gloves. "They mean well and I'm ninety-six percent sure they love me, but they won't believe I won't do as they say until I come home loaded with my textbooks. It's the only thing that has worked in the past."

Gabe stopped behind the couple's RV and cut the motor. Although he had a pretty good idea, he asked anyway, "What is it they want you to do?"

"To settle, to be less than I can." She pulled her coat over her shoulders. "I've seen too many people ruin their lives that way to allow the same thing to happen to me." She looked straight at him. "Like you, I'm going to follow my dream, regardless of what others think I should do."

"Are you sure?" he asked.

"I'm aware you don't know me very well, but I've always been a methodical person. I don't think I've ever done an impulsive thing in my life," she said softly. "Yes, I'm sure. Nothing is going to change my mind."

Least of all my brother, Gabe thought as he read the determination in her face, the set of her small shoulders. *Shelton, you're going to lose this time.* But Jessica would win. Gabe felt himself smiling at the prospect. "Then I wish you luck."

"Thanks." She returned the smile with interest, then reached for the door handle. "Come on and let's get the portrait inside. I can't wait to see what you've done."

. . .

The twenty-by-thirty portrait was as spectacular as Jessica had known it would be. There were a dozen animated black people sitting on colorful quilts or standing around talking, with a white-steepled church in the background. Their facial expressions were so lifelike, she felt they'd respond to her if she spoke to them.

Judging from the awestruck way Reverend Page stared at the portrait Gabe had placed on the easel he had brought with him, the elderly man agreed with her. His frail hand trembled as he pointed out various relatives. When he reached his deceased parents, his eyes misted and his arm tightened around his diminutive wife.

He insisted on calling his brother, who lived nearby. In a little over an hour the house was filled with friends and relatives who had come to see the portrait. There was nothing but praise for Gabe's work. With each accolade, her pride in him grew.

Standing in the midst of a small group of people, she glanced up and found Gabe watching her from across the room. The troubled expression on his bearded face cleared when she smiled at him.

Sipping her coffee, she still found it difficult to believe that with all the attention Gabe was receiving, he didn't forget her. She had been to numerous social functions, but she couldn't ever remember someone keeping an eye on her to make sure she was all right the way Gabe was. More often than not, people lost interest in her as soon as the social pleasantries were completed.

Not Gabe. He had introduced her as his friend. Not as the friend of his brother. Apparently, he didn't use the term lightly. She didn't even try to discount how pleased she was by the distinction of his phrasing. If the crazy idea occasionally slipped into her mind that she'd like for him to be much more, she wasn't foolish enough to dwell on it.

Some dreams were possible, others were inconceivable. Friendship was better than nothing, especially if the friend was Gabe.

· · ·

The lush scent of roses greeted Jessica the moment she opened her aunt's apartment door. On the glass cocktail table were two dozen deep red roses arranged among various cut flowers in a round crystal vase. She sneezed.

"Bless you," Gabe said, closing the door behind them. So Shelton had gotten around to sending flowers. Too little, too late.

Jessica sneezed again.

"Bless you." He frowned down at her. "Are you coming down with a cold?"

She shook her head and pointed at the floral arrangements. "Snapdragons. I'm allergic to them."

"Wh—"

Another sneeze cut him off. "Please take them out of here or I'll sneeze myself silly." As if to prove her point, she sneezed again.

Unsure of what to do with them, Gabe picked up the bouquet. She sneezed again. "Move away from the door and I'll set them outside."

Nodding, holding her finger beneath her nose, she did as he instructed. She sneezed again.

Coming back into the room, he handed her the card. "Will you be all right?"

"I'm not sure." She opened the envelope and read the message. "They're from your brother."

Gabe felt he'd be disloyal not to speak up on his brother's behalf. "I'm sure he didn't know about your allergies."

She sneezed again.

"Miss Ames, you're back," the maid said and glanced around. "Where are your beautiful flowers?"

"In the hallway. I'm allergic to the snapdragons in them," Jessica explained, waiting for the next sneeze.

"Oh, what a shame. They are so lovely," she said.

Jessica sneezed again. "Then please take them with my blessings."

She looked at Gabe. "Do you think you could stand to be with me for another hour or so until the air clears in here?"

He glanced at his watch. "It's only a little past seven. We can catch a movie."

"Marla, please see that the flowers are gone by the time I get back," she said, trying to hold back another sneeze.

"Right away, Miss Ames," the woman promised. "I'll turn the ventilation on."

"Thank you."

His arm around Jessica, Gabe led her back the way they had come. Poor Shelton, he was certainly batting zero.

Outside in the cool night air, Gabe stared down into her face. "Feeling better?"

"Much."

The corner of his mouth quirked. "Allergic to snapdragons, huh?"

"Very."

"So I won't make the same mistake, are there any other flowers to steer clear of?" he inquired.

Jessica's heart stopped, then raced wildly in her chest. He could send her a weed and she'd be happy. "That's about it."

"So my meticulous brother managed to send you the only flowers you're allergic to?"

She nodded.

"When Shelton makes a mistake, it's a doozie." Taking her hand, he started down the street.

Jessica shivered, her heart rate going crazy. The sexiest man in the universe was actually holding her hand. *Thank you, Shelton, for inviting me to New York,* she thought. Forgive me for all the unkind things I thought of you.

The street light changed to "Walk." Gabe released her hand, his arms curving naturally around her waist, drawing her closer to him. Jessica went willingly and without a moment's hesitation, a dreamy smile on her face.

FIVE

Elbows propped on her knees, the palms of her hands cupping her face, Jessica stared at the silent white phone in the living room. Sunlight had finally pushed away the smog that had covered the city most of the morning and it now shone through the wall of windows behind her.

She didn't particularly care. Her entire attention was focused on the phone since the clock on the mantel ticked past twelve and Gabe hadn't called.

In the past two days he had always called or dropped by by now. They'd talked about his work, her plans. She hadn't realized how much she enjoyed those times with him until they stopped.

Sighing, she glanced at her tiny gold wristwatch. Two minutes after one. He had told her he'd be busy completing a family portrait, but how long did it take to make one simple phone call?

Her shoulders jerked upright in her snake-print silk top as inspiration struck. Picking up the phone, she dialed information. Seconds later she was speaking to Shelton's secretary.

As Jessica had expected, the woman didn't hesitate to give her Gabe's address and phone number. Hanging up the phone, she decided there were certain advantages to being the boss's daughter.

Staring at the information, she came to a quick decision. Gabe had invited her to see his studio. Today was as good a time as any.

With a smile, she raced to the bedroom. Pulling on the stone-colored sueded silk jacket that matched her pants, she grabbed her coat and her purse. Passing the dresser, she happened to glance at the mirror.

Her steps slowed. Her smile faded. Not for the first time in her life she wished that she could have had a nodding acquaintance with pretty.

Her features were proportioned, but ordinary. The eyeglasses for her myopia didn't help. The only thing she had going for her was her unblemished, clear brown skin. Her shoulder-length black hair refused to hold a curl or stay styled the way she combed it, and had been a problem since she was in junior high.

Her salvation had been styling gel that kept her hair in place, or so she had thought. The French twist she had worn for years because of its neatness and practicality now seemed too severe for her oval face. The bangs covering her high forehead helped a little, but she needed something more.

Leaning closer to the mirror, she studied her reflection critically. Maybe if she wore makeup other than a lip gloss it might soften her face and bring out her dark brown eyes. They were kind of pretty at times. But here again, she never seemed to have the patience to apply it just like the fashion consultant did.

More time was spent trying to get the smeared mascara from beneath her eyelids than doing the whole makeup routine. Eyeliner was impossible, and dangerous. Afterwards she usually resembled a raccoon or a little girl turned loose in her mother's makeup kit.

She glanced at the closed train case on the dresser. Perhaps she should try again.

Becoming aware of what she was doing and thinking, she straightened and started for the front door. Gabe liked her the way she was. She hadn't tried to impress a man since Kendall Lawson in the eighth grade.

She had almost broken her neck in the high heels and she looked ridiculous in the frilly blue dress for the eighth grade dance. Kendall had laughed so hard he rolled on the floor.

She wasn't putting herself through that again. Gabe had to take her the way she was. Telling the maid she was leaving, Jessica went downstairs and hailed a cab. Friends accepted each other the way they were.

Jessica told herself the same thing in varying ways right up until she emerged from the cab in front of Gabe's brownstone and saw a beautiful black woman clinging around his neck. A woman who obviously had no problem with her makeup or her hair. Her short black hair was as stylish as the black leather miniskirt, which barely reached below her hips.

Everything Jessica had tried to convince herself of in the past thirty minutes was shattered. She wished she were pretty. Most of all she wished she were pretty for Gabe. Hands clenched, she turned to leave.

Smiling, Gabe pulled his newest client's arms from around his neck, took her elbow, and started down the steps again. He never thought giving someone a discount would get such a reaction.

"You're more than welcome. I—" He broke off as he saw a woman, head bowed, slowly walking away from him. He recognized Jessica and the long brown cashmere coat instantly.

He frowned, wondering why she was leaving without saying hello. As far as he knew, she didn't have any other reason to be in Harlem except to see him.

"I'm just so glad you're going to do my portrait, Mr. Jackson. My fiancé is going to be so pleased."

Gabe glanced at the excited Loraine and everything clicked. "I'm sure he will. If you'll excuse me, I see a friend of mine I want to speak with. I'll call to set up an appointment," he told the woman as he backed away, then turned and sprinted.

He easily caught up with Jessica. But since he wasn't sure what to say, he just fell into step beside her. He had intentionally not called or gone by today because he had woken up smiling, thinking about her, and anticipating the call. A sure sign of a man getting in over his head.

He didn't want a relationship. Certainly not one with a woman his brother thought he was going to marry. Gabe hadn't had time for anything serious with a woman since he decided to paint full-time. Painting had been his life and he hadn't felt the need for anything else. Until now.

It wasn't lost on him that Jessica hadn't gone by Shelton's office or house. Gabe knew it as surely as he knew his own name, as surely as he knew his feelings for the woman walking with her head bowed down were steadily growing deeper. He never wanted to see her upset or sad again. She asked for so little in life and gave so much.

"Hello," he ventured.

"Hello," she returned.

At least she's still speaking to me, he thought. "Did you come to visit my studio?"

"Yes, but I saw you were busy." Her voice was tight.

"Yes, Loraine's my newest client. I'm glad I only gave her a ten-percent discount instead of twenty. She might have squeezed the life out of me. I feel sorry for her fiancé."

Slowly Jessica came to a halt and finally met his gaze. "Her fiancé?"

"It's her wedding gift to him."

"I—" She glanced away. How could she tell him she had been hurt and envious?

Gentle hands on her shoulders turned her around to face him. "Since I'm free, would you like to come back to the house and see the studio?"

She wanted to, too much. "I don't want to keep you from working."

"You won't." Taking her hand in his, he started back.

· · ·

For his studio, Gabe had converted a bedroom on the second floor in the brownstone that caught the first rays of the morning sun. The large, rectangular room was surprisingly neat. On an easel was a covered work-in-progress. The walls were pristine white and un-adorned except for one. That was what drew Jessica.

She slowly walked from picture to picture, her respect for Gabe's talent growing with each one. There was a portrait of Billie Holiday in a gold dress, her trademark white gardenia in her hair; another of Louis Armstrong, his trumpet wailing while people crowded on the dance floor; happy children playing in the arch of water from an open fire hydrant; four black men playing dominoes on a crate in the front yard of a framed house. But the one that caught and tugged at her heart the most was that of a young woman with a let-ter clutched in her hand, tears streaming down her cheek.

"What's in the letter?" Jessica asked, feeling an instant empathy with the woman.

"Her future."

Jessica faced Gabe. "What?"

He stood beside her and gazed at the picture of the black woman in the faded dress seated at the scarred table, the windows bare of curtains behind her. One pane was covered with an oilcloth.

"People tend to see what they're feeling at the moment. Tears can come from more than fear or despair or pain. There are other emotions like joy, hope, excitement."

"Which is it for her?"

"That's for you, the viewer, to decide."

"Gabe," she said, exasperated.

He laughed at the mutinous expression on her face, wanting more than anything at the moment to be able to hug her. He couldn't. Shelton had to have his chance. *But if you mess up, little brother* . . . "You know artists have their quirks. Come on, I'll fix us lunch."

· · ·

They were cleaning up the bright yellow-and-red kitchen after eating corned beef and rye sandwiches when the phone rang. Throwing the towel he had been drying the dishes with over his shoulder, Gabe reached for the red wall phone.

"Hello. Hi, Shelly, thanks for the reminder. Hold on." Pressing the mouthpiece to his white-shirted chest, he spoke to Jessica, "I have an appointment to get a haircut. It only takes about thirty minutes. Do you mind?"

"No," she said, letting the dishwater out of the sink and trying to keep the disappointment out of her voice. "I've taken up enough of your time."

He smiled indulgently. "I meant, do you mind going with me?"

"Oh," she answered.

"Well?"

"Not at all."

He raised the mouthpiece to his lips. "I'll be there." Hanging up the phone, he picked up the last glass to dry. "The receptionist knows how busy I get painting so she gives me a call to make sure I keep my standing appointment. I think you'll like the salon."

"I'm sure I will," she answered, really not caring as long as she could still be with Gabe.

'Like' was putting it mildly, Jessica thought as she got her first view of Rosie's Curl and Weave. Jessica had been in some stylish salons before, but none compared with the subdued elegance of Rosie's place. From the moment they stepped onto the pastel blue-and-pink marble floor of the spacious, airy salon and were greeted by the receptionist who took their coats, she was impressed.

The relaxed, unhurried atmosphere reminded her of the European spas she and her mother had visited. She wasn't surprised to find the facility offered a day spa and an entire array of beauty treatments to pamper their clientele.

Only two of the chairs lining the white walls were empty. Women and men were being serviced with everything from weaves to permanents. Finished, they could view themselves in the huge mirrors in front of their chairs. Light came from the recessed lighting and elegant globes separating each booth.

A young woman wearing a black smock came up to them. "Good evening, Mr. Jackson. Anthony is ready for you." She smiled at Jessica. "Do you have an appointment or are you with Mr. Jackson?"

"She's with me, Dakasha," Gabe said and faced Jessica. "You're sure you don't mind?"

"No. I'll just look through some magazines."

"This way, Mr. Jackson."

Jessica took a seat. As time passed, her gaze flicked from one woman to the other. Each hairstyle caused her to wish she could do something different with her own. Surely she wasn't the only woman in the world with unmanageable hair.

A fashionably dressed woman with short braids passed. On the back of her head the braids were swept upward into an intricate French twist. Stylish and elegant. Jessica's fingers touched her own French roll. In her opinion, there was no comparison.

"Thinking about changing your hairstyle?"

Snatching her hand down, she jumped up. "It was just a thought. You finished quickly."

Gabe knew when someone wanted to change the subject. "Unlike most barbers, Anthony doesn't stop cutting my hair when he's talking. Let's get our coats."

"All right."

While the receptionist was getting their coats, Gabe couldn't help noticing that Jessica kept sneaking glances at the other women in the salon. He picked up the shop's business card and handed it to her. "If you ever change your mind."

Silently Jessica accepted the card and her coat and then said, "No one would notice."

Turning up the collar of her coat, Gabe stared down at her unhappy face. "So what? Do it for yourself."

"My mother doesn't like braids," she confessed once they were outside.

"She wouldn't be wearing them. You would."

"You make it sound so easy."

He stared down into her troubled face. "Sometimes you have to ask yourself what is more important, what others think or what you think? Somehow, I thought you had already asked that question and found the answer."

"This isn't the same as grad school."

"Isn't it?" he asked. "You have to stand on your own and know what you want about every aspect of life; otherwise someone is going to make the decision for you."

For some reason her parents' pushing her toward Shelton flashed into her mind. She had tried to tell them it wasn't going to happen, but had eventually caved in when the pressure became too much. "I don't like for people to be upset with me."

His mouth hardened. "Then get ready for your life to be run by others."

"I'll speak up for myself when I have to," she told him, a hint of anger in her voice. "The braids just aren't that important."

"If you say so, Jessica. It's your life." Taking her by the arm, they continued down the street.

Jessica didn't know why, but she felt sad. As if she had somehow failed Gabe.

Gabe didn't feel the elation he had earlier. He had thought Jessica wouldn't bow to the pressures of Shelton and her parents, but now he wasn't so sure.

"I can take a cab home from here," she said.

"Why would you want to do that?"

"I kind of think you're upset with me," she said.

"I'll get over it," he said. "In your trips to New York did you ever tour Harlem?"

"No."

"Then you're long overdue."

"Gabe?"

"Yes?"

"If something is really important to me, no matter how upset my parents get, I won't back down. I promise."

He squeezed her hand, not knowing if she realized her hand was trembling in his and that her quiet voice didn't sound the least bit sure. He only knew it disturbed him that she was frightened and he was going to do something about it.

"I want to show you what people were able to accomplish because they had faith in themselves and the determination to succeed," he told her. "I want to show you the Harlem I know."

SIX

Gabe showed her a Harlem she hadn't known existed, with clean, well-maintained homes, businesses, and streets. As New Yorkers, the residents still didn't make eye contact with strangers, but those who knew Gabe welcomed her warmly.

They drove past the legendary Apollo Theatre, then stopped by Sylvia's restaurant for some soul food. Words failed her when she saw the magnificent Cathedral of St. John the Divine. After one hundred years of construction, the edifice was only two-thirds finished, but when completed it would be the largest cathedral in the world.

On Monday she saw the original site of the renowned Cotton Club, where such musical greats as Lena Horne and Cab Calloway got their start. The Schomburg Center for Research into Black Culture took the rest of the day. Tuesday they went to the open air African market on 116th. She purchased so much that they had to get a cab from there and go back to the apartment.

With the passing of each day, he showed her how people with courage and faith in themselves had succeeded when others failed. She recalled hearing that only the strong survive, and it was certainly true of people of color. That night she called her parents and told them she was going to graduate school and Shelton wasn't a part of her future. Despite their protests, she was firm.

When she told Gabe Wednesday morning on the phone about notifying her parents that she was definitely going to grad school, he let out a wild cheer. He suggested they should go out and celebrate.

Aware of the short time left, she invited him to dinner at the apartment instead. He could bring the wine.

While she was at the market, Shelton called. Dutifully she had returned his call and was told he was in a conference and couldn't be disturbed. Her delight in his being unavailable didn't bother her at all.

Simply, there was nothing she had to say to him, she thought as she went about preparing dinner. Her parents had probably called him and dropped some broad hints. The poor man probably felt pressured to make some overtures.

She wished she had enough spunk to tell him not to bother. She held her tongue because she didn't want to be rude to Gabe's brother, and she owed him for inviting her to New York, even if it was to make points with her father.

She had just finished lighting the candles when the doorbell rang. Smoothing her hands over her long, midnight-blue velvet dress, she answered the door.

"Hello, Gabe. Come in."

"Hello," he greeted her, handing her a bottle of vintage wine. "Something smells almost as good as you look."

She blushed and took the wine out of his hand. "You must be starved. We can go in to dinner now."

Taking her arm, Gabe led her to the dining room and placed the wine in a waiting ice bucket. He had learned Jessica didn't take compliments well. It angered him because it was a sure sign that she hadn't received many in the past. He personally planned to rectify the situation.

They dined on sautéed veal cutlets with wild mushrooms and for dessert they had a fruit napoleon with raspberry sauce. Gabe insisted on helping with the dishes. Jessica refused. He challenged

her to a game of five-card-draw poker. The winner would decide
who did the dishes.

"I don't know how to play poker," she told him.

"Perfect."

Locating the cards in her aunt's game room was the easy part—
learning how to play was another thing altogether. Gabe couldn't
believe she hadn't learned in college. She politely informed him
poker wasn't considered appropriate for ladies at Vassar.

"And now?" he asked, a teasing light in his beautiful black eyes.

Jessica pushed her glasses farther up on her nose. "Deal the
cards."

She lost three games in a row. Gabe's stack of pennies was growing, hers dwindling. She stared at the three cards in her hand, determined to win this time.

The peal of the doorbell interrupted her concentration. The sound
came again. Sighing, she laid her cards down. "Marla has the night
off."

"Be sure to check before you open the door," Gabe cautioned.

Gazing through the peephole, her mouth gaped, then thinned
in annoyance. *Shelton.* Reluctantly, she opened the door.

Shelton smiled down at her. "Hello, sweetheart, how are you?"

Her brow arched at the endearment he had never used before.
"Fine. Is there something I can help you with?"

He tweaked her nose and stepped past her, removing his long
charcoal topcoat as he did. "I never knew you were such a kidder."

She resisted the urge to roll her eyes and tried to remember his
part in getting her to New York. "Neither did I."

"Gabe, I didn't expect to see you here," Shelton said.

"I might say the same thing about you," Gabe returned, and
leaned back against the silk upholstery cushion.

Shelton frowned. "I beg your pardon?"

"Have a seat, Shelton," Jessica invited, seeing he wasn't going anyplace. She sat back down on the sofa beside Gabe and picked up her cards.

Shelton, who had been about to hand her his coat, sat down in an armchair and drew it into his lap, studying the other two people intently. "What are my two favorite people up to?"

"Gabe is teaching me to play five-card-draw poker," Jessica explained, trying to concentrate on her cards instead of being annoyed at her unwanted visitor. She didn't want to share Gabe with anyone.

"Chess is much more stimulating," Shelton said.

Jessica glared over the top of her cards. "This is stimulating *and* fun."

Gabe tried to smother his laughter at the perplexed look on his brother's face. Obviously he had expected a more—what were the words he had used?—yes, "manageable and grateful" Jessica.

He didn't know squat about Jessica and was too full of himself to learn. Gabe had tried to warn him again this past weekend, but as usual Shelton hadn't had time to listen. Now it was every man for himself.

"Something the matter, Shelton?" Gabe asked mildly.

"No. Ah, Jessica, fix me a scotch," he requested, sitting back in his chair. "You know how I like it."

Her hands clenched. She laid the cards on the heavy glass table and turned to Gabe. "Do you want anything?"

"No, thank you."

Smiling, she rose gracefully and went to the bar in the far corner of the room. As soon as she lifted the heavy crystal decanter, Shelton jumped up and sat next to his brother. "What did you do to her? I've never seen her act this way."

"Maybe you didn't take time to look."

"Gabe, I haven't got time for this."

"For Jessica either. If anyone has done anything to her, it's you. You invited her to New York and haven't called in ten days."

"I called today and she was out. I sent flowers." Shelton glanced around the room. "Where are they?"

"Maybe you should ask her."

"I'm asking you."

"Your drink." Jessica held the squat crystal glass out to him.

"Thank you," he said, all smiles and charm. Jessica's dour expression didn't change.

"I'll hang up your coat."

"You're such a treasure. Thanks."

"You're welcome."

Shelton lifted the heavy glass to his mouth, all the time watching Jessica. When he thought she was out of hearing distance, he turned to his brother. "I don't know what is going on, but I want you to leave. The office opens in three days and I'd like to make an official announcement then."

"What announcement?" Gabe asked calmly, although he was anything but.

"You know damn well what announcement."

"Got the ring yet?"

Shelton actually appeared embarrassed. "Actually no. I haven't had—"

"Time," Gabe finished. "Do you know anything about Jessica? What her plans are, what she likes, her favorite color, food? Anything?"

"What difference does it make? I'm marrying her, aren't I?"

"Are you?" The softly spoken words were a direct challenge.

"Yes, I—" Shelton began to mutter beneath his breath and snatched his pager from his pocket. "Morrison. Damn! Where's the phone?"

"Behind you."

Jessica retook her seat and gathered her cards. If Shelton was like her father, he'd be gone in less than five minutes. She glanced at Gabe.

"Three minutes tops," he whispered.

She laughed. They were thinking the same thing.

Shelton, who had been deep in conversation, glanced up sharply at the sound and frowned. His frown deepened as they appeared to ignore him and went back to playing cards. The receiver rattled in the cradle as he hung up. "I have to leave."

Jessica jumped up. "I'll get your coat."

Shelton stared at her, then faced his brother. "What did you do to her?"

"Why do you keep asking me that?"

"Because I know you. You saw Jessica as one of your lost souls and you changed her somehow. I want her back the way she was," Shelton hissed between clenched teeth.

"Here's your coat."

He was all smiles when he turned and took the coat and tossed it casually over his arm. "Thank you, dear. I really hate that business has kept us apart. Did you get my flowers?"

"Yes. Thank you."

The wattage of his smile increased. "Where are they? In your bedroom?" he asked in a stage whisper, his voice low and husky.

Her black eyebrows lifted in obvious displeasure at the inference. "Actually, I don't know where they are. I gave them to the maid."

"You did what?" he shouted.

"They had snapdragons in them and they made me sneeze."

"Snapdragons? I told my secretary to send roses!" he snapped.

"She did, but among the roses were other flowers," Jessica explained. "Actually, the arrangement was very pretty. Please thank your secretary for me."

Shelton stiffened. His gaze narrowed. "I'm sure your father has had his secretary send you and your mother flowers on numerous occasions."

"That he does, and I always call to thank her and send her a gift for her birthday and Christmas," Jessica returned mildly.

Her calm explanation removed the lines from Shelton's brow. "I'm sorry if I appeared a little short. My patience hasn't been the best lately. I'm working long hours to get the office opened as scheduled."

Jessica smiled her forgiveness. "I know. Father is very proud of you and counting on you to do just that. We all have the utmost confidence in your business abilities."

Shelton's shoulders straightened in his double-breasted gray wool suit. "That's nice to hear."

She took him by the arm and steered him toward the door. "I'm sure you have things that need your attention. I wouldn't dream of keeping you."

"Yes," he said, stopping at the door and staring at her, the frown returning to his handsome face. "The party is Saturday and I want you looking your best. Why don't you get a new hairstyle and have your nails done? They have some fabulous salons in Manhattan that can do wonders."

Instead of being hurt or incensed as she would have in the past, she thought of Rosie's Curl and Weave on 125th Street. A smile blossomed on her lips. "Shelton, that sounds like a marvelous idea. I know just the place."

He patted her on the shoulder. "Good. I guess I better be going."

"Good night, Shelton," Gabe called.

His baby brother's eyes narrowed. "Good night, Gabe. I'll call you later tonight."

"Somehow I thought you might," Gabe said.

Impatient for him to be gone, Jessica opened the front door. "Good night, Shelton. I'll see you at the party."

"I promised your parents I'd pick you up," he said. "They're going straight to the hotel, where they have a room. The party is also being held there."

Her shoulders dropped, her lack of enthusiasm evident. "If you insist."

Shelton shot his smiling brother another mutinous look. Clearly, they were going to have a talk before the night was over. "I'll pick you up around five. I want to be there before the guests start arriving at six."

"Of course. I'll be ready."

Her quiet acquiescence pleased him. He showed his pleasure by patting her on the arm again. "Good girl. Good night."

Jessica closed the door, her teeth clenched. "You'd think I was a dog. Perhaps I should have barked."

A whoop of laughter from Gabe had her whirling in that direction. He was laughing so hard she feared he might roll onto the floor. She'd forgotten he always paid attention to her and what she said. Unease pricked her.

People had laughed *at* her rather than *with* her more times than she wanted to remember. A picture of Kendall at the eighth-grade dance came to her. "I didn't mean to insult your brother."

Gabe stopped long enough to wipe the tears from his eyes. "If you didn't, you're not the woman I've grown to admire. Shelton was being a jerk and we both know it."

"I'm sorry."

"He deserved it. There's nothing to be sorry for."

Shaking her head, she retook her seat. "Not about that. About doubting you were laughing at me instead of with me."

His smile was tender. "You should be. Now, let's get back to this game so I can beat you again."

She did as he suggested, her tongue poking out her cheek as she studied the three cards. "Not this time. I raise you another two pennies. Another card, please."

"I'll take another card, and raise you by five pennies."

"I'll see you and raise five. Another card please." She squealed on seeing the Queen of Hearts. *Perfect.* "Gotcha," she said, laying out a royal flush.

"Guess I'm a pretty good teacher."

"The best," she said, raking up the small pile of pennies. Being with Gabe had taught her to believe in herself. "Can I ask a favor?"

"Sure."

"Do you think you could take me to Rosie's if I can get an appointment for Friday?"

"No problem, and I can almost guarantee you can get in. The

owner is a friend of mine and I used to be his broker." He started gathering up the cards. "You're going to get a new hairdo?"

"Yes, but not the way Shelton thinks."

The corner of Gabe's mouth quirked. "You're going to get the braids."

"And the reddest nail polish they have for my manicure." He knew she had it in her. "This I want to see."

"Yes, Shelton," Gabe said *as* soon as he picked up the phone. At eleven-thirty P.M. it was a safe bet who was calling.

"I want you to stop seeing Jessica," his brother ordered.

Gabe had expected as much. "I can't do that."

"You only took her out because I asked you to, so why are you being obstinate?"

"I picked her up at the airport because you asked me to. I took her out because she's a nice woman and I thought you gave her a dirty deal," Gabe corrected.

"It comes down to the same thing, and I did not give her a dirty deal. Jessica knows what to expect," Shelton said, exasperation in his clipped voice.

"You haven't spent enough time with Jessica to know what she wants."

"Maybe not in New York, but we went out lots in Atlanta."

"Did you talk?"

"Of course we talked."

"So you know where she works."

"At a shelter," Shelton said triumphantly.

"Doing what?"

After a pause Shelton said, "Helping people."

Gabe had to give the lawyer in his brother points for being quick. "She teaches preschool children and she plans to obtain her Master's."

"She'll have to give all that up once we're married. She'll be much too busy."

"You're forgetting something."

"What?"

"You haven't asked her and she hasn't said yes."

"She will. You saw how easily she agreed to have her hair done. She'll do anything I ask her."

"You really believe that?"

"I'm considered a very good catch. Jessica is no fool."

"On that, we finally agree on something. Good night, Shelton. I have an appointment early in the morning." Gabe hung up the phone, then placed his entwined fingers behind his head and stared up at the ceiling. *Little brother, you're in for the shock of your life and I can't think of anyone who deserves it more.*

SEVEN

Jessica was nervous. What if it didn't work? What if she remained an ugly duckling instead of turning into a graceful swan?

"We're ready for you, Miss Ames."

She glanced at Gabe, her hand tightening in his. "Here goes."

"I'll stop by to check on your progress since the braiding is going to take a long time," Gabe told her, wishing he could take some of her anxiety away.

She nodded. "I'd like that." She took a deep breath and slowly released his hand and started after the assistant.

A few steps away, she stopped and came back to Gabe. There was something she had to say. "I'm not getting this done for Shelton."

His chest felt tight. "I know."

Smiling brilliantly, she turned and followed the assistant. "I hope this works."

"What?" the assistant asked.

"Making me over," she admitted.

"You have good bone structure and fantastic skin. You just need some help bringing it out." Smiling, she opened the door to the shampoo area. "You couldn't have picked a better place. We're going to pamper you sinfully today."

Jessica soon found out the woman wasn't exaggerating. After

her shampoo, she was shown to a quiet room where she was given a bone-melting massage, then served hot tea before she had her facial. She didn't have to think twice when asked about her nail color during her manicure and pedicure.

"The redder the better."

The staff soon caught on that they were in the process of a transformation. They got into the spirit of things. Three cosmetologists and the manager conferred on the best style of braids for her hair. A soft page boy for the front and sides, and for the back a triple twist in a figure eight for a dynamic impact.

Gabe came by about that time, saw the excitement in Jessica's eyes and smiled all the way back to his brownstone. He liked Jessica the way she was, but if a new hairstyle gave her more confidence, he was all for it.

Lunch was quick; the braiding was not. The time would have seemed unbearable if not for the friendliness of the braider, and the fact that by then the fashion consultant had done her magic with her makeup.

Jessica couldn't see herself because the beautician was standing behind her working, but she still remembered how good she looked with her makeup on. Since she was near the mirror, she had removed her glasses and put them in her purse.

Her anxiety grew for the woman to finish so she could see the end results.

"All done."

Slowly the chair revolved until she saw her reflection in the mirror. Trembling fingers with Exotic Red nail polish touched quivering Plum Red-colored lips. She hadn't known her cheekbones could be that dramatic or her eyes could look so mysterious. And her lips . . . they actually looked lush and inviting. She leaned closer so as not to miss one detail. She had already decided she was getting contacts as soon as possible.

"Oh my goodness. It worked," she breathed excitedly.

"You look terrific," said the salon manager as she walked up. "I knew you'd be sensational. When you start receiving all the compliments, please mention Rosie's."

Jessica glanced at the polished woman in her late fifties and smiled. "Thanks seems so inadequate."

"You haven't seen the bill yet."

Laughing gaily, Jessica rose from the chair. "Whatever it is, it's a bargain." Opening her purse, she handed the braider a tip. "Thank you."

"Thank you. It was a pleasure in more ways than one," she said, sliding the fifty-dollar bill into her pocket.

"You mind if I give you a little more advice?" asked the salon manager, her voice softly modulated.

"Please do," Jessica said.

"Get rid of the browns or accent them with oranges or yellows or other bright colors. They're draining you." She studied Jessica with a connoisseur's eyes. "I think you'd look great in red."

Since the woman talking was wearing a melon suit that was dramatic and flattering, Jessica readily took the advice. "Any suggestions of where to look for the clothes? I'd like to impress a friend."

The manager gave her the name of a shop. "Ask for Yvette."

"I will." She extended her hand. "If I lived in New York, you'd have another customer. Thanks again." She paid the bill and was fumbling in her purse for some change to call Gabe when she heard her name.

"Jessica?"

Instantly she recognized the hesitant voice. Taking a deep breath, she slowly turned, hoping neither of them would be disappointed.

"Jessica," Gabe whispered her name in awe and wonder. His black eyes that had always fascinated her roamed over her face as if the sight were something new and exotic he had just discovered, and the discovery was just for him.

She felt heated. She felt wonderful. Not even the quivering of her stomach could dampen her elation. To have Gabe look at her with desire was something she hadn't let herself believe could happen. She wished she had on something more flattering than the chocolate-brown tailored pantsuit.

Most of all she wished she could say she loved him. Loved him so much it hurt not to be able to tell him. Basically she was shy, but she'd find a way of letting him know. She hadn't met the man of her dreams only to let him get away.

Gabe's unsteady fingers touched those incredible cheekbones of Jessica's, then swept upward to her braids that barely skimmed her shoulders. Her brown skin glowed and her eyes sparkled as if she had suddenly discovered the secrets of the universe.

Knowing he shouldn't, but unable to help himself, he brushed his lips across hers, tasted something sweet and uniquely her, and felt her trembling breath brush over his own lips. Desire struck him hard and fast, but tempered with the emotion was a deep tenderness and unspeakable joy for her.

He loved her, wanted to cherish her and keep her happy always. He loved this changeling of a woman who was finally growing into her own.

A woman his brother wanted to marry.

Wishing he could tell her his feelings, but knowing he owed Shelton his chance, Gabe stepped back. But not too far back. When Shelton struck out, Gabe planned to be standing nearby.

Unsteady from Gabe's light kiss still pulsating through her body, Jessica did a slow pirouette. "I take it you like my hair."

"You're beautiful, but then you've always been beautiful to me," he told her honestly.

"Oh, Gabe," she said, her voice as wobbly as her lips. "If you make me cry and mess up my mascara, I'll never forgive you."

The pads of his thumbs brushed away the moisture in her eyes. "Since I'd like to take you out tonight, I'll behave."

She smiled, her heart soaring. "First, I have to do some shopping."

Gabe usually hated shopping, but the thought of *not* going with

Jessica never even crossed his mind. She was glowing, her energy and enthusiasm contagious. Her first stop was an optical shop for contact lenses. Next, they went to a boutique. "Nothing brown," she told the saleswoman on entering the posh shop in upper Manhattan.

From the number of packages she later handed him, she had found what she was looking for. When asked what she bought, she sent him a saucy look and said, "You'll see."

The slumbering sensuality in her eyes had his blood pounding through his veins. He wanted very much to lower his mouth and taste her lips again and keep right on tasting. The urge had steadily been growing all afternoon.

He couldn't. Not yet.

"Shoes are next."

She might not have wanted him to see her other purchases, but the shoes were a different matter. Red, high-heeled, and sexy. She had great ankles. The red patent leather evening sandals by an Italian designer had a tiny padlocked ankle strap that could only be opened with a key. When she handed him the key so she wouldn't lose it, he thought his heart would stop.

He was in trouble. Jessica was sending out signals a blind man could see. He'd have to do a delicate balancing act to keep from hurting her. Too bad her aunt wasn't due back until next week. He needed a buffer. It was going to be a long evening.

Gabe's reaction to seeing her in the fitted red silk chemise gown was everything she had hoped and prayed for. The hour she had spent on her makeup, and all the aborted efforts with her contact lenses had been worth the effort.

He couldn't seem to take his eyes off her then nor during their candlelit dinner in the quaint restaurant. Darned if he wasn't staring hungrily at her lips. When they danced, his heart beat as erratically as hers. Yet, when they were back at her aunt's apartment, he stopped at the door.

"Aren't you coming in for a drink?"

"No. You have a big day tomorrow. You need your rest," he said, sliding his hand into his pocket.

"Are you coming to the party?"

"No. I need to catch up on some work."

"Oh," she said, biting her lip.

"Here," he said, the key to her shoes in his hand.

Hurt and embarrassed, she lifted the key from his palm, making sure she touched him as little as possible. Love wasn't supposed to hurt. "Good night."

"I enjoyed our evening together. You looked sensational."

"Apparently not sensational enough. Good-bye, Gabe."

The palm of his hand caught the closing door. "I'll see you before you leave."

She wished for the courage to tell him that wasn't necessary. "If you want."

"Lady, you have no idea of what I want, but you will before you leave New York, that I promise." Whirling, he stalked away.

The sensual undertone in Gabe's voice sliced through her misery. He was angry, but she no longer doubted he wanted her. "If you break your promise I'll never speak to you again," she yelled, ignoring years of training again.

He turned, the lines of strain clearing from his face. "I won't. Good night, Jessica."

"Good night, Gabe." Stepping into the apartment, she closed the door, trying to figure out what Gabe had meant. He wanted her, yet he didn't even try to kiss her again. Even Shelton had kissed her twice on the cheek. She'd just have to wait. She trusted Gabe. That thought was the only thing that got her through the long, lonely night.

. . .

"My goodness! What did you do to yourself?" A wide-eyed, disapproving Shelton asked the moment Jessica walked into the living room.

"Just as you suggested," Jessica said, handing him the floor-length matching cape to her figure-revealing red beaded halter gown.

Automatically, he took the cape and held it for her. She turned. Breath hissed through his teeth. "This thing hardly has a back! I said nothing about braids or this kind of dress."

"I know. It's what I wanted, Shelton. Your opinion didn't enter into the situation." Drawing the cape around her shoulders, she pulled on her long red gloves and went to stand by the door. "We should leave or we'll be late."

"This is all Gabe's fault," he muttered beneath his breath as he opened the door.

Jessica heard him and decided to ignore the remark. She hadn't expected Shelton to like her makeover, but she hadn't expected him to be this annoyed. If this was his reaction, there was no telling about her parents.

The elderly Ameses were both speechless. As she had for Gabe, she pirouetted in the red gown, then raised her hands. "It's the new me."

Before her parents could say anything, her father's elderly partner, Oscar Koch entered the room. "Jessica, is that you?"

"Yes, sir," she answered affectionately. She had always liked the robust, no-nonsense man.

"Goodness, young lady. Where have you been hiding this other you?" he asked, his brown eyes twinkling.

She laughed. "I don't know, but I'm glad I let her out." She turned to her mother. "How about you?"

"What can I say except we should have sent you to New York by yourself years ago?" Smiling, Henrietta Ames took her daughter's hands in hers. "You look fabulous, even with the braids, doesn't she, George?"

"I suppose," her ultra-conservative, normally outspoken father said slowly.

"Coming from you, Dad, I'll take that as a compliment." Guests began to arrive. "Looks like we're on." Taking her parents by the arm, they went to greet them.

The party was a resounding success and so was Jessica's new look. However, the more compliments she received, the more Shelton glowered at her. Finally, she had had enough and took him aside. "What is your problem?"

"You."

"Me?"

"You've changed, Jessica. I thought you'd make the perfect wife, but I was wrong."

Her mouth worked for a long time before she could get the words out. "You thought what?"

"Keep your voice down," he warned, glancing around the crowded room as people turned toward them. "Your parents and I discussed everything. But that was before Gabe entered the picture. He changed you."

"Did you tell Gabe you wanted to marry me?"

"Of course. I asked him to keep you company." His mouth narrowed into a tight line. "Instead of doing just that, he somehow managed to change you. I'm sorry, but you won't do as my wife."

She laughed in his face. "I'm not and you're right. I'd do much better as a sister-in-law, if I can get your brother to ask me. Maybe I'll have to ask him."

"What?"

"Lower your voice, Shelton. You wouldn't want to create a scene." Patting his cheek, she then tweaked his nose for good measure. "Excuse me, I need to call someone." She started for the door just as it opened and Gabe walked in.

The smile started in her heart and bloomed on her face. "Gabe! I was going to call you."

"Then I'm glad I saved you the trouble." Gabe figured he had wasted enough time. "Did you turn down his proposal yet?"

"Yes," Jessica told him, her heart thudding again. He was dressed the way he was the first time they met. In a black leather jacket, jeans minus the paint, and aviator glasses. He looked hard and dangerous and gorgeous. She wanted to curl up in his lap and purr. This time, she was more than ready to tempt fate and go with him wherever he asked.

"Good, then I think it's time we went someplace and talked," he said, his gaze roaming boldly over her. "By the way, you look incredible."

"So do you," she said.

His gaze heated. "Let's go."

"Now, hold on a minute, Gabe," Shelton said, grabbing his brother by the arm as he turned to leave. "Do you mean to tell me while you were supposed to be watching my girl, you stole her from me?"

"I never was your girl, Shelton, so there was nothing for Gabe to steal," Jessica said indignantly.

Gabe's arm curved around her bare shoulder. "I gave you every opportunity to win her and I'll always be grateful you didn't. If you want to blame someone, blame your overinflated ego."

"What is going on here?" asked Mr. Ames, pushing his way through the gathering crowd with his wife by his side.

"My own brother stole Jessica from me," Shelton fumed.

"You can't steal what you never had," Gabe pointed out, drawing her possessively closer. "Besides, you'll make a much better brother-in-law than a husband."

"Wait a minute," Jessica said, pushing out of Gabe's arms, her hands on her slim hips, happiness soaring through her. Seems she didn't have to ask him to marry her, but there was something else she desperately wanted, needed, and she wasn't waiting another minute. "I'm not about to consider marrying a man who barely kissed me."

"I thought you'd never ask." He took her in his arms, his mouth finding hers, shaping itself effortlessly and beautifully. There was no hesitancy, no fumbling, just sweetness and fire.

Finally Gabe lifted his head, his breathing unsteady. "I love you with all my heart. Will you marry me?"

It took a second before Jessica could draw in enough breath to speak. "You talked me into it."

His lips found hers again.

Shelton folded his arms, glaring at the two. "If he thinks I'm going to be the best man, he has another think coming."

Gabe ignored his brother and apparently everyone else in the room did also. They were too busy watching this real-life drama unfold. "Please don't leave tomorrow. Stay and spend some time with me."

"I'd like to see anyone try to stop me."

"That's my girl. Get your coat and we can get out of here."

Jessica took off in a flash, grinning, her gown drawn up to her knees.

"Jessica, don't run," her mother admonished. She never slowed.

Gabe turned to her puzzled parents. "As you may have guessed, I'm Gabe Jackson, Shelton's older brother. I know this entire situation is a little crazy, but please know one thing: I love your daughter very much and I'd never do anything to hurt her."

Their expression didn't alter.

Gabe smiled. "It's the beard. My mother always said it made me look like a hoodlum. For the past thirteen days I've been with or spoken to Jessica every day. And did she appear the least bit reluctant to leave with me?"

"No, in fact, I've never seen her happier," her mother confided, slowly relaxing.

"I could have made her happy, too, given the chance," Shelton growled for good measure.

"You would have tried and failed and Jessica would have been the one to pay," Gabe said softly to his brother. "Do you remember all the things you said you wanted when you were growing up, only to get tired of them and stick them in the back of your closet and forget about them? I couldn't let you do that to Jessica. I love her."

Shelton snatched his arms to his sides. "I still want to punch you in the nose."

"For Jessica it would be worth it."

More than one woman aahed, Jessica's mother included.

"You're not playing fair." Shelton knew when he had lost. "It's a good thing I love you."

"Likewise." As if they were connected somehow, he turned to see Jessica struggling to get her cape on. He rushed over to help.

"What does your brother do, Shelton?" Mrs. Ames asked.

"He paints."

"Paints?" Mr. Ames repeated loudly, then shared a look of pure horror with his wife. Recently they had had the trim on their one-hundred-year-old mansion expertly restored.

"Portraits," Shelton clarified, watching Jessica and Gabe make a hurried exit out the door.

The frown on Mrs. Ames's perfectly arched brow lessened only slightly. "Is he solvent?"

The door closed behind the fleeing couple. Oddly, Shelton wasn't as ticked off as he wanted to be. Partly because Gabe was right. He hadn't exactly been looking forward to marriage with Jessica, but he fully planned on becoming a partner one day with her father's firm.

"Shelton, is he solvent?"

He glanced at his former-future in-laws. At least Gabe had kept Jessica all in the family. Actually this could work out better.

"My brother's not bringing down the high figures he once did as a stockbroker, but that's about to change. He's been commissioned by some very influential people to do their portraits. In the meantime, knowing Gabe, he has more pots of money in various funds than a leprechaun."

"Influential people?" Mrs. Ames asked, her eyes sparkling with interest.

"Funds?" Mr. Ames questioned, his interest equally piqued.

"Why don't we join our guests and I'll tell you?" Shelton said, a genuine smile on his handsome face for the first time that evening.

EPILOGUE

It was the longest and happiest day of Gabe Jackson's life. A sunny June day with the scent of magnolia in the air and the faint chirp of blue jays. He couldn't seem to get the smile off his face, nor did he try. Each time someone patted him on the back and congratulated him on marrying such a beautiful and vivacious young woman, he almost felt like thanking Shelton all over again.

"You think she's ever going to throw that bouquet or is she just teasing the horde of women waiting to catch it?"

Gabe, a silly grin on his darkly handsome face, winked at his wife, who winked back. "Shelton, your guess is as good as mine. Jessica has a mind of her own."

A manicured hand settled on his shoulder. "You're right about that. She's nothing like I thought she was."

"She's everything I thought and more," Gabe said softly.

Shelton chuckled. "Spoken like a man in love. That's one of the main reasons I forgave you, you know. I may not believe in it, but I know you do."

Gabe glanced at his brother. "When the right woman comes along, you will. And I'll tell you something else. You won't mind leaving the office and going home to her."

"Yeah, right," Shelton said, his disbelief obvious.

Shaking his head, Gabe turned to hear his bride of an hour ask the clamoring women if they were ready. Their shouts of "yes" shook the Rose Ballroom of the Grand Hotel in downtown Atlanta.

Jessica grinned, obviously giddy with happiness and simply beautiful in an elegant off-the-shoulder gown of ivory silk with beaded chantilly lace bordering the wide skirt. It was clearly her day.

She sent Gabe a secret look. "Just checking."

Turning her back on the crowd, she tossed the bouquet. Women squealed and jumped. The jubilant woman held her trophy of miniature red and pink roses aloft.

"It's time to throw Jessica's garter," advised Mrs. Applewhite, the bridal consultant.

"You'll make sure my best man is there, won't you?" Gabe asked, grabbing Shelton by the arm before he could make his getaway.

"Have I ever let you down, Mr. Jackson?"

"No, and thanks." Gabe made his way toward Jessica. From six months' experience with the forceful consultant, he knew he could count on her. Yet at times, between her, Jessica's mother, and his mother, he had considered eloping. Since Jessica was in grad school, he was probably more a part of planning the wedding than most men.

He was glad she was taking off the summer and was going to enroll in the fall at New York University near their home. Planning the wedding for the first of June had been perfect. For the rest of the summer, he had his wife to himself. He was more than ready.

"I believe you have something I have to take off?" he said teasingly, his fingers brushing across her smooth cheek.

She leaned within an inch of his ear. "I know you have some things I want to take off."

Resisting the urge to drag her into his arms and kiss her until they reached meltdown, he went down on one knee and reached for her foot to the applause of the women. Her white leather shoe settled on his tuxedoed thigh. Slowly she raised the hem of her dress. Gabe chastised himself, but he was unable to stop thinking she'd be taking the dress off shortly and he'd finally make her his.

His fingers trembling, he pulled the blue garter from her leg. Damn fine legs, too. To think he'd fallen in love with a woman before he'd seen her legs. He hadn't needed to. Her heart and soul were enough.

As he drew the garter over her ankle his heart rate kicked up. There was a tiny lock on the shoes, just like her red ones, and he had the key. Jessica had sent it to him just before the wedding.

Love shining in his eyes, he looked up, knowing she would be watching him. "I love you."

"Impossible as it may be, I know." Her trembling hand tenderly touched his face. He kissed her palm. Neither noticed the camera flash.

Garter in hand, Gabe stood. "Here goes." The dainty blue garter sailed straight to Shelton, who instinctively caught it, then dropped it. The men beside him were only too happy to return it to him.

Amid the laughter and teasing, Gabe and Jessica said their good-byes and made their way to the private elevator of the hotel. His hungry lips crushed down on hers. She melted into him.

The elevator pinged open on the top floor. They kept on kissing.

"I think this is your floor."

Gabe lifted his head to see an elderly couple smiling at them. "Yes, thanks." Picking Jessica up in his arms he strode to the door of the bridal suite. It took two tries to get the key in the lock because Jessica was biting and blowing in his ear.

Finally, they were in. He sat her down immediately and drew her arms away from him. He swallowed. "Do you need any help changing?"

"No."

Nodding, Gabe watched her go into the bedroom and close the doors behind her. His hands were sweaty. His throat dry. He had never wanted any woman like this or been so scared he'd mess up.

Jessica had such an expression of love and trust and, yes, pride, whenever she looked at him. He'd eat shredded glass rather than risk that changing. When she came over to his place last week to bring her things, the awesome responsibility he was about to undertake hit him.

He was going to be responsible for her the rest of his life—to love, to cherish, to honor in sickness and in health, on good days and bad days. He had looked up and she had been watching him.

There wasn't a shadow of doubt on her beautiful face or in her eyes. He had searched his heart and soul and found none as well. Wherever life took him, Jessica would be at his side and would be a part of him.

That's why he didn't want to mess up her wedding night. Both of them had wanted to wait and it had been hard. Now the time was here and he was nervous.

His hand jammed into his pocket. The key. She needed it to take off her shoes.

He knocked on the door. "Jessica."

"Come in."

"You for . . ." His words trailed off. She stood by the bed in something white, lacy, and decadent. He was profoundly glad he hadn't known during the ceremony that beneath her gown she had on a merry widow. "I-I knocked."

"I know."

His gaze roamed hungrily over her. "The key."

"Yes." She sat down on the bed and crossed shapely legs in sheer stockings and a garter belt.

He swallowed, then slowly walked toward her when he wanted to run. Kneeling, he took one shoe on his knee, removed the lock, then repeated the process and took off her other shoe. The light fragrance she wore stirred his senses more.

Her hand touched his face. "I love you, Gabe."

His control slipped a notch. His arms went around her, crushing her to him. "Don't be frightened."

She laughed, and laughed again at his strange look. She kissed him quickly on the mouth. "Frightened! I'd fight anyone or any-thing that tried to take me away from you, from this. I don't know what life holds, but I know with you I have the freedom to be me, not what someone expects me to be."

Love shone in her misty brown eyes. "You are my freedom, Gabe. You are my life, my love. Who could be frightened of that?"

"Oh, Jessica." His mouth found hers again, no longer hesitant. He drew her down on the bed, kissing her greedily. She met him boldly, her hands and lips as eager to touch, to taste, to savor, as his. Each caress was more desirable than the last.

Clothes were cast aside in heated urgency. Gazing into her eyes, he made her his, watched the surprise and momentary discomfort break across her expressive face, then watched the slow spiral of pleasure.

She came to him with all the innocence and fire he knew she possessed. She held nothing back. Neither did he. They both gave and in return received.

Much later, Gabe drew Jessica to his side, his hand tenderly stroking her. "Like I always said, you're incredible."

"If I would have known how incredible *this* would be, you would have had to fight me off."

Chuckling, he rolled her beneath him and kissed her. "Wel-come to my world, Jessica Jackson. I'll love you through eternity."

"And I'm going to love you right back, Gabe Jackson." Her lips touched his and it was a long time before either had enough breath to speak again.

a matter of

Trust

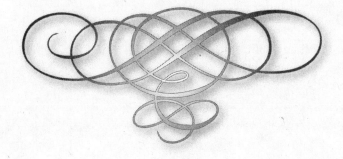

ONE

*Sebastian Stone was having the day from hell, and as the after-*noon progressed it showed no sign of abating. But having a flat with no spare, being splashed with dirty water in his new Brioni charcoal herringbone suit as he stood on the sidewalk waiting for the auto service mechanic, then getting a speeding ticket while rushing home to change for his morning meeting at the theater, and all the other crummy things that followed, in no way compared to this latest development. "Do you mean to tell me that Gregory isn't here?"

Tianna, the young receptionist at Della's House of Style who moments earlier had greeted him with a broad smile, noticeably swallowed, the smile in her attractive nut-brown face wavering. "He had an emergency, Mr. Stone."

Concern knitted Sebastian's brow. In their six-year association, the tempestuous Gregory had never canceled. "What kind of emergency?"

"Medical." The receptionist glanced away, her right hand fluttering upward to push the shoulder-length braids off her shoulder. "He sprained his ankle last night."

Sebastian's frown deepened. As far as he knew, the most strenuous thing Gregory ever did was operating the remote control for his entertainment system. He claimed standing in his Cole Haans for hours on end, twisting and turning to get the right angle to do people's hair, was enough exercise for him. If he needed to burn calories, he had a better way. "How'd he do that?"

Tianna's gaze settled in the middle of Sebastian's blue, pinstripe-shirted chest. "Jumping off a fire escape."

Knowing Gregory lived on the first floor of his apartment complex, and knowing his passion for the ladies, Sebastian decided not to question the obviously embarrassed woman further. Apparently Gregory had been burning calories with someone he shouldn't. "I see."

Tianna's braid-covered head quickly came up. She stared at him with pleaful, big brown eyes. "But I assure you the stylist your appointment is with is well qualified to cut your hair."

"Edge," Sebastian corrected, aware that he was splitting hairs and unable to help himself. "My hair only needs to be edged."

Her smile slipped again and Sebastian felt like the demon from hell in the last play he directed. He probably sounded like an irrational fool. But, despite her position, in Sebastian's opinion few women truly understood that letting someone loose with clippers, shears, or scissors on a man's head was just as traumatic for him as for a woman getting a cut. Once the hair was gone, no amount of apology would bring it back.

Sebastian had been in that unenviable position too many times in his past thirty-seven years to take it lightly. It had taken him five long years after his move from Los Angeles to New York to find Gregory. Once Sebastian found him, he had followed the gregarious Gregory wherever he went. Della's House of Style was his third move.

Gregory might wear a foot-long ponytail, but he knew Sebastian's taste was conservative. No fades or shags for him. His haircut hadn't changed since he graduated from Howard in the early eighties.

"Gregory said to tell you he had complete confidence in Hope," the receptionist offered.

"Hope?" Sebastian repeated, foreboding sweeping through him. A woman had never cut his hair. He wasn't a chauvinist. His mother and sister could testify to that. His father would disown him if he were. Sebastian simply believed men were more suited to some professions. This was certainly one of them.

"Hope Lassiter," Tianna finally said.

Maybe he was overreacting. Although this was only his second time in Della's, the salon had the highest reputation and it had a subdued elegance and airiness that he liked. The booths were spaced far enough apart so you didn't feel cramped or have to listen to your neighbor's conversation. . . . unless you wanted to. Mirrors abounded on the pristine white walls. A pink and blue marble floor sparkled beneath his Ballys. Fresh-cut flowers sat at every station. The setting was designed to be relaxing.

It wasn't.

Perhaps the fault was his. Even after ten years as a director in the theater, the last three mostly on Broadway, the start of a new play with all its myriad problems always put him a little on edge. He never completely settled down until after the final curtain call on opening night. With all the difficulties he was having casting the right actress for the crucial female lead in *A Matter of Trust*, if he wasn't careful, he'd be a basket case by opening night. "Which one is she?"

"Her station is the fourth one." Tianna's slim hand gestured to the left.

Sebastian's worried gaze followed. There were two women at the station, but he immediately dismissed the elderly, gray-haired woman in a trim-fitting sky blue suit. The younger woman standing by her side wasn't so easily discounted.

She was tall and shapely, and her black micro-miniskirt peeked from beneath her pink smock each time she leaned over to speak with the grinning little boy sitting in the chair. Momentarily, she glanced his way. His breath caught, then came out in a rush. The promise of her elegantly curved body and long legs was backed up with interest by her beautiful mocha-hued face.

Her pouting lower lip begged to be kissed. Chiseled cheekbones bespoke of a Scandinavian or Native American influence somewhere in her heritage. Unconsciously Sebastian took a step closer, hoping she'd turn to him again so he could see her face and determine the color of her eyes. Abruptly he stopped. His own eyes widened as the scope of his gaze broadened.

"Goodness gracious."

He might not be able to distinguish the color of her eyes, but he had no difficulty with her hair . . . black and tipped two inches in garish purple. Worse, it was spiked over her head as if she had stuck her finger in a light socket. He quickly turned to Tianna. "No way is that woman getting near my head."

"Oh, my, Hope, he's looking this way," Bridgett Swanson said, excitement ringing in her voice. "He's a handsome devil. His pictures don't do him justice."

"You gonna ask him, Mommy? Are you?" Four-year-old Jeremy Lassiter bounced in the chair with every other word.

"Of course she is," Bridgett answered, then leaned over to whisper in Hope's ear. "If I were twenty—no, make that ten—years younger, I might try out for the part myself. Next, I'd go after the man."

Hope laughed, and with the laughter, some of the tension she had fought all afternoon eased. Bridgett nodded her approval at the sound of the laughter.

Hope smiled at her two biggest supporters, Jeremy and their friend and landlady, Bridgett Swanson. Sixty years old and widowed for seven years, Bridgett was an invariable tease and absolutely wonderful with Jeremy. The best thing that could have happened to them was renting the upper floor of Bridgett's home on Striver's Row.

Leaning over, Hope kissed Jeremy's soft cheek and winked at Bridgett. "If he turns me down for the lead in *A Matter of Trust,* I'll let you work on him for me."

The older woman shook her head emphatically. "He's too smart for that. Those four Tony Awards he's received in the past attest to his ability to pick winners. He needs a versatile, powerful actress for his production and you fit perfectly."

"You're the best, Mommy," Jeremy said, his eyes wide. "Everybody said so last night and all the other times."

"Listen to your son, Hope. You were the hit of the show."

"Community theater is a far, far cry from Broadway," Hope said, doubt creeping into her voice again. "Reading in *Variety* that Sebastian Stone was doing open casting for his newest play, then having Gregory call and ask me to do Sebastian's hair, seemed as if fate were working for me to get back into real theater again."

"It is," Bridgett said with complete confidence. "You said Della said it was all right for you to broach the subject with him, so all you have to do now is approach Mr. Stone."

Hope drew a deep breath. "You make it sound so easy."

"It is." Bridgett reached for Jeremy's hand. Immediately the child grasped it and jumped down from the chair to land with a solid whack on the shiny floor.

Hope frowned down at him. "Jeremy."

"Sorry," he said, an unrepentant grin on his beautiful, chubby face, his black eyes twinkling.

Hope tried to appear stern, but a smile slipped through. Douglas, the father Jeremy had never known, could always get by her with the same look. And like his father, Jeremy was perpetually happy and mischievous. "One of these days that's not going to work with me."

Jeremy's grin widened. With his free hand, he beckoned Hope closer. When she neared his face, he kissed her loudly on the cheek. "I love you, Mommy."

Hope's heart melted. Bending, she enveloped him in a hug. Thank goodness he still needed and wanted those hugs as much as she did. "I love you, too. I'll be home by six with hopefully some good news."

"He'll let you play the part, Mommy, I just know he will."

She stood. "I'll know shortly."

"Good luck, Hope," Bridgett said.

"Thanks, and thanks for coming by with Jeremy to give me a pep talk."

Bridgett waved the words aside with a surprisingly agile flick of her wrist. Diamonds and emeralds glittered. "You've given me plenty of them. About time I returned the favor."

"You do that just by being there for me and Jeremy." Reaching out, Hope briefly squeezed the older woman's fragile, blue-veined hand. "I'll walk you to the front and meet Mr. Stone." Fighting the trembling that had suddenly invaded her legs, she turned and headed toward the front of the shop and what she hoped was the key to her future, Sebastian Stone.

"*But—but, Mr. Stone,*" *Tianna* spluttered. "Hope is one of our best stylists. Gregory personally selected her."

"That may be, but I want someone else." Sebastian glanced to the other side of the shop, looking for a male attendant whose hair and dress denoted some restraint. Although there were two other men there, neither inspired confidence. One wore clothes as loud as Hope's hair, the other had a pair of shears in his hand zipping over a man's head at only a fraction slower than the speed of light. "I'll reschedule."

"But—but—" Tianna stammered.

"Good afternoon, Mr. Stone. I'm Hope Lassiter. Gregory asked me to service you this afternoon."

Sebastian felt a strange, white-hot something slither down his spine. Slowly he turned. The husky, beckoning whisper of Hope Lassiter's voice went perfectly with the face and body. A combination like that had embodied man's dream of the perfect woman since the beginning of time . . . until he looked at the sobering sight of her head.

Unconsciously, he lowered his gaze to see the color of her eyes, and stared into a pair of heavily lashed almond-shaped black eyes. She was even more captivating close up. "You know who I am?"

"By reputation and from what Gregory has told me," Hope said, trying to tell herself to remain calm, that this was just another customer, albeit one who could give her back a dream that she thought was gone forever. However, his smooth, deeply compelling voice was sending her thoughts in an entirely, totally inappropriate direction.

"Gregory went to great lengths to ensure that I understood how to edge your hair correctly." Her black eyes narrowed as her expert gaze ran over his well-shaped head to give herself time to collect her thoughts.

Bridgett was right. He was a handsome devil. Devastating, in fact, with piercing black eyes, a strong jaw, a talk-me-into-anything mouth, and a no-nonsense chin. Just her luck that she was a sucker for a man with a mustache. Sebastian's was jet black and neatly trimmed.

Since Gregory hadn't mentioned it, Sebastian probably took care of it himself. However, Gregory *had* mentioned Sebastian's previous misfortunes with barbers. The way those black eyes of his were staring at her, he had lumped her in their number.

Trying to control the strange and unusual sensations swirling through her, Hope concentrated on the problem at hand, calming her potential client. This was no time to remember that the only males she had hugged lately were relatives.

"You have enough natural curl to use the scissors to shape your hair. The shears and clippers will be needed only to edge the back and sides. Moderation and restraint is what Gregory said you desired. At Della's we always give our valued customers what they desire."

Did her voice get even huskier when she said *desire*, the same way it had when she said *service*—or was it his imagination? Once he had arrogantly thought of women coming on to him as a great side benefit to being a well-known theater director, but as time passed and it happened more and more, the come-ons had quickly become an annoyance, then a nuisance. He preferred to do his own chasing. "My desire would be not to have to wear a baseball cap or a fedora for the next couple of weeks until my hair grows out," he said in a clipped tone.

In slow motion her smile withered. Her eyes narrowed and took on a distinct chill. "No one has ever been dissatisfied with my services in the past, Mr. Stone, but if you have reservations I'm sure Tianna can find someone else to assist you. As I said, at Della's we strive to give the customer what they desire. If you'll excuse me." With a slight nod of her head, she walked past him to the front of the shop, where the elderly woman and the little boy who had been with her earlier waited.

Stunned by her dismissal, Sebastian watched Hope hunker down to eye level with the young child and open her arms. The child didn't hesitate. Their shared laughter rang loud and clear. Somehow he knew the happy little boy clinging around her neck was her son.

For some odd reason he thought of his ex-wife, Celeste, who had thought children would ruin her model-thin figure. Celeste, beautiful and as selfish as they came. He had lousy taste when it came to women. That was something else his mother and sister could attest to.

"Mr. Stone, if you'd come with me, I can check the appointment book," the receptionist said.

Sebastian looked away from mother and child. "Certainly."

Hope was trembling, she was so angry. The compact, sturdy body of Jeremy giggling in her arms and against her body helped to calm her. The nerve of the man. To actually think she was trying to come on to him. She could tell from the sarcasm/flippancy of his statement, the piercing coldness of his gaze. She should know.

She'd used a similar tone and look herself many times in the past to discourage men.

"Hope?"

Hearing the concern and question in Bridgett's voice, Hope shook her head and stood. Bridgett would understand. Many times in their long association they had had to talk out of Jeremy's hearing. With a bright smile on her face, Hope rose and said, "I'll be home earlier than I thought. Why don't we eat out tonight, my treat?"

"To celebrate?" Jeremy asked, his gaze going from Sebastian, at the receptionist desk several feet away, back to his mother. "He's gonna let you?"

Hope's smile wavered, then steadied. "We'll see."

Bridgett, her mouth tight, briefly pressed her free hand to Hope's tense shoulder. "We'll talk later."

This time Jeremy didn't budge when the elderly woman tugged gently on his hand. "But you were gonna ask him, Mommy. What did he say?"

From experience, Hope knew her son wasn't easily put off when he wanted an answer. Since it was just the two of them, she had a tendency to discuss her plans with him. He had also been around adults all his life and his vocabulary and thought processes were advanced for his age.

He knew how important obtaining the part in the play was to her. To ensure that he did, she had compared it to his dream, that of becoming an astronaut and traveling to the farthest reaches of space. She hated to see the disappointment in the face she loved more than anything. "I didn't ask him, sweetheart."

"But you have to ask him, Mommy. If you don't ask him, you won't be able to—"

"Jeremy, let this *gentleman* pass," Bridgett said tightly, stepping aside and drawing Jeremy with her. This time he went, his gaze locked on Sebastian as he passed.

"He's leaving, Mommy. Mommy, he can't leave."

"It's all right, Jeremy," Hope soothed. Feeling Sebastian's hard gaze on her back, she hunkered down in front of her child again. She could easily detest him for upsetting Jeremy, but the blame wasn't his. It was hers. Somehow she had to make her son understand that sometimes dreams don't always come true, no matter how much you wanted them to.

TWO

Closing the salon's door, Sebastian still felt the disapproving glare of the elderly woman and even more so the pleaful one of the little boy. The small, stark face was a drastic contrast to the giggling expression he wore earlier. Jeremy. Hope had called him Jeremy.

Hands deep in the front pockets of his navy blue slacks, Sebastian headed for his car two blocks away. There had been a parking space directly in front of the salon, but the driver of a little red sports car had zipped around him and into the space. The gloating young man, not the least disturbed by Sebastian's honking horn or his glare, had gleefully waved. Either he hadn't been taught to be courteous or had forgotten the lesson.

Sebastian's thoughts returned to Jeremy. The child seemed genuinely upset that Sebastian was leaving. His steps paused. Would Hope be reprimanded for not keeping a customer happy? Although he didn't think of himself as such, other people thought of him as important. His ex-wife certainly had. But it was only after he had married Celeste that he'd finally figured it out. They'd spent two chaotic years together before she had found someone richer and more gullible. Frowning, he paused on the tree-lined street as he tried to recall exactly what Jeremy had said.

Something about "Mommy, you won't be able to—" then the

other woman had cut Jeremy off to let Sebastian pass. Sebastian had a sneaky suspicion that the interruption wasn't coincidental.

Tianna had said Hope was one of their top stylists, and he had no reason to doubt the receptionist, but something was going on. He glanced back toward the salon. Walking down the street in the opposite direction was the elderly woman and Jeremy. The child saw him and immediately stopped, bringing the woman to an abrupt halt.

From the hundred feet or so separating him, he couldn't see Jeremy's face clearly, but Sebastian had no trouble hearing the excitement ringing in the boy's voice over the traffic and other city noises. Even if he hadn't, the child was jumping up and down, his left hand pumping in the air. A lefty.

Sebastian was left-handed. If his ex-wife hadn't been so concerned with keeping her model-thin figure, partying with the rich and famous, and jetting all over the world, she might have become pregnant as Sebastian had wanted and he'd have his own child Jeremy's age. And he would've suffered the fires of hell not to disappoint him.

One step was followed by another, then another, back to Della's until he could hear Jeremy's thrilled cries of, "I knew it. I knew it." The woman trying to quiet him finally gave up. Sebastian felt himself smiling at the ecstatic boy, and hooked the thumb of his left hand upward. Grinning from ear to ear, Jeremy returned the gesture.

The day from hell had ten hours to go, but at least this time he knew what he was walking into. Wearing a baseball cap for the next couple of weeks in no way compared to disappointing a child. He opened the door and for the second time that day stepped into Della's.

Surprise hardly came close to describing the way Hope felt on seeing Sebastian reenter the salon. Pausing briefly at the receptionist's counter, he nodded, handed Tianna his sports coat, then started toward Hope, his long strides sure and purposeful. Despite her best efforts, Hope felt a distinct flutter in the pit of her stomach. Her hand closed tightly around the comb in her hand. No matter what an arrogant so and so she thought he was, he was an impressive so and so.

He topped six feet easily, but his physique was trim and athletic. Even without the jacket, he was a commanding figure in his blue pinstripe shirt and navy slacks. Heads, male and female, paused to watch as he passed. Each movement was rich with an irrefutable mixture of confidence, authority, and sex appeal that announced him as a man to be reckoned with even before he opened his mouth. He stopped two feet from Hope.

"Ms. Lassiter, Tianna tells me my appointment time isn't up for another thirty minutes," Sebastian said, his gaze direct and piercing. "If you're still agreeable, I'd like for you to service me."

Hope's eyes widened, then narrowed as a ball of heat rolled through her. She had used and heard the word *service* thousands of times, but never before had an erotic image of her entwined in a man's arms popped into her head. Her hand flexed on the comb. Her breathing escalated as she fought to get Sebastian out of her mind and his slow hands off her body. What was the matter with her? As a rule, she could take or leave men. Usually she left them.

But Sebastian was a different ball game. Nervously, she moistened her dry lips. Sebastian's onyx eyes followed the movement of her tongue with rapt attention. The heat shot higher.

"Sebastian, it's a pleasure to see you again."

With difficulty Sebastian tore his gaze away from Hope's lush red mouth and greeted Della, the owner of the salon. Beautiful and stylishly dressed in a figure-flattering suit the soft color of wisteria, she extended her hand. Gladly he reached for it. "Hello, Della."

She smiled. "I'm happy to see you were able to keep your appointment."

Sebastian noted the twinkle in her eyes and smiled. The first time he came to the salon, Gregory wouldn't have it any other way except to inform Della about Sebastian's haircut horror stories. After she left, Gregory had told him about the woman's business savvy and her close monitoring of the clientele. It wouldn't surprise him if she had seen him leave, then return.

Good. At least Della didn't think Hope was the cause, but it wouldn't hurt to reinforce that notion. "I've almost come to the conclusion that it's the shape of my head and not the barber's fault."

Della shook her head, her manicured nails lightly touching the delicate sterling silver chain around her neck. "Nonsense. You have a beautifully shaped head, and from all the acclaim your plays have garnered over the years, that head possesses considerable brainpower. I look forward to seeing your next play."

"Thank you." No matter how much trepidation or problems lay ahead with *A Matter of Trust,* including the most important one of casting the female lead, Sebastian had discovered early never to let his audience know. Learning the problematic side of the production of a play often took away from patrons' enjoyment. "Open auditions are set for later this afternoon."

"Then I better let you get finished. I have the utmost confidence that Hope will meet your every need." With a reassuring nod to Hope, Della strolled away.

"If you'll take a seat, Mr. Stone, we can get started," Hope instructed.

Sebastian took his seat. His back was to the mirror, but his gaze quickly swept the line of mirrors at every station across from him until he located Hope's reflection in one and watched her step behind him. Efficiently, she placed the black cape around his shoulders and secured it at the nape of his neck. She picked up a pair of thin pointed scissors with one hand and placed the other hand on his head.

Because he knew what was coming next, her touch should have made him tense. Instead he had to stop himself from leaning closer and rubbing against her soft hand like a preening cat. Her fingertips were entirely too gentle, entirely too smooth, and entirely too disturbing. He twisted in his seat.

The next thing he knew, her splayed fingers were beneath the cape on his shoulders, massaging. He jumped and tried to turn around in the chair to face her. "What are you doing?"

"Trying to get you to loosen up. This also helps blood circulation," she told him, continuing the ministration, the pressure of her hands keeping him facing away from her.

It was a good thing he had on the cape or she could tell he didn't need the blood circulating any better in one part of his body. Annoyed with himself for his lapse and her for being the cause, he leaned away from her unsettling hands. "If you don't mind, just stick with the hair."

"Of course, Mr. Stone," she said crisply.

His cell phone rang. Sebastian grabbed for the instrument like a drowning man for a life raft. His self-imposed celibacy must be finally catching up with him. Gingerly he settled back and said, "Sebastian."

"Hi, Sebastian. It's Roscoe Carroll."

Sebastian's life preserver turned out to be an anchor in disguise. Roscoe, wealthy and with a fondness for Havana cigars and imported beer, was the producer and major backer for *A Matter of Trust*. In their past associations Roscoe had adopted a hands-off policy, but this time he wanted in on every decision. Especially choosing the female lead. Maybe it had something to do with his recent divorce from wife number three. Fifty-three years old, bald, five feet six, tipping the scales at two-thirty, Roscoe loved to be in love. "What can I do for you, Roscoe?"

"It's my pleasure to do something for you," Roscoe said, the smile in his West Coast accent easily discernible. "This afternoon when you do the auditions, you don't have to worry about the female lead."

Sebastian's grip on the phone tightened. His back came away from the chair. "I thought we agreed to make the final decision together."

Good-naturedly, Roscoe chuckled. "We will. We couldn't have better than Margot Madison."

"What?" Sebastian leaned farther forward. Gentle hands settled on his shoulders and began massaging. Telling Hope to stop ran through his head only for a second, then he felt his tense muscles loosen. He leaned back in his chair. Hope returned to his head and he almost called her soothing hands back at Roscoe's next words.

"I want Margot and we're lucky to have her. There is no way you're gonna find better at the audition," Roscoe said happily. "She can have her pick of roles. She's a star."

Sebastian knew exactly what Margot was: conniving, manipulative, egotistical . . . and those were her good points. "Have you discussed this with her?"

"That's the fantastic part. She approached me. She'll make this play a hit before it opens."

She'd also make Sebastian's and everyone else's life hell every time things didn't go her way. He glanced around the salon. A few people were already watching him. This wasn't the time or the place to go into his objections. "We've already scheduled auditions for this afternoon. Why don't you come down to the theater and we'll talk before we make any definite decisions?" Sebastian suggested, knowing there was no way he was working with Margot again. It could be financially devastating, especially if Roscoe fought him, but if pushed he'd break his contract and worry about the damage to his bank account later.

"I'll come, but my mind is made up." The line went dead.

Punching the disconnect button, Sebastian returned his phone to his shirt pocket almost at the same time Hope pulled the cape from his shoulders, then briskly brushed around his collar. As soon as she finished, he stood up, pulled out his billfold, and handed her two twenties.

Instead of taking the money, she held out a hand mirror to him. "Don't you want to see?"

"I don't have time." A lopsided head at the moment would really have sent him over the edge. He gestured with the money.

Curling one delicate hand around the glass and the other on the handle, Hope brought the mirror to her chest. "I didn't mean to eavesdrop, but your call sounded as if it was about your play."

"It was. The female lead." His offer of the money was again refused.

Hope moistened her dry lips. "You haven't cast the part yet, have you?"

Sebastian was watching her pink tongue disappear back into her mouth and almost missed her question. "What? No. No, we haven't."

She smiled and his breath caught. "Great, because I happen to know the perfect woman."

"Who?" he asked automatically, his attention on her mouth again.

"You're looking at her."

"What?" Sebastian quickly surfaced back to reality.

"I said you're looking at her," Hope said, trying not to be discouraged by the absolute look of disbelief on Sebastian's face. "I was with the Edgar Evans Touring Company for several years before Jeremy was born. I've played comedy and drama. Even a couple of musicals, although my voice is not very strong."

Sebastian's gaze shot up to her black hair tipped in purple, then laid the money on her service area. Hope might tempt him with her body, but he wasn't crazy enough to cast her for the lead in his play. The day from hell might be trying to drive him crazy, but he wasn't there yet. "You're not right for the part," he said emphatically.

His dismissive words stung Hope's pride. Out of the corner of her eye, she saw Lynn, the stylist next to her, taking in every word. Lynn was a nice woman, but she was also an incurable gossip. Before the afternoon was over, the entire shop would know of Sebastian's curt rejection.

Trying to negate further embarrassment, Hope lowered her

voice. "But you haven't seen me act. I've played the lead part of Eleanor before and I—"

"Surely you can't be serious that you want to try out for the lead," he scoffed, causing several people around them to turn and openly stare.

Hope had been initially interested in playing Eleanor, but she would have settled for a minor role to get back into the theater after being out for so long. Now, seeing the incredulous expression on Sebastian's face, a face that had had her thinking erotic thoughts earlier, set her on a slow boil.

She might have had trepidations about asking for the role, but she had none when it came to her acting. Douglas, the loving husband she had lost unexpectedly almost five years ago to a brain aneurysm, had always maintained that if you didn't believe in yourself, you couldn't expect anyone else to.

Hope forgot all about Della's ironclad policy of deference to the clients no matter what. She forgot about the gossipy Lynn. "And why not?" she practically hissed, planting both hands on her hips.

Usually Sebastian tried to let down easy the unending number of would-be actors and actresses who approached him wanting a role, but his patience was in short supply at the moment. For some odd reason he felt betrayed that Hope and Jeremy wanted something from him like so many others.

It didn't help that Hope was also the eleventh person that day wanting him to help them get a part in his new play. Numbers nine and ten had done their part in continuing Sebastian's day from hell. Nine had been so busy talking, she had overflowed his water glass at lunch. He had thanked God it hadn't been coffee. Number ten had waylaid him on the elevator for fifteen excruciating floors.

And now Hope, a woman who, despite the ugly hair spiking on her head, effortlessly made his body want hers, was asking for the most difficult role he had directed in years. Well, if she wanted to know why she wasn't right for the part, he'd certainly tell her.

"Eleanor Cartwright is sophisticated, elegant, cultured one moment, then a scheming, conniving bitch the next. She can smile and cut your heart out, then cry over a sunset. She's a complex woman, and few actresses can master all the range of emotions she must carry. Certainly not a woman in your profession."

Hope's delicate nostrils flared with fury. "Are you trying to imply that because I'm a hairstylist, you don't think I have any brains or sophistication?"

"Acting is more than wanting to act," Sebastian said, fascinated in spite of himself by how anger heightened the color in her cheeks and made her beauty all the more alluring.

Snatching the money from the counter, Hope stuffed it in his shirt pocket behind the cell phone. "I can see why all the barbers messed up your hair. You head is full of hot air."

Her anger was hot, volatile. Almost tangible. He hadn't meant to hurt her, but it was better him than some slimy producer or director who would use her dream to misuse her body. Sebastian didn't like to think of Jeremy's expression when Hope told him she hadn't gotten the part. Obviously it was important to both of them.

His gaze never leaving Hope's, Sebastian slowly took the money from his pocket and placed it on the table again. It was the only thing he could think of to do to ease his own regrets, and maybe just not have Hope or Jeremy think too badly of him. Why it mattered, he wasn't sure. "I'm sorry."

Refusing to let the tears burning her eyes fall, Hope watched Sebastian and her dream walk away.

THREE

Sebastian couldn't get Hope's face out of his mind. She'd looked so defiant, yet so crushed when he had told her she wasn't right for the lead. He'd made the right decision, he just wished he could have made it easier for her. Her profession had nothing to do with it. Although most stage actors and actresses preferred working in the media off-season or while waiting to get their big break, some weren't able to find employment in that area. Subsequently, they came from all types of jobs. However, he honestly couldn't think of one who had been a hairstylist.

Now, sitting five rows back in the theater, watching woman after woman try out for the lead, he was again made aware of the depth and talent needed to bring Eleanor to life. He'd hoped having an actor bound and gagged in a chair might help the women bring more emotion to the crucial confrontation scene. So far, none of the women auditioning had a clue.

Hearing conversation behind him where there was supposed to be none since auditions were in progress, Sebastian twisted in his seat and saw Roscoe's portly body coming down the middle aisle. He wasn't alone.

Sebastian stood. The hellish day was nipping at his heels again.

"Hello, Sebastian," Roscoe greeted. "You know my lawyer, Shelton Jackson."

"Yes." Sebastian extended his hand. "Shelton. I don't have to ask why you're here."

Shelton smiled, showing even white teeth, and Sebastian thought he knew exactly how a trapped animal felt as it stared into the grinning jaws of a predator about to gobble him up. "Good afternoon, Sebastian. I'm just tagging along. We all want *A Matter of Trust* to be a success."

Sebastian's brows arched at the smooth-talking Shelton, whose meticulous style of dress in a three-thousand-dollar, handmade, midnight blue Brioni suit with white stripes made Roscoe in his off-the-rack plaid golf pants and bright yellow polo shirt appear out of place and very unlikely to have the brainpower to have amassed millions in the unpredictable entertainment industry.

Not so. Roscoe was as sharp as they came and had reached the enviable point in his life where he did things to please himself— much to Sebastian's increasing dismay. "Nicely said, Shelton, but we all know you're here to remind me that the contract I signed would be costly and difficult to get out of, and that Roscoe is the major backer for the play and without his money, we close before we open."

"Now, Sebastian, there is no need to be concerned," Roscoe said, easing his hefty weight into one of the blue-cushioned chairs. "We need each other. You pull out and we both lose a lot of money. You could find another backer, but why bother when we have always worked so well together in the past?"

"I don't want Margot," Sebastian said flatly.

Shelton casually unbuttoned his suit jacket, sat down, then placed his handmade leather attachè case by his highly polished wing tips. "The contract stipulates you and Roscoe are to be in agreement, but if an agreement can't be reached, as owning sixty percent to your fifteen percent, Roscoe gets the final call."

"You never interfered before, Roscoe," Sebastian reminded him.

The older man shrugged. "So, I'm entitled."

Sebastian glanced at Shelton. Shelton smiled.

Trying to keep the expletive locked behind his teeth, Sebastian sat in the seat beside Roscoe. "Try to understand that the woman needed for this part has to be able to display a wide range of emotions. She has to be able to appear innocent and vulnerable at the beginning, then despondent when she is betrayed, vengeful and enraged when she decides to pay Lawson back for framing her for embezzlement, leery of Nolan's interest in her initially, then indecisive when she has to choose between Nolan's love or revenge against his brother, Lawson."

Stretching out his short legs in front of him, Roscoe leaned back in his seat and folded his hands over his wide girth. "That's why my money's on Margot. That woman up there now sure can't cut it."

"We've just begun the auditions," Sebastian defended, hoping somewhere off stage was an actress who would blow their socks off. "Margot is a great actress, I grant you, but she can also cause havoc on the set. If you want this production brought in on time and on budget, then scratch Margot's name."

"I don't know," Roscoe said, shaking his head as another actress took the stage and began Eleanor's monologue. "Looks like we need Margot. She told me she wants this part very much. Seems to me she'd do as you suggested."

Sebastian barely kept from cringing as the hopeful actress on stage screeched her rage and flailed her arms around at the man who had sent her to prison for five years. Subtlety wasn't her strong suit. "Margot only does what anyone says as long as it pleases her."

Roscoe glanced at Sebastian out of the corner of his eye. "She said you might not like having her. I know it's hard since she broke up—"

Sebastian came up in his seat and gave Roscoe his full attention. "I beg your pardon?"

"Don't get huffy, Sebastian," Roscoe chided gently. "Even an aficionado like you strikes out sometimes. It was bound to happen sooner or later."

"Later, maybe—because it didn't happen with Margot," Sebastian said, tired of hearing again that Margot had dumped him after the play he directed her in closed last year. Usually he didn't bother correcting the lie Margot had spread. This time was different. Margot was using the lie to try to get the lead in his play. Never. "I was the one who called the relationship off."

Roscoe appeared thoughtful as he twirled his thumbs. The woman exited stage left and another took her place. "Then you don't mind if I take her out."

Sebastian's eyebrows bunched. "Don't tell me you're thinking of Margot being wife number four."

"Margot is too emotional for a wife. I like someone at home waiting for me with a nice dinner, my slippers, and my Havana," Roscoe said.

Shelton snorted. "You've been reading too many scripts, Roscoe. That woman no longer exists." He shook his dark head. "I thought my sister-in-law would make the perfect, efficient wife for me."

"You wanted to marry Gabe's wife?" Sebastian asked in astonishment. The three of them had known each other since Sebastian moved to New York. Gabe had once been Sebastian's stockbroker before he quit and became a full-time artist.

"Yeah," Shelton said, without a hint of embarrassment. "But that was before Gabe got his hands on her and turned her into Ms. Indestructible Independent. Now she's four months pregnant, on the president's list in grad school, volunteers one night a week at a shelter, and cooks the best meals you ever tasted three nights a week."

"Who cooks the other four?" Roscoe asked.

"Gabe does three and they eat out once a week at a different restaurant." Shelton shook his head. "Women. You just can't trust them to be what they seem."

All three men nodded.

"You can say that again," Sebastian said. "Just this afternoon the woman who edged my hair tried to convince me she could play the lead in *A Matter of Trust*."

"You're sure it wasn't just a come-on?" Roscoe asked with narrowed eyes.

"No. She was serious."

"Since you're not bald, you must have turned her down after she finished with your head," Shelton said jokingly.

"I did."

Sighing, Roscoe turned back to the stage. "Maybe you should have let her come. She couldn't do much worse than some of these women."

"This one may not be able to act, but with a face and body like that she doesn't have to," Shelton commented as he sat up and braced his arms on the back of the seat in front of him. "I'd like to know her better."

"My goodness." Sebastian slowly came to his feet. Even though she was wearing an auburn wig, he'd know those fantastic legs and that incredible face anywhere. "That's her."

"Her who?" Shelton asked.

"My barber," Sebastian said, unaware of his possessive tone.

"Are you sure?" Roscoe asked, leaning closer for a better look.

"I want her name and the address of the shop," Shelton said, coming to his feet as well. "That's one woman who could work on my head as well as any other part of my body she wanted to."

Not to be outdone, Roscoe rose. "You're stronger than I thought, Sebastian, if you turned her down. Maybe you were telling the truth about Margot."

Sebastian wasn't listening, he was watching as Hope, head high, shoulders erect, wearing a white blouse and little black skirt, crossed to center stage. She held something in her hand, but it was hidden behind her back. She stopped and looked straight at him.

He took an involuntary step backward. Hatred, pure and sharp, stared back at him.

. . .

This was it, Hope thought as she watched the shocked expression on Sebastian's face. This was her chance to prove to the snooty Mr. Hotshot Director that she had what it took to star in his play. Not good enough? She'd show him. Just thinking about his put-down made her blood begin to boil all over again.

Instead of trying to repress her anger, she used it to her benefit. Adrenaline rushed through her and she felt almost heady with its power. Fear was impossible. Her character, Eleanor, had no fear. Only a purpose.

By slow degrees, her hand came from behind her back to reveal the seven-inch blade of a mock butcher knife. Gracefully, she sank to her knees. The bound actor's shocked gaze darted from her to the gleaming blade.

"I'm going to kill you, Lawson." Eleanor's voice was icy cold and utterly controlled. "Not quickly, but slowly and with agonizing pain. You were so easy to lure here. You were actually stupid enough to think that you were such a magnificent lover that I could forget you were the reason I spent the last five years in prison. You were so eager to take me from Nolan, as you've taken all of your life from others, that you let your selfish greed lead to your destruction." Eleanor smiled, a flash of teeth and heartless black eyes.

"Struggle all you want, but the ropes around your wrists and feet won't budge. I thought it best, since before you die I intend to take that part of you that you value the most." She ran the knife in her hand up the inside of his thigh. "Are you whimpering behind your gag, Lawson? Not very manly of you. But then, you always were a coward. Worse, you're a treacherous coward, and now you have to pay."

Her voice hitched, wavered. "Nolan will be so distraught by your death, and so will I. I'll consider it my duty to console him. Comfort him."

Her head fell forward. Tears dropped on the tip of the butcher knife and slid to the wooden handle. Seconds later, laughter erupted as she threw her head back triumphantly, her eyes gleaming. "I thought I did that very well, didn't you? No one will suspect that I killed you. After you're buried, I will become Nolan's wife, sleep in his arms, and forget I ever allowed you to touch me. Now, which do you want to lose first, the right or the left?"

Eleanor brought the knife up and plunged downward again and again. Crackling laughter erupted. "You should have loved me. You should have loved me. Now you'll love no one."

"On second thought, I don't want to know how to contact her," Shelton said, his words hushed and unsteady.

"Shhhh," Sebastian said, not wanting to miss one word, one gesture, one nuance.

As gracefully as Hope had sunk to her knees, she rose. For a long moment she and Sebastian stared at each other. Her breath trembled over her slightly parted lips. Her reaction, she was sure, had more to do with the man than with the rush of auditioning on Broadway. But she had nailed the scene. She knew it from the look of rapt astonishment on his face and the stunned relief on the bound actor's face. She had accomplished what she had come for. Without a backward glance, she walked off the stage.

"If I can speak now . . ." Shelton began, then continued by saying, "your barber has been wasting her talents. She's nothing short of brilliant."

"Brilliant," Roscoe echoed.

"She's Eleanor," Sebastian said, excitement running through his veins.

"Too bad we can't cast her," Roscoe said, taking his seat.

Sebastian rounded on him. "What are you talking about?"

"I admit she's fabulous, but we both know we need someone with experience to play the role," the producer reminded him.

"She said she had acted before." Sebastian wanted Hope for the part and he intended to have her.

"Then why didn't you let her audition?" Shelton wanted to know.

"Bad decision on my part, it seems. Excuse me." Exiting the row, Sebastian rushed up to the stage. He looked among the group of audition hopefuls, but Hope wasn't among them. He went to his assistant, Roger Kurt. "Where is Hope Lassiter?"

"She left," Roger said, glancing at his clipboard. "I tried to get her to stay, but she said she had to go home. She was something, wasn't she?"

"Where are her credits?"

Roger handed Sebastian a neatly typed sheet of paper. "Figured you would want to see hers."

With each credit he read, Sebastian's certainty grew that Hope could play the lead. The list of New York performances and tours was impressive. The last notation was five years ago, when she had the lead in the off-Broadway production of *A Raisin in the Sun*. She must have stopped when she became pregnant with Jeremy, but why hadn't she returned? Where was the father?

Sebastian admitted his interest in the answers had nothing to do with casting her for the part of Eleanor, but asked anyway. "Do you know anything about her other than what's here?"

Roger shook his sandy head. "No. Sorry. You want me to try and find out from the union?"

"No, I'll do it," Sebastian said, studying the credits again as if that would give him the answers he sought.

"Shall we continue?" Roger asked.

Sebastian's dark head came up. He had his Eleanor, but she'd need an understudy. "Yes." The sheet of paper in his hand, he bounded down the steps off the stage, went back to Roscoe, and handed Hope's credits to him. "After you read this, you'll change your mind about casting Hope."

Roscoe scanned the page, then gave it back. "If she'll take the part."

Sebastian frowned. "Of course she'll take the part. Why wouldn't she? She approached me about it."

"And you turned her down," the producer reminded him. "I watched her doing her monologue. She was looking at you, Sebastian, and it wasn't with any fondness."

"I don't think I'd let her cut my hair again if I were you," Shelton put in.

"You're overreacting." Folding the paper, Sebastian put it in his pocket and took his seat beside Roscoe. "Hope will jump at the chance to play Eleanor."

"I hate to rain on your parade, Sebastian, but if she was as anxious as you said, she would have stuck around." Shelton nodded toward the stage as he sat back down. "I can see two other women who performed earlier, waiting off stage."

"She probably went home to see about her son, Jeremy," Sebastian said, hoping he was right. If Hope hadn't wanted the part, she wouldn't have tried out for it. Or would she have?

"Call her," Roscoe urged. "Her number is on her credits."

"She's probably not home," Sebastian hedged.

Roscoe turned around in the seat, his gaze narrowed. "I saw a mobile phone listing."

Annoyance pricked Sebastian. "Why are you pushing this?"

"Because I'm taking Margot to dinner tonight and I know she's going to ask me about the auditions." Roscoe tapped Sebastian's shirt pocket. "Make the call."

Pulling Hope's information sheet and his cell phone from his pocket at same time, he punched in her number. She answered on the second ring. "Hello."

The husky voice came through loud and clear. Sebastian immediately thought of her lush lips, then chided himself for his lapse. "Hope. Ms. Lassiter, this is Sebast—" Click. Incredulously, Sebastian held the dead phone out in front of him.

"What happened?" Roscoe asked.

"She hung up on me," Sebastian said, still not quite believing it.

Roscoe stood. "Guess I can tell Margot she's still in the running."

"Hope will come around." Deactivating the phone, Sebastian replaced it in his pocket.

"I wouldn't put money on it if I were you, Sebastian," Shelton advised. He picked up his attaché case and came to his feet. "I thought I knew what Jessica, my sister-in-law, wanted, knew how to handle her, but as it turns out, I didn't know squat. The other women I knew got excited over diamonds and influential men. I thought she'd be the same way. She wasn't then and she isn't now.

"Gabe had a small greenhouse built for Jessica because she likes to grow her own herbs, and from the way she was crying and kissing him you would have thought he had given her a rock the size of a golfball. His paintings are bringing in big bucks, and although she's happy people are finally recognizing what a great artist he is, she cares about Gabe, not the money. He always said she was different and had a mind of her own. I didn't believe him until it was too late. Now they're going to make me an uncle. Taught me a lesson that women are only predictable in their unpredictability."

"This is different." Sebastian came to his feet.

"I believe I said those similar words to Gabe, and instead of being the groom, I was the groomsman," Shelton said with a chuckle. "Once I got over the shock, I didn't mind losing, but I have a feeling you might."

"I'm not going to lose," Sebastian said. "I want Hope to play Eleanor."

"But does Hope want anything to do with you?" Nodding his balding head, Roscoe walked away with Shelton.

Deep in thought, Sebastian retook his seat. So he'd come down a little hard on her. It had been for her best interests.

Then he recalled the controlled hatred in her eyes and the knife in her hands, and repressed a shudder. She had ad-libbed that part of Lawson's kidnapping. Sebastian had an uneasy feeling it was for his benefit.

Hope Lassiter was turning out to be a woman as complex as Eleanor. Time would tell if she could be as vindictive.

FOUR

"Hope, I can't wait another second," Bridgett confessed as she sat in Hope's chair at Della's House of Style. "All you would say last night when you came home was that you had auditioned for the part, then you had to leave to perform at the community theater and we didn't get a chance to talk. I could tell you were upset and didn't want Jeremy to find out, so I didn't press you for information. The only way I could stand not asking what happened was knowing I was coming here this morning to get my hair done."

Pausing in the act of securing a soft white dry towel around Bridgett's neck, Hope met the other woman's worried gaze in the mirror. "I ruined any chance of ever acting in any production Sebastian Stone is ever associated with, that's what happened."

Bridgett's perfectly arched brows bunched. "How?"

"By ad-libbing a scene guaranteed to make a man shudder, then hanging up the phone on him," Hope told her friend.

"You hung up on him—but why?" Bridgett asked, keeping her words hushed.

Hope paused in sectioning the other woman's wet hair. "Because he put me down earlier in the shop and I didn't want to hear him do it again."

With the edge of the white towel, Bridgett dabbed a drop of

water from her temple. "Are you sure that's why he called? Maybe it was about the part. You're a marvelous actress."

Hope smiled with remembered pleasure, then spritzed the strands of hair in her hand. "Bridgett, I nailed the scene. Sebastian had this look of total awe on his face after I finished."

"Then maybe he was calling you for the part."

The smile on Hope's face faded. "No. I walked on that stage knowing I wouldn't get the part. I overheard one of the women waiting to audition say that her agent had heard that it was almost a certainty that Margot Madison was after the part and would get it."

"Didn't I read where they were involved once?"

"Yes." Hope's lips pressed into a thin line. The fact that Sebastian and Margot were once lovers shouldn't have bothered her in the least. It did. More than it should have. Reaching for a roller, Hope quickly wrapped Bridgett's hair around it, secured it with a clamp, then reached for another roller.

"Good morning, Hope."

Hope gasped and spun around. Standing there was Sebastian in all his stunning glory. No man should look that gorgeous in the morning. She caught herself before she sighed. Presenting her back to him, she picked up the roller. "Please leave."

"I apologize for what I said here yesterday, and would like very much to speak privately with you," he told her.

"I'm busy," she snapped, then clamped her teeth together. Della had been very understanding about the scene she and Sebastian had created yesterday, but she had made it clear she did not want a repeat performance.

"I see." This was not going well at all, Sebastian thought. Hope wasn't the least bit anxious to talk to him. Her hair was back to being spiked and purple-tipped. For some crazy reason, he liked it better this way. Perhaps because it showed how versatile she could be.

Trying to figure out how to proceed, he caught the glare of the woman in the chair. Instantly, he recognized her from the day before. If the elderly woman left with Jeremy, it stood to reason that she might have some influence on Hope. He smiled and extended his hand. "Good morning, I'm Sebastian Stone."

"If Hope doesn't like you, then I don't either, and that pretty smile is not going to help," the woman said without batting a lash.

Sebastian blinked, then laughed. Up-front and outspoken, just like his mother. He liked her immediately. "I'm trying to apologize, but she won't listen."

"Half the shop is looking this way. Please leave," Hope told him, but she couldn't help taking a peek now and then at him in the mirror. He certainly knew how to wear his clothes. This morning he had on a tan linen and silk sports coat, an ivory linen shirt, and cream linen pleated trousers.

"Has Margot Madison been cast for the part of Eleanor?" Bridgett asked.

"Bridgett!" Hope screeched. More heads turned.

Sebastian's lips narrowed into a straight line. "No, she hasn't. Nor will she be, if I have anything to say about it."

Resisting Hope, the elderly woman spun in her chair until she could look Sebastian directly in the eye. "From everything I've read, you have a reputation for honesty."

"That's right, and I'm proud of it. I don't lie."

Bridgett nodded her satisfaction and let Hope swing her chair back around. "Listen to what he has to say, Hope."

"I will not." Whirling, she picked up a clipper from her workstation. "Leave or I'll give you a buzz cut."

Sebastian didn't budge, his black eyes narrowed as he studied her face. "You're even more beautiful when you're angry."

Hope gasped, surprise and delight sweeping through her. It just wasn't fair that he could turn her to mush with a look or a few words. "Leave," she repeated, but her heart wasn't in it.

"Have dinner with me and I will." From behind his back, he drew out a fresh-cut flower arrangement of miniature yellow and pink roses, a mixture of tulips, and baby's breath.

"You have style, Sebastian," Bridgett announced. "Mind your manners, Hope, and take the flowers. My hair is getting dry."

Although Hope was aware that Bridgett was conning her, she put down the clipper and took the beautiful arrangement. Her friend also gave her a gracious out. Both of them had a weakness for flowers. "Thank you." Her voice came out unsteady. Before she knew it, like a schoolgirl, she had buried her face in the sweet smell.

"The pleasure is all mine," Sebastian said, grinning like a loon.

"I'm glad we're all happy," Della announced.

Hope shoved the flowers at Bridgett, shot an annoyed look at Sebastian, and picked up the spritz bottle. "Sebastian was just leaving."

"You didn't tell me what time to pick you up," he said, unmoved.

Hope swung back around. Della and most of the people in the shop were watching her. "I—I—"

"Seven, and make reservations at the Palm Court," Bridgett told him, and gave him their address, then held out her hand. "Bridgett Swanson, and I have a fondness for flowers and Swiss chocolate."

Sebastian chuckled and shook her hand. "I'll remember. Until tonight, ladies," he said, then spoke to Della. "Please don't blame Hope. I can be pushy when I want something."

Della folded her arms across the front of her red silk dress. She was no shrinking violet herself. "And what are you after?"

Everything in the salon stopped. Everyone leaned forward to hear the answer, including Hope and Bridgett.

"I want to discuss this with Hope first, but suffice it to say, she's one of the most brilliant actresses I've ever had the pleasure to see perform and I'd consider it a pleasure to work with her."

"You do? You would?" Hope heard herself say.

"I do. Until tonight."

Hands in his pockets, he strolled from the shop whistling.

· · ·

Hope was a nervous wreck. Bridgett had picked one of the most exclusive and expensive restaurants in the city and it was located in *the* hotel of New York, The Plaza. And Hope couldn't find anything to wear. After Jeremy was born she had added a few pounds, and the dress she now had on was too snug in the hips. "I look like a stuffed sausage in this."

"No you don't, Mommy," Jeremy said from where he sat in the middle of her bed strewn with clothes.

Hope turned from the full-length mirror in her bedroom and smiled at him. He thought it was fun seeing her small array of evening wear scattered on the bed, when she had always insisted he hang up his clothes after he took them off. She returned to studying her reflection in the mirror, then trying to smooth out the puckers in the side seams by her hips in the sheath. Yet, no matter how many times her hands swept over the wrinkled sky blue material, the fabric refused to remain smooth.

She barely repressed a sigh. "Jeremy, you're looking at me through the eyes of love."

"Won't Mr. Stone love you?" Jeremy asked, climbing off the bed to come and stare up at her.

Her heart racing, she gazed down at her son. "Why would you say something like that?"

"We're supposed to love everybody," he said innocently. "Isn't that what you always said I'm to do?"

Hope felt foolish, and realized she was getting in way over her head. Her eyes closed. This night meant entirely too much to her.

"Mommy, what's the matter?"

Her eyes opened. She tried to bend from the knees, couldn't in the tight dress, and wanted to groan. She glanced at the clock. Six-thirty. There wasn't enough time to call and cancel even if she knew Sebastian's phone number. "Nothing, sweetheart. Mommy is just having a little trouble finding a dress to wear."

"Not anymore," Bridgett announced after a brisk knock on the door. "Some things of Cynthia's were packed in the attic. How about this little number?"

It was a dream, chic, black, and hand-beaded. Hope reached out, then quickly withdrew her hand. "I can't wear Cynthia's dress."

"It's not her dress anymore, it's yours." Casually throwing the dress over her shoulder, Bridgett turned Hope around and unzipped the dress she wore to the midpoint of her back. "She always did have too many clothes. I called and she said to tell you to help yourself to anything you find. She's working such long hours with her residency, she doesn't have any time to go out."

"What about Peter Johnson?" Hope asked over her shoulder. The main reason Bridgett had advertised for a female boarder was because she was lonely, with her only child in med school. Cynthia, at the top five percent of her class, was already planning to do her internship and residency in cardiology at the famed Johns Hopkins Hospital in Baltimore, Maryland. The vivacious Cynthia was one of those women who had it all, beauty, brains, charm, and like her mother, was as down-to-earth as they came.

"Struck out, like all the rest," Bridgett finally answered with a sigh. "I may never be a grandmother."

"You got me, Aunt Bridgett," Jeremy said, having heard the story many times.

"Right you are," she said, smiling down at him, then handed Hope the dress. "Let's go downstairs and let your mother get dressed."

"Thanks, Bridgett. I'll call Cynthia tomorrow and thank her as well."

"When you do, tell her how much fun you had so maybe she'll take a hint and try to keep a man for more than a couple of dates. About time too—you're worse than she is about dating."

Hope frowned. "This is business. Not a date."

"If that were the case, you would have kept on the first thing you put on." The landlady glanced from the clothes scattered on the bed to Hope. "You didn't have this problem when you went to dinner with that school principal a couple of months ago."

"Some of them were too tight," she quickly defended.

"Some, not all," Bridgett said, then lightly touched Hope's cheek. "Tonight is important to you. Accept it and enjoy yourself. You deserve it. We'll be downstairs."

Sebastian got out of the backseat of the limousine, bounded up the steps, and rang the doorbell. Tonight he had pulled out all the stops. He planned on doing everything in his power to ensure Hope took the role of Eleanor. Nothing was too good for his future star.

Through the oval-shaped frosted glass in the door he saw Bridgett and Jeremy approach. The door opened.

"Good evening, Mr. Stone," Bridgett greeted with Jeremy by her side. "You're right on time. Punctuality is a good trait in a man."

"Good evening, Mrs. Swanson. These are for you." Sebastian handed her a long white box, and a small rectangular one wrapped in gold foil.

"Thank you, but you didn't forget Hope, did you?" Bridgett asked, taking the candy and flowers.

"In the limo," he said, then bent and held out his hand to Jeremy. "Sebastian Stone."

Jeremy reciprocated with all the manners he had been taught. "Jeremy Douglas Lassiter."

"Pleased to meet you, Jeremy." Since that morning Sebastian had learned that Jeremy's father, Douglas, had died while he and Hope were touring in Chicago. From all accounts, the couple had been very much in love.

"Would you care for something to drink, Mr. Stone?" Bridgett inquired, closing the door as Sebastian entered.

"No, thank you, and please call me Sebastian."

"Only if you call me Bridgett."

"I'd consider it an honor and privilege, Bridgett."

Pleased, she spoke to Jeremy. "Please show Mr. Stone into the living room and keep him company while I put these in some water."

"Yes, ma'am. It's this way," Jeremy said, unselfconsciously taking Sebastian's hand and leading him down the short hallway to the room on the left.

The room had style and warmth. The walls were painted a warm peach. Antique furniture graced the room, which was dominated by an immense bay window draped in pristine white sheers. A fresh-cut arrangement of tulips and lilies sat on the clawfoot coffee table. Photographs were everywhere. It was evident that in this home family was important.

Taking a seat on the sofa Jeremy indicated, Sebastian picked up a picture of Hope holding a baby in a long white christening gown. Tears sparkled on her cheek despite the smile on her face.

"That's when I was a baby," Jeremy said, standing by Sebastian with his hand on his leg. "Mommy said it wasn't a sad cry, but a happy one."

"She doesn't cry often, does she?" The thought disturbed Sebastian.

"No, sir. Just the time I got lost in the store and the time I fell out of the tree trying to get the cat," Jeremy confessed, then tucked his head.

Immediately concerned, Sebastian replaced the picture. "What's the matter, Jeremy?"

"Mommy might not like if I tell you," he said, his little head slowly coming up.

The black eyes were so much like his mother's, Sebastian would have done almost anything to help. But he didn't want to go against Hope's wishes. "Jeremy, we haven't known each other for long, but you can trust me. I'd like to help."

Jeremy threw a quick glance at the door, then leaned over and whispered, "I think she was crying last night."

Sebastian felt the bottom fall out of his stomach. Had he caused that?

"When she came home yesterday she wasn't happy like I thought she would be. She didn't get the part she wanted, did she?" Jeremy asked, his face somber. "She always gets me what I want. At least most of the time. I wish I could do something to help her. I could wash your car or something to help change your mind." His small face scrunched up. "I'm not very good at cleaning my room, so maybe we better leave that out."

Sebastian couldn't speak for a moment, his throat was so full. What a loving, selfless child. "Jeremy, can you keep a secret for a little while?"

He nodded.

"That's why I'm here. To offer the part of Eleanor to your mother." Jeremy opened his mouth to yell and Sebastian quickly put his fingers to his lips. "Our secret, remember?"

"I'll remember. Thank you, Mr. Stone." Jeremy threw his arms around Sebastian's neck.

Laughing, Sebastian hugged him back. The kid was all right. Then the noise of heels on the hardwood floor in the hallway caused him to turn toward the door. Hope appeared seconds later. Jeremy must have heard her also, because he loosened his stranglehold on Sebastian's neck and ran to his mother.

"Mommy, you're beautiful."

"Thank you," she said, her uncertain gaze going to Sebastian.

Sebastian, his heart doing a jitterbug in his chest, came to his feet. She was stunning, absolutely stunning. But what had she done to her hair?

FIVE

"What's the matter?" Hope asked, her heart sinking at his stunned expression. "Why are you staring at me?"

"Your hair," Sebastian whispered.

Hope's hand flew up to her head. She rushed to the hall mirror, with Jeremy and Sebastian behind her. Try as she might, she didn't see anything wrong with her hair she had spent an hour styling. Finally she turned to ask him. "What's wrong with it?"

"It's not purple and sticking all over your head," Sebastian told her, fingering the soft, sassy black curls framing her face.

Hope finally understood and would have relaxed if Sebastian hadn't continued to touch her hair. "I-it was washout dye for the play I was in. I left it in as sort of a walking advertisement. Neither Della nor my customers mind."

"Dye? Then you don't have purple hair all the time?" he asked, reluctantly drawing his hand away.

"No," she answered, trying to control her uneven breathing. The man definitely put her body into hyperdrive.

"Mommy's a motorcycle lady and gets to beat up two men," Jeremy said proudly.

Rubbing her hand across Jeremy's head, Hope smiled. "That's the scene Jeremy likes best."

"Sorry this took so long," Bridgett said, coming up to the three-some with the flower arrangement. "But I had a difficult time find-ing a vase big enough."

"Here let me take that." Sebastian lifted the large arrangement of mixed flowers, his gaze going back to Hope.

Bridgett frowned. "What did I miss?"

Jeremy giggled. "Mr. Stone thought Mommy's hair was purple all the time."

Sebastian looked momentarily chagrined, then laughed. "I had almost talked myself into liking the purple hair, but I have to ad-mit you look lovely with your natural hair." The smile vanished. "That is your natural hair, isn't it?"

Hope opened her mouth, but Bridgett said, "A woman never discusses her hair color or her age."

All the adults laughed. Jeremy peered up at them, puzzled. Se-bastian leaned over and said, "I'll explain it to you when you get older. Now, where shall I put this?"

Hope's nerves, which had been settling nicely, went haywire again. Walking down the steps to the open door of the waiting limousine, she couldn't get it out of her mind that Sebastian's words to Jeremy indicated he'd be around for a long time. Was he just mouthing words or did he plan to see them often?

She had to admit she hoped it was the latter, and she wasn't at all sure if it was just because of the play. The man was jaw-dropping gorgeous and always impeccably dressed. Any woman would be proud to be seen with him.

He had a style that denoted his wealth, authority, and power. Heads would always swivel when he entered a room. Rightly so. He possessed that special something that would forever set him apart from other men. The way he dressed added to his image. A measured fraction of crisp white shirt extended beyond the black tuxedo jacket. The collar of his shirt caressed, but did not bind, his neck. His black pants legs gently grazed the top of his immaculate shoes. Hope was both thrilled and a bit nervous about being in his company.

Thanking the uniformed chauffeur who held the door open, she got inside the car. Sebastian climbed in beside her. The door closed, enclosing them in a luxurious cocoon of comfort.

Despite the roominess of the backseat, she felt almost lightheaded because of Sebastian's nearness. The heat emanating from his body where their bodies touched, from shoulder to knee, wasn't helping. The subtle fragrance of his spicy cologne whispered and teased her senses to come closer. Swallowing, she inched away.

If Sebastian noticed her moving, he didn't comment. Instead he leaned over and picked up a white box from the leather seat across from them. "For you."

Accepting the box, she tugged the intricate white and gold bow on top free. She glanced at Sebastian and lifted the lid. A soft sigh escaped her. Inside was a white orchid delicately tinged with pink. Trembling fingers lifted the flower. "It's beautiful. Thank you. You didn't have to."

"You're welcome, and as we get to know each other better, you'll find out that I never do anything I don't want to."

There he went again, talking as if their association would be a long one. She couldn't wait another second. "You mentioned you admired my acting. Does that mean you have a part in *A Matter of Trust* or in a future play for me?"

"*A Matter of Trust.* I want you to play Eleanor."

Hope's eyes rounded in shock. "But . . . but . . . I know what you said this morning at the salon, but I'd heard Margot Madison had a lock on the part."

"I don't lie, Hope. Ever. If they want me to direct *A Matter of Trust,* Margot will have nothing to do with the production," he said tightly. Then his voice gentled. "The major backer for the play was there yesterday when you performed. He's agreeable if you want the part."

Sebastian went on to quote a salary that had her eyes widening again. He anticipated the cast to be finalized very quickly. Rehearsals would start in three to four weeks and the play would open six weeks later. He expected the play to run on Broadway six months, perhaps longer. "All you have to do is say yes."

Hope was speechless. She had hoped, prayed, but now that it was happening, doubts began to creep in. Her temper had had time to cool and the ramifications of carrying the success of the play on her shoulders wasn't comforting.

"Well?" Sebastian prompted.

Her fingers clutched the stem of the flower. "I wanted the role at first, but now I'm not so sure." She rushed on at his hard expression. "I don't guess I really stopped to consider that I couldn't schedule rehearsals around Jeremy as I do my appointments at Della's. Then there are the nightly performances and matinees. I never agree to a community theater play that will last over a week."

"You could hire a sitter," Sebastian pointed out.

"But it wouldn't be me." She twisted in her seat toward him, trying to make him understand. "Most of my relatives and those of my late husband are in Florida. I came here after my husband died, when I was barely two months pregnant. I'd always loved New York and decided to live here. Answering Bridgett's ad for a female boarder was a godsend. She's wonderful, but it's important that I be there at night to listen to Jeremy's prayers, tuck him in, read to him."

"Jeremy wants this for you, too," Sebastian reminded her.

"He may act and sound like an adult, but he's still a little boy." Hope glanced out the window at the glowing lights as the limo sped through the night. "He'd miss me and I'd miss him."

"But think of all the advantages you could give him with your increased income," Sebastian said, determined to win this argument. "He could attend the best private schools, eat at the finest restaurants, travel extensively. The world would be his."

"If the play is a hit and I get job offers afterwards."

Sebastian jerked his head back. "I've never had a flop in my career."

Hope smiled at the affronted expression on his handsome face, then sobered. "No offense, but this could be the first time. I've had the bad experience of having a play close on me. Fortunately for us when Douglas was alive, I kept my cosmetology license current and could find work. But nothing as exclusive as Della's."

Her hand briefly fluttered to her hair. "My job there is my only source of income. The booth spaces there are at a premium and highly prized. I had to wait almost two years before a position opened up for me. If I left, I couldn't expect to just walk back in. My spot would be filled and I'd have to start over someplace else trying to build up a clientele that may not be as loyal or tip as good as those at Della's."

While Sebastian understood her rationale, he wasn't a man to take no. "What if I could guarantee your salary for a year?"

She shook her head. "And then what? I can't gamble with Jeremy's future that way."

He studied her a long time. "I watched you on that stage. You were Eleanor and you loved it."

She twisted the flower in her hand. "You're right. The bright lights, the adrenaline rush. It was wonderful being on a real stage again. But nothing is as important as Jeremy's stability and happiness."

"You're amazing."

Her brows bunched. "What?"

"I said you're amazing," he repeated.

"I heard what you said, but why did you say it?"

"Because you are. I've met only a few women who were willing to put their children—or their husbands, for that matter—before their career," he said. His ex-wife certainly wasn't one of those women. "But in this case I think you're wrong. You could have the career and Jeremy could have his mother. The play will be a success, I can feel it. Once it closes, you'll be able to have your pick of roles.

You'll no longer be just an actress, you'll be a star, and Jeremy will reap the benefits. You'll be able to give him everything you've wanted for him. A pony, a swimming pool."

"How do you know what he wants?"

He shrugged. "Don't most children?"

"They grow up fine without them," she said.

"That may be, but that doesn't keep you from wanting to give them to him," Sebastian said.

Hope shook her head. "You certainly were right about being pushy when you want something."

"You haven't seen anything yet. I'm going to show you what star treatment is like." The limo pulled to a stop. Across the street was Central Park. "Starting now. Let's give people in the restaurant their first look at the next star on Broadway."

The restaurant was elegant and impressive. Immediately they were shown to a secluded candlelit table. The wine steward appeared after the waiter left with their food orders. Sebastian rattled off some French-sounding name of a wine to go with their filet mignon, which put a smile on the dour face of the steward. Hope bit her lip. Some star she was going to make.

"What's the matter?" Sebastian asked.

Hope saw what could have been a wonderful evening come to a screeching halt. The pads of her fingers stroked the white orchid on the table.

"Hope?" Sebastian reached across the table and covered her hand with his. She started, her gaze coming up to meet his. "If you're worried about Margot, don't."

"Actually, I have a more immediate problem." The heat of his hand was amazing and disturbing. Despite this, she felt her uneasiness increase. She'd never had this much difficulty before. Bridgett was right. Tonight did mean a great deal to her.

"What is it?"

Before she could answer, the wine steward reappeared, filled their glasses, placed the bottle in the cooler, then left. Hope pulled her hand back and watched Sebastian pick up his glass. He'd expect her to do the same. It was now or never.

"I've never developed a taste for wine. Especially dry red ones. Whites are a little better, but not much. The only one I found so far that I liked is a sweet white dessert wine one of Bridgett's friends sent her from a winery in California."

She held his gaze with difficulty. Now he'd think her gauche and probably take her home immediately. The school principal certainly had been miffed. Then she hadn't cared. Now she cared too much.

Sebastian set his wine down. "The fault is mine, not yours, Hope. I should have asked. I want you to enjoy yourself this evening, to be comfortable with me." Leaning across the table, he tipped her chin up with a long, tapered finger. "My first wine was Ripple. How's that for astute evaluation of bouquet and taste?"

Hope laughed.

His eyes darkened. "I like the sound of that."

She felt her cheeks heat. Without meaning to, she fluttered her eyelashes. Then flushed again. Goodness. She hadn't flirted since high school.

"What would you like to drink?"

"Iced tea."

He held up his hand and instantly a waiter appeared. "Please, take this away and bring two iced teas instead."

"Certainly, sir."

"See how easy that was?"

"Only because it was you," she told him.

"Probably." He glanced around the posh room. "The staff here is trained to cater to the whims of the rich and influential. To keep a straight face no matter what is asked of them."

"What about when they go in the back?"

Sebastian paused in answering as the waiter served their salad and tea. "Truth be known, I've never really thought about it and neither should you. Choosing the right wine isn't the most important thing in life. Raising a happy, well-adjusted child is infinitely more important and difficult," he said. "If I or the average person had to choose which one they'd value the most, it would be the child. You've done yourself proud. Jeremy is a wonderful little boy who shows every indication of growing into an intelligent, sensitive, and caring man."

"Thank you," she said. "He's my world. I want so much for him."

"I understand. That's why I'm going to talk you into playing Eleanor so you can show him more of it," he said, reaching for a dinner roll.

Laughing, Hope picked up her salad fork. "You never give up, do you?"

"Not when it's important." Sebastian broke his roll, but his gaze remained on Hope. "Make no mistake. You're under siege."

Her eyes widened. Her hand shook so badly she laid her fork aside. "I'm not sure I like the sound of that."

His slow, knowing grin curled her toes. "You will."

SIX

Sebastian proved to be a man of his word. Hope and Jeremy, and even Bridgett, reaped the benefits.

The inclusion of Bridgett in what Sebastian called "star treatment" endeared him to Hope all the more. He seemed to know instinctively that if she were to become a success, Bridgett, who had rented her a room at a tenth of what she could have gotten, would benefit as well.

Besides the fresh flowers each received every other day, a car and driver were at their disposal. To top it off, Sebastian had loaned them his own chef, Antoine. Hope and Bridgett were ready to send the arrogant little man away until they tasted his smoked salmon. It was to die for. His sinfully rich chocolate dessert was decadent and delicious. Not one word of objection was uttered when he returned the next morning to prepare breakfast. Since both women enjoyed good food, but not the preparation, he was greeted with open arms.

A couple of days later a man dressed as a sixteenth century French courtier, powdered wig, white stockings, and gold buckled shoes had entered the salon and presented her with an engraved invitation to dinner at Sebastian's penthouse apartment. She'd said yes in a flash. The trunk of Cynthia's had yielded the most divine long red dress.

She felt as beautiful as Sebastian's words and attentive gaze said she was when he picked her up. Everything—the star-kissed night, the scrumptious food, the sparkling fruit drink Antoine had prepared especially for her, the spectacular view of the city and Central Park—was absolutely perfect. But especially the man.

Sebastian could make her toes tingle just by looking at her a certain way. She'd kicked off her shoes and delighted in the experience.

The next morning Hope woke up with a smile on her face, wondering what Sebastian's next move would be. Downstairs she looked at the crepes Antoine was preparing for breakfast and worried about adding another pound to her hips. Yet somehow she let him coax her into eating two. Delicate and light, they were loaded down with freshly prepared whipped cream and plump blueberries. She asked for seconds.

At dinner that night, Antoine even did the impossible, Hope had thought, by cajoling Jeremy into eating the mushrooms that had been sautéed with tomato and goat cheese sauce on his breaded veal cutlet. The man was a culinary genius and was making all three of them into gluttons. Sebastian, who had been invited over for dinner, viewed the entire scene of them pigging out with a satisfied smile on his face.

Three weeks after Sebastian had come into her life, Hope sat in the bright lemon yellow kitchen at the breakfast table savoring the last bite of her delectable omelet loaded with cheese, ham, red and green bell peppers, and whatever else Antoine had thrown in. Finished, she sipped her freshly squeezed orange juice and vowed the next time she saw Sebastian she would tell him not to exploit her weakness and to take Antoine away.

Leaving the house fifteen minutes later to take Jeremy to preschool, she had her chance. Sebastian, arms folded, long legs crossed at the ankles, looking as yummy as the strawberries she had devoured the day before, leaned against his Mercedes. It quickly crossed her mind that she'd like the opportunity to devour Sebastian the same way. Instead of the flush of embarrassment that would have appeared a week ago, she thought of all the ways she'd go about tasting him.

"Sebastian," Jeremy yelled, and raced down the steps.

Laughing, Sebastian picked him up and twirled him around. It had become a ritual the two enjoyed ever since they had seen a man do the same with a little boy. The three of them had been at the park having a picnic. Sebastian had glanced over at Jeremy. Jeremy had grinned. Without exchanging a word, the two had gotten up from the blanket they were sitting on. Jeremy had run a short ways off, turned, and, grinning wildly, had run straight into Sebastian's outstretched arms. From then on, Jeremy had called him Sebastian.

Hope had been so pleased that Sebastian seemed to enjoy and understand Jeremy so well, she had taken him to task only briefly, when after leaving the park he had driven to a riding stable. Jeremy had surprised her by mounting the small pony with very little assistance from Sebastian. Jeremy had had the time of his life. Score another round to Sebastian.

Hope had no doubt that, if Bridgett weren't so proud of her prized flower garden in the backyard, Sebastian would have tried to talk her into putting in a pool. On learning Jeremy wanted to be an astronaut, he had arranged for Jeremy to talk with one of the astronauts on the last space shuttle mission. Sebastian was a tactical genius.

Shaking her head, she watched Sebastian set Jeremy on his feet, then rub his hand affectionately across the top of the official New York Yankees baseball cap on his head. Sebastian just happened to have tickets for the season opener. On Jeremy's dresser, proudly displayed, was a baseball signed by all the players. How did you fight a man who wanted to give you your heart's desire and fulfill the desires of those you loved as well?

"Morning. I'll take Eli's place and, if it's all right with you, drive Jeremy to school. I thought you might be tired, since I kept you out so late last night dancing. Eli will pick you up at ten-forty to take you to Della's," Sebastian said, his large hand resting comfortably on Jeremy's shoulder. It amazed him that he had come to care for the child so quickly, and how much he enjoyed being with and pampering Hope.

"I've tried to tell you I don't need Eli to take Jeremy to school, then me to work each day," Hope said.

"A star never walks when she can ride," Sebastian countered.

Hope wrinkled her nose. "Just the ones who don't care about their health. Walking is good for you."

"Mommy, can he take me to school? Please?" Jeremy said, his brown eyes pleaful.

"I don't know if I trust you two alone together," Hope hedged.

Sebastian smiled. "No more letting Jeremy steer the car. Right, Jeremy?"

"Right. We promised, and a man never breaks his promise," Jeremy said solemnly, quoting Sebastian verbatim. "Not even when there are no cars around like we did the other time."

"See? We promise to be good." He lifted Jeremy's Kente cloth backpack from his small shoulders. "Go back inside and relax. You said last night your first appointment isn't until eleven. I'll pick you up tonight at eight-thirty for the party at Roscoe's house."

A frown crossed her brow. "I still haven't decided about taking the part. Perhaps I shouldn't go wi—"

"You already said yes," Sebastian reminded her. "Promises shouldn't be broken."

"That's right, Mommy."

Sighing, she shook her head. "Since you two are ganging up on me, I guess I'll go."

"Great. We'll have fun. You'll see."

"Can Sebastian take me to school?" Jeremy asked again.

Hope conceded to a losing battle. Most of her son's conversation had Sebastian's name somewhere in it. He adored the man. "All right."

"Yeah!" Jeremy opened the door on the driver's side and crawled inside.

Sebastian got in behind him, not minding at all that the tennis-shoes-wearing child had crawled across the custom upholstery. Hope was unable to keep from comparing Sebastian's reaction—rather, nonreaction—to Russell's, the principal. He had been furious when Jeremy had gotten on his knees in the backseat of his BMW to look out the back window at a passing parade. Sebastian valued the person, not the car.

"Go back to sleep or have another cup of coffee," Sebastian advised, closing the car door. "Antoine makes the best."

"That's the trouble," she told Sebastian, walking to the car.

Sebastian frowned up at her. "Don't you like his cooking?"

"It's marvelous and fattening." Sighing, she put her hands on her hips. "I'll be a butterball if this continues."

Slowly, like caressing fingers, his gaze ran over her. "There's nothing wrong with your figure. All of you is absolutely perfect."

Hope flushed with pleasure and tried to keep her thoughts together. "Sebastian, I ate an omelet the size of Texas this morning. I have no willpower sometimes, but especially when it comes to food."

His gaze heated, narrowed on her lips. "I'll remember that."

Her throat dried.

"I like Antoine, Mommy." Jeremy had crawled back across the seat and was looking out Sebastian's window at her.

"Let him stay, Hope. You'd be doing me a favor." Sebastian started the motor. "He always complained in the past that I don't let him truly express himself in the kitchen because I ate the same things or was seldom at home for him to cook for me. Cooking for the three of you makes him happy. Good chefs are hard to find and harder to keep. I'd hate to lose him. Please let him stay."

"Please," Jeremy chorused.

How was she supposed to fight both of them? "He can stay, but if I get to be the size of Rhode Island, you two are to blame."

Sebastian chuckled. "You won't, but even if you did, we'd still care about you. See you tonight."

"'Bye, Mommy."

Sebastian drove off, leaving a shaky Hope on the sidewalk staring after them. Sebastian had used the word *care* so casually. But did he care about her as a woman or as an actress? She certainly cared about him, and it had nothing to do with him being a director and everything with him being a man.

Hope was running late. She had decided to lie down for a few minutes and had overslept. If Eli hadn't rung the doorbell, she'd still be asleep. Thank goodness she only lived a couple of miles from the salon.

Not waiting for Eli to open the limo's door, Hope dashed out of the car and rushed across the sidewalk and opened the door to Della's. Every eye in the place converged on her. Something was up.

It didn't take a genius to figure Sebastian was behind whatever it was. In the past week alone, Sebastian had sent a balloon-a-gram, a mime to act out that she was to get a full body massage and aromatherapy facial after work that day, and a ten-pound box of Swiss chocolates for her to share with everyone in the shop. Whatever it was, she didn't have time today. Mrs. Kent, her eleven o'clock appointment, was already there. Hope closed the door.

The music of "You Keep Me Hanging On" filled the air. A man with a top hat, cane, and tails came out from behind the receptionist's counter, where he had apparently been hiding.

Taking Hope's hands, he sat her in a straight-backed chair in the middle of the floor, handed her oversized black handbag to Tianna, and struck up a pose. The music changed to "Fame." The trim young man began to move his shoulders up and down, his eyes fastened on her startled face. At the first burst of "Fame" from his mouth, people in the salon began to clap and keep time with the music.

Hope's worried gaze flew to Della standing near the receptionist's counter. She was clapping as loud as anyone. She approved.

Della had personal knowledge of a woman wanting to be an actress. Her own daughter, Chauncie, had been bitten by the acting bug. Settling back in her chair, Hope prepared to enjoy herself.

The singer poured his heart into the lyrics. Whether he expected it or not, other voices joined in. People were dancing, popping their fingers, tapping their feet. Hope was doing the two latter and grinning like a nutcase.

For the finale, from fifteen feet away, the singer slid to her on his knees, his upraised white-gloved hands holding his cane and top hat. The music ended as he stopped a scant five inches away. "Be Eleanor and fame is just the beginning."

Hope momentarily palmed her face, outrageously delighted.

"What shall I tell Mr. Stone?" the singer asked, lowering his arms.

"That he's getting there."

"Perhaps this will help." He snapped his fingers and stood.

The rising murmurs of oohs and aahs from behind Hope had her twisting around in her seat. Two powerfully built men in skin-tight black leather pants, their hard muscles rippling across incredibly wide, bare chests, were moving through the crowd passing out long-stemmed yellow roses and candy kisses from baskets held by two attractive dark-haired women in long black dresses. If the group came to a man, one of the women would give the flower and chocolate.

Finished, they passed by her without stopping. Hope sighed. Sebastian certainly knew how to put on a production. The singer bowed and left as well.

She was about to get up when a lush white rose appeared over her left shoulder. She jerked her head around and stared up into Sebastian's piercing black eyes. "Sebastian." His name trembled over her lips.

"Hope." He handed her the rose. "Perfection for perfection."

Aahs and oohs came again, but this time Hope barely noticed, her entire attention on Sebastian. She was unaware of rising from her seat or of reaching toward him until their hands touched. She quivered as lightning zipped from her to him and from him back to her.

Someone began to clap and others joined. They jerked and glanced around self-consciously. The sensual spell was broken.

People gathered around them, but Hope wanted to tell them all to go away.

"Sebastian, I should cry foul," Della said, putting her arm around a shaky Hope. "How am I to compete with keeping one of my best stylists if you keep tempting her this way?"

"He can tempt me any day," said a female voice. Murmurs of agreement followed.

"You can say that again," agreed another female.

Sebastian heard the conversation as if from a long distance away. He was too busy trying to deal with his own erratic emotions and trying to decide if he had actually glimpsed naked desire in Hope's black eyes or simply saw what he wanted to see. Because, heaven help him, that's exactly how he wanted to see her. Naked and flushed with desire.

The knowledge hit him like a sledgehammer. He felt light-headed and something close to fear. Why hadn't he seen this coming and what was he going to do about it?

"The floor show is over, everyone. Back to work," Della ordered, using hand motions to send everyone about their business. "And you, Sebastian, leave so Hope can do Mrs. Kent's perm."

"Certainly. Right away." With barely a glance in Hope's direction, Sebastian fled from the shop.

Della frowned. "What's got into him?"

Hope flushed and looked away. She'd embarrassed him with her wanton thoughts. Usually she was able to keep a better lock on her growing fantasies about him. "Maybe he had an appointment. I better start on Mrs. Kent's perm."

Trying to maintain a pleasant expression on her face, Hope escorted Mrs. Kent to her workstation. As she passed her coworkers and their clients, she was regaled over and over about what a fine brother Sebastian was, and if she didn't want the part or the man, give them a chance.

Having heard it all before, Hope said nothing. She had told them numerous times there was nothing remotely romantic in Sebastian's attention toward her. He was simply trying to persuade her to play Eleanor.

Sitting Mrs. Kent in the chair, then draping the young woman, Hope wished she had paid better attention to her own words. She hadn't. Now she had to face the consequences of caring deeply for a man who looked at her as a challenge, not as a woman. Worse, he knew exactly how she felt about him.

SEVEN

Hands deep in the pockets of his tailored slacks, head down, Sebastian paced in front of his cherrywood desk in his Manhattan office. This couldn't be happening to him. He liked his life the way it was, uncomplicated. He went where he wanted, did what he wanted. He answered to no one in his personal life, and few people in his professional one.

His life was too full. He simply did not have time for this.

It was just a fluke. It wouldn't happen again in a hundred years. A million years.

Satisfied he had solved the problem that had caused him to flee Della's, he rounded his desk and sat down. The sight of the slender blue leather jewelry box stopped him cold. He stared at the box a long time before he picked it up and lifted the lid.

Diamonds winked and glittered. The ten-carat necklace and matching earrings were stunning. He'd seen them yesterday while shopping for his mother's birthday gift. It had been a simple matter of obtaining the jewelry on loan for Hope to wear to the party to-night. Stars did it all the time. But this was the first time he had initiated the request.

All the time that the papers were being prepared, he had envisioned the surprised delight on Hope's face, then her resistance to wearing them. He already had a story made up that they were fake. He'd take great pleasure in putting the stones around her neck, feeling her soft skin beneath his fingertips.

He enjoyed introducing her to new and different things, enjoyed seeing the open pleasure in her face, enjoyed making life a little easier for her. He'd catch himself smiling at her for no particular reason except it just felt good.

It felt right.

Rearing back in his chair, he took the box with him. That should have been his first clue. He tended to be serious. Everyone, including his baby sister, who thought he was "da bomb," often told him he needed to lighten up. And while he'd like to think he had treated the women in his life well, he couldn't truthfully say he relished each and every moment with them. Even during the last couple of days when he went a little overboard in trying to persuade Hope to take the role and she became annoyed with him, he was smiling inside.

Face it, Sebastian, this has gone way beyond you trying to entice an actress to play a part.

The door to his office burst open and his dark head came up abruptly. Dana, his secretary, glanced at him briefly, then brought her very perturbed gaze back to the woman beside her, Margot Madison.

"Mr. Stone, I'm sorry. I tried to tell Ms. Madison you were busy."

Leaning forward in his seat, Sebastian snapped the top closed on the jewelry box and set it aside. "That's all right, Dana. I'll take care of it."

With one last glare at the other woman, Dana left, closing the door behind her. Margot didn't move. Sebastian knew it was calculated on her part.

In the theater, timing was everything. So were the effects.

She had gone all out today to present herself as a theatrical star and a temptress. She was a striking woman with long auburn hair. At five feet nine, she still had enough confidence to wear four-inch heels. Her mahogany skin was flawless, her body voluptuous. Over the years she had learned how to use every asset she possessed to her full and merciless advantage.

The one rectangular pearl button on the severely tailored jacket of her Valentino ivory suit positioned just above her navel provided an unimpeded view of the curve of her generous breasts and flat abdomen. Most men would have probably been salivating. Sebastian was pleased to note he wasn't among them.

He dispassionately studied the jaunty hat with a curved ostrich feather, the Kieselstein-Cord brushed gold metal sunglasses with faux tortoise plastic temples, the textured calfskin bag and heels from Hermès. Dangling from her ears were sterling silver jewelry with rectangular mabe pearls set in fourteen-karat gold. On her wrist was a hinged cuff bracelet to match. On the other wrist a twenty-four-karat gold Cartier watch. Not counting the diamond rings she loved to wear on almost every finger, he was probably looking at forty thousand on the hoof. He'd take Hope's simplicity and honesty in a heartbeat.

"What is it, Margot? As Dana told you, I'm busy."

Taking the shades from her eyes, she crossed to him and leaned over his desk. The jacket opening widened. The scent of her cloying perfume wafted out. "There was a time when I could make you forget about being busy."

"Long ago and long forgotten."

Her practiced smile slipped for an instant, then blossomed again. Her voice lowered to a suggestive purr. "Why don't I refresh your memory?"

"I'd rather not." He leaned away from her and the heavy scent. He'd forgotten how much he hated her perfume. Hope smelled of sunshine and a scent that was uniquely hers.

Margot's attractive face hardened. She came upright and sneered, "I suppose it's that nobody little hairdresser you've been seen with lately."

A muscle leaped in his jaw. "Watch it, Margot."

The practiced smile returned. "Sebastian, you can't possibly be thinking of letting that woman star in your play. I was born to play the role of Eleanor. It's ludicrous to risk millions on a nobody because you're angry with me."

"Margot, this may surprise you, but the world does not revolve around you," Sebastian said.

She came around the desk, her attractive face filled with entreaty. "I've never stopped caring for you. If—"

He laughed and watched shock, then anger sweep over her. "Give it up, Margot. Even if Hope doesn't take the part, I'd break my contract before working with you again."

"I want that part," she practically hissed.

"Read my lips. You're not getting it." He picked up the signed contract for the male lead from his desk. "You know the way out."

"What's this?" Before he could stop her, she snatched the jewelry box from his desk and opened it. A strangled gasp escaped her. "Is this for her?"

Standing, Sebastian held out his hand for Margot to return the case. "That is none of your concern."

"They are, aren't they?" At his continued silence her expression went from fury to scorn, then hatred. "She must be really something in bed."

Angrily, Sebastian plucked the box from her hands and slipped it into his coat pocket. "Unlike you, she has enough character and talent not to stoop that low to get a part."

"Why, you!" Margot's bejeweled hand swept back in a wide arch.

"Don't let dramatics ruin your career, Margot," Sebastian warned coldly. "Try to keep what dignity you have left and leave quietly."

Her raised hand clenched, then lowered. Her eyes chilled. "I promise you. I'll find a way to make you pay for treating me like this."

"You have no one to blame but yourself. I'm one man you don't want to have as an enemy." Planting both hands on the desk, he stared across its wide expanse at her. "Don't make the mistake of taking weakness as the reason why I never bothered to try and correct the lie you spread about who broke off the relationship. It simply didn't matter. This does."

Without another word, she stalked angrily from the room. Seconds later he heard the outer office door slam.

Dana appeared in his office doorway. "I'm sorry, Mr. Stone. Is there anything you need at the moment?"

He started to say no, then felt the jewelry box in his pocket. "Yes. See that this is returned."

"Yes, sir." The door closed behind her.

If nothing else, Margot's visit had helped him remember he had lousy taste in women.

Getting ready for her date with Sebastian, Hope vacillated between panic, fear, and hope. She didn't want to look into Sebastian's eyes and see pity or, heaven forbid, wariness that she'd pounce on him. Perhaps he really did leave in a hurry because he had an important appointment.

She didn't understand what came over her when she was around him, she thought as she straightened her sheer lace top stockings, then snapped them to the garter belt. Who would have believed the quiet and proper Hope would turn into a love-starved, aggressive woman in her mid-thirties? She'd loved Douglas as much as she thought any woman could love a man, enjoyed their lovemaking, yet somehow her feelings for Sebastian were more intense, more needy.

Sighing, she reached for the shimmering gold dress with none of the enthusiasm she'd experienced when she had first seen it in the store. While thankful to Cynthia for her generosity in giving her carte blanche with her clothes, tonight Hope wanted to wear a gown no one else had worn.

The reason made her sigh again. She wanted her friendship with Sebastian to blossom into a new and exciting experience for both of them.

The long dress slid over her head and bare skin, shaping itself to the contours of her body as it drifted downward, then flaring out dramatically at the knee. Reaching behind her, Hope zipped, snapped, then stepped into her heels.

The doorbell rang.

Her gaze went to the clock on the radio. Eight-thirty. Sebastian was prompt as usual.

Trembling fingers gathered the silk organza stole and small gold beaded bag from the dresser. Without giving herself time to think, she swept out of the room, cutting the light off as she went. At least she didn't have to meet him with Bridgett and Jeremy watching.

Thankfully Bridgett had gone to her weekly Friday night bridge party and taken Jeremy with her. A couple of the other players had grandchildren and the women enjoyed spoiling the children when they got together. Jeremy had probably already eaten his third powdered-sugar lemon cookie, a batch of which Antoine had made for the occasion.

Halfway down the stairs, her hand paused on the hardwood rail. Through the frosted etched glass in the front door she saw the silhouette of a large man. Too large to be Sebastian. She stood poised on the stairs until the peal of the doorbell had her moving again.

Opening the door, her gaze went beyond Eli's burly body to the black limo parked at the curb. Sebastian wasn't standing by the car. The tinted glass prevented her from seeing inside. Her heart began to race.

He tipped his hat. "Good evening, Mrs. Lassiter."

"Hello, Eli. Where's Sebastian?" She hated the almost panicky note in her voice, but she couldn't seem to help it.

"He sends his apologies," the chauffeur informed her. "Work kept him at his office. He'll meet you at Mr. Carroll's house."

"He expects me to meet all those people by myself?"

"No, Mrs. Lassiter," the chauffeur quickly said. "He's taking a taxi. As soon as I pick you up, I'm to call him."

Something didn't jibe. "I know his penthouse is only a short distance away from Mr. Carroll's, but it doesn't seem possible that he'll have enough time to go home, dress, then meet us there. Besides, it's only a thirty-minute drive from his office to here. How much work could he have accomplished in that short length of time?"

The young man appeared flustered. Clearly, he wasn't used to people questioning Sebastian's dictates. "If you wish, once we're rolling I'll call to let him know, then you can talk to him personally."

"Why wait?" Picking up the hem of her gown, she went to the nearest phone located on the end table in the living room and dialed Sebastian's private number at his office. After the tenth unanswered ring, she hung up the phone and turned to the chauffeur hovering in the doorway. "What number were you to call?"

"The one for his cell phone."

She swallowed the growing lump of fear in her throat. "If he's in his office, why would he ask you to call him on his cell phone?"

"Mrs. Lassiter, I'm sure Mr. Stone has his reasons," he said. "If you'll just come with me, he'll explain everything when you see him at Mr. Carroll's house."

"No," she said softly.

"No?"

"I'm not going," her determination grew with each erratic thud of her heart. She had her answer.

There had been no appointment. Sebastian had left hurriedly because she had embarrassed him. He'd keep his promise to see that she went to the party because he had given his word, not because he wanted to. He'd probably continue to try and entice her to play Eleanor, but at arm's length. The wrenching pain of loss was almost crippling.

"But Mrs. Lassiter . . . Mr. Stone is expecting you," Eli said with some alarm in his voice.

"I'm sorry, Eli, that you had to drive down here for nothing, but I'm staying here," she said, desperately trying to keep her voice normal. Sweeping past him, she went to the front door and held it open until he reluctantly walked past her.

"Good night, Mrs. Lassiter."

"Good night." Her entire body shaking as if from a chill, she closed the door, her head falling forward in despair.

"She did what?" Sebastian *yelled* into the cell phone.

"She refused to come after she called your office and no one answered," Eli repeated as he sat inside the limo.

Sebastian said one crude word.

"I think she was about to cry, boss."

"Hell . . ." Sebastian sank heavily down on the padded bench on Roscoe's balcony. It had been so noisy inside, he hadn't been able to hear. "Where are you now?"

"Still outside the house."

"Good. Stay there. I'll be there in thirty minutes."

"Boss, you know taxis aren't fond of coming down here."

Sebastian stood, a determined look on his face. "With all the limos downstairs, I should be able to borrow one. Don't move, I'm on my way. If Hope tries to leave before I get there, stop her."

"How am I supposed to do that?"

"Cry. Appeal to her goodness. Tell her I'll fire you if she does."

The man laughed, then sobered. "You wouldn't do that, would you, boss?"

"I'm on my way." The phone clicked dead.

Sebastian had no difficulty obtaining a car. Because they were used to seeing him calm no matter what, his frantic request had his friends quickly volunteering their cars and drivers. In minutes he was on his way and had Eli back on the phone. It didn't make Sebastian any less anxious to hear the man say he had gone back and looked through the glass door, to see Hope, head bowed, sitting at the foot of the stairs.

Hanging up, Sebastian called Hope, as he had been doing since he'd gotten into the elevator to ride down to the front of Roscoe's apartment building, but at the sound of his voice she hung up. Her actions would have irritated him if he wasn't so worried.

Exactly twenty-seven minutes after he had gotten off the phone the first time with Eli, the limo Sebastian was riding in braked sharply beside Eli. Thanking the driver and handing him a hundred, Sebastian climbed out of the car. "She's still in there?"

"Yes, sir."

Sebastian rushed up the steps. The sight of her continuing to just sit there, head bowed, in a shimmering pool of gold tore at his heart. He jabbed the doorbell. "Hope. Let me in."

Her head lifted. Misery and the glimmer of tears were in her eyes. From out of nowhere he recalled Jeremy saying that he'd only seen his mother cry twice. Sebastian had known her for less than three weeks and he had doubled that number.

"I'm sorry. So sorry," he said, not knowing what the problem was but instinctively knowing he was the cause of her unhappiness.

Slowly she came to her feet. His pulse raced. She was going to answer the door. Lifting her skirt, she started up the stairs.

The sight of her turning away from him shook him to the core. "No," he yelled, twisting the doorknob. To his surprise, the door opened. He didn't waste time questioning his good fortune. He rushed through the door and toward her. He'd lecture her later on keeping the door locked.

She pivoted sharply on hearing his running steps. "Leave me alone."

He kept coming until she was in his arms despite her protests. "Whatever I did, I'm sorry."

She looked away from him. "Please, just leave."

"I'm not leaving. I can't leave," he said softly, his hand gently turning her face toward his. "I thought I could."

Hope was afraid to believe. "What are you saying?"

Tenderly, he palmed her face. "That I care about you very much, but I was afraid of getting in over my head. In the past I haven't had such a good track record with women. This morning at Della's I wanted to sweep you away and make love to you."

Her breath trembled over her lips. "You didn't come for me tonight."

"Because I was afraid I'd crack under the pressure of the close confines of the car and kiss you."

"I affect you that much?" she asked, going soft in his arms.

"More than you know."

Her bare arms wound around his neck. "Then why aren't you kissing me?"

His lips fastened to hers, hot and sweet and gentle. A mating of tongues and spirits. After a long time he lifted his head. "I hate that I waited so long."

She nipped his chin. "Same here."

"You're tempting a weak man," he warned, nibbling on her ear. "A very weak man."

Her breath hitched. "Is it going to get your mouth back on mine?"

"Come on, let's see." Taking her hand, he started down the stairs. Outside, he made sure the door was securely locked. Hand in hand, laughing like school children let out for the summer, they raced toward the limo. A grinning Eli held the door open for them.

Inside, Sebastian took Hope in his arms. "Now. Where were we?"

EIGHT

When Sebastian and Hope entered Roscoe's penthouse, she was blushing and he was grinning broadly. He had taken shameful advantage of the private elevator to explore the softness of Hope's sweet mouth. Each taste tempted, tantalized, beckoned him to return for another kiss, then another.

Hope was uniquely different from any other woman. Quite simply, he trusted her, and his feelings for her deepened with every beat of his heart. The only fear in his mind was the fear of never hearing the breathless catch in her voice when his arms were wrapped around her, never hearing her laughter or seeing her smile.

His arm curved possessively around her slim waist, he led her past the butler and entered the immense formal living area where the guests were gathered. Seeing him, several stopped and openly stared. Roscoe, standing with a small group of people in front of a large-scale fireplace with marble surrounds and a hand-carved mantel, excused himself, then crossed the plush white-carpeted floor to them.

"Roscoe Carroll, meet Hope Lassiter," Sebastian introduced. "The only woman, in my opinion, who can do Eleanor justice."

"Welcome, Mrs. Lassiter," Roscoe greeted warmly. "I was in the theater the afternoon you did the monologue and you were nothing short of brilliant."

"Told you," Sebastian murmured, a note of satisfaction in his deep voice.

Ignoring Sebastian, Hope smiled at their host. "Hello, Mr. Carroll. That's quite an honor, coming from you."

"Simply the truth," Roscoe said. "Might I add that you're even more stunning close up?"

Sebastian's arm around Hope tightened a fraction, bringing her closer to his side. The jealousy he felt caught him off guard, but he didn't shy away from it. Hope was his. "We don't want to keep you from your other guests, Roscoe."

Instead of leaving, the rotund man folded his arms, rocked back on the heels of his gently worn shoes, and smiled. "Trying to get rid of me, huh?"

"Yes," Sebastian said flatly. He'd never been jealous because of a woman before, but he had never been a lot of things until Hope came into his life.

The older man chuckled. "Never thought I'd see it, but I guess I should have known when you were demanding the loan of a car and driver. Never seen you so frantic."

Hope should have felt badly for putting Sebastian in such an awkward situation. Instead she was immensely pleased she had been able to crack through his legendary control, but she couldn't allow him to be cast in a bad light. "My fault. There was a mix-up in communication."

"Judging by your faces when you came in, I'd say everything was resolved," Roscoe stated.

A soft smile on her face, Hope gazed adoringly up at Sebastian. "Yes, it was." His arm tightened.

"Does that mean you're going to take the part?" Roscoe asked.

Hope felt the stare of both men. "I haven't decided. I've told Sebastian that I'll give him an answer on Monday."

"Let's hope it's the one we all want," Roscoe said.

"It will be," Sebastian said emphatically.

Hope remained silent.

"Come on and I'll introduce you to some of the other guests," Roscoe said.

It wasn't long before the room was buzzing. Sebastian left no doubt in the minds of anyone they met that he wanted Hope for the part of Eleanor. As the evening progressed, she felt the heavy weight of the burden he had placed on her. Sebastian might believe in her talent, but it was obvious the others in the room didn't. Excusing herself, she climbed the spiral staircase to the second-floor bathroom.

Her arm clutched around her churning stomach, she stared into the ornate gold mirror. If she took the part and the play flopped because of her, she had no doubts the critics would crucify both her and Sebastian. She'd damage both of their careers. Failure to a proud man like Sebastian would wound him deeply.

Failure would be just as devastating to her. She'd have to give up her dream of ever returning to the legitimate theater. No director would take the chance of letting her star in another production. The roles she'd be relegated to, if she could find them, would be few and the pay scale low. And by then she would have lost her secure job at Della's and have to take whatever cosmetologist job she could find.

Sebastian had offered her a year's salary, but as she told him, she couldn't accept the money. As a result, if the play flopped, the secure life she had worked so hard to obtain for Jeremy would be gone.

All because she had let her heart rule her head. Her feelings for Sebastian went beyond caring. From the very beginning she was aware that she had allowed him to be a part of her life more for personal reasons than professional ones.

He simply overwhelmed her. She wanted to please him, make him happy, give him that which he most desired. She loved him.

Denial was impossible. The gut-wrenching pain she felt told her more definitively than the misery in her eyes. With acceptance came fear. If she didn't accept the role, would he still want to be a part of Jeremy's and her life, or would he walk?

She was ninety-eight percent sure the man she had come to know in the past weeks had more honor than to walk out on them. The other two percent was tying her in knots. And if he did stick around, could their new relationship stand up to the test? Sebastian might continue to see her, but each time he did, she instinctively knew she'd see the disappointment in his eyes. She didn't want that, wasn't sure she could live with it.

She was damned if she did and damned if she didn't. But hiding wouldn't solve anything.

Straightening, she left the bathroom and started down the curved staircase. From across the room, Sebastian looked up and their eyes met. She couldn't lose him when they had just found each other.

Her gaze fastened on Sebastian's, she was almost upon the woman in her path before she realized it. Abruptly, Hope stopped. Recognition of the woman in the revealing, skin-tight red gown came almost immediately. "I'm sorry, Ms. Madison. I wasn't watching where I was going."

"Obviously," Margot said coldly, tossing her long auburn hair back. "So you're the little hairdresser who thinks she can act."

The statuesque black woman with short blond hair standing next to Margot giggled.

Hope never took her eyes from Margot Madison's face. Beautiful and vicious. "I'm proud to be a professional hairstylist."

"Really?" Margot said. She glanced at her companion. The two looked at each other and burst out laughing.

"Do tell us more," the blonde said, derision heavy in each word.

Hope folded her arms and smiled sweetly. "I'm not surprised you'd want to know. Your gray roots are showing and, Margot, your overprocessed hair looks like straw."

The women gasped.

"You're all right, Hope?" Sebastian asked, coming to her side and sliding his arm possessively around her waist. Margot watched the movement with tightly compressed lips and furious eyes.

"Fine. We were just discussing the merits of a good hairstylist. My schedule is full, but if you'd call Della's House of Style in Harlem on 125th, I'm sure you could get an appointment with another stylist." Hope waved her fingers. " 'Bye now."

Nodding, Sebastian started down the stairs with Hope. "Margot looked mad enough to go for blood. You're sure she didn't bother you?"

"Why talk about Margot when I hear there is a scrumptious buffet around here someplace?" she said evasively. With all the doubts running through her head, she didn't want a reminder of the relationship Margot and Sebastian once shared.

Sebastian peered at her closely, but all he said was, "Do you think you could wait for about fifteen minutes to eat?" They stepped off the last step of the stairs.

"Sure."

"Good night, Roscoe," Sebastian called as they passed their host.

"Good night, Sebastian, Hope. Thanks for coming."

"Good night," Hope said automatically, then frowned. Sebastian was heading straight for the front door. "We're leaving?"

"Yes," he said, going past the butler.

"You're taking me home?" Hope asked in disbelief as they stepped onto the elevator. The gleaming wood-paneled door silently closed behind them.

Sebastian pulled her into his arms. His eyes were fiercely possessive as he stared down at her. "No. I'm taking you to my place, where we can enjoy a quiet meal together and I can kiss you to our hearts' content. Any questions?"

"The same one I always have." She lifted her face to his. "What took you so long?"

. . .

"It's lovely," Hope said looking at the candlelit table on the terrace. On the pristine white linen tablecloth beside her plate was an orchid. Her finger glided over the lush, soft petal. "You always make me feel special."

"You are," he said, tipping her bowed chin upward to brush his lips across hers.

She'd promised herself she wouldn't ask, but somehow the question slipped out anyway. "Will I still be special if I don't take the part?"

His face harshened. "You think this has anything to do with the play?"

Now that she began, she couldn't seem to back down. "I'm almost positive it doesn't."

He backed up a step. "You think I'd stoop to something that low?"

"I don't want to think that," she cried, hating the flatness in his deep voice.

"I'll take you home."

A chill swept through her. She gathered the shawl closer to her body. "I can call a cab or Bridgett."

A muscle leaped in his brown jaw. "I brought you, I'll take you. I'll call Eli."

Hope watched a stiff-backed Sebastian walk back inside the penthouse. A stab of anguish pierced her. There was no way she could share the limo with him. Taking her courage in hand, she followed and saw him pick up the phone.

"Please tell Eli that I'll meet him downstairs. Good night, Sebastian. I'm sorry about everything." Not giving him a chance to reply, she hurried toward the front door.

When she was halfway across the room, an unrelenting hand closed around her forearm and turned her around. She stared up into a pair of stormy black eyes. "I said I'll take you home."

She shook her head from side to side. "Please don't."

"You're trembling. What's the matter?" Anger swiftly yielded to concern.

"I—I want to go home."

"You think I'd hurt you?" he asked in mounting disbelief.

"That's not why I'm trembling," she said, her voice husky and unsteady.

His eyes widened with the knowledge. Desire, not fear. His head swooped down, his lips fastening on hers. Her lips parted on a whimpering sigh, allowing him full access to her mouth. He didn't hesitate.

Bold and greedy one moment, gentle and persuasive the next, his tongue stroked, tasted, teased. With each brush of his tongue, each touch of his sure hand on her heated flesh, the need for more intensified. Her hands clutched the lapels of his jacket both to draw him closer and to give stability to her swirling world. This kiss was like no other they had shared. It burned. It demanded. It inflamed.

Hope moaned.

Sebastian shuddered.

His arms locked around her slim body, he lifted his head. "Do you trust me?"

Air rushing through her lungs, her thoughts scattered, Hope marveled that he had the presence of mind to form and ask a coherent question.

"Do you?" he rasped.

Pressed close to him, she felt the anger of his gaze, the rapid rise and fall of his chest, his hard arousal. Yet she also felt the tender way in which he held her despite his anger, but more than anything she felt the absolute rightness of being in his arms.

On tiptoes, she brushed her mouth across his lower lip, then bit. "Yes."

A hard shudder racked his body. His arms pulled her closer. "Thank goodness. Thank goodness."

His mouth found hers again. His hands were everywhere on her.

They seemed to know instinctively the places to bring the most pleasure. Hope reveled in the pleasure sweeping through her body. Clothes were hastily cast aside in a feverish rush to be as one. The pace was fast and wild and glorious. When completion came, the exquisite ecstasy brought tears to Hope's eyes. Holding her, Sebastian kissed each one away.

"What time does Bridgett get up on Saturday mornings?" he asked, his mouth moving across the damp skin on her shoulder.

"A-around seven." She arched her neck to give him greater access.

"Good," he murmured. "Then we have all night to enjoy each other."

Hope's answer was a broken whimper of need as Sebastian's hot mouth moved purposefully down the taut slope of her breast.

NINE

Hope had made her decision.

Her arms wrapped around her bent legs, her chin resting on her knees, she sat on the stone steps of Bridgett's house and waited for Sebastian to arrive. Like the schoolgirl she had compared herself to early in their relationship, she was too excited to wait inside for him. She didn't want to miss one second of looking at him, of being with him.

Lifting her head, she laughed out loud with the sheer pleasure of loving and being in love. The past three days had been magical. Saturday morning before dawn, Sebastian had awakened her with a kiss and breakfast, since they'd never gotten around to eating the night before. Sitting up, she had gasped in delight. Red, pink and white rose petals were scattered all around her. After eating, they had made love. The fragrant scent of the flowers enveloped them. Never again would she be able to see or smell a rose without remembering that morning.

After taking her home, he'd returned after Hope had gotten off work a little after twelve, to take them—Bridgett included—to his estate near Long Island. The Tudor-style home, with two formal gardens, a sweeping green lawn, and mature trees, was incredible.

She wasn't surprised to see a stable. They'd gone horseback riding, then swimming in the beautiful pool.

Late that evening, while Bridgett and Jeremy took a nap, Hope and Sebastian, hand in hand, had strolled the winding stone path in the formal gardens and talked about her good marriage, his bad one; the devastation of her husband's sudden death, his relief when his wife filed for divorce and, once it was final, her marriage to a wealthy banker three times her age. Both Hope and Sebastian had caught the acting bug while in high school, but while she continued to act, he had gone behind the scenes to direct. She was the youngest of three girls from Miami. He had grown up in Los Angeles and had a sister ten years younger. Sharing these details had brought Hope and Sebastian closer.

When they returned to Harlem late that night, Sebastian had carried a worn-out Jeremy up to his room, looked at her with longing and regret, then kissed her and left. Neither had wanted to say good night.

An hour later, her phone rang. It was Sebastian. They'd talked for two hours before she started yawning and he'd said good night.

He had spent Sunday afternoon with them playing board games. But today, Monday, was just for them. Jeremy was in school and Bridgett planned to work in her flower garden. Hope and Sebastian would have the penthouse to themselves with a wonderful lunch Antoine had prepared.

She couldn't wait.

A black limo turned onto her street. Hope shot up from her perch, then ran down to the sidewalk. There was no sense playing coy.

The car stopped. Grinning, she quickly bent and opened the door. "Goo—" Shock had her straightening abruptly and stepping back.

"Hello, Hope," Margot said.

"What are you doing here?"

"Get in and I'll tell you."

"Never mind. There's nothing you can say that I want to hear." Hope swung around.

"What about the ruination of Sebastian's career?"

Whirling back, Hope returned to the car, her heart thudding crazily in her chest. "What are you talking about?"

"Get in," Margot said, her voice demanding.

Hope got in and closed the door.

"Very smart of you. We both know what I want, so I won't waste time. After seeing a picture of you with Sebastian in the paper this morning, I thought you needed to hear some hard facts."

"Our picture was in the paper?" Hope questioned, unsure how she felt about it.

Margot's lips curled. "Don't flatter yourself. It was taken Friday night when you left Roscoe's. Apparently *Variety* had a need to fill space."

"Was your picture in the paper?" Hope asked, reasonably sure she knew the answer.

"My picture has been in newspapers and magazines all over the world," Margot snapped. "My fans adore me. I've proven what I can do on Broadway. You haven't, and if you try to play Eleanor you'll ruin Sebastian's career."

Hope's pulse leaped. "Sebastian has a fantastic career."

"You could ruin it. People were laughing after you two left."

Not by one flicker of emotion did Hope show her rising fear. She was as good an actress as Margot. "People like to talk. Roscoe is the major backer and he thinks I'm brilliant."

"One scene does not make a play," Margot said in a dismissive tone. "Did Roscoe actually say he wanted you for the part?"

"No," Hope had to admit.

"Of course he didn't. Roscoe is a smart businessman. Sebastian is a hell of a director, but even he can be led around by his pants."

Hope hadn't been expecting such a tasteless comment. She flushed. Margot had been watching her closely.

"Did he fix you breakfast in bed?" Margot wanted to know. "Sebastian is an inventive, exuberant lover, and always attentive."

This time Hope was ready for the vindictive woman. Jealousy clawed at her, but she refused to give vent to it. Her expression remained flat. "Sebastian believes in me as an actress. He wants me, not you, for the part of Eleanor."

The earlier satisfaction in Margot's eyes disappeared. Her mouth tightened. "Maybe so, but if the play fails, he's going to lose more than face. He's invested his own money. I know you care about him, so do him a favor and tell him no today."

"You know about the deadline?"

Margot's laugh scraped against Hope's frayed nerves like fingernails on a chalkboard. "Of course. Roscoe told me. He and I are very close. He wants a sure thing. If you think I'm lying, call him." Giving Hope the phone number, she had one last parting shot. "I have a lot of influence in this town and my friends have even more. We can do this the hard or the easy way. Tell Sebastian no and get out of his life, or try to hold on to him and play Eleanor, and I'll do everything in my power to discredit both of you. The next time you see your picture it might be in the tabloids, and I can guarantee the reading won't be tame."

Hope got out of the car, not noticing when the limo pulled away from the curb. She tried to dismiss Margot's words as jealousy, but deep down Hope had to admit there was truth in them as well. One short scene didn't make the play. Friday night she had seen the disbelief in people's faces.

Margot was one of them. Hope was an outsider.

Turning, she walked back into the house and started up the stairs, stumbled, and went down on her knees. Trembling, tears burning the backs of her eyes, her throat stinging, she wasn't sure she had the will or the energy to stand. For the second time in her life she had lost the man she loved.

"Hope?" Bridgett called, concern in her voice.

Hope heard her friend, but she wasn't able to make herself move.

"Hope?" Bridgett repeated, joining Hope on the stairs, her arm going around her waist. "What's the matter? Hope, you're frightening me."

"I—"

The peal of the doorbell cut her off. Sebastian. The trembling of her body increased. "T-tell him I'm not here."

"Why?" Bridgett questioned, her anxiety increasing.

"Please." With an effort, Hope pulled away and started up the stairs.

"I thought—"

"Please, Bridgett. I don't want to see him. Please." The doorbell chimed again. "Please."

"All right."

Hope's nod was almost imperceptible.

Bridgett watched Hope's slow, measured steps as she climbed the stairs. The doorbell chimed for a third time. Tugging off her garden gloves, Bridgett went to answer the door. The anger in Sebastian's face took her aback.

"Did you and Hope have a fight?" Her hand remained on the doorknob, blocking entrance into the house.

"Why do you ask?" he rasped, unease sweeping through him.

"Because she looked to be in worse shape than you," Bridgett answered.

His face contorted with fury. "Then that *was* Margot's limo Eli recognized."

"Margot Madison was here?"

"Where's Hope? I need to talk with her."

"Upstairs, but she doesn't want to see you," Bridgett said. "I'm sorry, but I have to respect her wishes."

"I need to know what she told Hope," Sebastian said, dread quickly overruling every other emotion. "You've got to let me see her. Margot is a vicious shrew. She'd do anything or say anything to hurt Hope and try to stop her from playing Eleanor."

"I—"

"Please, Bridgett. I've never begged for anything in my life, but I'm begging now." Hope meant too much to him to lose. He wanted her to be a part of his life, and that desire had nothing to do with her taking the part of Eleanor. But the decision should be hers. Not one influenced by Margot's lies.

"Ground rules," Bridgett began. "You talk from outside her bedroom door unless she asks you inside. No shouting. She's upset enough. And lastly, I'm going with you and if I feel Hope is becoming too upset, you'll have to leave. Take it or leave it."

"I'll take it."

Bridgett stepped aside. Sebastian rushed past her. His foot was on the fourth step before he stopped. He almost vibrated with impatience.

"Go on up. But remember, I have excellent hearing."

Giving her a smile of gratitude, Sebastian continued up the stairs. He rapped on the door. "Hope, it's me. Please let me in."

Silence.

"Hope, please. Margot is a shrew. She wants to play Eleanor and knows I'll walk before I direct her." His hand closed around the doorknob and clenched. "Hope, open the door."

The silence was painful and frightening.

His head and the flat of his palm rested on the door. "Hope, don't do this to me, to us."

"Sebastian," Bridgett said, her own voice unsteady.

Slowly he straightened. "Hope, I've always had lousy taste in women. Now that I've finally got it right, I'm not letting you toss away what we have. Sooner or later we're going to talk. I care about you. Just remember that, instead of the lies Margot told you."

His hand flexed on the door. He turned, started down the hallway, then stopped. "Take care of her, Bridgett. Neither Jeremy nor I like to see her cry."

"I will."

His hands deep in his pockets, he started down the stairs, then he whipped them out. Fury darkened his eyes. If he couldn't talk to Hope, he'd find Margot, and heaven help her when he did.

Curled up on the bed, Hope heard a soft knock on the door. Bridgett. Sebastian's knock had been sharp, and a bit desperate. "Are you alone?"

"Yes."

"Come in." The door slowly opened.

"Hope, you have a right to be angry with me, but Sebastian was so worried about you I had to let him come up. He cares about you."

She spoke without opening her eyes. "I know. That's why I can't see him ever again."

Easing down on the bed beside her, Bridgett stroked her hair. "You want to talk about it?"

Hope told Bridgett about Margot's threats, and ended by saying, "If it was just me, I'd spit in her eye and tell her to take her best shot."

"Hope, Sebastian is an influential man in his own right and can take care of himself," Bridgett reminded her.

Rolling over on her back, Hope crossed her arm over her eyes. "I know that, but you didn't see the hate in Margot's eyes. There's no telling what she'd do, the horrible lies she'd spread. There is going to be enough pressure on him without Margot stirring up problems. Sebastian was adamant about not giving Margot the part, but maybe if I'm not in the picture she'll calm down."

"So your mind is made up."

"Yes." Lifting her arm away, she rose and called Sebastian's secretary. "Dana, this is Hope Lassiter. Please tell Sebastian the answer is no and that I don't want him to contact me again." Slowly, she hung up the phone.

. . .

The short leash on Sebastian's temper shortened considerably when his secretary contacted him about Hope's decision. He called immediately, but she refused to talk with him. And the person who had started this mess wasn't to be found. After hours of fruitless searching, Sebastian went to the one person who would get a message to her.

"Roscoe, when you see Margot, tell her I'm putting the word out. I won't work with her ever. I don't even want to be in the same room with her. So if she's invited, don't expect me."

Sitting behind his massive desk in his home study, Roscoe jerked the cigar out of his mouth. "Now, wait a minute, Sebastian. You just said Hope wasn't going to take the part. What about the play?"

"I could give a flying leap."

"Let's be reasonable," Roscoe soothed, coming from behind his desk.

"Believe me, I'm trying. I warned you about Margot and you wouldn't listen," Sebastian accused. "Find yourself another director."

"What? I can't be held responsible for what Margot did. You can't walk out like this. I'll lose millions. I'll sue you."

"You know where to send the papers." Sebastian started from the room.

"Wait," Roscoe yelled, and quickly caught up with him and saw the determination in Sebastian's face. "You'd really toss away millions on this?"

"Yes." The answer was sharp and final.

"She means that much to you?"

"Yes, and unless you help me get her back, I'm seriously considering putting your name on the list beside Margot."

"How am I supposed to do that?" Roscoe railed, stuffing his cigar back in his mouth and mangling it badly. "You said she won't talk to you. Why is she going to listen to me?"

"I have a plan," Sebastian said, feeling the vise that had been constricting his chest since he'd left Hope that morning ease. "There's one place she can't run away from me."

Hope made herself crawl out of bed Tuesday morning, walk Jeremy to school, then go to work and get the inquisition over. She'd left work Saturday running to be with Sebastian. They'd see the dramatic difference as soon as they caught a glimpse of her face. Taking a deep breath, she opened the door and walked inside.

It wasn't until she was halfway across the floor that she noticed the absolute quiet. Her head came around. She spotted Sebastian immediately. Her heart leaped, then tumbled back to earth. Whirling, she started for the door. Bridgett, Antoine, and Eli blocked her path.

Sebastian stepped in front of her. "I told you we'd talk sooner or later."

Her hands clamped around her oversized handbag; it was that or fling them around Sebastian's neck and never let go. "Mrs. Fulton is due any minute."

"Lydia is going to take care of her. The charming woman graciously consented to change stylists even before I offered to send her and her husband out tonight for dinner and dancing. Now, about us."

"There is no us."

He stepped closer until his heat, his hardness, and the spicy scent of his cologne filled her nostrils. Her breathing quickened. "You want to say that again?"

She licked her lips. This time it was Sebastian's breathing that quickened.

"Hope." He uttered her name with reverence. "How did Margot get you to leave me?"

Margot's name effectively killed the sensual spell he had created. "I don't want to talk about it." She tried to leave and found herself without her bag, pressed against Sebastian's very disturbing chest.

"What lies did Margot say?" he questioned, rubbing his cheek against hers.

Weak woman that she was, Hope told him everything, her voice so breathless and soft, her words so disjointed she wasn't sure he heard her until she saw the rage in his black eyes. "I'm sorry."

"Margot will be the one who's sorry once she surfaces." He spoke without looking away from her. "Roscoe. Shelton."

Two men appeared on either side of her. "Roscoe, you're up first."

"I'm sorry for any unhappiness you might have been subjected to, and as the major backer for *A Matter of Trust*, I implore you to reconsider. You have my utmost support."

"Shelton."

"Good morning, Ms. Lassiter," Shelton said, holding up a sheet of paper. "This is the addendum to the contract that was drawn up between Roscoe and Sebastian three months ago. In essence it says that Sebastian has sole power to cast the female lead in *A Matter of Trust*, and unless he's completely satisfied, the production will be canceled."

Hope thought she heard Roscoe gulp. The rotund man looked greenish.

"As for Margot's other threats, they're just that: threats." Sebastian's eyes were sad. "You should have trusted me."

Misery welled inside her. "I'm sorry. It wasn't that I didn't trust you enough, it was that I cared so much."

"For a relationship to be strong, there has to be both." Touching her cheek with unsteady fingertips, he stepped back. "Margot's lies can't hurt me. Your leaving can." He held out his hand. "It's a matter of trust. The choice is yours. Take my hand and I promise you to never let go. For as long as I live, you'll be in my heart and by my side."

Hope blinked. Sebastian's words were the same ones Nolan said to Eleanor in the last scene in the play when he asked her to choose between a life with him or extracting revenge against his brother.

Eleanor had been ruled by hate; Hope had been ruled by fear. For both, love was the one answer that would set them free.

"Then I choose you."

Sebastian roughly pulled Hope into his arms to the wild applause in the shop, his lips finding hers for a long, satisfying time. How he loved this woman! He'd stopped fighting his feelings the night of Roscoe's party. Very soon he'd be able to show and tell her how much. "Does that mean you'll be my Eleanor?"

She grinned up into his face. "I'm going to knock their socks off."

EPILOGUE

The applause lasted for a full thirty minutes. Hope took curtain call after curtain call. Her prediction was correct. She had knocked their socks off.

Holding the large bouquet of red roses Sebastian had given to Jeremy to present to her at her fifth curtain call, Hope glanced in the wings where Sebastian stood with one hand on her son's shoulder. Happiness flooded her, but not contentment. She had her dream, yet there was something else she needed to make her life complete: Sebastian's love.

"May I have your attention, please?" Sebastian said into the stage mike at Della's Place. "First, I'd like to thank Della for allowing me to rent this fabulous nightclub for the opening night after-party of *A Matter of Trust.* I'll always have fond memories of the connecting salon."

"As long as no one else but Gregory tries to cut your hair," one of the stylists teased.

Laughter erupted. "True. I don't think I'd be lucky enough to find a woman like Hope twice."

Hope, sitting at the front table in a white Valentino gown, graciously accepted the many teasing comments from the women in the club.

Next to her, Bridgett leaned over and said, "I knew Sebastian had style. Aren't you glad I told you to accept his flower, then later helped him make you listen to reason?"

"More than you'll ever know," Hope said, her gaze locked on Sebastian.

"And thanks also to all of you for being here to help celebrate." He held up several newspapers. "In my hand I have some reviews. They all confirm what I've known from the start." His warm, proud gaze settled on Hope. "Because of the brilliant performance of Hope Lassiter, *A Matter of Trust* is a smash hit and a star is born."

The club erupted into another round of applause. Hope stood up, waved, and blew kisses. "I always wanted to do that."

Laughter joined the applause.

Sebastian silenced the audience. "I've been a director for thirteen years and seen hundreds of auditions. During that time I've never cast a role without seeing the work of the actor or actress first. Until tonight. Tonight I'm going to cast the most important role in my lifetime. Shelton."

People in the room turned to see a tall, good-looking black man enter the room from between two white columns. Murmurs grew as Shelton made his way around the tables to the front of the stage. He stopped directly beside Hope. In his hands was a blue velvet pillow with gold tassels. On top was a white orchid and next to it was a blue porcelain Limoges egg with twenty-four-karat gold feet and a hinge closure.

Sebastian left the stage, walked the short distance to a stunned Hope, then went down on one knee in front of her. Opening the egg, strands of Puccini's Aria to Madame Butterfly drifted upward. Inside gleamed a fancy yellow starburst diamond set in eighteen-karat gold. "I love you, Hope. I can't imagine living my life without you. I've already spoken with Jeremy and he is crazy about the idea of us becoming a family. Please mar—"

"Yes," she yelled, throwing her arms around him. "What took you so long?"

"I had to special-ord—"

"Never mind. Just kiss me."

He did.

Applause erupted again. This time it was thunderous.

Shelton shook his head. "She didn't even look at the ring."

"She has the man," Bridgett said. "That's what's important."

"Then I'd say Sebastian is one of the lucky ones."

"They both are." Bridgett glanced up at Shelton, a gleam in her eyes. "By the way, are you married?"

Shelton blinked, then spluttered, "N-no."

"Well, isn't that nice," Bridgett said, a speculative smile on her face.

Hope wasn't listening to anything but the joyous singing of her heart. She was where she belonged. Where she wanted to be, in Sebastian's arms, and the most marvelous part was that he loved her. Dreams did come true. All it took was a matter of trust.

sweet

Temptation

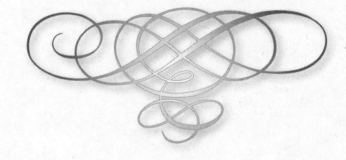

ONE

Time had run out for Chase M. Braxton. He knew it the instant he saw the neatly printed return address on the oblong box wrapped in plain brown paper stamped FRAGILE. An incongruent mixture of dread and anticipation swept through him. *Typical Monday,* he thought. The sigh that came from his wide chest was long and deep.

Shifting the unfamiliar weight of his briefcase to his left hand, Chase pulled the parcel from the black granite-topped front desk of Hotel George in the heart of Capitol Hill's business district. His thoughts unsettled, he strode through the two-story glass-and-stainless-steel lobby to the elevator and jabbed eight.

Less than a minute later the doors smoothly slid open on the top floor. Long, powerful strides quickly carried Chase to his door. Carefully shifting the bundle beneath his left arm, he pulled his plastic room key card from his shirt pocket and activated the lock. As soon as the light flashed green, he entered the room.

Decorated in cool beige and cream, the suite possessed a spacious sitting room with built-in wet bar, adjoining powder room, and custom-designed cherry wood furnishings. As a man topping six-foot-five, Chase welcomed the ability to move freely without bumping into furniture. That important aspect when he'd checked into the hotel eight extremely long days ago mattered little now compared with his current problem.

Skirting the lounge chair, he stopped on the other side of the coffee table positioned in front of a small couch. Tossing his brief-case on one of the cushions, he bent and edged over the twelve-inch-high, rickety stack of policy and procedure law enforcement manuals on the coffee table. He set the package down and straight-ened.

Hands on his narrow waist, he stared broodingly at the tele-phone a few feet away on the end table, then brought his troubled gaze back to the parcel.

He had definitely run out of time.

The phone call to Julia Anne Ferrington couldn't be put off any longer. Still, he hesitated at following through with action.

Indecisiveness was not a characteristic people who knew Chase would have associated with him. Few in law enforcement could come close to matching his outstanding reputation as a commis-sioned officer of the elite Texas Rangers. The wall behind his desk in Austin was covered with awards from civic organizations for his work with youth and with commendations for bravery in the line of duty.

Chase took special pride in the awards given for trying to make a difference in the lives of young people. As for the commenda-tions, the way he saw it, he simply did the job he had sworn to do. In his line of work a moment's hesitation could cost lives. In the thirteen years that he'd spent working his way up from Trooper One with the Texas Department of Public Safety to Lieutenant in charge of his own Ranger unit in Austin, he'd always acted quickly and decisively.

He'd never choked . . . until now.

His large, callused hand ran over his clean-shaven face as indeci-sion held him still. He didn't like the feeling. But neither was he thrilled at the prospect of calling a strange woman and making small talk. However, the neatly wrapped box with the Waco, Texas, postmark was a gentle reminder that he had to do just that. His procrastination for the past week since he had been in D.C. was about to come to an end.

Midnight black eyes narrowed as Chase stared longingly at the parcel. Mabel Johnson, the wife of his captain, Oscar Johnson, in Waco, had baited her trap well. She knew a gentle reminder worked better than a shove. Temptation worked even better.

Chase picked up the box and gently hefted its weight. He almost groaned in anticipation. Mabel made the best tea cakes his taste buds ever had the pleasure of meeting. He was probably holding at least three dozen of the delicious cookies the size of his palm. And unlike back in Austin when Mabel brought them to the station for all the Rangers to share, these were all his.

But first he had to make the phone call.

Pulling his billfold from the back pocket of his jeans, he plucked out Julia Ferrington's phone number. If Mabel had been the kind of lady to try to set him up, he'd have tossed the number despite the cookie bribe. But she wasn't. She simply was doing what she had always done, helping her husband take care of his men.

Chase had made no secret of the fact that he didn't want to leave his heavy caseload and come to D.C. for six weeks to teach a criminal law symposium at Howard University. Captain Johnson and his superiors hadn't given Chase a choice. They were honored that out of all the law enforcement agencies in the country the Texas Rangers had been chosen, and just as they had always done for the past 176 years, they sent their best, most qualified man to do the job. In their opinion, that was Lt. Chase Braxton.

Mabel, in her usual motherly way, had tried to ensure that Chase, who didn't know anyone in the city, not be lonely during his six-week stay. Mabel needn't have worried. Washington, D.C., like most metropolitan cities, had more women than men. Chase could have had a date, if he wanted one, even before the plane landed at Washington National Airport.

The pretty stewardess in first class had made him acutely aware she'd be more than happy to make his first night in D.C. a memorable one. Chase, still annoyed at his captain, had spent that night and the ones following alone . . . by choice. He wasn't interested in sex for sex's sake. He'd learned more sense than that by the time he graduated from high school.

He wasn't a monk by any stretch of the imagination, just selective and careful in more ways than one. He planned to be the fifth African-American in the history of the Texas Rangers to make captain, and that meant no women. Women had sidetracked the career of more than one man in law enforcement. They didn't like the crazy hours or the dangers their men faced. The excitement of dating a man in uniform, a man with so much authority, soon wore off and reality set in. Chase had seen it happen time and time again. In his opinion it took a very special woman to put up with being married to a man in law enforcement. The chances of finding such a woman were slim to none. His father and brother had tried and failed. Thirty-four-year-old Chase wasn't trying.

His focus for the next few years had to be the job, not trying to keep some woman happy. The pain and heartache that followed wasn't worth it.

Mabel understood his plan and applauded him for his determination. She also understood he hadn't wanted to go to D.C., and in her own thoughtful way she wanted to see that his stay in D.C. was as pleasant as possible. Since a lady, in Mabel's old-fashioned opinion, never called a gentleman first, she had asked Chase to initiate the call. The cookies were both a reminder and an enticement if he had not.

His blunt-tipped forefinger traced the clear plastic tape. Mabel was well aware his conscience wouldn't allow him to rip into the box and satisfy his notorious sweet tooth if he hadn't done as he promised: called Julia Ferrington before he left D.C.

Sighing, Chase picked up the receiver and punched in Julia Ferrington's number. He should have known Mabel would realize he hadn't been specific in his promise. He had planned on calling the day before he left.

He wasn't much on small talk, and frankly, after hearing Mabel chatter about Julia Ferrington and her family's deep political and financial connections and clout, Chase didn't think he, a Ranger and a rancher, and Julia, a Washington socialite, would have much in common. The way he figured, he was saving them both a painful ten minutes, tops, of each trying to be polite and pretend interest in what the other was saying.

As the answering machine clicked on, a grinning Chase quickly stashed the phone between his ear and shoulder, then shoved his hand in the front pocket for his knife. By the time the electronic voice had asked him to please leave a message, the sharp blade had sliced through the wrapping paper and he had a golden brown tea cake in his hand.

"Ms. Ferrington, this is Chase Braxton. Mabel Johnson asked me to call and say hello. I'm at the Hotel George on Capitol Hill. You have a good day. Bye."

His duty done, he took a sizable bite out of the cookie, closed his eyes, and savored the taste. By the third cookie he was thirsty. Picking up the phone, he ordered milk from room service. Some decisions weren't that difficult. Propping his booted feet atop the table, Chase reached for another cookie.

Later that evening in her high-rise condo near the wharf, six miles from Hotel George, Julia Ferrington listened to the messages on her answering machine with her notebook in her hand and her black-and-gold Mont Blanc pen that had been a college graduation present from her oldest sister, Suzanne, poised. There had been five messages thus far.

Her handwriting was a reflection of Julia, elegant, neat, and precise. She had worked hard to change the insecure, awkward teenager into someone she and her family could be proud of. At age twenty-seven, her poise and self-assurance were as much a part of her as her sunny, caring nature.

The deep baritone of Chase Braxton's drawling voice brought her head up. She recognized the authority behind the rumbling sound, the confidence. She had grown up with and been around people just like him all her life. It was with a small bit of pride that she could now count herself in that number.

She recognized something else in his voice: impatience. Obviously the phone call to her had been made under duress. It appeared Mabel Johnson had been completely mistaken in her assumption that Chase would be lonely and homesick during his stay in D.C.

Mabel Johnson had called several weeks ago and asked Julia's permission to give Chase her phone number. Julia had been hesitant at first, until Mabel had said Chase didn't know anyone in the city. Julia had friends now, good friends, but she still remembered times when she did not. No one should be lonely with so many people in the world. It still saddened her that people were lonely.

She'd like to think she made a small positive difference in the lives of the residents in a nearby nursing home by visiting and reading to them twice a month. Her practical-minded family of bankers and politicians thought her time would be better spent crusading to raise volunteer awareness. Julia didn't. Her family might take pleasure from the spotlight and a calendar full of social events, but she enjoyed a quiet, simple life. More importantly, the people in the home would be left with no one if she weren't there.

"End of messages."

Clicking off the machine, Julia leaned back in her antique Queen Anne chair and stared out the window at the distant lights of Virginia. People visiting D.C. for the first time usually were surprised that Virginia and Maryland were so close. Just as her family was surprised that she chose to live in D.C. instead of Virginia as they did.

The crowded city of D.C. was a government town with literally thousands of office workers. Yet because of the high cost of living and poor parking facilities, many people elected to live in one of the surrounding suburbs or cities, with their leisurely lifestyle, quaint shops, and deep historical presence.

No one expected the shy baby sister to leave the shelter and security of her family. But her parents and her two older sisters had made their mark. Julia had just begun to make hers with Sweet Temptation, her gourmet chocolate-and-candy shop. A small chain of Sweet Temptation stores was her dream, just as a house in the suburbs and a family were a dream to some. She was on her way. Her first store was a resounding success.

After triple-digit profits for the past four years, she now felt comfortable enough to start scouting for a second location in Virginia. That way she could keep a close eye on both businesses and maintain her residence. If some people said she had used her family's far-reaching connections to become so successful so quickly, that was all right. This was Washington, where who you knew weighed just as important as what you knew. But she had little doubt her business had thrived because of the care she gave to the smallest detail and the excellent service. She took pride in knowing that when you purchased from Sweet Temptation you got much more than a delicious box of the finest candy money could buy.

The antique grandfather clock in the entryway chimed the half hour. Eight-thirty. She might as well get her own obligatory phone call over with. From the sound of his voice, he didn't want or need her help in becoming acclimated to the city or in fighting loneliness.

Flipping back through her telephone message book, she found the number of the Hotel George. In the past she'd had clients who stayed there, and she had worked with several conventions hosted there. Chase Braxton certainly hadn't given her the number, and judging by the high regard Mabel Johnson had of him as a Texas Ranger, he wasn't a man who forgot details that were important to him.

After the fourth ring, the message center activated. Emulating the same manner in which Chase had spoken, she said, "Good evening, Mr. Braxton. This is Julia Ferrington. Welcome to D.C. I'm sorry I missed your call. Good night and enjoy your stay in our fabulous city."

Hanging up, Julia stretched and walked into her bedroom, her retreat. She spent long hours away from home, and when she returned she enjoyed indulging herself with things that delighted the eyes as well as the other senses.

The elegantly romantic soft peach room held a mixture of Louis XVI and Empire furniture. On a glass-topped table were fresh flowers. French chairs flanked the cozy nook. Silk brocade ran the length of her picture windows and pooled on the thick cream carpeted floor. The fine old drawings and art by African-Americans hanging on the soft white walls had taken months to locate but were well worth the effort and expense.

The focal point was a huge four-poster canopy bed draped in peach silk. On the hand-made imported duvet were restored antique throw pillows. If romance was not in her immediate future, she could still enjoy the trappings by having beautiful, sensuous surroundings.

Stepping out of her high-heel Italian pumps, she placed them in a specially designed shoe box, unbuttoned her plum-colored double-breasted jacket, then her knee-length matching skirt. Hanging the clothes on a padded hanger, she felt a twinge of guilt about the call to Chase, then pushed it away. Although she had sounded like an overworked representative of the Visitors Bureau, the call had served its purpose. She had other things to worry about.

Like trying to come up with a unique concept to add Leo's to her growing lists of clients. If she could acquire the "in" supper club in D.C., it would be quite a coup.

Noah Hardcastle, manager and one of the four owners of Leo's, demanded only the best for his restaurant. Since his and Julia's business philosophy was the same, they got along fabulously. Her name and their friendship might get her an appointment, but she had to deliver the goods.

Finished undressing, she slipped on a white terry cloth robe with peach piping and headed for the bathroom, ideas running through her head. As water gushed from the mouth of a gold swan into the oversize marble tub, there wasn't a doubt in Julia's mind that when she and Noah met on Thursday she'd have an idea that would meet with his approval.

It was after ten that night when Chase returned from his jog and saw the red message light on the telephone in the sitting room. Although the hotel had an exercise and steam room, he preferred the unrestricted outdoors and fresh air. Pulling his perspiration-dampened gray sweatshirt over his head, he mopped the trickles of moisture gliding down his face and chest. Leaning over, he hit the speaker button and dialed for his messages.

Black eyes narrowed as he listened to Julia Ferrington's cool, cultured voice. *Iceberg* was his initial impression. He tossed in *snooty* and *stuck-up* by the time she said good-bye. Deleting the message, he went to the wet bar and chugged a glass of mineral water. After turning the TV to the evening news, he headed to the bathroom. A soak in the Jacuzzi had become as much a part of his nightly ritual as his jog, and just as pleasurable.

As the water filled the oversize tub, Chase promised himself again that as soon as he returned to his ranch he was going to install a Jacuzzi in his bathroom. His modest home was large enough to give him room and small enough for him to be able to keep fairly clean by himself.

His extra money went to pay a ranch hand to take care of his growing herd of Herefords and horses. By most Texas ranch standards, a ten-acre spread wasn't much of a ranch, but to Chase it was a small piece of heaven on earth. He had another fifteen years of a twenty-year mortgage and it would be his.

Stripping off his pants, he climbed into the swirling water, stretched out his long legs, and leaned his head against the rim. Through the wall speaker in the bathroom the reporter's voice came through loud and clear, but the one Chase heard was Julia's. Cool, polite, distant.

Closing his eyes, he tried to come up with a face to match Julia's voice. Within seconds he visualized a thin nose, pinched features, an unsmiling mouth. Rich laughter filled the room. Thank goodness he had missed her call and hadn't had to talk to her. He certainly wasn't going to call her again and try to meet her. He'd kept his word to Mabel and now he could enjoy his tea cakes and put Julia Ferrington out of his mind.

Chase had a good day at Howard and planned a better evening. Not even the tailgating and lane-switching of fellow motorists trying to beat the inevitable bumper-to-bumper rush-hour traffic could dampen his mood. He and his students were finally on the same page. They'd gone from being faintly suspicious of his qualifications and vocally wanting to know why the law symposium class wasn't being taught by a person from the FBI or CIA to respectful and genuinely interested in what he had to say.

Chase stopped for the traffic light. Tires screeched. Horns honked. People yelled out of open windows. The cars on the other side of him went through the yellow caution light. Cars illegally followed on the red. Glancing across the street, he saw Howard University Hospital. At least they wouldn't have far to go for medical attention.

The light changed and Chase pulled off. This afternoon several students had followed him into the hall after the lecture and then to his car, their mood angry over the accounts he had given them of injustices to minorities. He'd told them to channel their anger into becoming involved in the political arena and the justice system and changing laws. A few promised they would. He believed them.

To celebrate his breakthrough and the distinct possibility that his superiors had been right about the necessity of his teaching the class, he was going to indulge himself with a meal from room service, watch some football on TV, and, if he were lucky, find someone who wanted to check out the hotel's billiard room.

Chase was smiling in anticipation as he pulled up in front of the hotel. Saying hello to the jovial valet on duty, he tossed him the keys and quickly crossed the sidewalk. He pictured the blood-red, two-inch-thick porterhouse he planned to order, the mound of French fries with catsup piled on top.

"Mr. Braxton."

Chase stopped on the steps and looked over his shoulder. Henri held his briefcase in his hand. "Sir, you forgot again." Light amusement trickled through in the valet's heavily accented French Creole voice.

With a shake of his Stetson-covered head, Chase bounded back down the steps. He never took paperwork home from the Ranger office, so he had problems remembering he had to do so now. Teaching meant notes and lesson plans.

For the first time, Chase didn't shudder at the words. Smiling, he reached for the briefcase. "Thanks for catching me. This time someone won't have to be bothered with bringing it to my room."

"No problem," assured the valet as he turned to get into the Jeep Cherokee. By the time he'd pulled away from the curb, Chase was walking through the automatic glass doors and whistling softly. Another thing the department had been right about was choosing the "boutique" hotel over a large chain. The staff was small and friendly. He knew everyone by the end of the first week there.

"Mr. Braxton," called the desk clerk. "Could I see you a moment, please?"

Chase paused, trying to figure out why Simone had called him, then figured the quicker he took care of the matter, the quicker he could get to his steak. He switched direction and went to the desk. "Yes, Simone."

"You have another package, sir."

Black brows bunched. "Another one?"

"Yes, sir. I'll get it for you."

Chase placed his briefcase on the desk and wondered who might have sent this one. He was close to his father and brother who lived in Austin, but all three preferred using the telephone to keep in touch. They did enough paperwork on the job to abhor writing letters. Sending a package to him would be out of the question.

The department had shipped all the materials, too much in Chase's opinion, that they thought he'd need to teach his six-week seminar. There was no woman in his life who might want to make him think he'd be much better off with her in his life permanently. He was genuinely puzzled.

His thoughts came back to the present and his frown deepened as Simone returned with a large brown wicker basket wrapped in clear plastic and tied with a big red, white, and blue bow. There was a white star on the blue, just like the Texas flag. Although the clerk's slim arms were stretched to capacity, they were unable to encompass the basket.

"You're sure this is for me?"

White teeth flashed in Simone's ebony-hued face. "Positive." Her red nail tapped the envelope. " 'Chase Braxton. Hotel George.' "

His puzzlement growing, Chase opened the envelope. He stared at his name and the neat handwritten note welcoming him to D.C. Below in small, discreet gold print were the words: "Created by Julia A. Ferrington."

"Why would she send me this?" he mumbled.

"Since I don't know who 'she' is, I can't very well say, Mr. Braxton," Simone answered with open amusement. Her black eyes dancing with lingering humor, she glanced around the lobby, then leaned over and whispered, "But if you don't want it, I'd be delighted to take it off your hands. I'm a chocoholic and Sweet Temptation is renowned for their gourmet chocolate goodies."

Replacing the card, Chase picked up the basket and briefcase and flashed her a grin. "I'll be sure and keep that in mind."

"Please do that," Simone said, moving away to help another guest.

In his suite, Chase's gaze immediately zeroed in on the telephone, as if that would give him the answers he wanted. Seeing the red message light on, he quickly crossed the room and retrieved his message.

"Chase, this is Mabel. You sweet man. You must have made quite an impression on Julia. She called this morning to ask if you had any food allergies and if you liked candy. I told her no to the allergies, yes to the candy. If I don't miss my guess, you should be very happy by now. Enjoy and don't eat it all at one time."

Chase stared at the basket he still held in his hands. There were five sections, each filled with a different kind of candy. He recognized three: pralines, chocolate-covered peanuts, and divinity. The question remained, Why would she send him a gift basket? He knew enough to know that it hadn't been cheap, and although Julia Ferrington came from money, why would she want to spend it on a stranger?

Placing the basket on the coffee table, he removed the heavy card again. Seeing a telephone number on the back, he picked up the phone and dialed.

He needed answers. He prided himself on reading people correctly. In his profession it was almost second nature. It didn't set well that Julia Ferrington had somehow managed to prove him wrong.

"Sweet Temptation," answered a cheerful-sounding woman.

"Is this some kind of a candy shop?" Somehow he couldn't reconcile himself to the cool woman on the phone last night designing gift baskets.

"Sweet Temptation is more than just candy. As the name implies, it's a fabulous treasure trove of delicious and decadent goodies guaranteed to tempt the untemptable," she explained.

Her answer told him nothing. "Can I speak with Julia Ferrington, please?"

"I'm sorry, sir, she's not here."

"She works there, doesn't she?"

"Yes, sir. Is there a message?"

Leave it up to a woman to leave a man hanging. "Please have her call Chase Braxton at Hotel George. She has the number."

Hanging up the phone, he poked at the cellophane. The rich, tempting aroma of chocolate and other candies drifted out. The fat pralines, loaded with big pecan chunks, glistened like spun honey. He could see similar pecan chunks in the divinity. If he didn't miss his guess, macadamia nuts were in one of the other chocolate candies.

He loved nuts. People liked to joke about policemen eating doughnuts, but he preferred nuts any way he could get them.

What the heck. Ripping open the cellophane, he plucked out a praline and bit. His taste buds exploded in sheer ecstasy. The woman who'd answered the phone hadn't exaggerated. The sugary candy was as good as any he had ever tasted.

He still didn't understand why Julia Ferrington had sent the candy, but he intended to find out. Unanswered questions annoyed him.

Speaking with Julia Ferrington wasn't as easy as he'd imagined. Over the next two days he called Sweet Temptation four times and each time she was out. They either got tired of him calling or took pity on him, because the fifth time he was informed she was out of town.

Hanging up the phone, he decided that, come what may, he was seeing Julia Ferrington before he left Washington. And he was getting some answers. She might be cool, but she was also exasperating, even though he had yet to meet her. But he would. That he promised, and Chase never broke a promise.

TWO

"You've made a wonderful choice, Mrs. Howard. Your mother will enjoy the Bavarian chocolate cream mints, and each time she reuses the crystal dish she'll think of you." Handing the young woman the white shopping bag with SWEET TEMPTATION in bold red script, Julia held the shop's glass front door open for her.

"Thank you, Julia, for gift-wrapping it for me." The model-thin woman laughed and adjusted the strap of her Fendi bag on her shoulder. "She'll take forever trying to unwrap the lilac paper without tearing it. Then she'll store it and the lavender ribbon and silk orchid in her closet saying she'll use it, but she never will."

Julia smiled warmly. "I believe I've made the same prediction myself a time or two."

"So have I," the shopper agreed. "Thanks again."

Closing the door, Julia glanced around the shop to see if anyone needed help. When she was assisting a customer she always gave them her full attention. Nothing annoyed her more than a salesperson's impatience or curt dismissal if they saw the potential for a bigger sale.

An older couple browsed contentedly in Aladdin's Cove, a corner of the store that was devoted entirely to interesting and unique containers for the store's confections. A little boy of about four stared thoughtfully through the glass case, trying to choose which candy he wanted. At the register a well-dressed gentleman was checking out with a two-pound box of assorted chocolate creams. Since all the customers appeared content and taken care of, Julia decided she could go to her office for a few minutes.

Discreetly signaling Georgette, her assistant manager, who was patiently waiting for the little boy to walk down the twenty-foot glass candy case, Julia went to the back. She took special pride in everything in her shop and always saw that it came first. It had taken her a long time to finally decide in which direction she wanted her life to go, so she didn't treat her business lightly.

Two years after college, most of her friends had already started to make their mark in the world while she'd wandered aimlessly from job to job. It hadn't helped that her older sisters never seemed to have any doubts about their career choice. Suzanne was a lobbyist, and Amanda worked for the State Department.

The idea for Sweet Temptation had sprung from filling in for a sick friend for two weeks as a volunteer in the gift shop of a hospital. Julia had always been fond of people and soon learned she had an eye for detail and the unusual. Nine months and a small business loan later, she had opened Sweet Temptation. Her parents had been upset that she hadn't wanted them to help financially, but she had wanted to do it on her own. And she had.

She truly enjoyed being around people and helping them pick out just the right gift, whether the reasons were personal or business. Because she strongly believed it was equally important to please the eye as well as tantalize the taste buds, she was always looking for unique ways in which to package her goods. Thus the occasional buying trips.

Her wrapping paper changed with the season and never repeated itself; her baskets and containers, from paper to brass to crystal, came in an array of colors and shapes and prices. For those who became confused when offered so many choices, Julia, Georgette, or one of her assistants was there to gently guide them. This afternoon, however, Julia was the one in need of guidance.

Sitting behind the neat desk in her office, Julia stared at the five messages from Chase. She was more than a little puzzled. There had been five on her answering machine when she arrived home from her business trip last night as well. Of course, there were other messages from friends and family, but for some unexplained reason she felt the pull of Chase Braxton's messages more.

A manicured pale pink nail tapped the notes lying on the antique Chippendale desk. Never in her wildest imagination had she expected the distant, impatient man of three nights ago to try so hard to contact her. He certainly wasn't turning out to be what she had initially thought.

Leaning back in her chair, she bit her lower lip and felt somewhat guilty for putting him through so much trouble in trying to locate her. Since she lived alone, she never wanted the general public to have knowledge of when she was out of town. Her gated condo had security guards on-duty at all times, but it never hurt to be careful.

She had sent Chase the basket to make up for her less than cordial behavior when she returned his phone call. The bottom line was that regardless of her initial unflattering impression of his brash impatience, he was a friend of a friend. More important, just because his behavior was suspect, there was no reason for her to follow suit.

Besides, she'd learned long ago that first impressions could often be influenced by variables the other person wasn't aware of. Mabel Johnson was as kind as they came, but she wouldn't put up with a rude, arrogant man, nor would she subject Julia to one. The logical answer, she had concluded after a good night's sleep, was that there was another reason for Chase's abruptness.

Looking at the messages spread out on her desk, Julia was glad she had sent him the basket. Not many men would be that persistent in trying to contact a strange woman. It seemed Chase wasn't a man who gave up.

A smile lifted the corners of her mouth. With a name like Chase she should have guessed. Leaning forward, she flipped through her Rolodex until she found the phone number for Chase's hotel. She listened incredulously as the hotel's message center clicked on. *Figures*, she thought and blew out an exasperated breath.

This was ridiculous. She wasn't playing phone tag another day.

"Mr. Braxton, if you're as tired of talking to machines as I am, I'd like to offer a solution, if your schedule permits. I have a late appointment at Leo's, a supper club here in the city. I should be finished by nine, and then you and I could have drinks. I'll wait for you until nine-thirty. If you're able to come, just ask Erin, the hostess at Leo's, to direct you to my table. Good-bye."

Julia hung up the phone and sat back in her chair. She didn't make dates with men, certainly not with men she had never spoken with, but someone had to take action and since he had tried to contact her so many times, she felt it was her responsibility.

Leo's was perfect. The elegant supper club was a fabulous place to wine, dine, and unwind. Movers and shakers, working-class and corporate types frequented the restaurant. Maybe, just maybe, she'd finally get to put a face with a voice.

Chase wasn't coming.

Julia took another sip of the white wine she had been nursing for the past thirty minutes. She glanced again at the tiny eighteen-karat gold watch inlaid with diamonds on her wrist. Nine-forty-five. She had given him plenty of time if he planned to show up.

Her meeting with Noah Hardcastle had gone extremely well. He liked the idea of Sweet Temptation supplying him with special desserts during the holidays, starting with a chocolate cranberry upside-down cake topped with cognac whipped cream for Christmas. In the meantime they would partner on a gift basket. She would supply the basket and giant chocolate-covered strawberries, Leo's the vintage wine, crystal glasses, and signature linen napkins. Leo's would be the exclusive outlet.

The popular supper club was already known as the happening place to meet, relax, and have fun, so why shouldn't it, Julia reasoned, also be known as the place where romance begins? Glancing around the room bathed in soft light, the smooth sound of jazz flowing over the intercom, couples snuggled next to each other, their rapt expressions illuminated by the Tiffany lights on the round tables, or dancing on the intricately patterned parquet floor, she didn't doubt for a moment the success of the baskets.

People fall in love every day. And one day, when my business is solidly successful, I might let myself fall in love, too. But for now, Sweet Temptation is my only *temptation,* she mused. Smiling at her little play on words, Julia ran her finger around the rim of her wineglass. Across the room, the double mahogany front doors opened. She straightened, then sat back in the chair. An elderly gentleman crossed to the elongated rosewood bar and slid onto one of the tall, padded stools.

Groans emanated from the four women at the table directly behind Julia.

"It's certainly slim pickings tonight."

"He's old enough to be our grandfather."

"There's a football game on tonight."

"It was drizzling when I came in."

Julia listened to the four women and tucked her lower lip between her teeth. Was that where Chase was, watching a football game? Married and single female friends had told her, "Never try to compete with a football game. Even if you win, you lose." Perhaps she should have scheduled their meeting later in the week.

The front door opened again and she glanced up sharply, unaware of the hope shining in her brown eyes. A tall, broad-shouldered man stood poised in the doorway. His black Stetson-covered head moved in a slow arc as he searched the room. His gaze paused briefly on her, then moved on. A sudden gust of wind pressed the long black rain slicker to his athletic body, then away. Julia got an immediate impression of strength and leashed power. A little shiver raced up her spine.

Jeans lovingly encased muscular thighs and long legs. His skin was the color of burnished teak. The white shirt emphasized his wide chest.

"Mercy, look what the rain drove in."

"Now there's a man who looks like a man."

"If any of you are wondering what to give me for my birthday, you can stop."

"Since I'm your friend, why don't I make sure he's in good working condition first?"

Laughter drifted from the table behind her. They were unabashedly man-watching but until now Julia hadn't paid much attention to their rating scale. This time she did and wholeheartedly agreed with them.

This man was spectacular, and for some reason, she thought, dangerous. Perhaps it was the way his gaze encompassed the room in a single all-consuming glance. She could almost feel the intensity from across the room.

Finally, he let the doors swing shut and came farther into the restaurant. Erin stepped forward to greet him, then moments later turned and looked in Julia's direction. Julia felt her breath catch. Tipping his Stetson to Erin, he started toward Julia.

"Oh, goodness, he's heading in this direction."

"If he passes us, I may grab his leg."

"If you grab one, I'll grab the other one."

"Just make sure that's all you grab."

The women erupted into bawdy laughter. Julia briefly wondered why their laughter sounded muted, as if from a long distance away. She didn't seem capable of anything except watching the man's slow, purposeful stride toward her. The brim of his hat shaded the upper half of his clean-shaven face, but she easily distinguished the strong jaw, broad nose, mobile lips. His eyes were hidden from her, but for some odd reason, she felt their pull.

Another tiny shiver raced up Julia's spine. Instinctively she wrapped her arms around her. The long-sleeved red suit jacket did little to help. Moistening her lips, she reminded herself it was always on the cool side in Leo's and continued to watch the stranger who was creating such disquiet within her.

With each step that brought him closer, she hoped the man heading straight for her wasn't Chase Braxton. She had asked to be seated near the back of the restaurant because she hadn't wanted to appear conspicuous while she waited for Chase. There were three other tables behind her besides the one where the four women were seated. Maybe he was going to one of them.

Her hope died when he stopped directly in front of her and removed his hat. She almost groaned. The women behind her did.

No man should be that handsome. His lush black eyelashes were longer and thicker than hers. His eyes were black and entirely too intense. His mouth was full and sensuously inviting. Worst of all, he had a charming and irresistible dimple in his stubborn chin.

How could Mabel have done this to her?

"Julia Ferrington?"

Her throat went dry. This man was nothing like she had expected and everything that could make a woman act very, very foolish. "Chase Braxton?"

He nodded, his handsome face unsmiling. "You're not what I expected."

"Neither are you."

THREE

Studying the flawless oval face of Julia Ferrington, Chase tried to reconcile what he was seeing to what he had imagined. He couldn't. She was . . . lovely. It was not a word he used often, but he could think of no other way to describe the woman in front of him. Her smooth skin was the warm, inviting color of cinnamon. The eyes watching him warily were a deeper shade of brown. So was the lustrous curly hair that brushed her tense shoulders. He had never thought of bangs as being flirtatious. Hers were. The red suit was another surprise.

He'd thought she'd be buttoned-down, hidden from the prying and unwanted eyes of men. Again he had guessed wrong. She was dressed completely in red. Here was a woman with enough confidence to draw attention to herself with an eye-stopping combination of sexy style and classy elegance.

"May I sit down?" He thought that best since his legs weren't all that steady.

"Of course," she said, her voice smooth and oddly breathless.

Pulling out a chair, Chase sat down across from Julia and studied the becoming flush on her face. Another surprise.

"We meet at last," she said.

Chase grunted in the affirmative. There was nothing cool about her voice now. The tone was soft, shy, and enticing.

Julia twisted uneasily in her seat, trying to understand whatever it was about Chase that made her decidedly . . . restless and scattered. Then she decided it was his eyes . . . dark, hot, and mysterious.

To combat the feeling, she took a sip of wine and quickly discovered her mistake when his gaze shifted to her mouth. The scorching intensity had her gripping the stem. "I—I didn't think you were coming," she said, hoping to avert his attention from her lips.

Slowly his gaze widened to encompass her face once again. "I was out with some friends from the university and didn't get your message until about thirty minutes ago."

Julia's eyes widened. The hotel was a good thirty minutes away in the best of travel conditions, and with the rain . . . "You must have rushed over here."

Chase shrugged, then leaned forward in his seat and braced his arms on the table, telling himself he was just getting comfortable and not moving to get closer. "Why did you send the basket?"

She fiddled with her wineglass, then looked straight at Chase. She had always demanded honesty of herself and others, even when it was difficult to face. "I had been less than cordial and rather austere when I returned your phone call, and I wanted to make amends."

Chase never took his eyes from Julia. Cordial, austere, amends. More words he didn't hear or use. But he admired her honesty. She didn't shift blame, just took responsibility for her actions. Since he admired those qualities and tried to emulate them, he had to admit he shared in the blame. His phone call to her had been impatient at best. "Then I should have been the one to send the basket. I was less than cordial and rather austere first."

A slow smile curved her magenta-colored lips. "Now that you mention it."

Did she know her mouth was enough to make a man weep? Somehow he didn't think so.

"No wonder she was waiting so long."

"Some women have all the luck."

"Maybe she'll throw him back."

"Would you?"

Julia's eyes widened in embarrassment. Her gaze skirted to Chase, then away. She had forgotten about the women. Heat pooled in her cheeks. "Chase, I'm sorry."

"Why? You're gonna throw me back?" he asked, enjoying the husky sound of his name on her lips.

She blinked.

"Forget it," he said, annoyed with himself because for one crazy moment he had toyed with the tantalizing idea of her wanting to keep him and wanted her to disagree with him.

"I'm not much of a fisherman, but even a novice knows you have to catch something before you can throw it back," she countered, trying not to be affected by the sensuous mouth, the dimpled chin, the drawling voice that stroked the skin and the senses. Most of all by the little voice in her head wondering what it would be like to "catch" a man like Chase Braxton.

His gaze strayed to her lips again. What was the matter with him? He went for the fun-loving, no-strings type. Somehow that wasn't stopping him from fantasizing about how Julia Ferrington's mouth would feel beneath his. He barely kept the scowl from his face.

What was the matter with her? Julia wondered. This man was a stranger. An annoyed-looking one at that. Perhaps she shouldn't have had the wine on an empty stomach. All she'd had to eat today was a bagel and a cup of tea. Her first day back after a trip was always hectic. Noah had offered her dinner, but she'd declined. She had been afraid dinner might run over the time she expected Chase.

"Would you like another glass of wine?"

Opening her mouth to say, "No," she yawned instead. "I'm sorry," she murmured, covering her mouth with both hands in abject embarrassment and apology. "I caught the red-eye last night so I wouldn't miss another day in the shop. I've only had a couple of hours' sleep."

"Surely your boss would let you off another day."

Julia smiled. "I *am* the boss."

Chase straightened. Black eyes widened. "You own Sweet Temptation?"

"Yes," she answered proudly. "We celebrated our fourth anniversary two months ago."

Chase floundered. "I thought you just did the baskets."

"I do it all, including sweep floors and wash the windows," Julia said without shame. "If I don't take pride in the store I can't expect my employees to."

Chase stared at the well-dressed, elegant woman in front of him. "But Mabel didn't mention you owned a business."

"It's no secret," Julia said, but she wondered why herself. Mabel had always seemed so proud of Julia.

"I guess," he said, then watched Julia fight back another yawn. She had to be exhausted, yet she had waited past the time she had stated to meet a stranger. Certainly not the action of an iceberg, but he had already discovered his mistake in judging her.

Julia Ferrington was turning out to be a complex, fascinating woman. Too bad he didn't have time to explore the possibility of getting to know her better and learning if her mouth was as sweet as it looked.

Standing, Chase closed his hand around the back of her chair. "Come on. I'll walk you to your car."

Oddly reluctant, but aware that her body wanted to sleep, Julia picked up her briefcase from the corner of the table. "Thank you. I apologize."

Strong fingers closed around her elbow. "No need. I'm just sorry I kept you waiting."

"I didn't mind," she said, looking up at him. "I wanted to meet you."

The genuine sincerity and warmth in her voice caused Chase's fingers to tighten briefly on her arm. He felt the fine bones beneath his calloused fingers, the silk of the tailored suit, and loosened his hold. Wrong woman. Wrong time.

Outside they stopped beneath the restaurant's awning and watched the steady downpour. Julia turned to Chase. "Good night. I'll have to make a dash for it."

Chase didn't release her arm. "Where's your car?"

"In the back I'm afraid."

He pulled off his rain slicker and placed it over her shoulders in one easy motion. "It's a little big, but it will keep you dry."

Julia felt enveloped by his compelling, clean male scent, the lingering warmth from his body. It was almost like being in his arms. She flushed at the thought. "I couldn't take your coat."

"I'm wearing a hat, Julia," he told her. "Besides, my clothes can take a little rain; that suit you're wearing can't."

The dry cleaner could probably handle getting the Dior back in shape. What she couldn't handle was Chase's unnerving nearness or the way her pulse sped up when he said her name. Shaking her head, Julia reached up to take the slicker off.

"The coat stays." With surprising gentleness, his hand closed over hers. Again Julia felt the tiny shiver.

The door behind them opened. Automatically they moved in tandem to one side, the motion bringing them closer. The nearness of the man was intoxicating. But his stubbornness was annoying. "I will not take your coat."

"Then we'll share it." Before Julia could answer, he lifted the coat from her shoulders, stepped beside her, and raised it over their heads. "Now we both stay dry."

His muscled thigh brushed against hers, sending more little tingles of awareness up and down her spine. The coat over and around them became a seductive cocoon. She had the ridiculous notion to step closer, press her lips to the dimple in his chin, then to his lips.

The door opened again. A young couple came out, nodded in greeting to Julia and Chase, then ran hand in hand laughing into the hard-driving rain. They were soaked within seconds. Carefree laughter drifted back to Chase and Julia. Clearly neither cared about being wet if they were together. Unexpectedly Julia felt a pang of envy, then pushed it away.

"Unless you want to follow their example and get drenched, we better get moving."

"If you insist." Julia turned briskly away from Chase, the cause of her strange and unwanted mood, and headed down the sidewalk to the parking lot just off the street. Chase's long, easy strides easily matched hers.

Approaching her white unmarked minivan, she removed the key from the pocket of her suit jacket and disengaged the lock. Chase reached the door handle before she did, inadvertently pressing his long muscular frame against her. The intense heat and hardness was impossible to ignore.

Quickly she climbed in, as much to escape Chase's disturbing presence as to let him get out of the rain. She was well aware that he had shielded her from the rain at his own expense.

Starting the vehicle, she let the window down. "Good night, Chase, and thanks for seeing me to my car."

"I'm in a black Jeep Cherokee a couple of rows up front. Wait for me on the street. I'll follow you home."

"Ha—" He was already turning away. Julia let the window up and pulled out of the parking space. She could ignore his command couched as a request, but why bother? As it happened, she didn't have a chance even if she wanted to. As soon as she hit the street, the Cherokee pulled out behind her.

Ten minutes later she pulled up to her condo building. Letting down her window, she waved good night to Chase and drove through the black iron security gates. It hadn't escaped her attention that

Chase had not asked to see her again, which was just as well. She was honest enough with herself to admit she was attracted to him. And practical enough to see that any relationship was impossible. According to the information Mabel had given her, he had only a little over four weeks in D.C. remaining.

Too bad, she thought as she parked the van and got out. Chase had a kind of sexy magnetism that she found absolutely fascinating, if a bit overpowering. Or perhaps that was what attracted her to him.

She wouldn't have minded getting to know him better if the situation were different. The intriguing thought stayed with her all through getting ready for bed and followed her into a restless sleep.

For four days Chase tried reason, and when that failed he tried exercise, which also failed. He couldn't get Julia Ferrington out of his mind. She was nothing like he'd expected. Her warm, caring nature invited a man to get closer. Then there was the vulnerability he'd glimpsed in her dark brown eyes, eyes that could quickly change into fire if she was crossed.

She was a woman of contrasts.

Hands stuffed in the pockets of his jeans, Chase stood outside Sweet Temptation on Monday afternoon. The day was beautiful. Blue skies stretched forever.

Unlike the sweltering heat in Texas in September, the temperature in D.C. was in the upper sixties. Best of all, after the past few days of showers no rain was in the forecast. Judging by the heavy crowds passing by, people fully intended to take advantage of the good weather.

Watching people enter and leave the shop, most of the time with a handled shopping bag with the Sweet Temptation logo, he debated his options. He was a man of action, a Texas Ranger whose courage was well documented. He didn't have to be nervous about seeing a woman. Besides, if he stood beneath the pin oak tree much longer, the birds might decide to try to roost on top of his Stetson.

He had to get a grip, and fast.

He'd been the same way, indecisive and unsure of himself, when he went to the flower shop to order her flowers the morning after he met her. In the past he'd faced a crazed, knife-wielding junkie high on crack with less concern. But then he had known to expect the unexpected.

In selecting the flowers he'd had nothing to go on. There was just the driving need from somewhere that the flowers be just right. He instinctively knew she had put a great deal of thought into his basket, and he wanted to do the same with the flowers. It was impossible to do less. By the time he'd left the florist, the poor woman working there had practically pushed him out the door.

Julia Ferrington was changing him, and it wasn't for the better. What was it about her that tugged at him? Had him thinking about her throughout the day? Maybe it was because she didn't act or look as he'd expected and that had captured his attention and interest.

He was a seasoned law enforcement officer. He knew how to step back and analyze a situation. This was no different. He just needed to see her again to figure out what was happening to him; then he could get on with his life.

Without further hesitation, Chase crossed the busy sidewalk and strode into the shop, sure he would find the answer he sought . . . until he saw her. And seeing her, he wanted to touch, to taste.

She wore a lemon yellow dress that reminded him of the daffodils that shot up yearly around the perimeter of his ranch house. Although he didn't particularly pay attention to flowers, at least until three days ago, he'd always admired the way the daffodils foreshadowed spring, their delicate beauty, their tenacity for life.

Across the room, Julia gracefully bent from the knees to pick up a crystal bowl from the lowest shelf of a six-foot glass-and-brass étagère. The silky material flowed down the gentle curve of her back to lovingly cup her hips. Standing, she traced her delicate fingers over the fragile curved glass, her touch reverent and loving.

Grace. Beauty. Strength. She was all that and more.

Would she touch a man the same way or with greedy anticipation? Chase rammed his hands deeper into his pockets because he couldn't fool himself any longer as to why he had come.

He wanted Julia Ferrington. Wanted her badly. There wasn't a thing he could do about it. The fact that she was out of his class and that he had less than four weeks left in D.C. didn't seem to matter.

Julia felt him. She didn't understand how; she simply knew Chase Braxton was in the shop watching her. Her hands trembled. Carefully she set the crystal bowl on a nearby table.

Forgetting one of her ironclad rules, she shifted her attention from a client. Chase stood ten feet away, watching her. The impact of seeing him again, this time in the bold revealing light of day, stole her breath and scattered all thoughts, but one. He affected her as no other man ever had.

He was impossibly handsome. Once again he was in jeans that appeared to have been sculpted to his muscled legs and a white long-sleeved shirt. The cuffs were rolled back to reveal a gold watch on one powerful wrist and a thick gold link bracelet on the other. If *GQ* or *CODE* could get him to pose, he'd certainly set the style and have the magazines flying off the shelf.

He slowly crossed to her and paused a few feet away. "Hello, Julia."

"Hello, Chase," she answered, trying to calm her racing pulse and booming heart. "Welcome to Sweet Temptation."

Midnight black eyes glanced around the crowded upscale shop that gleamed in the bright sun like a multi-prism jewel. "You have quite a place here."

"Thank you."

He shifted from one eel-skinned boot to the other. "I'd like to talk with you, if you have time."

"Certainly." Did he ever smile? "Just as soon as I finish with my customer."

"Sure. I'll just look around."

"All right." Julia followed him with her eyes as he moved away, much in the same way she had seen so many children in the shop stare with such intense longing at the wide array of candy behind the glass casing, wanting to taste everything but resigned that it was not to be.

With an annoyed shake of her head, Julia went back to helping the customer, making sure her attention didn't wander. Admiring a good-looking man was acceptable; letting it interfere with business was not. Certainly not a man who wouldn't be around long. Five minutes later, she rang up the sale.

Satisfied she had whatever crazy musings she had about Chase under control, she turned to seek him out. One glimpse and her heart thumped sharply against her breastbone. So much for control. He made her restless. He made her contemplate throwing caution to the wind.

Brushing her damp palms on the sides of her dress, she went to Chase. He was in Toyland watching a working replica of a chocolate Ferris wheel. Thankfully, no children or adults were nearby. She had a feeling the conversation might get heavy. "I hope I didn't keep you too long."

Hands still firmly in his pockets, his gaze shifted to her. "No."

"Thanks again for the flowers, Chase. They're lovely."

"They reminded me of you," he said, then frowned as if annoyed with himself.

For the first time since he had walked in, Julia relaxed. She could because Chase was nervous enough for both of them.

For a man who had single-handedly captured three bank robbers and rescued their hostage, according to a proud Mabel, a nervous Chase seemed incongruent. He was also annoyed. Somehow it made her erratic emotions easier to deal with. Neither one of them was entirely comfortable with what was happening between them.

Her eyes had foolishly teared up on seeing the dozen white roses. She'd taken half of them home so she could enjoy them there as well while she watched the tight, perfect buds blossom into an aromatic profusion of white. She'd been touched by his thoughtfulness and unspoken apology. She also understood perfectly his dilemma because it mirrored her own.

"You didn't want to come here, did you?"

His gaze sharpened. "No."

"Then why did you?"

"Because I wanted to more than I wanted to stay away."

Her heart sighed. "Chase, that's the most beautiful thing anyone ever said to me."

His scowl deepened.

She laughed.

"This isn't funny."

"Believe me, I know."

"I'm leaving in less than a month." He tossed the words almost as if they were a challenge.

"Yes, I know."

"I don't want to get involved."

"Neither do I."

He nodded as if that settled everything. "Would you like to meet for a drink or something after work?" he asked, then rushed on. "You understand it wouldn't be a date or anything."

"Of course." Whatever this was, they were going to pretend it wasn't there. She decided to show him she understood the unspoken rules. "Why don't we meet at Leo's around seven?"

"I could pick you up."

"I can get there myself. It's not a date or anything," she said, giving his words back to him.

"All right. See you at seven."

"Fine."

Still he didn't move, simply frowned at her as if she were an annoying puzzle he had yet to figure out. The front door opened and three shoppers came in. "I better get back to work," she told him.

"Yeah." Tipping his Stetson, he spun on his booted heels and left the shop. The interested gaze of the three women followed. Julia didn't blame them.

Now *that*, Julia thought as she watched Chase through the glass storefront, was another kind of sweet temptation.

FOUR

Chase was waiting for Julia when she arrived at Leo's. Seeing her walk through the double mahogany doors smiling and looking beautiful somehow calmed the doubts that had plagued him all day. It was natural for a man to be attracted to a friendly, attractive woman. Feeling more confident, Chase leaned back in his chair and studied the woman who was seldom far from his thoughts since he had met her.

She wore a long-sleeved jacket in jewel tones over the yellow dress. She had a way with colors that drew the eyes and made a man think of what lay beneath. Desire, fierce and hard, hit Chase low and fast. Grimacing, he rocked forward. His logic of moments ago went out the window. The deep intensity of his attraction was unreasonable, undeniable, and, worse, uncontrollable.

Her progress across the room was slow. First one man, then another stopped her. Her warm, open smile never faltered despite the continued apologetic glances she kept throwing in Chase's direction. It didn't help his mood that all the men she stopped to speak with were young, well dressed, and good-looking.

Finally, she made it to the table. "Hello, Chase."

Standing, his mood decidedly testy, he held out her chair. "Do you know everybody in this place?"

Her black eyebrows lifted regally at his brusque tone. "Three of the men I was speaking with are co-owners of Leo's. We were discussing business. The other is an old friend. Any other questions?" Her tone was civil but tinged with frost.

Her message came through loud and clear: *Back off.*

She was absolutely right. It shouldn't matter to him if she talked to a thousand men. She had waited much longer for him and greeted him with a smile instead of an accusation. If it had been another woman, he wouldn't have been bothered by the length of time it took to reach their table or the number of men she spoke to on the way.

But it wasn't another woman. It was Julia, and therein lay his problem. A problem he was determined to rectify. He just had to figure out how.

"Sorry," he muttered.

She smiled, sending his heart thumping in his chest, and placed her small yellow handbag on the corner of the table. "Long day."

"Yeah." Long because he had wanted to see her, kiss her. *Concentrate, Chase, concentrate.* "What do you want to drink?"

"White wine. I took the precaution of eating a quick sandwich around four, so I shouldn't fall asleep on you."

"You work too hard," he told her, then signaled a waitress to take their drink orders.

"True, but I enjoy what I do." She leaned forward, wondering if she'd ever get used to the little leap in her heart when she saw him. "So do you, I heard."

"Mabel?"

"Mabel," she confirmed, accepting her wine. "She says you have quite a reputation as a Texas Ranger."

"I have a good unit. We work together as a team to get the job done." Chase sipped his mineral water. He never drank while on duty, and in his opinion the six-week assignment in D.C. was duty. "There's only the four of us, myself and three sergeants, assigned to the Austin area. We investigate major felony crimes and other related incidents. You already know I report to Captain Johnson in Waco. I fought the assignment of coming here. They sent a replacement for me, but since there are only six field captains and seven lieutenants out of one hundred and seven commissioned members in the entire Ranger force, someone's job had to go lacking to do mine."

"You'd rather do the job yourself, wouldn't you?"

He frowned into his glass. "My temporary replacement is a good man."

"But he's not you."

"Yeah. Captain Johnson says I should learn to delegate more," Chase told her, not sure why he was telling her this except she listened well.

"Chase, you don't appear the type of man to take your responsibility lightly. You'd want to make sure every detail is taken care of."

He arched a brow. "How did you know?"

She sipped her wine and sat back. "I used to be the same way. I've just learned to let my assistant manager do what I had hired her for. I found out the hard way I couldn't do it all and do it all well. This time away from your unit should convince you that it won't fall apart without you there."

Black eyes narrowed. "You're saying I'm not needed."

"I'm saying I can't imagine you having people working under you who didn't know what they were doing or who don't have the intelligence to act independently."

Studying her closely, he leaned back in his chair. "Every time I think I have you figured out, you say or do something that baffles me."

"Is it so important to figure me out?"

"Yes."

Julia was afraid she knew why. He hated the attraction between them, and with his analytical mind he was probably trying to figure out the how and the why to put an end to it. She wasn't waiting around until he did. She'd had enough rejection in her life.

She picked up her purse. "Let me know if you come up with an answer."

He frowned. "You're leaving already?"

"Yes."

"You just got here."

"I have a feeling things won't be any different an hour from now," she said sadly and stood.

Slowly coming to his feet, Chase signaled the waitress. What had he said or done to make Julia leave so abruptly? "I'll see you to your car."

"No need. I promised Noah I'd stop by his office on the way out." She extended her hand. "Good night, Chase."

Her hand was soft, smooth, her grip surprisingly strong. He didn't want to let go. He had a sinking feeling that she was saying good-bye, not just good night. But he didn't know the words to stop her or if he should.

"Good night, Julia."

Pulling her hand free, she headed for Noah's office in the back of the restaurant. *Keep walking*, she told herself. *Keep walking away from temptation and heartache.*

Chase got as far as the parking lot. The area was well lit, but lighting in itself wasn't enough of a deterrent to a determined criminal. Retracing his steps, he positioned himself in the deep shadow of the building beside the restaurant and waited for Julia. She might not want to talk with him and they may not have had a date, but he was going to make sure she got home safely.

Ten minutes later, she came out. One of the men she had spoken with earlier was with her. Chase gritted his teeth in annoyance when Julia held up her keys and firmly refused the man's offer to see her to her minivan. Lord save him from stubborn, independent women.

Brisk steps quickly carried Julia to her minivan. By the time she reached the first signal light, Chase was a car length behind. She drove fast but competently. When she pulled into her complex, Chase lagged back and watched her speak briefly to a security guard, then proceed through the black iron gates into the underground garage.

Chase felt a strange something in his chest as the taillights of her vehicle disappeared. Probably the chili dog he had for lunch. Putting the Jeep into gear, he drove to his hotel and went to bed.

Two hours later a wide-awake Chase stared at the ceiling and finally gave in to the inevitable. Whether he liked it or not, it wasn't over between him and Julia.

The next morning Chase was standing in front of Sweet Temptation when Julia unlocked the door. "May I come in?"

She debated only a second. "Of course." She stepped aside, noticing that he didn't look as if he had slept any better than she had.

He glanced at the other young black woman in the shop, then faced Julia. "Is there a place where we can speak privately?"

"Georgette, I'll be in my office if you need me." Julia went to the back, past the gift-wrap area, to her small office. She didn't offer him a seat. "We don't have long, Chase."

"Tell me something I don't know."

"Chase, you're not making sense."

"Right again." His hands closed around her upper forearms with surprising gentleness and undeniable strength. "Wanting you is not making sense, but I can't seem to help it. I go to bed thinking of you. Wake up thinking about you, wondering about how you'd taste. I'm tired of wondering."

His determined mouth came down on hers, demanding a response. Julia didn't hesitate. Her tongue greeted his with greedy anticipation and bold acceptance. Fierce pleasure swept through her.

With a ragged groan, his arms tightened around her waist, anchoring her to the hard length of his muscular body. On tiptoes, she strained to get closer, her arms locked around his neck.

The kiss was fire and heaven, bliss and hunger.

Chase finally lifted his head, but as if he couldn't bear to be away from her, his hands palmed her face as he pressed soft kisses to her mouth. "I'm not sure what I would have done if you had slapped my face."

"Too Victorian. Kneeing is the modern method for unwanted advances."

"Ouch. Then I'm doubly glad." He kissed her again. "This is crazy. I'll be gone in a few weeks."

"I've told myself the same thing, but I don't think I'm listening."

Black eyes stared down into brown ones. "Maybe it'll wear off."

"Maybe," Julia answered, her hands now on his wrists. She turned her head to brush a kiss against the top of his hand, the dimple in his chin, his soft mouth.

He shuddered, then captured her lower lip and suckled. "I want to see you tonight."

"W-what?"

"Tonight. What time?"

"Six," she murmured, seeking his lips again.

He barely lifted his mouth from hers. "I'm picking you up at your place and taking you home."

"So this is a date?" she asked breathlessly.

"You better believe it, and just so there'll be no misunderstanding . . ." His mouth came back down on hers.

By four-thirty that afternoon Julia knew she'd never leave the shop by five and be ready for Chase by six. As sometimes happened, they'd had a rush. Men who had forgotten birthdays or anniversaries. Women who had forgotten the same thing. Or customers who simply wanted the best chocolate on the East Coast.

Smiling at her own boastfulness, Julia gave a final pat to the pink ribbon bow on the basket she had just finished, then carried it out to the waiting hands of a young man. "Happy first anniversary. I wish you many more."

"Thanks," he said and moved to get in the growing line at the register.

Julia glanced around the shop to see who needed help next. They were four deep. She barely refrained from glancing at her watch. She needed to call Chase and tell him she'd be late, but the customers always came first. Why since Chase had come into her life did she have to keep reminding herself of that fact?

The little tingles of awareness that swept through her at the mere thought of him were her answer. She'd just have to learn how to deal with whatever was between them. She definitely wasn't going to turn her back on it.

Moving to help an elderly couple in Toyland, she saw her older sister with her cell phone glued to her ear as usual, a briefcase in the other hand. Suzanne capably juggled the four two-pound gold foil boxes of truffles under her arm just as she did her hectic life as a lobbyist.

With a sigh of resignation, Julia scanned the store. Still full, and Georgette was on the phone by the register. She didn't have time to go to her office. She switched direction.

"Hi, Suzanne." Careful not to disturb the delicate balance of her sister's packages, Julia gave her a hug. Taller by two inches, Suzanne was stylishly dressed in a black Prada pantsuit and shoes by the same designer.

"Can I ask you a favor?" Julia preferred not to involve her overprotective sister in her personal life, but at the moment she had no other choice.

"Hold on, Harold," Suzanne said. "What's up?"

"Please call Chase Braxton at the Hotel George and leave a message that I'm running late and I'll call."

Suzanne lifted one naturally arched black brow in a face that had been known to stop traffic on the busy D.C. streets and said into the receiver, "Harold, let me call you back." She disconnected the call. "Is he a client?"

"No." Julia moved away before Suzanne could ask questions but knew they would come later. She hadn't had a meaningful date in over five years. Since she had opened Sweet Temptation, the store had always been her top priority. Dating took a back seat. Socialization was work- or family-related.

Ten minutes later when she was in the gift-wrap room in the back, someone tapped her on the shoulder. She glanced around.

"Chase said to tell you he'd wait for as long as it took."

"You actually talked to him?" Julia asked, surprised and impossibly touched by his words.

"Yes." Suzanne's intelligent brown eyes narrowed. "He seemed surprised by the fact also. He says he's a Texas Ranger."

Julia was well aware that Chase had not volunteered the information. He wasn't the talkative type. Suzanne wouldn't have let that stop her. She made her living ferreting out secrets and obtaining information. "He's a lieutenant in charge of his own unit," Julia told her. Unabashed pride rang in her voice.

"So this is a date?"

"Yes," Julia answered, sure of what was coming next. She was not disappointed.

"How long have you known him?"

Julia rolled her eyes and tore off a two-foot length of wrapping paper with footballs scattered on a white background, then set a specially constructed box with a hollow chocolate replica of a Washington Redskin football inside on top of the paper. "Suzanne, I love you dearly, but I'm busy."

"Two years ago, I could have probably gotten the answer," Suzanne said with a hint of annoyance.

Julia sealed the wrapping paper around the box with invisible tape and spoke without turning. "Yes, you could have."

"Even before you opened this shop, you never went out much. You need experience in the trenches, so to speak, to be able to tell if a guy is on the level. Experience you don't have. Sweet Temptation is a testament to your being a savvy businesswoman, but when it comes to people, you're too trusting and naive," Suzanne said, obviously worried. "There are some real dogs out there. They get sneakier and more underhanded each year."

"Chase isn't one of them," Julia defended him, turning at last to face her sister.

"You sound serious about this guy." The words came out as an accusation.

Julia returned to wrapping her package. "Suzanne, I really am busy."

"Do you know how difficult it is to have a good relationship with a man when you're in the same city? Long-distance romances are doomed. You're setting yourself up for heartache if you let yourself become involved. I've seen it happen over and over again."

"Do you think the white or the brown ribbon? Brown, I think." Quickly Julia made the bow and attached a referee whistle. "Their six-year-old grandson will love the whistle, but his parents may want to strangle me."

"I can certainly empathize with them," Suzanne said, glaring at Julia. "I'm calling in the morning."

Accepting the thinly veiled threat and the love behind it, Julia reached for a Sweet Temptation sticker. "I love you, too."

Chase's black eyes narrowed as Julia's vehicle came barreling around the corner of her condo building at ten miles over the speed limit. In a town crowded with expensive imported cars and SUVs of the same makes, her white Caravan minivan stood out. He applauded her sense at not putting her store's name on the side, since she obviously drove the vehicle all the time. Too many thieves would view a woman driving it as an easy mark.

Julia pulled to one side and braked across from the white guard-house where he and Percival, the security guard on duty, had been talking.

"Hi, Percival. Hi, Chase. Sorry I'm late."

"Evening, Miss Ferrington," the guard greeted her.

Chase took his time answering. She looked beautiful, delectable, and harried. He wanted to kiss the frown from her face, watch her fall asleep in his arms. Each time he saw her, she surprised him by causing some new emotion to churn within him.

Slowly, when he wanted to run, he went to her van. "You were speeding." She had been speeding last night when he had secretly followed her home as well.

She had the audacity to grin. "Unless you park in a restricted area the police here are very liberal."

"I noticed on my drive in from the airport and every day since. People jaywalk and disobey traffic laws at will." He shook his head in disgust and placed his hand on the roof of the vehicle. "Driving in this city is a real challenge. My brother and father in the Austin Police Department would have a field day issuing citations."

"They'd have to catch us first."

"They would."

Julia easily heard the assurance in his voice. "Any other siblings?"

"It's just the two of us."

"There are three of us. All girls. My father always joked that he could open a clothing store if he ever left banking. Suzanne is the oldest."

He chuckled. "The interrogator."

Julia put her head on the steering wheel, then glanced up. "I knew I was taking a chance when I asked her to call."

"No problem. It showed she cares."

"Thanks for understanding. As the oldest, she grew up watching out for me. Unfortunately, at times she forgets I'm a grown woman. I hope you'll be equally understanding if you meet Amanda, who can be just as bad as Suzanne. Amanda is two years older than I am and works in the State Department."

"You're the baby."

She wrinkled her nose. "Guilty."

"So am I, and in their eyes we never grow up."

"True."

"We'll have to show them differently." He studied her closely. "I have a feeling you already have with your shop."

"You're right. At first they thought I had lost my mind," she said.

"I remember something similar when I decided to go into the Department of Public Safety instead of the Austin Police Department."

"You broke tradition."

"The same for you?" he questioned.

She nodded. "Politics and high finance. Those were the choices. My mother actually has records dating back to 1886 where my great-great-great-uncle loaned money."

"My brother is a third-generation city police officer."

"But you're still in law enforcement."

"Not the same branch. Each of us takes pride in his area of enforcement and thinks he can do better than the other."

"But I bet you both can't stand the FBI."

"True."

They stared, grinning, at each other. "My family still can't believe I'm not in some form of politics like my sisters." Her brown eyes twinkled. "If they only knew how diplomatic I have to be sometimes with customers trying to decide on a gift."

"From what I saw today, you're very good at your job."

Pleasure shone on her face. "Thanks. I try. Hopefully they'll realize we want to make a difference in a different way, but that difference is still important."

"You have a nice way of putting things."

"Practice," she said with feeling.

Chase had noticed something else very nice. Julia's mouth. He felt its inexplicable pull. He wanted his mouth on hers again. Instead of acting on his desire, he glanced around at the approaching darkness. "I thought we might do a little sightseeing since I changed our dinner reservation to eight, but it's too late now."

She shook her head. "D.C. by night is even more beautiful and powerful. I'll be ready to go in fifteen minutes."

He stepped back from the vehicle instead of leaning closer and sampling her mouth. "Take your time, I've enjoyed talking with Percival."

She smiled at the gray-haired man in the booth. He was lazily flipping through several sheets of paper on a clipboard. "He's a hoot and a good man."

"He thinks highly of you as well. Says he's known you since you were in diapers," Chase told her.

Julia wrinkled her nose. "He knows the whole family. He was one of the security guards at my father's bank until five years ago when the board decided to replace all the guards with off-duty policemen."

"I think he likes it here better so he can keep an eye on you."

Her smile returned. "We keep an eye on each other."

"So I'm finding out." Chase had also found out from the outspoken Percival that Julia seldom dated. "Get going. We might as well put off the sightseeing until after dinner. You probably were too busy to eat."

"I was," she said, delighted that he had thought of her.

"Then go on and we'll see if we can get seated early."

"Yes, sir." Putting the car in gear, she backed up, then drove past the black iron gate, down the slight incline, and abruptly stopped. Expecting that she had forgotten to tell him something, Chase started toward her.

Her door opened, and out she came at a fast clip with a small Sweet Temptation bag in her hand. Without a glance in his direction she went straight to the booth. After a brief conversation with a grinning Percival, she gave him the bag and planted a kiss on his heavily lined cheek. Waving to a watchful Chase, she ran back to her car.

His gaze followed. He openly admired her ability to run in three-inch heels, the graceful way she moved, the sway of her hips. He watched until she got in her van, then turned and started for his Jeep.

"Chase."

He spun back around. This time she was running straight for him. Seeing the anxiety in her face, he quickly sprinted to her. Automatically his hands closed over her shoulders. "What's the matter?"

"I forgot to tell you where to park."

He barely managed to keep from laughing aloud. "Percival told me."

"Oh. Of course. Then I'll just run along. I'll leave the door open."

Chase's hands tightened, his expression changed. "No, you won't. Percival says there's a seating area by the elevator. I'll wait there."

"You can't wait in the hall," she protested, outrage in her lovely face.

"I can and will." He pointed her toward her car. The driver's door was still open. "Now get going and don't worry."

"I'll hurry."

This time Chase watched until she rounded the corner in the parking garage. Still shaking his head, he started for his Jeep. He'd just seen another side of Julia: flustered. The idea pleased him immensely, especially since he had felt the same way that morning before entering her shop.

Percival waved Chase down as he walked past. "I get off at ten. You make sure Miss Ferrington gets home safely."

"I will." She also had people who cared about her. Her sister had politely asked where they planned to go, then inquired if possibly she had met him. Chase had gotten the distinct impression that if his answers hadn't satisfied her, the pleasantries would have abruptly ended. "You don't have to worry."

"Miss Ferrington is a fine young woman," Percival said. "She cares about people."

Chase rubbed his stomach with remembered pleasure. "I found that out before we met when she sent me one of her special baskets."

"Sounds just like her. She saved my life," Percival said quietly, then continued, "The stress and tension of my job at the bank had me hitting the bottle pretty hard. I blamed everyone but myself. Then came the layoff and I started reaching for the bottle more and more. Miss Ferrington came by my place one day to visit me and saw what a mess I'd made of my life. She didn't preach or turn away in disgust, just fixed me a decent meal and kept coming back, kept encouraging me to go to AA and get help. Finally I listened."

Percival held up his bag. "My reward for sticking with the twelve-step program. I haven't had a drink in almost four years." He inclined his head toward the eight-story building behind them. "After my first AA meeting she got me the job here."

Chase's expression saddened. "I've had friends and associates who couldn't or wouldn't turn away from the alcohol and drugs and ended up losing their family, their jobs, their self-respect, and, as you said, their lives." His sigh was long and telling. "Being in law enforcement isn't easy, but it's a job that has to be done."

"I agree." Percival's eyes narrowed. "There are a lot of mean, unscrupulous people in the world who won't hesitate to take advantage of others."

Chase lifted a heavy brow. Had Percival's comment been a veiled insinuation? "I'm not one of them."

"Never said you were, but just so you know, I keep a close eye on Miss Ferrington." Percival leaned closer, his gaze direct. "Don't you go forgetting she's a lady."

"That's one thing neither of us have to worry about. Good night, Percival." Chase continued to his Jeep and got in, his face thoughtful.

The lady and the lawman were an impossible mix, but he was finding that with Julia the impossible became possible. That was another thing he didn't understand. He wanted to lay her down and make love to her in every way known to man, but he also wanted to protect her, cherish her. He had a sinking feeling that he could do one but never both.

True to her word, Julia was ready in fifteen minutes. Slowly Chase rose from the settee in front of the elevator and watched her walk gracefully toward him. She literally took his breath away.

Her knee-length, long-sleeved black knit dress bared smooth brown shoulders. The clinging material flowed irreverently over her body. His mouth watered. A man could spend a lot of time debating what was under the dress and how fast he could get it off.

She stopped inches from him. As if the dress weren't enough, her perfume reached out and punched him in the gut. "I hope I didn't keep you waiting."

"You made it worth the wait."

"Thanks," she said, hoping her voice didn't sound as giddy as she felt.

His gaze wandered down her shapely legs to the high-heeled sandals on her feet. "If we decide to check out some sites after dinner and walk, will you be comfortable in those?"

"My other shoes are in here."

Chase glanced at the small bag in her hand. "In there?"

She pulled out a pair of soft-soled black ballerina shoes. Carrying a canvas bag would have ruined what she hoped was the impact of the dress. Usually she wasn't so vain, but she was honest enough to admit her attraction to Chase wasn't the usual.

"Next time, bring sturdier shoes."

Next time. Julia's heart soared. "I will."

The food, the ambience, the soft jazz music in the background at Leo's were absolutely perfect. Julia cherished every moment and eagerly looked forward to being in Chase's arms again, to having his lips on hers again. Apparently so did he, because he took her straight home after they left the restaurant, and as soon as she opened her door he pulled her into his arms.

Standing on tiptoes, Julia clung to Chase, her senses alive and her body humming. When he asked her to go out with him the following night, she eagerly accepted.

In the days that followed they spent every possible moment together. The place didn't seem to matter. They had just as much fun playing billiards at Chase's hotel as they did at a Howard University faculty get-together, helping with a birthday party at the nursing home, and wandering the many museums and national monuments D.C. had to offer.

An unexpected pleasure for Chase was going with her to see *Swan Lake* at the Kennedy Center. Ballet wasn't his thing. He had little doubt his eyes would cross with boredom and he'd embarrass Julia by falling asleep before the end of the first act. However, instead of watching the dancers, he'd watched the play of emotions on Julia's expressive face. He'd never seen anything more beautiful or more heart-wrenching. His pleasure came from seeing her happy. His hand closed over hers. Inexplicably he felt content and restless at the same time when she laid her head on his shoulder at the swan's metamorphosis into a beautiful woman. Caring for Julia was ridiculously easy and undeniably foolish.

He had never wanted to love a woman or to be loved by one. He had always thought the risks for both of them far outweighed the brief span of happiness they might share. His family and friends in law enforcement had taught him that. However, when he touched Julia, held her, looked into her eyes it was difficult to remember he never wanted that heavy-duty responsibility. He had to.

His life was in Texas, just as hers was in D.C.

The next afternoon, when he went with her to Virginia to scout out a possible location for her second store, he felt more at ease with their situation. They were just enjoying each other's company. Neither one of them could afford to forget that their futures lay in different directions.

After dating Chase for almost two weeks, Julia now well understood why couples sat across from each other instead of next to each other. You wanted to see the person's face, catch, learn, then study all the little nuances that made them who they were.

You also just liked looking, liked getting that little quivering sensation in the pit of your stomach when they looked back, like the way your senses were heightened yet somehow strangely muted and focused on that special someone across from you.

They were dining at what was becoming their favorite table at their favorite restaurant, Leo's. Wearing a charcoal gray sports jacket that fit his broad shoulders perfectly, Chase looked dangerously handsome. She'd certainly been right about the place being conducive to romance.

Blissfully happy she sipped her white wine and accepted the growing sexual awareness between them, the pull that she realized would only become stronger if she continued to see him. She searched her mind for a reason to pull back besides the obvious one.

"Would you like to dance?" Chase asked. He laughed at the flash of surprise that crossed her face. "In high school, dancing was a sure way to get the girls into your arms," he confessed with a roguish grin.

"I'd say it still works." Setting her glass down, she placed her hand in his and allowed him to lead her to the crowded dance floor.

Slowly he pulled her into his arms. She fit perfectly with her head resting over his heart. They moved as one, as if they had always danced together, as if they always would.

The live music curled around them like the arms of a jealous lover. Raw, possessive, driven. The slow, mournful wail of the sax warned them of a lost love, of a love gone bad, of the pain and heartache that replaced the joy of falling in love.

Julia lifted her head from Chase's jacket and stared into midnight black eyes. Yes, she could understand the pain and heartache, but she could also see that sometimes your heart made a decision without consulting you.

"What are you thinking?" he asked, his thumb lazily stroking her back.

"Different things," she answered evasively, then laid her head back on his chest, following his steps with her thoughts elsewhere. Could it be possible that her heart had decided already?

Lips, warm, gentle, and fleeting, brushed across her temple. Shock waves of pleasure and surprise had her lifting her head.

"That's what I was thinking," Chase murmured.

She studied the passion burning in his coal black eyes. Sometimes your heart and mind made a decision they both could agree on. "How fast can you get us back to my place?"

He grabbed her hand and started from the dance floor. "Not fast enough."

"Then maybe you should let me drive."

FIVE

She was having second thoughts.

Her increased nervousness as they neared her condo, her silence on the ride up the elevator, made that fact abundantly clear. Her reaction helped to explain and solidify what he had suspected even without Percival's comment or Suzanne's interrogation: Julia's experience with men was minimal.

She stood several feet inside her condo, her bottom lip caught between her teeth, her hands gripping her purse. The sight tore at him. He wanted to give, not take, and only then if she wanted. He went to her and traced a long, lean brown finger down her cheek. She trembled beneath his touch and he breathed easier. Her unease hadn't destroyed her desire.

"We can always leave."

"You must think I'm silly."

His fingers followed the curve of her jaw and pressed against her lips. "I think you're a beautiful, desirable woman who might be having second thoughts."

She wasn't. At least not about kissing Chase. It was where the kisses might lead that had her a bit nervous. "Do you want—"

"Yes." Slowly Chase pulled her into his arms, his lips lowering toward her, giving her time to retreat if she wished. She didn't. Closing her eyes, she sighed and leaned into him.

Her lips were sweet, soft, yielding. Chase took his time tasting and learning her mouth, getting reacquainted with their taste and texture, savoring each new discovery, nibbling as a child miserly bites his favorite candy.

Something dropped to the floor. Chase realized it was Julia's purse when her hands pressed flat against his chest. He rewarded her by suckling her lower lip. She rewarded him by sinking more heavily against him.

One arm locked securely around her waist, he gave his full attention to her mouth and took her on a slow glide into passion, building the heat, degree by incredible degree. Slowly he backed her toward the sofa.

Julia felt the yielding softness of the silk sofa at her back and Chase's hardness above her. A moment of unease swept through her; then he deepened the kiss, his hand running boldly over her body, and thinking ceased to be important.

She whimpered. Her fingers clutched his lapel, telling him of her need.

Boldly his tongue swept into her mouth. His hands moved down to cup her hips, molding her to his rigid hardness. When he moved against her in the same slow rhythm as his tongue inside her mouth, she shuddered.

One hand closed over her breast, his thumb flicking over the turgid point of her nipple, again and again.

She was on fire. She needed. She wanted.

Julia wanted the dress gone. She wanted his hands on her body, hers on his. She whimpered in growing frustration.

"The dress stays!"

Her eyes flew open and she stared into Chase's equally wide ones. His outburst was a direct contradiction to what she'd been thinking, what she wanted.

Groaning, he buried his face between the crook of her neck and her shoulder. "Sorry. I don't usually argue with myself." His mouth brushed tantalizingly against her neck.

"I don't understand?" she stammered.

"If the dress comes off, only an act of God will keep me from making love to you."

Julia was caught between being indignant that he thought she was that easy and trying to come to grips with the possibility that she just might be when he continued speaking: "Percival was on duty when we came back."

Her puzzlement increased. "Percival? What has he to do with this?"

Chase lifted his head, stared down into her open face, felt the softness of her body beneath his, and knew it was the wrong way to have a conversation. Sitting up, he pulled her into his lap. "Besides being a Saturday night, it's the first time we've come back from a date before he got off duty." There was no way he would embarrass her by telling her of Percival's initial warning. "Then there is the interrogator."

"I can handle Suzanne," Julia said with confidence. "She asked about you after the first time we went out. I didn't tell her anything."

"Because there was nothing to tell," he told her, accepting that there would be nothing to tell about tonight, either. "You're not very good at hiding your feelings and I don't think you'd like people knowing we had been intimate."

Julia bit her lip. He was right. She laid her head back on his chest, her fingers idly toying with a white button on his shirt. "Not very modern, is it?"

"No." Chase brushed a kiss across the top of her head to soften his pronouncement. "But in your case, I approve."

"You're not angry?" she asked, softly angling her head up to see his face.

"A woman should always be able to say no."

Julia heard what he said, but she was sitting on very hard proof that his body was saying something vastly different. He wanted her. She wanted him. But she needed more.

Men tended to think with their eyes, women with their hearts. At the moment, hers was telling her she was falling in love.

"What do you want from me, Chase? Besides the obvious?" she asked, making herself maintain eye contact with him.

His large hands cupped her face. "I stopped having sex for sex's sake in high school. If I didn't care about you, I wouldn't be here. As for what else I want, I don't know. All I know is that I can't wait to see you, and when I'm not with you I want to be."

"Oh, Chase." Her voice trembled. "What are we going to do?"

"Steal each moment we can to be with each other," he told her.

"Then what?" she asked, dreading the answer but voicing it anyway.

For the first time that night, his gaze wavered. "For as long as I can remember I've wanted to be a Texas Ranger. It's not just a job; it's what I believe, what I'm good at. Just like you are with your customers at Sweet Temptation. I watched you and them. They're not just there because of the candy; they're there because of you. You plan to open a second store soon. Your life is here."

He was right. "You have your family and job in Texas and I have mine here in D.C.," she said, her voice unsteady.

"Yes."

There it was. When it was over, it was over.

Julia stared into Chase's set features and took a deep breath. He was leaving her with no false illusions about their relationship. Could she continue seeing him and risk her heart, as Suzanne had warned against?

"I know it's selfish," Chase said, interrupting her thoughts as he pulled her back into his arms. "But is it wrong to want to see you, hold you, kiss you, make love to you?"

The rapid pounding of his heart that matched her own answered her question and his. Sometimes the greatest risks yielded the greatest gain. It wasn't wrong. She wanted to be with Chase, felt alive as never before in his arms. She was mature enough to give him part of what he wanted, what *she* wanted.

"Excuse me." As gracefully as possible, she got off his lap.

Chase came to his feet, surprise, frustration, and disbelief in his eyes. "You're throwing me back."

The desolate words stopped Julia two feet away. She came back to him, her gaze locked with his every inch of the way. "Like the woman said, only a fool would do that."

He frowned. "Then where were you going?"

She grinned. "To the kitchen to set the timer. Percival gets off at ten, and until then I intend for you to be too busy paying attention to me to care about the time."

He flashed her a roguish smile. "Julia Ferrington, you never cease to amaze me."

"After I set the timer, you can show me how much you appreciate that fact."

He wasn't going to make it.

Jumping into the Cherokee, Chase started the engine, then shoved the vehicle into reverse. He threw a glance at the digital clock on the dashboard before straightening and shifting into second: 10:06.

He had followed Julia into the kitchen to cut off the timer; then she had kissed him. They'd immediately become more interested in each other than the passage of time. Regaining some control, he'd gone to the door, turned to say good night, and looked at her lips glistening and pouty from his kisses, her eyes dark with passion, and hauled her into his arms.

His jaw set, he drove out of the garage wishing he were holding Julia instead of a steering wheel. He fully intended to bypass Percival. If not for his interference, Chase would still have Julia in his arms, seeing how close he could take them both to the edge and not go over.

The elderly security guard apparently had other ideas. Stepping out of the booth with the other guard, Percival directed Chase to pull over to one side. With ill-concealed annoyance, he did as directed.

Percival stared at Chase's profile long and hard; then the older man's dark, leathery face split into a wide grin. He slapped Chase on the shoulder with surprising strength. "I knew I could trust you."

Chase cut him a look.

"Now don't be angry." The older man looked back at the new guard on duty, then leaned closer and opened his gray metal lunch pail. "Have some of my candy. Luther's got hands like a linebacker. If he saw, I'd lose half. I figure you deserve a reward, too."

Chase looked at the candy, which the older man no doubt greatly enjoyed, hoarded, and looked forward to but was willing to share to show his appreciation. Chase's annoyance changed to gratitude. Percival would always watch out for Julia. Chase reached for a chocolate and popped the cream-filled candy in his mouth.

Percival nodded. "You'll do."

"Thanks," Chase said, acknowledging the older man for more than just the candy.

"My pleasure." Percival straightened. "Miss Ferrington backed me, believed in me. There isn't anything I wouldn't do for her to keep her safe and happy. So if I seem nosy, I am."

Chase grinned. "The thought had crossed my mind."

"I'll just bet it did." Humming, Percival walked off.

The phone was ringing when Chase entered his room. He rushed to the end table in the sitting room and jerked up the receiver. "Hello."

"So you're finally home."

"Oh, it's you." Disappointed, Chase plopped down on the arm of the sofa.

A deep chuckle came through the receiver clearly. "Don't tell me you've been out of my sight four weeks and you let some woman get her hooks into you."

"Don't start, Colt."

"Dad, Chase is having women problems!" Colt yelled. "No wonder he didn't come home this weekend or last."

"I thought you two were always telling me to stay here." Chase plucked a chocolate peanut cluster from the basket and eased onto the couch.

"That was before we knew about her. So give."

In between bites, Chase briefly told Colt about Julia, intentionally leaving out the last hour of heavy petting. He and his big brother were extremely close and shared a lot, but neither of them discussed the intimate details about the women they dated.

"Watch it, Bro," Colt warned once Chase finished. "The candy was just to soften you up."

"You are too suspicious." Chase polished off the candy and considered another piece. "You sound like her sister, who, by the way, could beat you at interrogation."

"Sounds like a busybody," Colt said. "Stay away from that family."

Chase knew it was useless arguing with his brother. Ever since he'd caught his ex-wife in an affair, he'd been distrustful of women. With a start, Chase realized some of Colt's resentment had rubbed off on him—until he met Julia. "From experience, I'd say this is one family I wouldn't judge until I met them in person."

"Maybe Dad and I should come up there to make sure you aren't getting in over your head."

"Big brother, I can handle it."

"See that you do. Marriage and lawmen don't mix." Bitterness tinged Colt's words.

Chase straightened, all thought of the candy forgotten. "Who said anything about marriage?"

"You're the noble, romantic type. All those mystical, heroic stories about the Texas Rangers are what attracted you in the first place," Colt told him. "I'm surprised you've stayed single this long."

"You're just mad because you have to wear a uniform and I don't."

"But I'm cuter."

"So is a baby elephant to its mother."

Both men laughed and settled down to talk. From time to time Chase's father, Charles, got on the phone. An hour later Chase hung up the phone and pushed to his feet. Restless, he opened the cabinet doors of the entertainment center and turned on the TV. He channel-surfed for several seconds, then shut it off. The remote control still in his hand, he stared at the telephone.

He knew why he was edgy, what would take the edge off; and just as certainly knew it wouldn't happen tonight. If ever. Crossing the room, he picked up the phone and dialed. With Julia he was finding he wanted much more than her body. However, by the eighth ring he vacillated between anger and concern.

"Hello. Hello," she finally answered breathlessly.

"Where were you?" Chase asked, his voice sharp and accusatory.

"In the shower. I tried to hurry."

If she had wanted to pay him back, she couldn't have chosen a better method. He didn't have to close his eyes to imagine droplets of water rolling down her sleek body or imagine his tongue lapping them from her skin. He groaned.

"Chase. Chase, are you all right?"

"I hope you grabbed a towel."

"I, er, actually—"

"If you're trying to put the screws to me, you're succeeding," he told her, then plopped on the edge of the sofa. "Go get a towel." He tortured himself further by visualizing her running naked to the bathroom.

"I'm back," she said, her voice as breathless as the first time. "I'm sorry it took me so long to answer. I couldn't hear over the shower."

"Julia, let's not talk about the shower, if you don't mind."

"Sorry." Securing the oversize bath towel between her breasts, she pushed aside the antique throw pillows, then drew back the duvet and sat on the bed. Chase sounded grouchy, and she fully realized why. She wasn't at her best, either. She was beginning to fully understand the term *sexual frustration.*

"Not as sorry as I am," Chase said. "You have any plans for tomorrow afternoon?"

"No."

"You want to go to a movie or take a drive?"

"Why don't I prepare a picnic basket for lunch? It will give me a chance to try out a new enterprise I have with Leo's. Is twelve all right?"

"Fine. What should I bring?"

"A huge appetite."

He chuckled. "That shouldn't be a problem. See you at twelve."

"Good night, Chase. I had a wonderful time before and after."

"So did I. Good night, Julia." Letting the phone drop into the cradle, Chase went into the bedroom, gazed at the king-size bed's wide expanse of emptiness, and went to the closet for his sweat suit.

He was going jogging. Maybe if he got tired enough his brain and body would shut down and he'd stop craving what he couldn't have: Julia, hot, naked, and needy beneath him.

The flat of his hand slammed the closet door closed. It was going to be another restless night.

"Will you leave so I can get dressed?" Julia requested for what seemed to be the fifth time since her sisters had followed her home from church.

Neither Suzanne nor Amanda moved from their side chairs in Julia's bedroom. Both were strikingly attractive, with flawless skin, intense brown no-nonsense eyes.

"It isn't like we haven't seen you before, Julia," Suzanne said, sipping her favorite Earl Grey.

"She's right," Amanda agreed, critically assessing the two outfits in her sister's hands. "Wear the magenta."

"Thanks." Ignoring her sister's unsolicited advice, Julia hung up the magenta pantsuit and laid the flowing tangerine dress on the bed. The wide belt would accent her waist, and the drop shoulders would certainly keep Chase's attention. Her matching flats would allow her to keep pace with him without having to wear her unflattering walking shoes.

Suzanne set her porcelain cup on the table. The sisters traded worried glances. In the past, Julia had always followed their advice on clothes and men. It seemed both might be changing. "You *really* like him."

"Yes." Julia unbuttoned her skirt and went to the closet to hang it up. Her jacket followed.

"I downloaded a picture of his unit from the Internet last night and I can see why," Amanda commented. "Even in the grainy black-and-white picture he looked handsome, strong, and tough."

"He *sounded* the same way," Suzanne said.

There was no sense reprimanding her middle sister for what some might see as snooping. With her connections she could have gone much deeper into Chase's file, if she had wanted. Going to the high chest, Julia pulled out fresh undergarments and turned. "Amanda, aren't you supposed to be flying to Camp David this afternoon?"

"The plane isn't scheduled to leave until late," she stated. "I have plenty of time."

Julia's annoyed gaze fastened on Suzanne. "Don't you have someone's arm to twist about their vote on a bill or something?"

"We aren't leaving until we meet him. You've been evasive about him and out every night. It's time we checked this brother out. You know Mother and Father always told us to watch out for each other." Suzanne crossed long, well-shaped legs. Her slim black skirt inched up higher. On her feet were four-inch heels. "Stop fussing and go get dressed. You don't want us to meet him without you, do you?"

The threat worked. Grabbing the dress, Julia rushed into the bathroom to change. "Don't you dare embarrass me in front of

Chase!" she yelled, pulling off her slip and flinging it carelessly in the direction of the marble countertop. Her hands were unfastening her bra when she heard the doorbell.

"Don't worry!" Amanda called sweetly. "We'll get it!"

"No!" Grabbing the dress, Julia pulled it over her head and raced out of the bedroom, zipping as she went. Bra or no, she wasn't about to let Chase meet her sisters without her being there.

SIX

Chase's gaze lingered on Julia's flushed face, then moved to the two beautiful women behind her who were staring daggers at him. Interrogation time again. Looked like Suzanne had brought reinforcements. He'd learned long ago to start as he intended to finish.

"Hi, Julia." Leaning over, he brushed his lips across her cheek, then straightened. Two pairs of assessing brown eyes openly sized him up. He didn't mind. He was doing the same.

The one in black would be the lobbyist; the other one in pale gray would work for the State Department. Classy and elegant, both women would draw a man's attention and have enough spunk to cut him to the quick if necessary.

"Hello, Suzanne, Amanda." He extended his hand. "I'm Chase Braxton."

Their handshakes, as he had imagined they would be, were firm. "Chase," they greeted in unison.

Her stomach still doing little flip-flops from Chase's unexpected kiss in front of her sisters, Julia opened the door wider, hoping they would take the hint. "I'll talk to you later. Bye."

Neither took her gaze from Chase. Amanda spoke first, "I pulled your photo up on the Internet."

"That's what it's there for." Chase's gaze went to Julia. "Where's the picnic basket?"

Julia frowned at her stubborn sisters. "In the kitchen."

"Why don't you get it, and your sisters and I can become better acquainted?" he said easily.

Indecision held Julia still. Because she had been shy, awkward, and insecure growing up, her family, especially her sisters, had always been protective of her. Now that she had grown up, they still thought she needed them to watch out for her.

Chase reached behind him and closed the door. "The Rangers have a motto: 'One Ranger. One Riot.' I'll be fine."

Julia looked at Chase, jaw-droppingly handsome in a chambray shirt, jeans, and blue jeans jacket, and noticed none of the nervousness her pitiful few dates had suffered when confronted with Suzanne and Amanda while Julia was in high school and college. Chase could hold his own. The kiss should have told her.

She relaxed. "Excuse me; I won't be but a minute."

Chase, Suzanne, and Amanda waited for all of ten seconds. Chase got the first volley off. "Julia is a unique young woman who knows her own mind and doesn't need you or anyone else telling her what to do or looking over her shoulder."

"Wait a minute, buster," Suzanne said, stepping forward.

"No, you wait a minute," Chase replied. "How do you think she feels knowing you're here to check out her date, as if she is still in high school? She knows what she wants."

"And I suppose that's you."

Chase cut his gaze to Amanda. "Whether it is or not, she has to make the decision. And all you can do is be there for her. Sometimes you have to let go."

"She's our baby sister and much too softhearted and trusting."

"She's also a grown, intelligent woman, in case you hadn't noticed."

"I hate to interrupt, but here is the basket," Julia said sweetly, handing it to Chase.

He hefted the weight and grinned. "I see you've packed enough."

"I hope you like it."

"I will. You better get something to sit on. While you're at it, grab a pair of walking shoes."

Julia stopped and turned; the long skirt of the dress swirled around her shapely legs. "These shoes are fine."

"Not if you decide you want to traipse through monuments again."

"Chase, I'll be fine."

"Indulge me and grab the shoes, and don't forget your keys."

She made a face, muttering as she went, clearly not pleased.

He looked at Suzanne and Amanda. "See? She's no pushover. For that you probably should take some of the credit, but it's time to back off and let her make her own mistakes, if it comes to that. But I don't think she will."

"I was prepared not to like you," Suzanne said with a sigh. "I'm just realizing that about her myself."

"Me, too," Amanda agreed.

"Why did you see it and we didn't?"

"Because, as you said, you still see her as your baby sister and not the woman she has become."

"She grew up on us." Thoughtfully Amanda folded her arms.

"That she did," Chase said with frank male appreciation. "Does this mean we call a truce?"

"For now," Amanda said, a slow smile curving her lips.

"Good. I didn't want to argue with my brother *and* you."

"What's your brother got to do with this?" Suzanne asked, a frown on her beautiful face.

"Absolutely nothing, but he's as opinionated as they come." Chase shook his head. "After I told him about our conversation, he thought you were a busybody."

Suzanne's brown eyes flashed. "Opinionated and annoying."

Chase chuckled. "At times. However, in Colt's defense, he was only trying to look out for my best interest, just as you and Amanda were doing for Julia. All of your intentions were good, but unnecessary and unwanted." Looking over their heads, he saw Julia. He suppressed a smile when he saw the canvas bag in her hand. He took the things from her. "You'll thank me tomorrow."

"I suppose," she admitted.

He took her hand in his, pleased by the slight tremble he felt. "Ladies, would you like to join us?"

Julia shook her head and mouthed, *No.*

"We can tell when we're not wanted, can't we, Amanda?" Suzanne went to the sofa and picked up her oversize black purse and slung the twin straps over her shoulder. "Have fun, you two."

Amanda's gray purse was a fourth of the size and bulk of Suzanne's. She stuck the bag under her arm. "I have a plane to catch. Nice meeting you, Chase."

Chase's arm lifted to circle Julia's shoulders, his eyes direct and sincere. "I'll do my best to make sure you always feel that way."

"We believe you." The door closed softly behind them.

Julia gazed up at him in amazement. "How did you do that?"

"First things first." His lips settled on hers, his tongue slipping inside her mouth to gently mate with hers. Long seconds later, he lifted his head. "You taste sweeter each time I kiss you."

"So do you," Julia breathed, curling her arms and her body closer to his. "You could make me a kissaholic."

"That . . ."—he nipped her lower lip—"works both ways." Stepping back, he opened the door. "Come on. Let's get out of here while I still have some willpower left."

The morning was sun-kissed and magical. Julia freely admitted it was because she was with Chase. She selected a sunny spot on the lush grass of the Mall, the popular corridor between the Capitol and the Lincoln Monument, for their picnic. People strolled its length, played baseball, soccer, jogged.

Chase placed the basket on top of the plaid blanket, then helped Julia sit. She came down on her knees and immediately began dragging food from the hamper. "I hope you like chicken salad."

Propped on his side, Chase watched her economical, graceful movements. "I love food, period."

Laughing, she looked up at him, felt the familiar pull, and ducked her head. If she wanted him to wait, she had to stop staring at him as if she could eat him with a spoon.

Chase's hand settled over hers, causing her to jump. "It's all right to want me. Lord knows I want you."

Some small part of her wanted to tuck her head and shy away from the words. Another part of her wanted to embrace his words as she wanted to embrace him.

She had overheard Chase talking to her sisters. He saw the woman that she so desperately wanted to be, the woman she hoped she was. Not for anything would she give him cause to think he had been wrong. "I don't know what to say."

"You don't have to say anything," he said, his eyes and his words tender. "I've heard the practiced words too many times in the past. I've forgotten them and the women who said them. Your honesty and, although it might annoy you, your vulnerability are much more appealing."

She made a face and reached into the basket for a Thermos of lemonade. "You make me sound pitifully childish."

"A childish woman wouldn't keep me awake at night, and I certainly wouldn't arrive thirty minutes early for a date."

"You did?" she questioned, delight and amazement in her animated voice and face. "You arrived at the door on time. Where were you?"

Seeing the joy shining in her brown eyes banished the mild annoyance he had felt with himself. "With Percival. He had a good laugh watching me try to decide if I should go up early or play it cool and wait."

"He likes to tease."

"So I found out," Chase said. "The important thing is that I'm where I want to be."

"So am I." That she was sure of. "And next time come on up."

"I will." He gave her hand a gentle squeeze before releasing it to rummage in the basket. He came out with the thermal cooler containing chocolate-covered strawberries. He held one up to her lips.

Her eyes locked with his. She bit. Juice ran down one corner of her mouth. Her tongue followed. So did Chase's hot gaze.

She began to tremble. Leaning toward her, he slowly traced the path her tongue had taken with his tongue, then sat back and bit into the strawberry, chewed, swallowed. He closed the container with hands that were not quite steady. "Why don't we save them until we get back to your apartment?"

It took a couple of moments for her to speak. "I'd like that."

A soccer ball rolled onto the blanket, breaking the tension-filled moment. Coming to his feet, Chase expertly shot the ball back to the young man loping toward him.

Catching the ball, the ponytailed player began rolling the ball in his hand. "Wanna play?"

"No, thanks," Chase told him, then sat back down.

"I don't mind if you want to play." She poured the lemonade into a slender glass.

Chase popped an olive into his mouth and accepted the glass. "I would."

She paused in unwrapping the thick sandwich loaded with chunky chicken salad, lettuce, tomatoes. She had purposely left out the sweet onions. "I don't understand?"

"To play, I'd have to be away from you."

Her insides went shivery. Her eyes misted. "Chase, you say the most beautiful things to me."

His knuckles tenderly grazed her cheek. "If you cry I'll have to kiss the tears away, and one thing might lead to another. It wouldn't look good on my record or on yours if we were arrested."

Julia brushed away the tears forming in her eyes. "No, it wouldn't. So why don't you tell me why you broke tradition to become a Texas Ranger?"

"I think it was probably after my hundredth or so rerun episode of *The Lone Ranger* when I was ten," he began, regaling her with stories as they ate their lunch. He told of playing the Lone Ranger and riding Silver, the kitchen broom, to capture the neighborhood kids playing outlaws. He'd cut holes in his father's best black socks to make a mask. Although his father had tanned his backside, he'd still gotten the holstered guns and hat set he'd asked for for Christmas.

"What did your mother have to say?" Julia asked, smiling.

His face and body tensed. "She left when I was nine and Colt was twelve. Daddy and his partner answered a domestic dispute that went sour. Daddy's partner was killed and he was wounded. Mama left as soon as he was released from the doctor. She said she couldn't take the possibility of Daddy not coming home one night."

"Chase, I'm sorry. I didn't mean to pry."

He shrugged broad shoulders and sat up. "It happens."

"But that doesn't make it any less painful," she said, placing her hand over his.

It always amazed him how intuitive and supportive she was. His hand turned, enclosing hers within his. "We did all right."

"I'd say you did more than all right," Julia said, wanting to take the shadows from his eyes. "I haven't met your father or Colt, but from the way you speak about them I know they must be wonderful men, and the three of you must be very close. That took hard work on your father's part to raise two responsible, honorable, hardworking men."

"He never missed a day telling or showing us how much he loved us," Chase said. "I've counseled too many kids not to know how it could have turned out. Policemen's kids or not."

"It must have been hard at times on all of you."

"For a long time, Daddy blamed himself."

"Did you?"

"Oddly enough, Mama helped me to understand. He wouldn't have been happy doing anything else, and if she had taken his children thousands of miles away it would have killed him. She loved us all enough to sacrifice. Not a week went by that she didn't call or write. Sometimes both. In the summer, off we'd go to Pittsburgh."

"It sounds as if she loved you very much."

"She did. Losing her when I was in high school to a ruptured appendix was hard on all of us." His gaze bore into Julia. "She never remarried. She fell in love with the wrong man and paid the price the rest of her life."

Julia listened, her heart growing heavier with every word Chase spoke. He was warning her against falling in love, but it was already too late. "Was your father ever injured again in the line of duty?"

"No."

"Your mother chose her way to deal with her fear, but another woman might choose to stay and cherish each minute, each second," Julia said with feeling. "If given the opportunity, another woman might choose to fight to hold onto what she loved most."

He pulled his hand free. "Maybe. Let's repack the basket and you can drag me through another museum."

Sighing, Julia began putting things back in the basket. Chase wasn't going to give them an opportunity to find out if it was left up to him.

"Chase," she said softly, waiting until his dark gaze met hers. "What would you say if we skipped the museum and went back to my place and finished the rest of the strawberries?"

"I'd say pack faster."

His hot, hungry mouth was on hers the instant the door closed behind them. Holding nothing back, she met him with passion and greed, her slim body pressed eagerly against his. He felt the difference immediately. High, firm, unrestrained breasts pushed against his chest. He groaned and thanked the increasing temperature that had made him leave his jacket in the Jeep.

Nibbling her lower lip, he slid his hand from her waist to close possessively over the soft mound of her breast, felt the nipple harden instantly. The pleasure pulsating through him doubled as she pressed against him. Her eyelids drifted shut for all of five seconds before they flew upward. Eyes wide, she blushed and stumbled back.

"Julia, what is it?"

She shook her head and backed up a step.

Worried, Chase matched her step for step. "Honey, what's the matter?"

Somehow the endearment only made her predicament worse. Her mouth opened, then closed. Several seconds passed before she stammered, "I don't have on . . . I forgot . . . I mean I didn't have time." She swallowed. "Y-you were at the door and Suzanne and Amanda were going to answer it. I didn't have time."

A slow smile of understanding spread across Chase's handsome face. He reached out, his hands gently settling on her shoulders to keep her from backing up farther. "You weren't thinking of leaving your guest, were you?"

"I—"

His lips brushed across hers. She swayed closer, her mouth lifting to his. "Because I'd be very disappointed if you did."

"But—"

He kissed her again, scattering her thoughts and sending heat and desire racing through her bloodstream. "Do you trust me?"

"Yes. It's me I don't trust."

For some odd reason her words disturbed him. "Never say anything like that to any man."

"I wasn't saying them to any man."

His hands on her shoulders tightened a fraction. He stared into her wide eyes and felt the floor shift beneath his feet. "I told you when I leave, this is over."

"I know."

"Then stop looking at me as if you expect this to continue."

Biting her lower lip, she tucked her head. So much for good intentions and maturity, for believing she could enjoy what they had, then let him go. It wasn't what she wanted or what she could accept. "I'm sorry."

"You have nothing to be sorry for," he said, angry at the impossible situation. "I can't give you what you want."

"How do you know? You haven't tried," she told him tightly.

"And I won't," he shot back.

She recoiled from the harshness of his voice. "I see."

"No, you don't. I don't have time for anything but the job," he riled. "When I leave D.C. and go back to Austin I'll have to catch up on six weeks of work that was already behind six months. I'm on call twenty-four/seven. I can't remember the last time I had a full day off."

"I'm sure other single men in the Rangers find time to date."

A muscle leaped in Chase's jaw. Why was she being so stubborn? "The women they're dating aren't four hours away by plane, nor is there the likelihood that they run their own successful businesses. Both of us have too many obligations for this to continue."

"I don't mind the trip, and as you've seen, I make time for the things that are important to me," Julia told him, hoping it didn't sound as if she were begging and afraid it did.

Chase's mouth flattened into a narrow line. "What about when you open your second shop?"

Doubt that Julia was unable to hide flickered in her eyes. "I didn't say it would be easy."

Wearily he shook his head. One of the things he admired about Julia was her dogged determination. He just wished she wasn't now using it against him. "Both of us have too many responsibilities. It couldn't work."

She met his hard gaze with more courage than she had imagined. "How can you be so positive? You won't even try."

"No, I won't." His hands dropped to his sides. "When I leave in two weeks, I won't be back."

Her small hands clenched. She hadn't imagined the pain, the immense sense of loss, could be so intense. "I thought I could be very modern and adult about this, but I can't. Making love should mean something between a man and a woman, not just passing time."

"I never lied to you, Julia."

"No, you didn't. I lied to myself." She lifted her hand, extending it as though she expected nothing more from him than a perfunctory businesslike handshake. "Good-bye, Chase."

He stared at the delicate hand with narrowed eyes; then his gaze glanced up to her. "So this is it?"

Her hand and voice wavered. "Yes."

With a curt nod, he turned to leave.

Pain and disbelief rushed through Julia as Chase opened the door. How could he just walk away without trying? She knew he cared.

"I thought Texas Rangers were fearless," she tossed out, then rushed on when he whirled back toward her, his eyes sharp and cutting. "You're not giving either of us enough credit. We both go after and fight for what we want. Make no mistake, you're what I want, but not for just a brief interlude. If you ever find you feel the same way, you know where to find me."

For a long moment, he simply stared. Hope leaped in Julia's heart; then he opened the door, walked through it, and closed it softly behind him.

"Oh, Chase!" Julia cried, finally letting the tears fall.

SEVEN

Chase was in a foul mood. The Saturday afternoon rush-hour traffic wasn't helping. There had been a full moon the night before, and the lingering effects seemed to have carried over into the full light of day. People were zipping in and out of lanes, tailgating, honking horns, and in general being nastier than usual.

His hands clenched and unclenched on the steering wheel. He wasn't at his best himself. He didn't like the restless, edgy feeling. It was as if he had overdosed on caffeine or was coming down from the aftermath of an adrenaline rush. But he was honest enough to admit it wasn't caffeine or adrenaline that had him uncomfortable in his own skin but a woman who wanted something from him he couldn't give.

He wasn't afraid of anything. He was just doing what was best for both of them. You knew fire would burn without sticking your hand in it!

Thirteen days! It had been thirteen miserable days and unbe-lievably long nights since Julia had politely kicked him out of her life and issued her impossible challenge. The thought still had the power to make his temper rise. How could she stick out her hand to him as if he were a stranger when they set each other on fire every time they kissed?!

He wanted that fire again. But in twenty-two hours he was taking a flight home. Why couldn't she accept and understand—

Suddenly a BMW coupe darted in front of him. Chase slammed on his brakes to keep from hitting the sports car and heard the squeal of brakes behind him. He jerked his gaze sharply to the rearview mirror, fully expecting to feel the Mercedes that had been on his bumper for the past ten minutes ram into him.

Instead the Mercedes took the sidewalk, giving the cab behind him enough time to safely stop. *Good reflexes*, Chase thought and waved out the open window.

Shifting the Cherokee into gear, Chase had started to pull off when he saw the car that had cut in front of him do the same thing to another driver in a Maxima. This time the BMW didn't make it.

The car clipped the Maxima's left fender, causing both cars to spin out of control and careen into cars in front and on the side of them. The impact pushed automobiles through the approaching stop sign into the oncoming right-of-way traffic. The sickening sound of metal crashing into metal filled the air.

Chase had his car phone in his hand, dialing 911, when everything within him went icy cold and still. A white Caravan minivan was heading straight for the pileup.

The phone slipped from his hand. *Please, no!*

In an instant he was out of the car and running. He had barely taken a step past his Cherokee when the minivan slammed head-first into the other cars.

"Julia!"

Chase hated hospitals. He'd lost his mother in a hospital.

Hands deep in the pockets of his jeans, he stared out the window of the surgery waiting room and tried desperately to remember that his father's life had been saved in a hospital. He couldn't. His mind was too busy remembering the agonized screams of a woman in pain and his frantic attempts to pry open a door with his bare hands.

"Chase."

He spun around, his hands coming out of his pockets. His heart leaped before he could tell it to do otherwise. Julia stood ten feet away from him. Safe. Alive. Healthy. She wasn't in surgery fighting for her life. She could have been.

He felt stinging in his eyes and fought to keep the moisture at bay. There was nothing he could do about the trembling in his legs, the knot in his throat.

"Chase. Are you all right?"

Chase briefly shut his eyes and thanked God that he had heard his name on her lips one last time, because no matter what, nothing had changed between them.

"Thank you—"

He shook his head. He didn't want to hear the words of gratitude again because then he'd have to relive the fear. What he desperately wanted was to take Julia in his arms and keep her safe. To keep from doing just that he picked his hat up from the chair he had never bothered to sit in.

"Your friend is still in surgery. Her father finally talked her mother into going down to the cafeteria for a cup of coffee. I told them I'd stay in case any family members or friends came."

Julia's hungry gaze searched Chase's drawn face, the jagged tear in his shirt, the dirty jeans. He seemed so cold and distant. She clenched her hands to keep from touching him to reassure herself that he was all right and fought to remain calm.

She'd been in her office when she heard the radio broadcaster announce that a Texas Ranger, disregarding his own safety, had single-handedly rescued a young couple from a burning van after a traffic pileup. He was also credited with saving others with his swift action to get bystanders to help accident victims to safety before the police and fire departments arrived.

Until Georgette's mother called, Julia hadn't known the couple was her assistant manager and her husband, Michael, who had borrowed Julia's van to pick up a sofa they had purchased. Julia had barely been able to understand what the woman said because she was crying so hard. Georgette was bleeding internally and had been rushed into surgery.

"How is Michael?"

"Broken leg. He'll survive."

"Because of you," she whispered softly.

Chase rolled his shoulders; his large hand crushed the brim of his Stetson. "Any law enforcement officer would have done as much."

Julia didn't think so. It took a special man to risk his life again and again for strangers. "Perhaps."

Chase's gaze bounced off the wall, the door, the floor. Anyplace except where he most wanted it to be. He slipped the hat on his head, tugging down hard on the misshapen brim. "Since you're here, I'll be going."

"Chase."

He stopped but didn't face her. "Yes?"

The door behind them opened. Millie Watkins, Georgette's mother, saw Julia and began to weep.

Instantly Julia went to the older woman and pulled her into her arms. Reaching behind the older woman's back, Julia briefly squeezed Mr. Watkins's hand. His usually smiling face was ravaged with fear. Georgette was their only child. "Georgette is a fighter. She'll make it."

Julia felt Mrs. Watkins's nod of agreement against her shoulder and pulled the frightened woman closer, comforting both of them. Georgette was only thirty-six. She had two adorable children and a husband who worshiped her. Her whole life was ahead of her.

Looking up, Julia met Chase's impenetrable stare. A shudder went through her. His mother had had two children and a husband. Life offered no guarantees.

Trying to hide her own fear, Julia helped a distraught Mrs. Watkins to a seat, then sat beside her. Mr. Watkins remained standing, his gray head bowed. Instead of leaving as he had said, Chase walked over to the father and began quietly talking to him.

Julia was glad Chase had decided to stay. His presence comforted her. Obviously he didn't feel the same. He wouldn't even look at her.

Chase stoically accepted the torture of being near Julia. He thought he could leave. He couldn't. Not while she was bravely comforting Georgette's parents and obviously in need of reassurance herself. But he already knew Julia put those she loved before herself. A rare woman. If her friend didn't make it, he wanted to be there for her. He could give her that at least.

Two hours after Julia arrived, a woman in a scrub suit entered the waiting room. Mr. and Mrs. Watkins rushed to her.

"I'm Dr. Durant. We had to remove the spleen and tie off several bleeds, but none of the vital organs were involved. Your daughter is a very lucky woman. She'll be fine."

Julia closed her eyes in thanks. When she opened them Chase was gone.

Chase couldn't deal with the situation. More accurately, he didn't want to deal with it. Each second that ticked by made him more acutely aware of his own limits, of the fragility of life, and of the uncorrectable mistakes fools make.

Head bowed, he slowly went up the front steps of the hotel, feeling wearier than he ever had in his life.

"Mr. Braxton, there's someone here to see you."

Head still bowed, Chase kept walking. He didn't want to see anyone or talk anymore. What he wanted was blissful oblivion. His jog had done nothing to smooth the jagged edges since he had seen Julia's minivan pile into the carnage of mangled vehicles.

"Chase."

He pivoted. Julia. He read the weariness in her beautiful face, saw the puffiness in the eyes that searched his. She had been crying. He felt a pain in the region of his heart. "Yes?"

She flinched at the brusqueness of his voice. "I just wanted to make sure that you were all right."

"You saw that at the hospital."

"I . . ." She seemed to falter, tucking her lower lip between her teeth.

His hands slid into his pockets to keep from reaching out for her. How much misery could one man take and remain sane? "Go home. It's getting late."

She didn't move.

The automatic doors directly behind him whooshed open. Two men came barreling through. One of them held a camera. The other carried a microphone.

Chase let out an expletive and turned his head.

The bright light of the camera flared, centering on the other man who now held the microphone under the nose of the desk clerk. "Good evening. I'm Harold Kent, reporter with Channel Eight at WFRA. I understand Texas Ranger Chase Braxton is registered in this hotel. I'd like to interview him."

Not in this lifetime, Chase thought. He wasn't reliving that hell again just to be a sound bite on the nightly news. "Come on." Spinning on his heels, he headed for the elevator. Silently she followed. Neither spoke until they were in Chase's suite.

"Once the reporter finds he can't get any information on me from Simone, he'll try to find other guests or acquaintances to pump. I was afraid he might try to talk with us next."

"Chase, are you sure you're all right?"

His hands came up to keep her from touching him. He saw the pain in her eyes and turned away from it. "I'm sweaty. I'm going to take a shower. I'm sure I don't need to show you the way to the door."

Her chin lifted. "No, you don't."

Nodding briskly, he went through the sitting room and into the bathroom. Stripping off his clothes, he stepped into the shower stall and turned the blast on full force. Maybe, just maybe, it could wash her from his mind.

Julia stood in the living room listening to the shower, her stomach churning. She'd been that way since she heard the news of the accident.

Her hand clutching her stomach, Julia sank in the nearest chair. Several cars around the van had been badly charred, but thanks to Chase no one had lost their lives.

After he'd left them in the waiting room, she had called him several times and had always gotten the hotel's message center. Worried, she'd taken a cab to the hotel after leaving the hospital. She called him again from the lobby. Getting the message center again, she had decided to wait. She needed to touch him.

Seeing him at the hospital, disheveled and distant, had broken her heart. But he wanted nothing from her.

Her gaze strayed to the closed bathroom door. He had shut her out. The sensible thing, the proper thing, to do would be to leave as he requested. But love wasn't sensible, she was finding out.

Standing, she slipped off the long cranberry-colored jacket, heedlessly letting it fall to the floor, and walked into the bathroom. Steam fogged the frosted glass. Through it she could still distinguish the shape of Chase's powerfully built body.

She might have lost him today. The terrible thought still made her weak. Trembling fingers tugged the silk blouse from her skirt.

She had managed three buttons when the door swung open.

Water glistening on his skin, Chase stopped in mid-stride. His hand gripped the shower door. "What are you doing?"

"I don't want to live with regret. If this is all there is to be, then I'll take it."

"Julia—"

"I'm not asking for a commitment," she rushed on, cutting him off.

He brushed by her and snatched a towel from atop the marble countertop and wrapped it around his waist. "Put your clothes back on."

"No."

"Leave!" he shouted, his hands braced on the counter, his head bowed.

"Don't worry. You don't have to stop this time."

Shaking his head, he pressed his hands against the countertop. "Why are you being so stubborn about this?"

"Because I think I love you, and if something had happened to you this afternoon, I would have lived with regrets the rest of my life." The other buttons slipped free. The blouse fell to the floor. The skirt followed. "You'll have to help with this."

Chase heard the rustle of clothes. Despite his best effort, he was unable to keep from lifting his head. His breath snagged. She was all that he desired, all that he had tried to convince himself that he couldn't have.

He saw her reflection in the mirror. She wore a scandalous lacy black bra, bikini panties, and thigh-high stockings edged in lace. Need struck low, fast, and hard.

He wanted to tell her to go, but he wasn't capable of pushing the words through the tight knot in his throat. Then she tenderly placed her hand on his arm and he was lost.

Whirling, he pulled her into his arms, crushing her in his embrace. "I thought I'd lost you. I didn't know it wasn't you until I wrenched open the van's door."

Julia held him tighter, listening to the tortured words that echoed her own misery. She rubbed her chin against the dampness of his wide chest, felt the muscled warmth, and tried to get closer. "I was at the office when I heard. I could have shaken you, but I was so proud. I didn't know Georgette and Michael were involved until her mother called."

Setting her away, he stared down into her eyes. "They weren't sure when they wheeled her into surgery."

Her trembling hand palmed Chase's tense jaw. "You gave her another chance at life, Chase."

As Chase remembered Georgette's husband's gut-wrenching sobs in the Emergency Room, his arms tightened around Julia. "It could have gone the other way."

"I know," Julia said. "That's why it's important to live life to the fullest when you have the chance. I realize that now. Tomorrow isn't promised."

"No, it isn't." His gaze softened. "I don't know what tomorrow brings, but I know I don't want to go through another day without knowing you're going to be there for my tomorrows."

"Neither do I. Please take me to bed."

"I can do nothing less." His voice shook. "You're all that I desire." Sweeping her up in his arms, he carried her into the bedroom and placed her gently on the bed. With exquisite care and tender kisses he finished undressing her, then tugged the towel from his waist.

His mouth slowly settled on hers again, both aware that their time had finally come. There was no need to rush. Each kiss, each feverish touch, was simply a prelude to fuel the need, heat the blood, fire the passion until their hunger could only be satisfied in one way. Their eyes and hands locked, he brought them together.

The fit was perfect, the sensations exquisite. He took her on a ride that was at times slow and lazy, at times fast and frenzied, but always, always, deep and hot and immensely pleasurable for them both. Release came in a torrent that left both shaken and too weak to speak.

Rolling to one side, Chase pulled Julia into his arms. Trustingly she curled against him and drifted into sleep. His body relaxed, but his arms didn't. He found himself unwilling to let her go now or ever. There was only one way that was possible.

He accepted his fate and tightened his hold.

. . .

Julia woke up the next morning a little after eight with a smile on her face. Usually she never slept past seven. But she had never made love half the night, either.

Laughing, she hugged the feather pillow to her hot cheek. Her skin still felt sensitized, her senses heightened. Afraid that reporters might have hung around, Chase had insisted that they leave the hotel separately. He'd picked her up down the street from the hotel, then taken her home and to bed again.

Her heart beat wildly in her chest in remembrance of the things they had done, things she couldn't wait to do again.

Laughing again for the sheer pleasure it gave her, she rolled on her back and stared up at the silk canopy. Loving someone made you reckless and daring and needy. You desperately wanted to please, but in the pleasing, you also pleased yourself.

They were on two separate paths, had two separate career goals in cities miles apart. But when Chase looked at her, touched her, and gave her one of those toe-tingling, thought-scattering kisses, practicality was the last thing on her mind. All she could think about was getting closer, grabbing, and never letting go.

Now they'd have a chance to run laughing in the rain; to feast on chocolate-covered strawberries and each other. And it had all begun at Leo's. She'd always known there was something uniquely wonderful and romantic about the supper club.

The phone rang on the bedside table. *Chase.* He had gone to his hotel to pack. She eagerly reached for the phone. "I miss you already."

"Julia?"

Eyes wide, she sprang up in bed. "Mabel!"

"Yes," came the southern-accented voice. "Do you have any idea why Chase called this morning to talk about resigning?"

"What?" Throwing back the covers, Julia sat up on the side of the bed. "Chase's whole life is the Texas Rangers!"

"We all thought so, too," Mabel said, unhappiness in each word. "Oscar would roast me alive if he knew I listened to his conversation, then told someone else, but I know how proud of Chase he is, how proud the entire force is. For Chase to be planning to resign is unthinkable."

"Then he hasn't resigned yet?" Julia asked.

"No. From what I heard, Chase just wanted to prepare Oscar. He's going to formally resign when he returns to work tomorrow."

Julia breathed a sigh of relief. "Tell Oscar not to worry."

"Do you think there's a chance you can change his mind?"

"I'm certainly going to try my best, but we both know how stubborn Chase can be."

"Oh, dear."

"Good-bye, Mabel." Hanging up the phone, Julia headed for the shower undaunted by the worry in Mabel's voice. She didn't know the reason behind his sudden decision, but he *wasn't* quitting the Texas Rangers. Not if she had her way.

She was stepping into the glass enclosure of the shower when she heard the doorbell. She started to ignore the summons, but judging by the repeated rings, the person wasn't leaving. Pulling on her robe, she stalked to the door, determined to get rid of whoever it was.

"Chase!"

Grinning, he came in. Taking the door from her, he closed it behind him and kissed her lips. "I see I'm in time to join you in the shower. These are for you."

Julia automatically took the bouquet of white roses.

Chase took the opportunity to untie the belt of her robe. His gaze narrowed with hungry appreciation at the expanse of smooth brown skin.

"I won't let you do it."

Lazy amusement danced in his black eyes. "Wanna bet?"

Julia realized they were talking about two different things. "I don't mean that. I mean resign from the Texas Rangers."

His hands settled heavily on her waist. "Mabel."

"You can't do it. The Rangers mean too much to you."

"Sweet Temptation means just as much to you."

"What has this to do with my shop?" she asked with a frown.

"I have no intention of trying to have a long-distance marriage."

Her eyes widened. "M-marriage?"

"Yes, I told you that last night."

"Chase, do you think I could sit down?" Without waiting, she went to the sofa.

Frowning, he stared down at her. "You all right?"

"A great deal happened last night, but I would have remembered you asking me to marry you."

He shifted uncomfortably. "I didn't exactly ask, but I thought you understood. We made love, didn't we?"

"Several times, as I remember," Julia said.

"Then there you are," Chase said triumphantly.

Julia stared up at Chase's long length, trying to understand his reasoning. "Chase, perhaps you should help me remember."

"Last night you told me you thought you loved me and I told you I wanted you to be there for all my tomorrows and you agreed."

"But I thought—"

"You accepted and you can't back out now after I finally stopped fighting it," he said fiercely, coming down in front of her.

"What did you stop fighting?"

"That I love you completely, irrevocably," he answered, his voice and gaze softening. "The accident opened my eyes. Life isn't promised, so you have to grab hold of the one you love and never let go. That's what I'm doing." Tenderly his hand closed over her free one. "I love you and you love me. If you didn't, you wouldn't have made love with me."

Everything fell perfectly into place. "No, I wouldn't. I love you more than I ever thought possible."

His hold tightened for a brief moment. "The accident showed me something else. I don't ever want to see you scared or worried about me again. I don't want you going through what my mother went through." Pausing, he took a deep breath. "With a Master's in Criminal Law, I shouldn't have any difficulty getting a job here."

Love and tenderness and determination filled her. "You're not resigning. I can handle the dangers of your job. You're staying a Ranger."

His mouth took on a stubborn slant. "My ranch is isolated. Here you have people who watch out for you, a secure place to live."

Laughing, she kissed him. "You can't tell me your ranch doesn't have security, and I happen to know every year you have to qualify on the shooting range. I bet you're a crack shot, and you can teach me."

His lifted eyebrow told her he was. "Mabel tell you that?"

She grinned. "The Texas Ranger Internet site."

He glanced around her stylishly furnished condo. "My house is comfortable, but it's nothing like this."

"As long as you're there, I'll be happy. The only thing I definitely have to have is my bed." Her grin widened. "I have a lot of warm memories of being in it with you and I plan a lot more."

Passion blazed in his black eyes. "That's not fair."

"By whose standards?" she asked with a regal tilt of her chin.

Shaking his head, he said, "I still don't like the idea of leaving you alone so much."

"I have the perfect solution. People in Washington have been doing it for years and it will be a great tax deduction. I'll get a place in town for us, and if you have to work late, we'll spend the night in our second home," she told him, then continued as his gaze sharpened. "Don't tell me you're one of those men who cares if a woman pays her own way or earns more than he does?"

He looked abashed. "I did. I finally figured out that's probably why Mabel didn't tell me you owned Sweet Temptation. You'll keep *it* and open your second location as planned. I don't intend to start our lives with regret or recriminations."

"Neither do I," she said. "The accident taught me something as well: we don't always get a second chance."

His lips brushed across her hand clasped in his. "I'll always be thankful I got another chance to get it right."

"No more than I. Virginia's loss is Austin's gain. It will be a unique marketing concept. The flagship store in the national capital and the other in a state capital. I have family and friends with contacts everywhere," she told him, the excitement growing in her voice. "I wanted a chain of Sweet Temptations. Austin will be my second location."

"You'd do that for me?"

"Not for you. For us."

"You're sure?"

"Well, I may need some convincing." Smiling, she walked to the bedroom. The robe dropped at the door.

Grinning, Chase hurried after the sweetest temptation he'd ever known.

EPILOGUE

How deeply could a man love a woman?

Chase asked himself that question when he saw Julia coming down the aisle of the crowded church toward him wearing a moon white ball gown embellished with rose appliqué of lace around the scooped neck and scattered over the wide hem of English net. In the glow of the candlelight with the scent of vanilla candles in the air she appeared eternal and breathtakingly beautiful. In her gloved hand was a single long-stemmed white rose.

Like most brides she had kept her choice of gown a secret, but he did know that the diamond tiara in her chignon had been worn by her mother and her mother before her at their weddings. The long embroidered lace veil from France was a gift from her sisters. The double strand of pearls circling her throat was a wedding gift from him.

She'd cried when he'd given her the necklace last night after their wedding rehearsal. With the pad of his thumb he had brushed the tears from her cheeks and tried to keep any more from falling by teasing her that he hadn't cried when she'd surprised him with his wedding gift. Impish woman that she was, she'd seductively whispered that her motives were partly selfish, then sent his blood singing in his veins by telling him some of the things she planned for them in the Jacuzzi.

How deeply could a man love a woman?

As the minister asked, "Who gives this woman away?" and Julia's father answered, "I do," then stepped back, Chase pondered the question again. Love meant sharing as Julia's father shared his daughter with a man who loved her. Love meant leaving home, friends, family, as Julia was doing for him.

With Julia's hand in his, Chase slipped the wedding band on her finger next to the heart-shaped two-carat diamond he'd given her a week after he'd asked her to marry him. Whenever she looked at the ring, he wanted her to be reminded that his heart belonged to her. The heavy gold intricately carved wedding band she slid on his finger was perfect. So was the inscription inside: J.A.F. ALWAYS & FOREVER, C.M.B.

"You may kiss the bride."

He'd meant to keep it light, a brush of lips, but something happened when their lips met and she leaned eagerly into him. This woman was his; he was hers. The kiss deepened into a vow, a pledge of forever, of need that would never die.

"Uh, hm, there will be time enough for that later," the minister whispered.

Laughter boomed from beside him. Chase lifted his head and shot Colt a hard look. Nonplussed, he shrugged, still grinning.

Julia's squeezing of his hand and the recessional music had him turning away. With his arm around his wife's waist, they went back down the aisle. Outside, the June day in Virginia was perfect, with blue skies and a light breeze that ruffled Julia's veil as she and Chase ran laughing down the church steps to the waiting limousine that would take them to Leo's for their reception.

"How about we skip the reception and see if we can get the pilot to take off early?" Chase suggested, nibbling on Julia's lips.

Julia moaned. "Do you think we could?"

"No, but it's nice to know you'd go." A jet, courtesy of Julia's parents, was standing by to take them to Monterey. From the airport a car would take them to a resort on the beach. Her parents had wanted to pay for their accommodations as well. Chase had politely refused. The only reason he'd accepted the jet was because they'd have privacy while traveling and they wouldn't have to worry about the hassle of checking and claiming baggage or changing planes in Los Angeles.

Her eyes filled with love when she said, "I'd follow you anywhere."

He kissed her. He couldn't help himself. Nor did he want to. There was no longer a question in his mind whether she was sure or had any regrets; love had a way of overcoming problems and establishing trust. "One dance, one quick trip around the room to meet everyone, and we're out of there."

"You lead. I follow."

He'd tried, but too many people wanted to kiss the bride, congratulate the groom. Julia, as always, took time to greet each and every one of them. Percival had proudly told Julia's family that he'd known all along Chase and Julia would end up getting married. A fully recovered Georgette was there with her husband, Michael, and their two daughters, who had been flower girls.

Chase had hired a bus to bring the residents from the nursing home where Julia volunteered. They were having a ball. She hadn't rested until she had found another volunteer to take her place.

Violins serenaded the guests, waiters plied them with vintage champagne, chefs tempted them with delicacies in the room decorated with tall, gilded candelabras that were overgrown with flowers in muted antique tones. No one seemed inclined to leave, but if they did waiters were stationed at the door to present them with a specially prepared gold-foil box of chocolate candy. The label read: SWEET BEGINNINGS, CREATED BY CHASE & JULIA.

Two hours and countless handshakes and hugs later they left for the airport in a shower of birdseed and soap bubbles. Once aboard the plane Chase thought he showed admirable strength when he undid the twenty-eight buttons on the back of Julia's gown, then left her to change in private. The next time he took her in his arms he didn't plan on letting her go for a long, long time.

Instead he used the time to unpack the hastily gathered dinner and set the small table in the main cabin. As usual Julia had been too busy seeing to others to see to herself. He'd have to see that she took better care of herself now that she had two stores.

Sweet Temptation had been an instant success when it opened in Austin a month ago. If things continued to go as well, she planned on publishing a catalogue next year.

He glanced up the moment the door opened. Surprised delight shone on her lovely face as her gaze touched the huge slice of wedding cake, succulent slices of roast beef, smoked salmon, rolls, and champagne. "You always think of me."

"And I always will."

Lush flowers in the deepest hues scented the salt-tinged night air. A gentle wind rustled the palm trees. Standing on the stone terrace leading to the private beach two hundred feet away, Julia listened to the sounds of the waves crashing against the shore. Overhead, a full moon shone.

The secluded cottage was perfect for a honeymoon, Julia thought. As soon as they had arrived, she'd changed into her nightgown. After sharing a glass of champagne they had gone outside to enjoy the night. Happiness flooded her. No woman could be happier.

Chase's strong arms slid around her waist from behind and pulled her up against him. His cheek rested against hers. "You want another glass of champagne?"

Snuggling closer, she felt the warmth and security and, yes, the temptation of his hard muscular body through her long sheer white robe and nightgown. Soon she could freely explore those temptations, but for now she was content. They had a lifetime ahead of them. She shook her head. "I have everything I want."

His hold gently tightened. "Same here."

"The wedding was beautiful."

He slowly turned her and stared down into her face. "*You're* beautiful."

"Oh, Chase. You make me feel so special."

"You are." He kissed her forehead, her nose, her lips. "Not many women could open a new store and find a town house in a strange city while coordinating a big wedding hundreds of miles away."

She grinned. "These past eight months have been busy, but my mother and sisters helped. I had a strong incentive to get everything done by May. Once we were married I didn't want to be away from you."

"Me neither. There's nothing in the world more important than us. I plan to spend the rest of my life loving you." His hands tenderly palmed her face. "Ever since you started down the aisle toward me, I've asked myself the question of how deeply could a man love a woman."

"D-did you find an answer?" she asked, her voice tremulous.

"Partially." Picking her up in his arms, he went into the bedroom, then placed her on the four-poster bed and came down beside her. "I finally figured out that discovering the answer will take a lifetime of loving you, watching our children grow inside you, growing old beside you, and it all begins now."

"It all begins now," she repeated, lifting her face to meet his kiss. Their journey was about to begin, a journey that had all started with a sweet temptation and would last a lifetime.

southern

Comfort

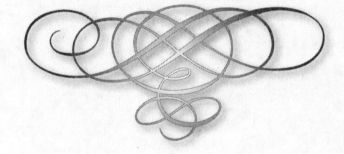

ONE

Charlotte Duvall was a charmer. She was the kind of woman men noticed, and women aspired to emulate. It was impossible to remain detached and impersonal once you saw her and had been graced by her eloquent presence.

Vincent Maxwell had heard the flowery accolades often from his cousin, Brian, so much so that Vincent often wondered if his young and still highly impressionable twenty-four-year-old cousin was half in love with Charlotte. Vincent hoped not. Especially since Brian had recently announced his engagement to Emma Hamilton, a rather shy kindergarten teacher.

Vincent had liked Emma immediately when Brian brought her by his office several weeks ago. Sweet-faced with a lovely smile, the woman obviously adored Brian. She even laughed at his lame jokes. They seemed so right for each other. They were the same age and attended the same church.

However, in the weeks that followed, Brian had become increasingly vocal in his adoration of Charlotte. When Vincent mentioned his concerns to Brian, he always laughingly denied any romantic interest in Charlotte and assured Vincent that he would understand once he met her. With Brian's wedding six weeks away,

Vincent, as Brian's best man and eldest cousin, felt it past time for him to meet this paragon of virtue and desire.

"I'm so glad you and Charlotte's schedules have finally worked out so you can meet each other," Emma said with a smile, her nut-brown face glowing with love and happiness. "I was afraid you two wouldn't meet until the wedding rehearsal."

"So am I," Vincent said, sipping his tonic water. As tired as he was after a ten-hour day, if he drank anything alcoholic, he'd be asleep in an hour. In his briefcase, which he'd left in his car, was a three-inch stack of paperwork he needed to go through before a meeting at eight the next morning. He'd never been late with a report and he didn't intend to start now. He'd pulled an all-nighter before. He could do it again. It was in Brian's best interest that Vincent meet this Charlotte Duvall person ASAP. Even the name sounded seductive and mysterious.

Although Vincent hadn't been around his cousin for years, he doubted Brian had much experience with women. Vincent had. Women could be as vicious and as devious as men in getting what they wanted.

His mouth tightened as he thought of Sybil Lamount. Beautiful, cunning, and heartless. A viper if ever there was one. She could ruin a person's career and never lose a moment of sleep. Spoils of the game, she always said.

Vincent took a sip of his tonic water and found the taste as bitter as his thoughts. *Forget her, forget the past,* he chided himself. He had survived when others had not. His mind had to be on one thing and one thing only: re-engineering Ora-Tech Petroleum Company's entire financial structure. The task was monumental, but in his three-month-old position as vice-president of finance, it was his job, and what he had been wooed away from Standard Securities in Boston to do. As with every job Vincent undertook, he planned to do it and do it well, no matter what.

"Charlotte works as hard as you do," Brian put in from his place on the far side of Emma.

"Mmmm," was all Vincent said. He doubted that very seriously. Women simply didn't have the force of will or the single-mindedness that a man had. Most were too easily distracted by emotions. Of course, a few had made it to the top, but in doing so, in Vincent's humble opinion, they had to compromise in some way. Their path was littered with broken relationships, rebellious children, and ant-acid bottles. Working sixteen hours a day or being gone ten to fifteen days out of a month didn't go very well with caring for a family. Something went lacking. He'd seen it happen too many times in the past.

Or if they were as heartless as Sybil, they didn't worry about any emotional attachments or the people they stepped on on their climb up the corporate ladder. The job was all that mattered and to hell with anything or anyone else. *That* was something of which he had personal knowledge.

"Charlotte's almost as fantastic as Emma," Brian said, his handsome face wreathed in a boyish grin.

Vincent easily shifted his thoughts back to the present. His onyx eyes narrowed on his cousin. There it was again, that open praise bordering on worshipfulness in Brian's voice.

Even as a boy Brian had been impressionable. He'd been reared by easygoing, good-natured parents who believed the best of everyone. Vincent's father, his namesake, often commented that William, his younger brother and Brian's father, was every con man's dream.

Vincent's father had worried when William Maxwell moved his family from Connecticut to Dallas twenty years ago to teach philosophy at Southern Methodist University. Vincent's father, a high-powered banking executive, was pragmatic. Vincent's mother, the quintessential executive's wife with a liberal arts degree from Vassar who could hold her own with Martha Stewart or B. Smith, was sensible. No one got to them. They had reared Vincent to be the same way.

"Oh, look. Charlotte's here."

Vincent glanced in the direction Emma was staring, but all he saw was the broad, black-tuxedoed back of the maître d'. Then the man moved and Vincent, renowned for keeping his calm in any situation, barely kept his mouth from dropping open.

Surely he wasn't seeing what he thought he was. No woman would be that bold. But as he stared all he could see was a smooth toffee-toned body draped in an oversized fringed shawl. The soft, iridescent material in shimmering bronze tones slipped off one golden brown shoulder revealing more bare skin and the lush swell of Charlotte's breasts.

A hot ball of healthy lust rolled through Vincent. It seemed he had been right to be concerned about Brian. Few men would probably be immune to such an obvious temptation.

Smiling warmly, Charlotte said something to the overly attentive maître d', then turned toward them, waved and started in their direction. For a long moment the man she walked away from stared wistfully after her, only looking away when a waiter came up to speak to him. Vincent could understand why.

The view from behind was probably just as enticing as the one in front. Her walk was a mixture of strut and saunter on impossible high-heeled leopard sandals that bared her feet and showed off trim ankles.

"Charlotte."

Charlotte glanced around at the white linen-draped table-for-two she had been about to pass, then stopped abruptly and bent to hug the matronly woman in pearls and diamonds who had greeted her. Nimbly, Charlotte scooted around the table to the gray-haired man who had risen and gave him a hug as well.

In the three months Vincent had been in Dallas he'd noticed that people in the South were high on hugging and emotionalism. Bostonians as a rule weren't so enthusiastic or demonstrative.

However, at the moment he was annoyed to find he also noticed how the deep fringe on the shawl lazily parted to provide a tantalizing glimpse of Charlotte's shapely brown leg each time she bent over. It annoyed him further that as he glanced away he saw the rapt attention of several other men in the restaurant doing the same thing. It wasn't difficult to see the open speculation in their faces as to what, if anything, lay beneath the shimmering shawl and if the material would rise further to give them the answer.

Vincent sat back against the leather booth, picked up his glass and studied the small fresh-cut floral arrangement on the table. He'd met that type of flamboyant woman before. Women like that held little interest for him. He preferred his women to be feminine and demure. Provocativeness belonged in the bedroom. Apparently no one had told Charlotte about subtlety. He would be civil to her because he had no choice. She was Emma's maid of honor. *He* didn't have to be her new best friend.

"Hi. Sorry I'm late."

Despite his best effort to remain detached, the slow, husky Southern drawl stirred something within Vincent. It was the kind of voice lovers used when they were hot and sweaty and tangled in moonlight and each other. Because of his hectic schedule those nights were a distant memory.

"I'm just glad you're here." Laughing, Brian stood, his long, lanky arm curving affectionately around Charlotte's slim waist as he kissed her offered cheek. Vincent cut a look at Emma to see if she disapproved of her fiancé kissing a woman who wore seduction so brazenly. To his surprise, Emma was smiling warmly.

"I'm just glad you and Vincent are finally meeting each other," Emma said, her hand reaching out for Brian's. He grasped it immediately. "The wedding is only six weeks away."

"I wish it were tomorrow," Brian said, squeezing Emma's hand.

For a moment the two of them had eyes only for each other. Vincent almost breathed a small sigh of relief. Charlotte wasn't an issue as he had suspected.

"I think they've forgotten about us," Charlotte said lightly, her voice a smooth mix of silk and honey and magnolia blossoms. The pouty lower lip fit the seductive image the voice evoked—and so did the rest of the face, with its sharp cheekbones, thick black lashes over slumberous hazel eyes, and dainty nose.

Emma and Brian laughed, then he finished the introductions. "Charlotte Duvall, political fund-raiser extraordinare, long-time friend of the bride and maid of honor, meet Vincent Maxwell, financial wizard and Vice-President of Finance for Ora-Tech Petroleum Company, my favorite cousin, and best man."

Vincent slowly came to his feet. It had been rude not to do so earlier, but he had reached that point in his life when he followed his own dictates in his personal life. "Ms. Duvall."

A smile spread across Charlotte's beautiful face. He noticed a tiny mole near the corner of her mouth. The top of her head barely reached the middle of his chest. She was smaller and daintier than he realized. More trouble. A man would feel protective toward a small woman, and he just bet Charlotte Duvall used that to her best advantage.

She held out her slender, French-manicured hand. "Please, call me Charlotte. It's a pleasure to meet you. I was afraid you were a figment of Brian's imagination."

The way she seemed to center her attention entirely on a man had probably caused many to succumb and throw themselves at her feet. Vincent was made of sterner stuff. Courtesy, not interest, dictated his next movements. Her soft hand barely settled in his before he released it and stepped aside. "If you'll have a seat, we can order."

Charlotte kept the smile on her face with difficulty. She earned her living by being able to read people quickly and correctly. She'd bet the platinum card tucked in her Hermés bag that Vincent Maxwell didn't like her. The limp handshake, the slight curl of his sensual upper lip, the disapproving black eyes all told the story. His loss.

She reached for her shawl. His broad shoulders stiffened.

Her brows puckered, then cleared as the reason came to her. She smiled to herself. The attire was designed to draw a man's attention. It did the job extremely well and as her mother had always said, why wear something that no one notices?

The first time she had worn the outfit at a fund-raising dinner for the Sickle Cell Anemia Foundation, she'd been inundated with requests from women to have the designer's name. She'd happily given them her sister's name and address in Charleston, but the dress was one-of-a-kind, as were most of her clothes.

Charlotte smiled into Vincent's tight face and slowly pulled the shawl from her shoulders, knowing that as she did she'd reveal her bare skin inch by inch until the light material slid over the low bodice of the leopard-print strapless dress. His eyes rounded.

After twenty-nine years she had gotten used to men's reaction when they saw her breasts: She was top-heavy, but she no longer slumped her shoulders or wore oversized tops to hide what God had given her. Women went under the knife to get what she had naturally.

Sure the disapproving expression on Vincent's face would vanish, she watched and waited expectantly. If anything, his mobile lips tightened even more. She admitted the bustier-style of the clinging dress plunged a bit, but it was in no way indecent. *Stuffed shirt*, she thought.

Only an uptight Yankee would think a Southern woman would appear in public so improperly dressed or disapprove of a little cleavage. To think, she had looked forward to finally meeting him. Dismissing Vincent, Charlotte slid into the booth. "Emma, I told you the meeting might run late and to order."

Emma waved Charlotte's words aside. The two-carat round diamond on the third finger of her left hand reflected a rainbow prism from the crystal chandelier several feet away. "It's only a little past nine and since tomorrow is Friday, I can sleep in late on Saturday."

Charlotte shook her head of shoulder-length auburn curls. She hated to be the bearer of bad news, but she had to do her duty. A duty that she had performed eight times in the past four years.

With difficulty she shook away the unsettling memory of people's comments at the last wedding where she had been the maid of honor, wanting to know when she was going to be a bride. She wondered the same thing.

"Saturday you and Brian are meeting at your parents' house at ten to go over the final guest list and get the wedding invitations in the mail. Then at two you meet with Pastor Bailey in his study to confirm the ceremony details."

Emma's brown eyes sparkled with humor. "Sleeping late for me is any time past eight. I get up at six on school days."

Charlotte shuddered delicately. "You always did get up with the chickens. Brian, why don't you get the waiter?" The words were barely out of her mouth before the waiter appeared. Somehow she knew the reason was the silent man sitting next to her.

"Please bring another menu," Vincent requested.

"If you all know what you want, that won't be necessary." Charlotte smiled up at the waiter. "Hi, Louis."

A flush climbed upward from the banded collar of the man's white shirt. His Adam's apple bobbed. "Good evening, Ms. Duvall. It's nice to have you dining with us again."

"Always a pleasure." Putting her elbows on the table, she linked her slender fingers. "My friends were waiting on me. Please tell Pierre I'd consider it a favor if he'd do his magic and get our orders out as soon as possible."

"Certainly, Ms. Duvall."

She sent the young man another hundred-watt smile, then turned to Emma, who had a tiny, knowing smile on her own face. "You first."

In less than a minute the waiter had hurried away to put in their orders, then returned almost immediately with Charlotte's white wine. In less than two minutes their mushroom appetizers appeared. Aware that another customer's order would be late, Charlotte guiltily speared one. But as was her understanding with the chef, the other customer's appetizer was now complimentary and the cost billed to

Charlotte's account. While she enjoyed the ability to pamper her clients, she understood that the integrity and high standards of the five-star restaurant had to be maintained.

Although this wasn't business, for some perverse reason she wanted to show Mr. Stuck-up he wasn't all that. Just because he was an executive with a large firm didn't mean squat. So what if he didn't approve of her? There were plenty of people who did. She had clout, too.

But as the meal progressed and they were served their entrées, Charlotte became aware that not once had Vincent spoken directly to her. He smiled and chatted with Brian and Emma, but acted as if she wasn't there. When she tested her theory and asked him a question, he gave the answer in precise diction as if he were reciting to his English teacher. One he didn't particularly care for.

Charlotte, as the youngest of three sisters, had never taken being ignored very well. She took being judged unjustly worse. Combined, the two offenses hit her boiling point midway through her blackened catfish. The ladylike thing to do was to ignore the rude man. He was a Yankee and didn't know any better. She, on the other hand, had been raised to be hospitable, ignore offenses, and never forget she was a Southern lady. But as the meal lengthened she recalled she had also been taught that if a woman were smart enough she could get her point across and remain a lady.

"Vincent." Charlotte drew out the first syllable of his name, then ended the second in a soft croon. She waited until he slowly turned to face her. She wondered briefly what that sensual mouth would look like relaxed, then dismissed the thought. "I certainly hope our hot Texas summers aren't too brutal for you. Boston's climate is so different."

Unyielding black eyes narrowed. "I was in Saudi for two years."

"Then you can take the heat. How nice," she said drolly. Dismissing Vincent, she reached for the crystal salt shaker and brushed her bare arm against the fine cotton blend of his jacket. He stiffened as if something vile had touched him.

"Excuse me, sugar," she smiled into his taut face. He certainly hadn't liked being called "sugar," but then neither did she care for being treated as if she were something repugnant.

Immediately she made up her mind—the challenge was on. For the next five minutes, she "accidentally" brushed against Vincent every chance she got and called him "sugar." Her lips twitched. If he became any stiffer, he'd crack.

A delightful prospect.

With that thought in mind, Charlotte decided a two-pronged attack was in order. She leaned toward Vincent to ask him his party affiliation. The twin assaults would surely send him over the edge. Relishing the outcome, she grinned.

Vincent chose that moment to reach for the bread basket near Charlotte's plate. Instead of her brushing against his shoulder, his right forearm grazed her breast.

Charlotte froze out of embarrassment and the unexpected thrill of pleasure that shot through her. Her sharp intake of breath hissed through her clenched teeth.

Time stood still, then started again as she slowly faced him. The apology on her lips died under his accusing glare. Hot shame flooded her cheeks and made her speechless for one of the few times in her life.

Vincent scooted over. "Sorry, I didn't mean to crowd you."

She felt inexplicably worse by his unexpected gallantry. She opened her mouth to say it was her fault, then inwardly shrank from the anger boiling in his stormy black eyes. He thought she had done it on purpose.

Charlotte realized she had no comeback. Her childish act of teasing him had gotten her into this predicament. Mutely, she turned to Brian and Emma and was relieved to see that they were too involved with each other to see what had happened.

Vincent picked up the roll from the linen-draped silver basket with his left hand, broke the bread in half and placed it on his bread plate without taking a bite. Charlotte had the feeling he wished the crusty roll were her neck.

"Brian, should I plan to go with you and Emma to see the pastor Saturday?" Vincent asked.

Smiling, Brian shook his head. Apparently he didn't notice Vincent's strained voice. "It will be more like a counseling session to make sure we're ready."

His jaw tight, Vincent nodded solemnly. "Well, if you'll excuse me, I have some paperwork that I have to get to tonight. The bill has been taken care of."

"You haven't finished your meal," Charlotte blurted.

Cold eyes stabbed her. "I've lost my appetite."

Charlotte flinched.

"Thanks, cuz, for dinner and for coming," Brian said, then asked, "Do either of you ladies want any dessert?" At the negative shake of the women's heads, he tossed a fifty on the table. "Then we'll walk out with you. Emma was up late last night with PTA."

Emma leaned her head against his shoulder and stared worshipfully up at her fiancé. "Charlotte, I hope you find someone like Brian."

"One can always hope," Charlotte said.

A snorting sound came from the direction of Vincent, but when Charlotte looked around, his expression was bland. "Did you say something?"

"Nothing you'd want to hear."

Realizing he was probably right, Charlotte stepped in front of him and headed out of the restaurant. Outside, as luck would have it, Vincent's car arrived first from the valet. She had hoped she might get a chance to apologize. Curtly, he dipped his well-shaped head in Charlotte's direction before warmly saying good-bye to Brian and Emma. Then he went around and got in the driver's seat of his late-model Lincoln Town Car and drove off.

"I'm afraid I didn't make a very favorable impression on your cousin, Brian," Charlotte said, staring at the taillights of the luxury sedan before they disappeared as Vincent turned onto Houston Street.

Perpetually easygoing, Brian slung his free arm around Charlotte's tense shoulders. "Don't worry. I admit Vincent is the serious type, but he's an all right kind of guy. The reason he hasn't been able to meet you until now is that he's reengineering his company's entire financial organization. He's got a lot on his mind. It'll be different the next time you meet him."

"Brian's right, Charlotte," Emma said from beside Brian, who had his other arm around her trim waist. "Vincent just has a lot on his mind. He's a great guy. Besides," she said with a grin, "there's not a man alive who's immune to you."

Charlotte smiled as Emma had intended, but it was forced. All her friends thought she was some kind of femme fatale. But Charlotte knew all too well she wasn't, just as she knew that men *were* immune to her. While her friends were getting married right and left, she was going home alone.

Hugging Emma, Charlotte went to her Lexus, tipping the attendant as she got in her car. Traffic was light in downtown Dallas and soon she was on Central Expressway heading north and home. It might have been her imagination, but every car she saw seemed to have a couple snuggled together inside.

Pulling into the garage located in the rear of her house, she went straight to her office off the kitchen and checked messages. There were seven since she had retrieved the last one before she went into the restaurant. That was light, but it wouldn't remain that way.

Her party needed money to ensure that when the time came their presidential candidate won the White House, and when he did he'd need the votes of senators and congressmen and women he could count on. Her job, her passion, was to ensure that that happened. And that meant money, and lots of it.

By law, fund-raising could only be conducted while the Senate was in session, from January to June first. It was May twenty-fifth.

And although fund-raising didn't usually get into full swing until late fall, things were already happening.

Cutting off the light, Charlotte stopped by the bright kitchen done in celery green with creamy oyster accents, pulled a bottle of water from the refrigerator, then continued to her bedroom, yawning as she went. She'd been up since six working on a volunteer project for Brian's House, a home for children with AIDS. But it would be worth it. The budget would be met for the following year and then some.

Fighting back another yawn, Charlotte reached for a padded hanger in her mirrored walk-in closet. Out of the corner of her eye she saw the rose silk taffeta maid of honor gown for Emma's wedding hanging in a thick plastic bag emblazoned with the name *Yvonne's Wedding Gowns.*

Melancholy hit Charlotte without warning. She had a beautiful, tastefully furnished, brick four-bedroom home, a nice car, a closet full of clothes for each season of the year, and a job that allowed her to work out of her home and set her own hours. And no one special to share her life with.

As a political fund-raiser, she not only helped in a small way to shape the policies of the country, but met influential and often famous people in the process. In Dallas, there was something going on every weekend and almost every night. Her social calendar was full, but her personal life was empty.

Only her immediate family was aware of how much it hurt when people continued to ask when *she* was going to walk down the aisle as the bride. She wished she knew.

Most of the men she met were either out for what they could get, already in a relationship, or thought she was too outspoken and aggressive. They wanted a woman who stayed in the background, who was nonthreatening and demure. She'd never be that.

She sighed. Those attributes, some would say faults, she admitted to herself, were what had gotten her into her present predicament. But you couldn't get political donations by being timid.

Especially since she was only five-feet-two in her stocking feet. She'd learned to walk gracefully in stiletto heels because she'd been taught that a lady always wore heels, but they also added inches to her height.

To those who said she had a Napoleonic complex, she said bull. She'd just learned early to speak up for herself in a house full of women who all wanted to be heard. She often wondered how her daddy, a loving, soft-spoken man, had stood it. But he had, and he'd appeared to relish being around so many women.

Charlotte was the only one of her sisters still single. She'd absolutely refused another blind date or to be hooked up. If Mr. Right was out there, she'd wait until God placed him in her path. But patience had never been Charlotte's strong suit.

At the last wedding she'd attended as maid of honor—number eight—Ira Hadnot, a reporter for the "Lifestyle" section of the *Dallas Morning News*, had asked Charlotte about doing a story on the number of times she had been down the aisle and not married. Thankfully, Ira had been joking and why shouldn't she? Ira had a wonderful husband who adored her. She had someone to go home to; someone to wake up with.

Tossing the hanger on the king-sized bed, Charlotte unzipped her dress. She, on the other hand, woke up to the sound of an alarm clock. She was twenty-nine with no prospects. But that wasn't her biggest concern at the moment. Her biggest concern was facing Vincent Maxwell and apologizing.

She strongly believed a person should take responsibility for their own actions, even if it meant getting their head chopped off. Vincent looked as if he could chop with the best of them.

TWO

Vincent stepped into the chrome-and-glass elevator on the third floor of Ore-Tech Petroleum Company, nodded absently to two men he recognized from marketing, and punched nine. Vincent's mind was on the thick stack of fan-folded paper he'd just picked up from accounting.

The data he held was just another piece of the larger puzzle that was needed to complete the financial reorganization of Ore-Tech. After working sixteen-, sometimes twenty-hour days for more weeks than he cared to remember, the financial plan was finally coming together. When he and his team were finished, they'd save the company millions.

People not in the corporate world tended to think that all executives did was play golf and have five-martini lunches. If that were true, the company they worked for would go bankrupt. Truth was, they worked their butts off. They saw little of their families. The trade-off for the family was a higher standard of living.

When he wasn't traveling, there wasn't a night that he didn't take work home. However, he was well compensated for his hard work and diligence.

The high six-figure salary he earned easily went to seven figures with bonuses and profit sharing. If things went as planned he could retire in twenty more years at fifty-five, if he wanted. He didn't see that happening. He liked what he did, and if he did say so himself, he was very good at it.

The elevator door opened on the fifth floor and the men got out. Vincent's destination was the top executive floor and his corner office that looked out onto picturesque Lake Carolyn that meandered through Las Colinas, an upscale office and residential complex. As the elevator door closed, Vincent's thoughts went to Brian.

His cousin wanted the high salary, the corner office, but Vincent wasn't sure the easygoing man was cut out for the stressful, hectic pace that could crush a man and his marriage. Vincent had been raised to believe that a man took care of his family. The man worked and the wife stayed home. That's what the men in Vincent's family did—until Brian.

Emma planned to continue teaching. According to Brian, she liked to cook for him, and enjoyed going to the movies. If Brian continued his climb in the marketing department of the telecommunications company he worked for, she'd be cooking for one, and the only movies they'd see would be the ones rented from a video store. Vincent couldn't remember the last time he'd seen a new release, with or without a woman.

Although he had no thoughts of getting married, when he did decide to take the plunge, he planned to follow tradition. His wife would stay at home.

Vincent liked Emma and while she seemed practical, he wondered if she could handle the pressure of being married to a man gone more than he was home. Vincent shifted the papers and wondered about something else: how a nice, sweet woman like Emma had a friend like Charlotte.

Charlotte. She was completely unacceptable, but that hadn't kept him from thinking about her. She'd been on his mind when he finally drifted off to sleep last night, then in his dreams.

His hand closed over the spot on his arm where her breast had touched. The soft imprint had burned into his flesh and left him wanting to remove the cloth barrier and place his mouth there. He scowled. He'd known she was trouble the moment he'd laid eyes on her.

His scowl deepening, Vincent bumped the closing elevator door with his shoulder and stepped off. It wasn't like him to let a woman distract him. Not even Sybil had managed to do that.

Determined steps carried him down the wide hallway filled with contemporary art and lush tropical plants. Six offices were located on the floor. His was at the far end. Opening the heavy mahogany door to his outer office, he took two steps, then stopped abruptly. The last person he expected to see perched on the edge of his secretary's desk was Charlotte Duvall.

Her hazel eyes widened. Mulberry-painted lips parted in surprise, then she seemed to glide off the desk and onto her feet. Multiple layers of white swirled around her, then settled, but not before he'd seen those shapely legs that had helped deny him his sleep. He closed the door with a crisp snap.

"Vincent, I know we don't have an appointment and that you're a busy man, but if you'd give me five minutes I'd like to explain about last night," she said in a rush, eyeing him warily.

"You have fifteen minutes before your next appointment," Millicent informed him. "I could get you and Ms. Duvall some coffee, if you'd like."

Charlotte glanced back at the older woman and smiled. "Please, call me Charlotte."

Millicent smiled back, a real smile full of warmth and pleasure.

Vincent's gaze went from one to the other. He felt as if he was in the Twilight Zone. His secretary, Millicent Howard, was cool, crisp, and a bit remote. But obviously not with Charlotte. He'd inherited her from the previous vice-president and since his secretary in Boston hadn't wanted to relocate, he'd agreed to keep Millicent.

The first time he'd met Millicent, the diminutive sixty-year-old had politely informed him that she was a secretary, not a waitress or an errand girl. She typed 120 words per minute, spoke five languages, had an in with all the departments needed to get his reports done quickly and correctly, knew all the word processing programs, and didn't mind working late.

Aware of what his schedule was going to be like, Vincent figured he could get a housekeeper to shop and do errands for him, so he'd kept Millicent on. In the months since, not once had she ever offered to bring him coffee.

"Vincent?" his secretary questioned, peering at him from behind her tortoise-frame glasses, none of the gray hair that she wore scraped back in a tight bun out of place.

"No, thank you, Millicent." Another thing about Dallas was that all the employees seemed to be on a first-name basis. Balancing the papers in his arm, he opened the door to his office. "You have five minutes."

"Thank you." Charlotte passed him in a flutter of white, the exotic scent of jasmine trailing softly behind her.

Need nipped him in a place he didn't want to think about. He'd let her have her say and then she was out of there.

Closing his door, he nodded his head in the direction of one of the matching navy blue leather seats in front of his massive desk. Then he rounded the desk and placed the papers on the corner. His hand settled on the back of his executive swivel chair and pulled it back. He glanced up before taking his seat and discovered Charlotte, her posture rigid, still standing.

He folded his arms, uncaring that the posture was confrontational and rude. She deserved no less. "You have five minutes," he reminded her.

Her chin came up. "My behavior last night was reprehensible. There is no excuse for it and I apologize. I set out to provoke you initially, but the last incident was totally unplanned and embarrassing for both of us. I hope we can put the incident behind us for Emma and Brian's sake."

He studied her a long time. The stunning face and clenched

fists. She didn't want to be here. They were even. He didn't want her here either. He'd rather keep his very low opinion of her. It was easier and safer.

He didn't have to think back to remember the hot stab of lust that touching her breast had caused or her wide-eyed stare of embarrassment. Faked, of course. But one thing he was sure of was that the imprint of her nipple pressing against her dress afterward hadn't been there before. The last thing he wanted to be aware of was that she was aware of him.

"Why would you want to provoke me?" His voice gave no quarter and usually sent those under him scurrying to get out of his way.

Charlotte's small chin inched higher. "Because you acted as if I was a contaminant, and I foolishly tried to get back at you."

Unfolding his arms, Vincent placed his hands palm down on his desk and stared across it at the woman who stirred something not quite tame in him despite his best efforts. Reluctantly he had to admire her courage. Not many people stood up to him. "Is that how you usually react when someone doesn't like you?"

The question was deliberately provoking. "No."

He kept his gaze steady. To let it wander was dangerous. The white dress draped seductively over her voluptuous body. Whoever thought white was virginal hadn't seen Charlotte in that dress that fluttered, whispered, beckoned with each graceful movement. "Then why me?"

For the first time she seemed to lose her cool and bit her lip. Something he'd very much like to do for her. He tried to look sterner, but it was difficult with this heat coursing through his veins.

"Poor judgment on my part."

Vincent straightened. If Brian was correct, poor judgment was not a characteristic people associated with Charlotte. So there had to be another reason.

There was a brief knock on his office door. There was only one person in the company who Millicent would allow to disturb him. Vincent rounded his desk. "Come in."

The words were barely out of his mouth before the door opened and the CEO of Ora-Tech and his boss, Sidney Hughes, entered. Hughes wore his sixty years well. Despite the ups and downs of the oil industry, his silver hair was as thick as it had been thirty years ago. His shoulders were arrow-straight beneath his crisp, pointed-collar white shirt. The shirt was open at the throat, the sleeves rolled up to reveal a thick gold watch on one tanned wrist.

In contrast, Vincent's blue-and-white-striped cotton shirt was buttoned, his woven silk weave tie with discreet flower motif in periwinkle was knotted precisely, his sterling silver cuff links fastened securely in the French cuffs. Beneath his gray, pinstriped double-breasted jacket were silk braces. Dressing was the one area Vincent had no intention of altering.

"Hello, Sidney."

"Hello, Vincent," Hughes greeted in his Arkansas twang. His gaze had already shifted to the woman standing just behind Vincent.

It figured, Vincent thought in rising irritation. Charlotte attracted men like a steel magnet drew metal shavings. Any man who was interested in her would always have to worry. "Charlotte Duvall, please meet Sidney Hughes."

Hughes was already reaching out his large manicured hands and smiling. "No need for the introduction, Charlotte and I are old friends." He gently squeezed her soft hands in his. "It's nice seeing you again."

"Hello, Mr. Hughes, nice to see you too," Charlotte said. "How's Mrs. Hughes?"

"Helen is bursting with happiness. That dealer in Europe finally located that antique Chippendale table and chairs she wanted."

"I love antiques! Especially Chippendale. The rich carving is bold and energetic, yet beautiful," Charlotte said.

"You said it. I warned Helen that the housekeeper might quit when she saw the chairs and table with all that fancy carving, but they trade off days dusting." Sidney shook his head in obvious puzzlement. "In any case, we're having all of the executives of the firm and their spouses over tomorrow so she can show them off."

Charlotte twisted her head to one side. The gold hoops in her ears glittered in the afternoon sun. "And you just adore her and enjoy giving her what makes her happy."

"She keeps life interesting," Hughes said, his green eyes twinkling. He looked at Vincent. "I didn't mean to interrupt."

"You didn't," Vincent reassured his boss. "Charlotte and I were finished."

Sidney's keen, intelligent eyes went from one to the other. "I didn't know you two knew each other."

"We just met last night. His cousin is marrying one of my dear friends. I'm the maid of honor and Vincent is the best man," Charlotte explained, aware that Vincent had just given her her walking papers. She might have known that the first time he said her name he'd have his nose out of joint.

"Helen can't wait for the day our children decide to settle down." Sidney shook his head. "I just got off the phone with her and promised I'd remind Vincent in person about tomorrow night. The last time, he got there when everybody was about to leave. Almost missed out on the barbecue."

"I'll be there and on time." That night he'd been caught up in finishing an analysis and lost track of time. He didn't plan for that to happen again. In the business world, socializing was a necessary part of the climb. Vincent considered it a necessary evil.

"You said that before." Sidney rubbed his chin thoughtfully and stared at his newest executive. "You still dateless?"

"Yes," Vincent answered slowly, hoping Sidney wasn't about to do what he thought he was.

"Well, then I have the perfect solution to ensure you get there." The older man smiled and turned to Charlotte. "Why don't you come with Vincent? Helen would love to see you and show off her latest acquisition."

"I'm sure she has other plans," Vincent quickly interjected. He could see why they called Sidney the Silver Fox. He had left Arkansas with nothing and had amassed a fortune in the oil industry with brain, grit, and ingenuity.

"I do have plans," Charlotte said dutifully, not meeting Vincent's gaze.

Hughes' shrewd eyes narrowed on Charlotte. "There's going to be a lot of people there. Some of them you may not have met. Fertile ground, Charlotte. Might be able to get a few donations. You know the political coffer could always use money and the excitement of new blood."

Charlotte didn't have to think long. People working in the political arena often became discouraged and fell by the wayside. If there was a chance to benefit the party, she couldn't turn her back on it. Vincent might be upset, but business was business. "I can be there later, if that's all right."

Hughes' green eyes sparkled with triumph. "We'll see you when we see you."

"Until tomorrow night, then. I won't keep you from business." Bracing herself, she turned to Vincent and almost sighed. Did he ever smile? His black eyes didn't look too happy behind his silver-rimmed glasses. "Thank you for seeing me. Good-bye."

"Good-bye."

"Good-bye, Mr. Hughes. I'll see you Saturday night."

"I'll call Helen when I get back to my office and give her the good news."

Charlotte stole another look at Vincent and caught him scowling at her. She offered him an apologetic smile. His expression didn't change.

Sighing, she walked from the office, aware that Vincent watched her with disapproval. Stopping briefly at Millicent's desk, she found out the affair was formal. Helen Hughes intended to show her eighteenth-century table and chairs off to their best advantage. Waving good-bye to Millicent, Charlotte headed for the elevator, her mind going back to Vincent.

Despite the hard gaze and occasional dark look from behind his glasses, Charlotte couldn't help but notice his handsome face and the lean, rugged body in beautifully tailored clothes. Vincent was one fine brother.

He was also trouble.

Impatient and somewhat annoyed with herself, she jabbed the elevator button. She didn't like the thoughts going around in her head or the answer to Vincent's question of why she had reacted to him the way she had. Leave it to a Yankee to cause a Southerner grief.

Saturday night Charlotte was typing on the computer and talking on the phone headset with the campaign manager for their party's candidate for city council when the red light by her keyboard began to flash. The doorbell.

Not for the first time did she experience mixed feelings about having the electrician install a signal light for the front doorbell. But she had a habit of tuning everything out when she was working on a project and had missed several important deliveries.

Not that there had been a chance of that happening yesterday or today. No matter how hard she tried, her mind kept straying. She knew the reason and it irritated her all the more because she knew *he* wasn't thinking about her.

She was in the middle of ten things as usual, but unlike usual she wasn't doing any of them well. Ending the phone conversation, she pulled off the headset and saved the list of possible donors to a fund-raiser for Senator William Upshaw.

The clock on the computer read 7:15. By eight-thirty she could probably get dressed and go to the Hugheses' party. She'd get there by nine-thirty, spend an hour socializing, then slip out. She didn't want to impose on Vincent's territory any more than necessary, but she had a duty to her party.

The doorbell rang just as she stepped onto the cool sandstone marble tile in the wide foyer. "Coming. Keep your shirt on."

Throwing the two dead bolts, she yanked the door open. "What is—" That was as far as she got. On her porch, in a tuxedo that sculpted his wide shoulders and long muscled legs perfectly, was the man who had distracted her all day.

She snapped her mouth shut. "Why aren't you at the Hugheses' party?"

"Because Helen and Sidney think the only way to get us both there is if we come together." His gaze unhurriedly tracked her from her mussed hair, to her white oversized blouse, to her black stretch pants and stopped at her bare feet. Her toenails were painted the same electrifying, eye-popping red as her fingernails gripping the door.

He lifted his head. "It seems she was right."

Charlotte's toes curled on the cool floor and she wished she had her heels on. It was a distinct disadvantage when craning your neck back to stare up at a man who easily topped six feet when you wanted to stare down your nose imperiously at him. "I have never missed an engagement and not called to cancel."

"Helen asked me to stop by to pick you up to make sure. She said she had called twice and your line was busy." He slid his hands into the pockets of his black pants. "It seems you don't have call waiting."

The way he said it made it seem like an accusation. "I do on my personal line, not on my business line. A person who calls me has my undivided attention." Why did the handsome ones always have to have something wrong with them? Vincent was too rigid and too judgmental.

The phone rang. The perfect excuse. "If you'll excuse me, I need to answer that. Good night. I'll let Helen know you dropped by." She started to close the door, but his hand stopped her.

"I think you better answer that first."

"The machine will get it."

"It might be Helen."

"I'll call her back once you leave."

"You're missing the point." Vincent frowned down at Charlotte with open impatience. "She wants you there tonight. She's as determined in her own way as Sidney is when he wants something. She says you liven up a party and Mary Lou wanted you there. I'm to bring you."

Charlotte's hazel eyes widened. "Mary Lou is back from the spa?"

"Isn't that what I just said?"

Charlotte thought of giving Vincent a look that would set him back on his polished heels, but the prospect of seeing Mary Lou was too delightful. Mary Lou was Sidney's eighty-nine-year-old mother. She was a hoot and a half. Mary Lou Carlaise from Pine Bluff, Arkansas, was a diamond in the rough and a very free spirit. "Why didn't you·say so earlier? I wouldn't miss it." She started to close the door again. Again, Vincent's hand stopped her.

"You've delivered your message," she said pointedly.

His black eyes narrowed. Charlotte could almost hear his teeth grind. "As I said, I'm to escort you."

Her eyebrow went up. "Sugar, since when did vice-presidents begin to double as escorts?"

"Since now, so just get dressed and we can leave."

Folding her arms, she stared up at him. "I don't take orders very well."

"Sidney said to remind you of the fertile ground."

He'd slipped that in nicely. Charlotte could almost admire him if he didn't irritate her. "I don't need you to take me."

"I never said you did." Vincent looked at the gold watch on his wrist. "I don't like being late, please get dressed so we can leave."

"Sugar, you must be hard of hearing, because I'm not going anyplace with you."

The scowl Charlotte expected didn't materialize. "Correct me if I'm wrong, but weren't you the one who came to my office yesterday offering words of apology? Was that just talk or did you want us to be friends?"

Charlotte gazed into the black eyes watching her and felt an unmistakable tug in the region of her heart. She honestly didn't know what she wanted them to be. "I'm sure you must be a busy man."

"That didn't seem to stop you from coming to my office and getting Millicent to let you stay so you could see me."

He had her there. What the heck? "It'll take thirty minutes for me to shower and get dressed."

"I was prepared to wait forty-five." He lifted a laptop.

Charlotte burst out laughing, then stepped aside. Perhaps there was hope for Vincent to lighten up after all. "Come on in and make yourself at home. Would you like something to drink?"

"No, thanks."

"The kitchen is this way. You can set up on the dinette table." She led him through the living room of comfortable overstuffed chairs, crystal, and fresh floral arrangements. "I'd hate to see you hunched over and getting a crook in your neck."

"I'll bet."

Since he had said the words without his usual sarcasm, Charlotte let them ride. "If you change your mind about something to drink there's an assortment in the refrigerator. Glasses are in the cabinet next to it."

"I'll be fine."

"Somehow I don't doubt that. I'll call Helen and tell her we're coming." She turned away and went to get dressed.

Vincent placed the carrying case on the round glass dining table, took out the laptop, and booted it up. He didn't get much further. It was difficult to work with abstract facts and figures when he was visualizing a very full dimensional figure getting dressed.

He slipped the single button free on his tuxedo and worked his shoulders. He wished she hadn't mentioned the part about taking a shower. The other night at the restaurant he might have thought she had done it on purpose, but now he wasn't so sure. Sidney was no fool; neither was his wife—or his secretary, for that matter. A woman of loose morals would not be accepted in any of their lives.

Leaning back in the chair, he glanced around the neat celery green and creamy oyster kitchen, then into the living room that carried out the same color scheme. The house was warm and inviting. The kind that you feel comfortable in taking off your shoes and kicking back. There was nothing showy or loud.

He'd been in enough homes to know that money couldn't buy taste. There were even a couple of antique pieces of furniture, including a Queen Anne corner chair and a Hepplewhite demilune table mixed with art by Arthello Beck, Jr., and Carole Joyce. And the style worked.

She hadn't been blowing smoke when she'd said she loved antiques. Oftentimes people trying to impress you said what they thought you wanted to hear or things to ingratiate themselves or to show how intelligent they were. He was forced to admit that apparently Charlotte did none of those things.

Who was the real Charlotte Duvall?

Rubbing the back of his neck, Vincent went back to the laptop, determined to complete the financial data for the benefits programs. If there was a way to reduce costs and still give the employees excellent coverage, it would be done. If not he'd look elsewhere. A company was only as good as its employees. He wouldn't jeopardize their health.

"Thirty-seven minutes."

Vincent looked up and was suddenly glad he was sitting down. The lady packed a wallop.

She wore a long, strapless black dress that fit over her lush breasts. Her hair was pulled back, silhouetting her beautiful face. Her lips, lush and inviting, were painted the same eye-catching red as he'd seen earlier on her nails. Long black gloves that reached almost to her shoulder completed the outfit.

She was elegant and alluring—and trouble.

Vincent did the only thing he thought safe. He turned back to the laptop and concentrated on shutting it down instead of gawking at the striking woman a few feet from him. Placing the laptop back in the case, he stood, picked it up, and finally turned to Charlotte.

"Do you need a wrap?"

Her smile wavered for a split second. "In the living room."

"Shall we go?" He walked toward her, but was careful not to touch.

"Certainly, we don't want to be late." Swirling, she went to the sofa in the living room and picked up her purse and a black silk chiffon scarf.

Vincent followed, his eyes somehow straying to the easy sway of her hips. Charlotte Duvall, as he had thought, definitely looked as tempting going as she did coming.

THREE

The smooth voice of Ella Fitzgerald filled the silence in the car as Vincent drove to Sidney and Helen's home. Charlotte, usually a brilliant conversationalist, could think of nothing to say. From the overhead lights on the freeway, she snuck peeks at Vincent. She came to the same conclusion she had when she first saw him: He was a handsome brown-skinned devil. And after so many men had tried to get her attention, it rankled a bit that he didn't seem to notice her . . .

There it was, she thought, finally admitting the reason for her inexcusable behavior at the restaurant. She hadn't liked being judged and dismissed by a man she found attractive. She could blame it on melancholy from Emma's impending wedding or blame it on what it was, a lapse in common sense. Vincent got to her. Of all men, why did her body have to pick a stuffed shirt? She sighed in frustration.

"You all right?"

"Yes," she quickly told him, and searched her mind for something to say to keep the conversation going.

He nodded and returned his attention to the busy traffic on Central Expressway. He drove competently and smoothly.

"You drive well," she said.

He cut his gaze to her again and Charlotte could have banged her head against the padded dash. Of course he drove well. He was from Boston. He'd have learned to drive in heavy traffic, snow, and ice. Dallas hadn't seen any appreciable snow in the five years she'd been here, and only one small ice storm that had all melted by the next afternoon. They didn't even close the public schools, much to Emma's students' dismay. Even with the infamous crazy motorists on the expressways, this was a cakewalk for him.

"Thanks," he finally said.

Charlotte had never considered herself a quitter. "We've already discussed the weather."

This time she got a small smile from him. "Yes, we have. You probably know more than you ever want to know about me, but what about you?"

"Youngest of four daughters from Charleston. Mother was a schoolteacher who quit to have my oldest sister, Ondine. Mama went back when school started in the fall. Since Ondine was late, as she always is, she was only six weeks old. Mama cried so hard at work, my father had to go pick her up. Daddy, a Realtor, took the opportunity to turn the garage into an office and open his own business. Mother became his secretary." Charlotte twisted toward Vincent as far as the seat belt would allow and smiled at the retelling of the story.

"Turns out it was the best thing that could have happened to the Duvall family. Daddy, as they say, can sell snowshoes in hell. But he's the most honest, loving man I know. By the time my third sister arrived, Daddy had an office and a secretary with two other Realtors."

Vincent hit the signal indicator and exited the expressway onto Loop 12. "My kind of man. How did you get into politics?"

"My cousin Jeb, my mother's youngest sister's oldest son, ran for city councilman in Charleston, and we all pitched in to help. I was a senior in high school. It was fun, and I found I had a knack for selling too, but what I sold could make the world a better place for people to live. So I majored in political science."

Vincent pulled up in front of a three-story mansion. Light blazed from every window. A valet dressed in a white polo shirt and dark slacks rushed to open his door. "I take it Jeb won."

"By a landslide."

Grinning at each other, they got out of the car.

A butler opened the heavily carved front door. Almost as soon as Vincent and Charlotte stepped onto the three-story foyer with limestone and marble flooring, Sidney was there to greet them. By his side was an elderly woman with coal black hair who was even more petite than Charlotte. She was dressed in a sequined red gown. Diamonds and blood-red rubies encircled her throat, wrists, and hung in shimmering color from her ears.

"'Bout time you got here!" she said by way of greeting.

Charlotte grinned and enveloped the small woman in a gentle hug. "Mary Lou, it's good to have you back. The spa must have been wonderful. You look sensational."

Mary Lou waved a hand. A ten-carat diamond winked. "I'm going to live until the day I die."

"Which will be a long, long time," Charlotte said, then glanced over her shoulder. "Have you met Vincent Maxwell yet?"

Sidney's mother held out her hand. "How do you do, Mr. Maxwell. Welcome to my son's home."

Vincent took the offered hand and held it as gently as he had seen Charlotte do. "Thank you. It's a pleasure." Releasing Mary Lou's hand, he leaned down to her. "Charlotte hadn't planned to come, but once she heard your name she couldn't wait to get here. I can see why."

Pleased, Mary Lou fluttered her lashes again. "Well, Sidney, it looks like you've finally found a live one. What do you do, Mr. Maxwell?"

"Please, call me Vincent." He looked at Sidney before continuing.

"Your son has given me the privilege of being Vice-President of Finance, in charge of reorganizing the financial structure of Ore-Tech, among other things."

"A number cruncher." The way Mary Lou said it wasn't a compliment.

Vincent surprised Charlotte by smiling. "Someone has to see that the lights stay on."

Shrewd gray eyes stared up at him. "I bet you do it very well, don't you?"

"I do try, Mrs. Hughes."

"Call me Mary Lou." She took his arm and looped her other hand through the curve of Charlotte's arm. "You've already met the rest of the guests. Charlotte can meet them before we go in to dinner. I'm dying to tell her about the young masseur I met in Hot Springs who wanted to be my boy toy."

Sidney's mouth gaped. Mary Lou turned away and missed the indulgent smile that followed.

"You think I shocked him, Charlotte?" Mary Lou asked, her steps slow on the gleaming hardwood floor as she led them to a window seat covered in a fresh spring blue and cream plaid fabric near the stone fireplace in the living room. The other guests were enjoying before-dinner drinks on the terrace.

"Definitely," Charlotte assured. "Vincent even has his mouth open," she teased.

Mary Lou squinted at Vincent. She refused to wear her glasses and didn't trust contacts. "Must have closed it."

Vincent laughed, a rich joyful sound that curled through Charlotte and warmed her like mulled wine. Her heart thumped in her chest. *Easy, girl.*

"I like you, Vincent." Mary Lou sat on the seat. Charlotte pushed one of several tapestry footstools scattered through the room under Mary Lou's small feet. "You won't be disappointed if I didn't have a shocking story to tell, will you?"

"I'll survive."

"Good. Now, Charlotte, what's going on with the party and what can I do to help?"

Charlotte told her. Check donations from companies might be illegal, but not from relatives of people who owned the company. Mary Lou had wisely let her son reinvest her money in his company and subsequently she was worth millions.

Fifteen minutes later, Helen announced dinner, beaming proudly as the guests got their first look at her mint-condition eighteenth-century Chippendale dining table and chairs. The lavish dining room offered a beautiful view of the lighted outdoor pool and gardens beyond. The table, set with Baccarat crystal and heirloom china, sparkled as much as Helen in her silver gown. Sidney was visibly pleased and proud.

Dinner was scrumptious. And although Charlotte hadn't gotten a chance to search out potential donors, she was enjoying the evening. Vincent, sitting to her left, was a good conversationalist and not once had she felt he disapproved of her in some way.

They were almost through with dessert, a marvelous chocolate mousse that Charlotte knew she'd have to work on her StairMaster to get off her hips, when tranquility screeched to a halt. Across from her, Ashley Green, the assistant vice-president of marketing services for strategic accounts, turned green, slapped her hand over her mouth, and rushed out of the room. Her husband ran after her.

Charlotte was already pushing back her seat. Vincent and the other men stood as she did. "I'll go see if I can help."

"Thank you," Helen said, but Charlotte had already turned away.

Charlotte found the couple in the powder room off the hallway near the kitchen. Ashley's full-skirted lavender-colored taffeta gown was billowed around her. Beside her on his knees as well was her husband, holding her long auburn hair out of her face and harm's way with one hand and the other around her waist. He looked almost as pale as she did.

Charlotte wet one of the thick hand towels on the black marble vanity and knelt beside them to press the cool cloth to the woman's face in between her bouts of illness. Mutely, her husband offered his thanks.

Soon there were only dry heaves from Ashley. Still on her knees, she leaned weakly into her husband's arms. Tears coursed down her pale cheeks.

"Please don't cry," Charlotte soothed.

Tears fell faster. "I'm so sorry, Anthony."

"Shhh, you and the baby are what counts," he consoled.

"But this position is what I've worked for. I've only been assistant vice-president for a year." Ashley shook her auburn head in despair. "This shouldn't have happened. We just bought the new house—"

"It doesn't matter," he interrupted, brushing his lips tenderly against her forehead. "Things will work out."

Charlotte felt as if she were intruding on a very private moment. She pushed to her feet and stepped away from the couple. "Shall I tell the valet to bring your car around?"

"Thank you," Anthony said.

Ashley's weak voice stopped Charlotte when she was almost out the door. "Charlotte?"

She turned. "Yes?"

"Please don't tell anyone."

"Honey, they'll have to know sooner or later."

"Please," she repeated, her pleading gaze on Charlotte.

Another woman trying to break through the glass ceiling and having a rough time. "I won't."

To Ashley's obvious embarrassment, everyone came out to the car to see her off. She mumbled apologies about something she ate for lunch, then ducked her head. Her husband said nothing, but his tight lips told the story. He wasn't too pleased with his wife's not telling them she was pregnant. When they walked back inside, one of the wives mentioned that Ashley had been sick at the barbecue two weeks ago as well.

"Would anyone care for coffee?" Mary Lou asked.

"I'd love a cup," Charlotte said, catching a thankful look from Helen.

However, as the evening progressed, Charlotte sensed by the preoccupied looks on the other guests' faces, and their hosts', that they were all thinking of the possible reason for Ashley's illness and coming to the same conclusion. These men were shrewd and observant. Ashley's attempt to conceal her pregnancy had probably been futile. She was only fooling herself.

Charlotte knew she was right when Sara, the wife of the vice-president of human resources, whispered, "I think she's pregnant."

Charlotte didn't have to ask why the middle-aged woman was whispering. The men were in the game room shooting billiards. Mary Lou, spotted ten points, was partnered with Vincent. Helen had gone in to see if they needed anything. The women in the enclosed terrace amid tropical plants that reached the apex of the twenty-five-foot ceiling nodded in agreement.

"Poor thing." This from Nancy, wife of the president of business markets. She was in her mid-thirties and her balding husband looked to be in his early sixties. He seemed to be as taken with her as she was with herself.

"You make it sound as if it's the worst thing that could happen to her," Charlotte said, aware that she was the outsider here, but that had never stopped her from speaking her mind in the past.

"They live off Ashley's salary. Anthony has been trying to make a profit from that bookstore of his for years." Nancy Brisby fingered her blond hair behind her ear. The diamond in her ear was as big as a dime. "She could have done better."

Charlotte clamped down on her lower lip to keep her thoughts behind her teeth. *So could your husband.*

Sara threw Nancy an annoyed look, but the other woman was gazing in a jeweled compact mirror, putting on an unnecessary layer of plum-colored lipstick, and didn't notice. "Ashley has another child, David, the cutest three-year-old you'd ever want to see. Her husband didn't like her going back to work when David was six weeks old, but they adjusted because Ashley has always aimed to shatter the glass ceiling and thought being out longer might jeopardize her job," Sara explained.

"So, they'll adjust again," Charlotte said, but Sara and the other women looked doubtful. Remembering Ashley's words in the bathroom, Charlotte was afraid the women might be right.

They heard the clicking of Helen's heels on the hardwood flooring and Sara launched into the latest rebellious act of her thirteen-year-old: wanting to get her eyebrow pierced. Everyone laughed as the women traded stories on the trials and tribulations of parenthood, but from their smiling, proud faces none of them would change a thing.

"None of you work outside the home?" Charlotte asked, although she was reasonably sure of the answer.

They all shook their heads of perfectly coiffed hair. Their reasons were varied, but mainly it was because of the husband's job. By the nature of their man's position, they entertained a great deal, and then there were the children. There were just so many hours in a day to get things done.

Charlotte thought it was rather sad that two of the women had given up their own promising careers to be at the beck and call of their busy husbands. Although they were quick to point out they hadn't minded, Charlotte wasn't so sure.

It had been her father's suggestion but her mother's *decision* after Ondine was born to stay home. No man was going to dictate to Charlotte that she *had* to give up her career to stay at home with the children unless that was what *she* wanted.

As the conversation progressed it became abundantly clear that, though the women might empathize with Ashley, not one of them could truly understand why she just didn't chuck it all and go home to raise David and his future little brother or sister. Charlotte thought it was more than money. None of them seemed to understand that you might give up on a dream quietly, but if someone tried to take it away, you'd fight with everything to stop them.

With the exception of Ashley becoming ill, Vincent had had a surprisingly enjoyable evening. Charlotte had blended in well with the women. She had certainly been a hit with the men. Even Paul Brisby, who had recently married a much younger woman, couldn't seem to keep his eyes off Charlotte.

Men noticed Charlotte. Any man who married her would always have to wonder and worry about her, but that wasn't his problem. For him, life was good. He was settling in nicely at the firm, and he and Sidney got along well. And it appeared he was liked by Mary Lou as well. Vincent shook his dark head and chuckled.

"What?" Charlotte asked, surprised by the sudden sound of Vincent's laughter and the jittery feeling it sent through her nervous system.

"Sidney's mother is a hustler. She no more needed to be spotted ten points than the Black Widow."

"Black Widow?"

"The moniker of women's world billiard champion Jennifer Chen," he answered, then maneuvered around an SUV on the five-lane Central Expressway. "It's a good thing we weren't playing for money."

Charlotte's lips curved upward. "She likes to tease."

"She likes you. You took up a lot of time with her tonight."

"She's fun; besides, elderly people are revered in the South. And if they're a little unorthodox like Mary Lou, they give the family character and color." Charlotte chuckled. "We don't hide our relatives who are different; we enjoy and appreciate them."

"So I noticed." Vincent's friends and associates would have been horrified to have their elderly mother flirting with their business associates, then hustling them at pool. "Nothing Mary Lou did seemed to embarrass or annoy Sidney."

"Did it embarrass or annoy you?"

Vincent thought he heard a bit of censure in Charlotte's voice. A quick glance told him he wasn't mistaken. Her hazel eyes glinted. "No. As you said, she livened things up." He paused. "It was nice of you to check on Ashley." At the time he had been surprised that none of the other women who had known Ashley longer had gone to help.

"Anyone would have done the same," Charlotte said simply.

Vincent wasn't so sure. Deep in thought, he turned onto Charlotte's tree-lined street. "Ashley is top-notch at what she does. It would be a shame to lose her."

"Why would you lose her?"

Vincent favored Charlotte with a look that intelligent people bestowed on those with less than two brain cells to rub together. "The company is going through a transitional phase. We need every key person at the top of their game."

"You heard her; it was something she ate. She'll be better tomorrow." Charlotte hoped she was right. Ashley had looked so desperate.

"She's been late every day this week, and twice I've been trying to work on a report with her and she had to rush to the ladies' room," Vincent said. "Doesn't sound like it's something she ate that's the problem."

Poor Ashley, Charlotte thought. *Everyone knows.*

"She's lucky she's advanced this far. Maybe it's time she stayed home. Her little boy must miss her terribly."

"I'm sure she makes up for the time spent away from him and her husband when she's home."

"Time lost can never be regained," he said pragmatically.

"Women can work and take care of their families."

Vincent was shaking his head before Charlotte finished. "A

woman's place is in the home. Women trying to prove they're as good as men in the workplace is what's contributing to the breakdown of the family."

Charlotte almost bit her tongue off trying to remain calm before speaking. "Then you believe a woman should stay at home and have a gourmet meal and well-behaved children waiting for her husband when he gets home."

"Exactly."

"Bull!"

Vincent's head whipped around so fast Charlotte thought he might get whiplash. It would serve him right for his antiquated way of thinking. "Women have just as much right to a career as men," Charlotte pointed out fiercely. "What's wrong with a man cooking a meal or changing a diaper? This isn't the Stone Age where the woman stays home to birth and raise the kids and the big, strong man protects them and drags home T. Rex's hindquarter to roast over a spit."

"Men are supposed to care for the women and the home. My mother never worked. Yours didn't after your sister was born, and neither will my wife," Vincent said heatedly.

"With that attitude you probably won't get one."

His mouth tightened. "I'm not looking for one."

"That's good, because no woman in her right mind would have a husband as antiquated and stuffy as you." Folding her arms, she turned to look at the window. *Opinionated sexist.*

She remained in that position until Vincent's car stopped in the circular driveway in front of her double doors. Charlotte didn't wait for him to open her car door. By the time he caught up with her, she was halfway up the steps.

Opening the front door, she turned, her body rigid with indignation. "Good night, Vincent, and thank you for picking me up."

"You've never met Ashley before tonight; why are you being so difficult?"

"Injustice is injustice. I don't have to know the person," she flared. "But I guess coming from the North, you wouldn't understand."

His mouth had that pinched look again, but all he said was, "I think you should go inside before one of us says something that can't be taken back."

Her chin lifted at his annoying way of ordering her around. Light brown eyes narrowed. "Sure thing, sugar." Going inside, she flicked off the porch light and threw the dead bolts, angrier than she ever remembered being in her life. Stripping off her gloves, she headed for her bedroom. She reached the doorway and pulled up short, a sudden thought of Emma and Brian, and why she'd been trying to be nice to Vincent in the first place, coming to her.

Heck! She had done it again.

Whirling, she raced to unlock the front door, then rushed through it and straight into something hard and unmovable. A scream tore from her throat.

"Charlotte, it's me."

While her heart tried to beat out of her chest, she felt the alignment of his hard, muscular body against her, his large hands on her bare arms. Her heart then raced for an entirely different reason. Awareness shimmered though her. "I–I was afraid you'd already left."

"I was waiting until the light came on at the other end of the house."

"Oh," was all Charlotte could manage as fear turned to other more dangerous emotions.

Vincent made no move to release her. Her luscious breasts were pillowed against his chest, one of her legs sandwiched between his. Her face, tipped up to his, was shadowed by the ornamental shrubs on either side of the small porch. Someone had watered the grass recently and the smell was earthy and elemental and oddly arousing.

"You make me angrier than any person I've ever met," he finally said.

She had to moisten her lips before she could speak. "You seem to have the same effect on me."

"Why do you suppose that is?"

"You're from the North and I'm from the South?" she ventured, trying to hang on to the conversation and not keep wondering what his mouth would taste like against hers.

"Perhaps." His hand lifted to her face. She trembled beneath his touch. Her eyelids drifted closed. Vincent stared at temptation and trouble. He could afford neither. Gently he eased her away. When her eyes opened, he released her and stepped off the porch, and took a deep breath, hoping it would clear the tantalizing scent of jasmine and the wrong woman from his nostrils, from his mind.

"Was there something you wanted to say?" he asked quietly, trying to forget how warm and soft Charlotte had felt in his arms.

"I–I wanted to apologize." She couldn't see his face clearly, but she imagined his eyebrow shot up. She sighed heavily. "For Emma and Brian's sake, I hope this is the last time."

"One can always hope."

Charlotte tried not to sigh again. "One of the women tonight had some unflattering things to say about Ashley and it made me angry. I didn't say anything to her, then I jumped all over you."

He folded his arms. "Why me and not her?"

"Because I didn't want to jeopardize your standings in the company, but when we began talking about women in the workplace I got upset all over again," she explained. "You are wrong, you know."

"Never bite your tongue for me," Vincent told her. "I can take care of myself and furthermore, I'm not against women in the workplace, only those in positions that require them to be away from home more than they are there."

"Please stop." She held up both hands. "We'll be arguing again, and I'll have to apologize again."

Smiling, he unfolded his arms. "I guess we agree that we disagree and let it go at that."

"Deal."

"How long do you think this time will last?"

"Depends on how long it takes you to annoy me," she said with complete honesty.

Sudden laughter rippled from his mouth. "Charlotte, as Mary Lou said, you do liven things up."

"I'm glad we got this settled," she said.

"So am I."

She stared at him; he stared at her. "Well, I guess I'll say good night."

"Good night, Charlotte."

Charlotte hesitated for a moment longer, then went inside the house and locked the front door. Then, remembering what Vincent had said, she went to her bedroom and turned on the light. She didn't hear the sound of his car starting and wondered if he had gone, just as she wondered why he hadn't kissed her, and if the opportunity would present itself again.

Plopping on her bed, she stared up at the ceiling, a slow smile curving her lips. She certainly hoped so.

FOUR

She was all that he desired, all that he wanted. She responded eagerly to the lightest touch of his hands, the gentlest brush of his lips. He'd fantasized, planned, and now she was in his arms, draped only in moonlight. Her breathing was as ragged as his, her need as great. He'd give them the release they both craved, but not yet. He wanted to savor the taste, the textures, the scent that was uniquely hers.

"I need you," she said, her voice low, hushed, urgent.

"I need you too," he answered, his voice tight and guttural. He reveled in the demanding nails raking his back.

"Vincent, is that you?"

Vincent came awake instantly. He stared at the phone clutched in his fist as if he had never seen one. Groaning in part embarrassment, part disappointment, he sucked in a gulp of air and spoke into the receiver. "Yes."

"I—I didn't mean to disturb you. If you're busy I can call back when you . . . er finish . . . I mean later."

Vincent closed his eyes, then opened them and stared down at the papers scattered on the desk in his home office in his condo.

He'd fallen asleep while working on them. A rarity. His body didn't usually shut off until he allowed it to do so. Instinctively he'd answered the phone while still asleep. And dreaming, a very erotic dream.

"Vincent, should I call back later?"

His eyes opened at the continued hesitancy in Charlotte's voice and realized what she must have thought when he answered the phone the way he had. His hand rubbed the back of his neck impatiently. She was the reason behind his loss of sleep for the past week. He kept dreaming that they were in bed together with nothing separating them but a thin sheen of perspiration after a marathon bout of hot sex just like tonight.

"Vincent?"

"I'm here." He took three long breaths, hoping to focus his mind elsewhere and forget about the problem below his waist. It didn't work. "What is it, Charlotte?"

They hadn't spoken or seen each other since he had dropped her off at her home last Saturday night.

"Brian and Emma had a fight. Brian is overdosing on coffee at a restaurant around the corner from her house, and Emma is probably crying her eyes out. We have to do something."

Vincent rubbed eyes burning and gritty from lack of sleep. "We?"

"You're the best man and I'm the maid of honor," she told him unnecessarily. "It's our duty to see them through any problems that may stop them from getting to the church on time and getting married."

"I'm not sure helping them over an argument qualifies." He glanced at the Seth Thomas clock on his desk. 2:15 A.M. Just one night he'd like to get to bed before midnight.

"Anything qualifies. I should know."

"Meaning?" He waited for an answer, but none came. "You're still there?"

"I'm still here." Her voice had definitely taken on a weary note.

A frisson of unease went through Vincent. Had he been right about Brian being attracted to Charlotte? "Are you telling me everything? Why didn't Brian call me?"

"He didn't want to disturb you."

"Apparently you didn't feel the same way," he told her, feeling lighter despite the situation.

"I thought he meant paperwork. I didn't know he meant you'd have company."

Vincent was caught in a delicate dilemma. He could explain he was alone, but then he'd also have to explain why he'd answered the phone the way he did. "Never mind that. Where's Brian now?"

"At the Yellow Rose. It's off Interstate 20 and Westmoreland."

"I'll find it." Vincent came to his feet. "Go back to sleep. I'll call you in the morning."

There was a slight pause. "Thank you, Vincent, and I'm sorry about disturbing you." The line went dead.

Vincent rolled down his shirt sleeves, feeling inexplicably like a coward who had kicked a puppy.

Twenty-three minutes later, with the help of his car's navigation system, Vincent pulled up in front of the all-night restaurant. The neon sign of a single stemmed rose winked on and off. Several cars and trucks dotted the parking lot. One of them was Brian's Alfa Romeo. Vincent had been hoping that his cousin had already gone home.

Getting out of the car, he activated the lock. His usual brisk steps slowed as he walked to the glass double front doors. He had no idea what he would say to Brian or if he should say anything at all. Perhaps this was for the best. Yet, somehow the obvious concern in Charlotte's voice had pulled him here as much as his love for his cousin.

Inside he scanned the Formica-topped tables looking for his cousin. A clean-shaven man in his mid-thirties with close-cropped black hair wearing a white shirt and black slacks came out from behind a glass casing filled with pies and rushed up to him. "Are you Vincent Maxwell?"

"Yes."

Relief clearly shone on the man's dark face. "Great. They're over here."

They. It appeared the lovers' tiff was over and Charlotte had gotten him here for nothing while she—

Charlotte glanced up, saw Vincent glaring at her, and her spirits plummeted even lower. They had been spiraling downhill ever since she'd called and he had a woman with him. At two in the morning, it wasn't hard to guess why.

She nudged Brian. "Vincent's here."

The young man's head came up and he stared at his cousin with misery in his brown eyes. "I don't know what to do."

Charlotte patted his lanky arm. "We'll think of something, won't we, Vincent?"

Vincent slid into the booth on the other side of Brian. "I thought you were home."

She shrugged elegant shoulders beneath a black shirt that clung to all the places Vincent had dreamed of touching. "Fred called me and here I am. But that's not important; we have to get Brian and Emma back together."

"She gave me back my ring." Brian's hand was clutched in a fist on top of the table beside a half-empty mug of coffee.

"Charlotte, can I see you for a moment?" Vincent didn't wait for an answer. He slid out of the booth and went to a corner table for two in the back of the nearly empty restaurant. Holding a chair for Charlotte, he waited while she sank onto the padded seat, then took his seat across from her, pushed his glasses up on his nose, and placed his folded hands on the table. "Explain to me why you're here?"

She started to say that wasn't of any consequence, but the stubborn set of Vincent's jaw told her she'd just be wasting her time. "Fred Bowers, the manager, is a good friend to all three of us. We go to the same church and are in the same singles group. After Brian had been here for an hour, refusing to go home, Fred called me. I called Emma, but her phone is off the hook. I got here about thirty minutes before I called you because Brian still refuses to go home. The rest you know."

"Any idea what caused the problem?"

Charlotte ran her hand through her hair. "None. Brian's not talking."

"Maybe her parents know." Vincent shook his head to the waitress who appeared. Charlotte did the same.

With a weary sigh, Charlotte leaned back against her seat. "If so, they probably won't help. Emma is an only child and adored by both parents. She's always led a sheltered, protected life. She went to school at a local university and still lives at home. Her parents made it no secret that they thought she was too young to get married and that she and Brian should wait a couple of years. Neither would object if the wedding were canceled. Especially her father."

"They *are* young," Vincent said, drumming his fingers on the table.

"But neither of them are impulsive or stupid. They love each other and what's more, they're good for each other." Arms braced on the table, she stared across at Vincent. "Except with her kindergarten class, Emma was painfully shy and had few friends. Brian introduced her to his many friends and she's helped him find the direction he needed in life. He's not just about having fun anymore, but doing something worthwhile with his life. He's mentoring at her school and has definite career goals."

"You've never had any of those doubts, worries, or hang-ups, have you?"

"No, I've been fortunate and very, very blessed," she answered, wondering where the conversation was going.

He stood. "Wait here and let me have a go at it."

"Thank you, Vincent." She bit her lower lip. "I'm sorry about disturbing you."

He stared down at her. She was beautiful, sensitive, and caring. He was coming to understand why Brian's opinion of her was so high. She'd never turn her back on a friend. Fred had known that, and Vincent finally knew it too. "I'm not."

Going back to the booth, he slid in beside his despondent cousin. Brian had his head bowed, his hands in his lap. Vincent had negotiated deals in the past and figured he'd treat this the same way he did when they hit a snag. Go for broke.

"You still love her?"

Brian nodded without lifting his head.

"Then are you going to sit here and mope all night or are you going to go back to her house and try to straighten out whatever it is that caused this?"

"She doesn't want to talk to me."

"Then just tell her to listen," Vincent said. "Negotiate. Find common ground. Your love for each other should be a good start. Apologize. Then kiss her until she gives in."

His cousin lifted his head and stared hard at Vincent.

"What?" Vincent asked, warily.

"I just never figured you had to spend time soothing women," Brian answered.

Vincent saw no reason to tell his cousin he was right. He simply didn't have time for that sort of thing. "Come on. I'll go back with you. At least, if her parents call the cops, I can post bail for you."

Vincent hadn't thought Charlotte would go home and let him and Brian go see Emma, but he had given it a good try. As he suspected, she'd adamantly refused. She could ride with him and Brian or follow in her car. His choice. Since Vincent worried about her being on the road by herself, he told her to get in the backseat and put Brian in the front.

In the end, Charlotte's presence was what saved Emma's father from calling the police and having Brian *and* Vincent arrested. Charlotte had one simple request of the irate man: Could he please see if Emma was asleep? If she was, they'd leave, but if she was still awake and as miserable as Brian, then please allow her to speak with him. Emma's happiness was what they all wanted.

Emma's father had closed the front door without commenting, but a short while later the door opened and Emma stood there in her stocking feet, her eyes red and lids swollen, her blue dress wrinkled, her shoulder-length light brown hair mussed.

Brian took one look at the miserable picture she presented and said, "I'll die if you don't love me."

Emma turned into her waiting father's arms.

Brian's hand unclenched. The engagement ring fell from his fingers onto the sidewalk. His body wavered as if he might fall, then he turned and slowly walked back toward Vincent's car.

"Emma, if you let him get away instead of working out your problems, perhaps I was wrong about you," Charlotte said fiercely. "Perhaps you *are* too immature to know how to love a man. Running away never solved anything. Make sure this is what you want because you may not get a second chance. Once word gets out he's available, the single women in church will be all over him."

With fire in her eyes Emma whirled around. "Teresa already was."

"What?" The shocked word erupted from Vincent, Charlotte, and Emma's parents.

Midway down the sidewalk, Brian spun back around. "She came on to me at the movie theater and I told her to get lost. She saw you, and you played right into her spiteful hands."

"You were about to kiss her when I came out of the ladies' room," Emma accused, stepping away from her father in her righteous anger.

"No, I wasn't. I was trying to get her arms from around my neck. Why would I want to touch another woman, let alone kiss her, when I have you?" Brian said, coming forward until he was almost nose to nose with Emma. "I love you. Can't you get that through your stubborn head?"

Emma spluttered. "Don't you dare call me nam—" He jerked her into his arms, silencing her words with his lips.

"Take your hands off her!" Emma's father started toward them but Charlotte threw her arms around his neck. His wife grabbed him around the waist from behind. By the time he managed to untangle the arms of the determined women, Emma was clinging to Brian as desperately as he was clinging to her.

"He might make a go in labor relations after all," Vincent murmured with a pleased smile.

"He was fooling around with another woman!" Mr. Hamilton shouted.

Mrs. Hamilton touched his arm and quietly asked him, "Douglas, were you fooling around with Charlotte a moment ago?"

Much as his daughter had done earlier, he spluttered his outrage. "Melissa, you know darn well I wasn't. I was trying to get her arms from around . . ." Understanding dawned. With one look at the embracing couple, he shook his head in obvious defeat and curved his arm around his wife's shoulder. "Looks like there's going to be a wedding after all."

"Don't you just hate it when women are right?" Vincent said with a grin. He looked at Brian and Emma still locked in each other's arms, the kiss showing no signs of ending, then thumped his cousin on the back. "There'll be enough time for that. Now, we need to find Emma's ring."

"Oh, my goodness!" Brian straightened, panic in his face.

"My ring!" Emma cried frantically, pressing the palms of her hands over her face.

"I'll get a flashlight." Emma's mother rushed back into the house.

"Oh, Daddy, we'll never find it!"

Her father lovingly patted her on the back. "Don't you worry, baby girl, we'll find your ring if we have to take up every blade of grass."

They didn't have to do that, but it did take fifteen minutes of searching on hands and knees, fingers combing through thick blades of St. Augustine grass that hadn't been cut in a week.

Vincent located the ring, stone down in the tiny crevice between the grass and the edge of the sidewalk. "Found it."

With a cry of delight, Emma rushed over. Brian snatched the ring from Vincent's hand, gallantly went down on one knee, and slipped the ring on her finger. "I'll love you always."

"Brian, I'm so sorry," Emma said, tears in her voice and in her eyes. "I'll never doubt you or take my ring off again."

Vincent glanced at Charlotte and Emma's mother. Both were sniffing. He looked at Emma's father, who looked as perplexed and uncomfortable as he felt. He handed Charlotte his white monogrammed handkerchief with one hand, then, with the other, lifted Brian to his feet.

"Charlotte needs to get home and I doubt you want to tax the patience of your future in-laws any further. Good night, everyone."

Grinning, Brian allowed himself to be pulled away. "Thank you, Mr. and Mrs. Hamilton. Emma, I'll call you as soon as I get home."

She threw kisses and would have followed her fiancé to Vincent's car, but Charlotte caught her by her dress. "Brian lives twenty minutes from here. That'll give you just enough time to pick out a sensational outfit for church tomorrow, roll up your hair, then put some cucumber slices on your eyes. You don't want to give that shameless Teresa any reason to think her plan might have worked, do you?"

Emma turned to Charlotte. "It almost did."

Charlotte smiled. "Almost doesn't count."

"Thank you and Vincent for caring." Emma gave her a hug. "I couldn't have chosen a more perfect maid of honor."

Loneliness hit Charlotte again. Always a maid of honor and never a bride. Somehow she managed to smile, then rushed to

Vincent's car and got into the backseat trying not to think of the empty house waiting for her.

When Vincent pulled up behind Charlotte's white Lexus in the circular driveway it was almost four in the morning. He met her on the sidewalk as she dug into her oversized black purse. "What are you looking for?"

"My house keys."

"They aren't on your key ring?" He frowned as she continued to rummage through her bag.

Shaking her head, she never looked up. "Too easy for some un-scrupulous person in valet or the auto shop to make a duplicate. Here it is." Lifting the key, she opened the door and turned. "Well, good night and thanks again."

"You don't have an alarm system?" he questioned. From down the street came the barking of a dog.

She made a face and pushed her curly auburn hair behind her ear. "Yes, but I forgot to activate it when I left tonight."

"It wasn't on last Saturday night when I brought you home ei-ther," he said, censure in his voice. "It's senseless and careless having a system and not turning it on."

"Don't start being difficult again."

He peered down at her. "I'm never difficult."

She rolled her eyes. "Spoken like a man."

"I am a man."

She had no comeback to that. He was a man and a very tempt-ing one at that, but he was taken. Southern women never poached. "Good night, Vincent. Your friend is probably still waiting on you." Charlotte knew she would have been.

He stepped closer, surrounding her with his arousing clean male scent. "There is no one waiting for me."

Instead of assuring her, his words had the opposite effect. "You're into one-night stands?"

The horror and accusation in her voice had him grinding his teeth. "No."

"But I—"

"I was dreaming! All right?" he practically snarled.

She blinked, then her lips curved upward in a slow sultry smile. She dreamed too. "All right."

He stared at her lips, glistening and inviting. "You're trying to tempt me, Charlotte."

"Whatever do you mean?"

Her Southern accent had thickened. He thought of long lazy nights of loving with him deep inside her and her straining to get closer. His body went as hard and as stiff as forged steel. He would have sworn neither of them moved, but somehow their faces were closer, their lips almost . . . All he had to do was . . .

Their lips touched, the gentle joining of mouths. Their bodies gradually sank together as first one tongue then the other tentatively explored the shape, the heat, the drugging desire to have more, to taste more.

On tiptoe, Charlotte wound her slender arms around Vincent's neck. One of his strong arms slid around her tiny waist and anchored her snugly against his hardness. His other hand tunneled through her thick hair. He deepened the kiss, taking them both deeper into passion, into need.

With consummate expertise he plundered her mouth and scattered her thoughts. Her body quivered like a taut bow, caught and held by the will of this man. A willing, eager participant, Charlotte pressed closer to the hard, muscular length of him. He felt good and made her feel even better.

Vincent held on to his sanity by sheer force of will. Somehow, he got them through the door and shoved it closed behind them. A kiss had never taken him under so fast or so completely.

Charlotte was fire and desire in his arms, burning out of control and he was enjoying every mind-blowing second. He couldn't get enough. Groaning, his hands slid under the black spandex top and closed over her breasts. She moaned and he moaned right along with her.

He had to see. He looked down and almost lost it. The black scrap of lacy confection didn't even try to hide the creamy swell of her lush breasts. His thumb grazed over a nipple. It pouted immediately for him. Charlotte's breath hissed through her teeth. So sensitive. Probably tasted like chocolate mixed with whipped cream.

Lips parted, his head bent. He had to taste and find out.

The phone rang.

The strident sound was like a blast of frigid air. It rang again. Eyes closed, Vincent reined in his desire with an iron will. Straightening, he withdrew his hands and pulled down her blouse, then looked up into her dazed eyes. "Should I say I'm sorry?"

She drew in a gulp of air past lips that were damp and swollen from his kisses before she could speak. "Only if you are."

For once in his short relationship with Charlotte, Vincent didn't have to ponder his answer. "No."

Relief swept across her face. "Good, because neither am I."

The answering machine activated on the fifth ring. "Charlotte, this is Emma. Brian is on the other line. We wanted to make sure you got home safely. Hope we didn't disturb you."

"Thanks again, Charlotte," Brian said. "I know Vincent made sure you got home all right, so we'll call him."

Quickly crossing the living room, Charlotte snatched up the receiver. "I'm here."

She stared back at Vincent and wished she was still in his arms, letting him drive her crazy with his mouth and hands. Who would have thought a conservative man like Vincent could kiss like the scoundrel every woman secretly dreams of finding and taming? He certainly didn't dress like one.

Tonight he wore a pink diamond-patterned shirt with a white collar and cuffs. He even had on a properly knotted tie at four in the morning. On another man, she would have thought the shirt too feminine, but on Vincent anything looked good. But she'd bet he'd look even better without anything on.

His black eyes darkened as if he knew exactly what she was thinking. The temperature of her body shot up again.

"I'm sorry, what did you say?" she asked, having no idea what either Brian or Emma had said after she answered the phone. "No. You didn't disturb me. Yes, I'm fine. Good night. I'll see you in the morning at church." She replaced the receiver, then linked her fingers and stared across the room at Vincent.

"I suppose this has happened between a maid of honor and a best man before," he said casually.

All the mellow feeling inside Charlotte shattered. "Are you making a generalization or an accusation?"

"Watch it or you'll be apologizing again," he told her, the corners of his mouth slanting upward.

"Since I hate redundancy, good night, Vincent, and thanks for your help." She went to the door, opened it, then stepped to one side. "Church starts at eight."

He didn't move. "We were doing pretty good for a while tonight. You think we'll ever make it for an entire evening without an argument?"

Because she saw amusement instead of censure, she answered honestly. "I continue to hope so."

Crossing the room, he stopped in front of her. Strong, elegant fingers lifted her chin. "So do I." His kiss was as fleeting as it was sweet. "Good night, Charlotte."

Her eyelashes slowly fluttered back upward. "Good night, Vincent."

With a gently teasing smile he stared down at her. "At the risk of starting another argument, make sure you lock the door after me."

With a reckless smile like that he could probably ask her anything, she thought. "Since you put it like that." She locked the door behind him, then raced down the hall to cut on the light in her bedroom.

Vincent was turning out to be very interesting. She couldn't wait until she saw him again, kissed him again. He'd probably call after church, maybe ask her to dinner. She couldn't wait.

Vincent didn't call Sunday or Monday. By Tuesday Charlotte vacillated between annoyance and concern. By Wednesday afternoon she knew he hadn't been unexpectedly called out of town on business nor was he lying broken in a hospital. He was well and working hard, according to Brian, who had been at Emma's house when Charlotte went by to take Emma for the final fitting of her wedding gown.

Thursday morning, Charlotte frowned down at the blue phone in her office. She was tempted to just pick it up and call, but that was as far as it went. Southern women did not chase men. It was acceptable to let them know that you were interested by a look or a comment that you hoped to see them again, but that was the extent of things. Their kiss had certainly said that and more.

Why hadn't he called? She knew when a man was interested in her. Had she done something to turn him off?

The phone rang. Her heart gave one hard knock against her rib cage before caller ID identified the call as coming from Senator Upshaw's office. Annoyed with herself *and* Vincent, she picked up the phone. She wasn't wasting another second trying to figure out why Vincent hadn't tried to contact her. Nor was she letting him stop her from doing her job.

Thirty minutes later, she hung up the phone, the date for the senator's fund-raising dinner finalized. The western-themed gala would take place downtown at the venerable Adolphus Hotel's posh grand ballroom on August eighteenth.

Spinning around, she picked up a disk with the names of businesses that had political action committees and shoved it into the disk drive. As she worked through the list of companies with PACs, Ore-Tech's name came up. Her mouth firmed, then she continued. Vincent apparently wasn't giving her a thought. She was going to do the same with him and do her job. If he came to the shower the singles group from their church was giving Emma and Brian on Friday night, she'd show him a thing or two about tampering with a Southern woman's affection!

Vincent heard Charlotte's laughter before he saw her. He worked his way through the friendly crowd of young people in the sprawling ranch house of the senior pastor of their church until he was only a few feet away from her. As he had come to expect, she was surrounded by four attentive men in the spacious kitchen. In the past jealousy had never been an emotion he'd had to deal with in his personal or business life.

He was dealing with it now.

He had purposely stayed away from her since last Saturday night. He told himself he had too much work to do, which he had. But it was also to see if he would miss Charlotte. He had. Constantly.

He had come tonight because Brian had not wanted a bachelor party and his singles group at church had decided on a joint shower for the engaged couple. Brian had informed Vincent his attendance was a necessary part of the duties as best man. However, seeing Charlotte, Vincent knew he wouldn't have been able to stay away even if he wanted to.

She had on white again. This time it was a backless ruffled silk dress that was also strapless. Fleetingly, he wondered what kept the dress up and how soon it was going to be before he found out. He started toward her.

Charlotte had seen Vincent across the room staring at her. *Good.* Despite the men surrounding her, she managed to make sure

Vincent got a good look at her dress. She'd teach him not to kiss her like his life depended on it and then not call.

"Oh, Henry, sugar, you do say the funniest things." She'd known Henry for five years and the other three men almost as long. They were as safe and comfortable as a ratty bathrobe. Not like the dangerous man approaching.

"Good evening, Charlotte, gentlemen. I don't believe we've met." Vincent extended his hand to the man nearest him, and in a matter of seconds the handshakes and introductions were complete. "Do you mind if I steal Charlotte for a moment or two? As maid of honor and best man, we need to talk. Reverend Bailey said we could use the game room."

In his usual high-handed way, Vincent didn't wait for an answer. Gently encircling her upper forearm with long, lean fingers, he pulled her away from her admirers. Shivers of awareness raced up her arm from his fingertips.

Charlotte didn't want to be alone with Vincent, but she didn't wish to make a scene either. She wasn't as detached toward him as she would have wished. He looked too good in his wheat-colored suit and her body recalled too well the pleasure he could give. He closed the door to the game room behind them. Her uneasiness increased dramatically.

"What's so important that it couldn't wait?"

"This." His lips descended.

Charlotte twisted her head. His lips missed her mouth, but she trembled as they brushed across her cheek, sending an undeniable shiver of longing down her spine. "If that's all you have to say, I've heard it before," she said, hoping he didn't hear the shakiness or need straining her voice. "I'm sure this isn't what Pastor Bailey thought you had in mind."

"You're angry with me again."

Lying wasn't her style. "As a wet hen. Go kiss someone else."

"I don't want to kiss anyone else," he said, the truth sinking like tenterhooks deep into his soul. His eyes slowly ran the length of her. "You look absolutely wicked in that dress. Planned for me to suffer tonight, did you?"

Her chin went up. "The thought had entered my mind."

"You succeeded." He pulled her into his arms. "I missed you."

She lasted for one long breath, then she softened against him. "You didn't call."

"I was trying to see if I could get you out of my mind." He held her away from him, his dark eyes intense. "I couldn't."

"Does that annoy you?" she asked, afraid of the answer, but realizing she had to know before she fell any further. She was half in love with the conservative scoundrel already.

He kissed her on the tip of her nose. "Not since I walked in, heard you laugh, and wanted to punch four men I'd never met in the nose. I've accepted my fate."

She tried to appear shocked, but she was too pleased to pull it off. She'd never expected a staid man like Vincent to be jealous. "They're just friends."

His handsome face became serious. "But you were sharing your laughter and smile with them, not me."

Her bare arms looped around his neck. She tilted her face toward his. "I'm here now."

He didn't need another invitation. His mouth took possession of hers. This time there was nothing sweet about the kiss. It was blatantly arousing, a mating of tongues, a duel of desire where each became the victor. When Vincent finally lifted his head they were both shaking.

He held her tightly. She was small, but gloriously built and absolutely perfect in his arms. "I suppose we better go back and join the party."

Still pressed against him, she stroked the curve of his jaw with her finger. "I suppose."

Unable to resist, he nuzzled her neck and delighted in her soft sigh that ended on a ragged moan. "Any objections to my following you home?"

"None at all." Charlotte lifted her face. "But I have out-of-town houseguests."

"What if I offered to put them up in a hotel?" he asked, only half teasing.

On tiptoes, she kissed his chin. "Nice try, but since it's two of the bridesmaids, I don't think I could do that."

"How long are they staying?"

"All weekend."

Vincent groaned.

FIVE

Now that he had seen her, he didn't want to go the entire weekend without seeing her again. He wasn't leaving the game room until they had a firm date. "How about I take you ladies to breakfast?"

"That's very sweet of you, Vincent, but Emma's mother has already invited us over."

"Lunch?"

"We're going shopping after breakfast and I don't expect we'll stop until either our feet or our credit cards give out."

Vincent was not a man who gave up. "Dinner?"

"I promised Beverly and Carolyn to take them to The Place, a new dance club in Deep Ellum. They have a buffet there."

"Just you ladies? No men?"

"Just us."

Vincent frowned. "That doesn't sound like much fun, watching other people dance."

"Finding a dance partner won't be a problem for either of them." Charlotte played with the button on his jacket. "You'll understand once you meet them."

Vincent didn't think Charlotte would have any problems either. The thought of her being in some other man's arms annoyed the hell out of him. "Do you mind if I stop by?"

The pleased smile on her face came and went in a blink of an eye. Uncertainty took its place. "I don't think you'd like the music."

"It's not hip-hop or rap, is it?" he asked, the distaste clear in his Bostonian accent.

The worried expression didn't clear from her face. "No, it—" The knock on the door interrupted them. She stepped back. "Come in."

The door opened and Henry stuck his head in. "Sorry to disturb you, but Emma and Brian are about to start opening their gifts."

"My goodness." Grabbing Vincent's hand, Charlotte hurriedly left the room. "Thank you, Henry."

Vincent allowed her to lead him back to the den decorated with streamers and balloons, then assign him to his duty. He was to make sure Emma and Brian always had a gift ready to open. Charlotte would keep track of the gifts and the givers' names.

As the happy couple unwrapped gifts from the useful to the useless, Vincent caught himself laughing just as hard as everyone else and truly enjoying himself. However, occasionally when he glanced at Charlotte, she'd have a pensive look on her face. He pondered the cause behind the faraway expression. He didn't like the idea of her being unhappy when she went to such great lengths to ensure the happiness of those around her. He'd find out tomorrow night what was bothering her. Because as sure as his name was Vincent Albert Maxwell, he was going to that dance club and make sure some cowboy didn't try to make a move on Charlotte. Deep Ellum was the undisputed avant-garde district of Dallas. In the shadows of multi-billion-dollar corporations in downtown Dallas, Deep Ellum was populated with million-dollar businesses and those on the verge of bankruptcy, five-star and no-star restaurants, designers renowned and unknown, the prerequisite tattoo shops, clubs on the cutting edge or no edge. New Yorkers might have called the area "funky." Bostonians would have called the area "urban blight."

Vincent parked his car on the side street, and hoped he could call it safe.

He heard the music at the bottom of the three curved steps. His eyebrows lifted at the sound. The fast tempo of the Latin beat was easily distinguishable. He breathed a little easier. Charlotte obviously thought he wouldn't enjoy being there, so he hadn't known what to expect.

He bounded up the step under the red-and-black-striped awning and prepared himself for whatever. The room was spacious with strobe lights in the ceiling, and surprisingly smoke-free. People were pressed together at the bar, on the dance floor, and clustered around the tables circling the wooden dance floor. Arms were in the air, feet seldom were on the floor. The steps were quick and intricate.

"Vincent, over here!"

Peering through the crowd, Vincent saw Charlotte's house guests. Beverly and Carolyn were identical twins, and built like warrior princesses with the sultry beauty to match. When asked about their unidentical names he was told their mother had always been unorthodox. Shaking his head, Vincent thought the trait had passed on to the daughters, who were having the time of their lives dancing and bumping hips with two grinning guys on the dance floor.

He waved. The women hooked their thumbs over their shoulders. Nodding that he understood, he wove his way through the crowd. He didn't see Charlotte, but he did see three guys clustered around a table. With a shake of his head and a curve of his mouth, he headed over.

"Hello, Charlotte. Mind if I sit down?"

Her head whipped around. Her smile blossomed, then grew strained. "Hello, Vincent. I'd like you to meet these nice gentlemen who've been keeping me company."

Vincent's expression remained pleasant as Charlotte completed the introductions. It was obvious the three men wished he'd keel over with a coronary. It was just as obvious that Charlotte was worried about something.

"Would you like something to drink?" she asked when the three men had finally accepted that she wasn't available and moved on.

"Scotch and soda," he told her and watched in fascination as she managed against all odds to get the attention of a waiter and gave him the order.

She bit her lip, then said, "It can get rather hot in here. You want to take off your tie?"

"I'm fine," he said, then watched her sneak another glance at him. Finally, he'd had enough. He took her hand. "If my being here bothers you in some way, I'll leave."

Her hazel eyes widened with obvious distress. "It's not that."

The waiter returned and set down his drink. Vincent let go of her hand and reached for his wallet.

"That's all right, Charlotte has a running tab," the man said, then was gone.

Vincent picked up his drink, his gaze on Charlotte. "You come here a lot."

"My second time actually." She twisted the stem of her margarita glass and eyed his red silk tie with navy stripes. "You're sure you're not hot?"

"I'm fine." Vincent took a sip of his drink. Charlotte seemed to acquire friends wherever she went. The three men who had just left had struck out, but Charlotte had remained polite and cordial so they didn't feel belittled or angry. In fact, the only time he'd ever seen her irritated or annoyed was with him. Just as she was now. Interesting.

The music changed to the hot and spicy beat of the salsa. Most of the dancers moved off the floor, including Carolyn and Beverly. They slumped into their seats on the other side of Charlotte and reached for their fruity drinks.

"Would you care to dance, Charlotte?"

Charlotte, who had just turned her glass up, choked. Vincent pounded her on the back as she stared wide-eyed at him. "W-what did you say?"

"Would you care to dance?" he repeated, telling himself again that he was going to find out what was troubling her before the night was over.

Grinning, she gave him a quick kiss on the lips. "I should have known a scoundrel would know how to dance, even the salsa." Standing, she reached for his hand and led him on the floor to the loud applause and yells of the twins.

"You go, girl!"

"You were worried about me?" he asked as he curved his hand around her waist.

"I didn't want you feeling uncomfortable," she admitted.

"Thank you," he said, then he began to move to the pulsating music.

"For what?" she asked as he made a sudden stop, twisted her away then back to him.

His eyes burned down into hers. "For caring."

That's all the time they had for conversation, as Vincent moved her across the floor, first maddeningly slow, then like the onslaught of a torrent. Each movement was filled with grace and power and seduction as their bodies moved first away then back to each other, the passion raw and impetuous as they teased and coaxed each other, then offered solace once again when their bodies joined.

Only once before in her life had Charlotte felt so vibrant, so alive, and it had been in Vincent's arms as well. The dance became more than a dance. It was as if Vincent were wooing her, making love to her as he held her body and matched his steps to hers as elegantly as he matched their bodies. She lost herself to the throbbing beat of the music, lost herself to him. Where he led, she effortlessly followed, and when he spun her away, she yearned to be in his arms, held against his body.

The end came suddenly with the strum of a Spanish guitar. Applause erupted around them. Face to face, body to body, their breathing labored, Charlotte and Vincent stared at each other and each knew their relationship had shifted, changed into something hot and needy.

Charlotte had always known Beverly and Carolyn were good friends. The women proved it when Vincent and Charlotte finally reached their table after all the congratulations, handshakes, and pats on the back from the crowd. The twins insisted they were worn out and wanted to go home. Charlotte knew her protest was weak at best. She wanted nothing more than to be alone with Vincent. One look at Vincent and she knew he felt the same.

If they didn't go someplace where they could get their hands on each other soon, they'd both explode.

Thankfully, on the drive to her house, Carolyn and Beverly kept chattering. Considering they were litigation lawyers for one of the largest law firms in Houston, they had no trouble talking. In their church singles group before they moved, they had lovingly been referred to as motormouths.

Charlotte parked the car in the garage, sent the twins a thank-you-for-understanding look, and rushed to open the front door. Vincent was coming up the walkway.

Charlotte rubbed her hand on the side of her red chiffon dress. "I thought we'd sit out on the patio."

"All right."

Closing the door after him, she turned and caught the twins grinning at them. "If you need anything, Vincent and I will be outside."

Carolyn yawned. "I'm going to bed."

"Me, too." Beverly stretched.

Charlotte walked through the den, then opened the French doors leading to the backyard. Lights followed the winding path around the yard. She kept walking until she reached the double chaise lounge.

She turned and was in his arms, his mouth on hers, before she could take her next breath. It was heaven. It was hell. The yearning was almost a physical pain.

"I want you, Charlotte."

All she could do was whimper. She wanted him too, but both knew that was impossible.

He nipped her lower lip. "Do you think they're watching?"

"No." Her breath hitched as he used his teeth on the delicate lobe of her ear, then worked his way downward. His tongue licked the upper curve of her breast. Her legs buckled.

Picking her up, he gently placed her on the lounge chair, then came down beside her. Even in the semidarkness, she could see the fire and passion burning in his eyes. She swallowed.

"I won't take you tonight, Charlotte, but I'm going to come very, very, close."

She swallowed again, thought of what a proper Southern lady should do when faced with temptation, the words of her mother and grandmother about remaining chaste until marriage, then Vincent closed his hot mouth over her nipple and she was lost.

Beverly and Carolyn had a ten-fifteen flight the next morning out of Love Field. Due to bad weather in Houston, the plane didn't leave until two hours later. When passengers in their seat rows were called, Charlotte gave them a hug, and quickly headed for the parking garage. Vincent was taking her sailing and she could hardly wait to be with him again.

He was waiting for her when she arrived home. In less than an hour they were in the water of Lake Ray Hubbard. She couldn't have asked for a more perfect day. Skies were blue and the wind gentle.

Later he'd taken her to dinner at a restaurant on the pier.

They'd talked for hours, but were comfortable in their silence as well. When he'd taken her home, he'd driven her just as mad with longing as he had the night before. She knew she was tempting fate, but it felt too good to stop.

During the next couple of weeks, both of their schedules became hectic and they only saw snatches of each other. During those times, they'd often wonder which of their pagers was ringing, and who would be called away first. It became a standing joke between them, but it also made them appreciate their precious time together.

Vincent delighted in having a woman who understood his work and didn't pout if he had to cancel a date. No matter what, Charlotte always greeted him with a smile and asked how his day went. She accepted that business might interfere with their plans and never made him feel guilty. He began to look forward to being with her. He'd catch himself rereading her handwritten notes on scented stationery saying she was thinking of him. Charlotte made him feel special and he enjoyed every second of it.

However, the first time Charlotte had to cancel because of an unexpected meeting with her party chairman, Vincent took her home from the theater as grumpy as a grizzly with a thorn in his paw. Much to his increased annoyance, he'd told her how he felt the moment they walked through her front door.

"Vincent, I'm sorry," Charlotte placated, then stood on tiptoes to kiss his jutted chin. "But this couldn't be helped. I have just enough time to pack before the car picks me up."

Vincent was usually a very reasonable man, but tonight he couldn't quite seem to find that quality in himself. Not when Charlotte was standing before him in a mauve-colored, clinging slip dress, looking delectable and tempting. He had been looking forward to spending an uninterrupted evening with her. "This is Saturday night, for goodness sake. Can't you get out of it and fly down to Austin tomorrow?"

"You know as well as I do that Saturday and Sunday can be just another workday for us. Besides, could you get out of a meeting with your employer if you had key information they needed?" she asked.

"No, but I don't have to like it," he grumbled.

Charlotte laughed and kissed him again. "I do admire an honest man, but I'm afraid I have to throw you out."

"I can take you to the airport," he suggested. He didn't want to let her go. He was surprised how strong the feeling was.

She shook her head. "Thank you, but there's a car coming."

He didn't move. "How long will you be gone?"

"Probably just overnight. I'll be back before you miss me." She glanced over his shoulder as a limo pulled up behind Vincent's car. "Get going, so I can pack."

His hands fisted on the soft chiffon scarf around her neck that was almost as soft as her skin. The back of his knuckles lightly grazed her breasts. He forced himself not to increase the contact. "Would it destroy your image if I kissed you?"

Hands that weren't quite steady circled his wrists. "I'm not sure, but I'd be disappointed if you didn't."

The kiss was long and hot, leaving her breathless. "I—I'll call when I get back."

"You better." Releasing the scarf, he walked back to his car and drove away.

Vincent wasn't in a very good mood by Tuesday afternoon. After Charlotte had gone, the weekend hadn't been that much fun; since she was still gone, the week wasn't shaping up much better. Tossing the papers on his desk, he got up and went to the office window, annoyed with Charlotte and himself.

He missed her.

Slipping his hands into the pockets of his slacks, he sent an accusatory glance at the silent phone. When they'd talked last night, she'd said she'd call when she got back into town. She was returning on a private jet with a group of major political contributors.

He'd bet, by the time the plane landed, Charlotte would have gotten the maximum contributions allowed.

She was a charmer. And he was enthralled by her. What was the matter with him? Women did not interfere with his work. Charlotte's fault again. She simply got to him.

It was his conversation with her that had him trying to cut Ashley some slack. At least she had stopped being sick every day and finally confessed to being pregnant. But if her department figures weren't on time in the future, he'd have to take a second hard look at the situation. But in the meantime, her performance was exemplary.

Vincent had run into her husband and their little boy one day when they came to take Ashley to lunch. They had all looked happy. Perhaps it could work for some couples.

Pulling out his chair, Vincent sat down and picked up the financial report of a new natural gas discovery in Oklahoma. When Charlotte finally came home he wanted his work done so he could spend some time with her tonight. He had an early morning flight to Atlanta for a business meeting that could last through the rest of the week. If Charlotte was delayed, he might not see her until the weekend. The thought had him snarling at the papers in his hands.

Five minutes later he was up again, pacing in front of the window behind his desk. This was Charlotte's fault. That's what came of women having jobs that took them out of town for extended periods of time. If she had a regular job, she'd be in town and he wouldn't be edgy and needy. They could have spent more than a handful of hours together so he wouldn't feel like scum if he made love to her the way their bodies craved.

The intercom buzzed and he pounced on it. "Yes?"

"Vincent, Sidney called. You were supposed to meet him at the Racquet Club ten minutes ago. If you're not there in ten minutes to play against the guy from CityCore, you lose by default. Sidney doesn't like to lose without at least playing," Millicent said.

Vincent's mood went from irritated to feral. He had won the round-robin tournament for his company and was now being pitted against other company winners for the grand championship. The real winner would be the high school students who received college scholarships from the ten thousand dollars each company donated to participate. "Tell Sidney I'm on my way."

Kevin Harris, Vincent's opponent, never posed a real threat. Vincent came out of the box like a demon and never let up. Company employees and members of the Racquet Club gathered to watch. Both men were soaked with perspiration when Vincent hit the winning shot. Kevin swung valiantly for the speeding ball and ended up sprawled on the floor.

"Game!" shouted the referee.

Breathing hard, Vincent walked over to Kevin and extended his hand. "Good game."

"Yeah, right," Kevin said, then smiled, took the offered hand and came to his feet. "Is it a woman or business that has you steamed?"

Vincent flicked a glance at the bearded man. "Why do you say that?"

"Last week you came out to have fun. This week you came out with blood in your eye." Kevin grasped the door handle. "That could only come from one of two reasons."

Vincent didn't say anything, just waited for Kevin to open the door. When he did, the first person he saw standing there was Charlotte, a wide grin on her face, pumping both fists. He didn't think, he just grabbed.

He felt her start of surprise, then the melting of her body against his. He kissed her like the starved man he was. She kissed him the same way.

Only the congratulatory thumps on the back brought Vincent

back to reality. He realized what he was doing and where he was doing it. Surprise went through him. He'd never been the demonstrative type, especially in public.

Lifting his head, he slipped his arm around Charlotte's waist and felt her tremble. What they both needed was a heavy bout of hot, mindless sex. Come tonight, that was exactly what he planned for them.

Thankful she still had the car service, Charlotte left Vincent a note saying she had errands to run, then slipped away when he went to the locker room to shower and change. Still shaken from his kiss and her own desire, she hadn't been sure she would have made it home if she had to drive.

As promised, she'd called Vincent when the plane landed. On learning where he was, she'd gone to watch and cheer him on. She'd marveled at his athletic prowess and the muscular strength and coordination of his graceful body that made her want to run her hands and her lips over every inch of him.

Being conservative, he'd surprised her by wearing only white cotton shorts which, against his toasted brown skin, made him even more striking. The kiss had been another surprise. She'd hungered and thought of little else except being in his arms again while she was away.

Then what?

Vincent, as he had said, was a man. Men wanted intimacy. She had vowed to wait until marriage. With Vincent, she was seriously thinking of abandoning that vow . . . if he loved her. For she was no longer falling in love, she was *in* love. If he loved her, if there was a chance for them, she'd take the risk that what they felt for each other was forever.

Curling up on the four-poster, she tried to shut out the little voice that warned her that when you compromised one principle, others would surely follow. Unsuccessful, she threw back the quilt her grandmother had made for her, and dressed in her jogging shorts, sweatshirt, and tennis shoes. Time to stop feeling sorry for herself and do something that she'd been putting off for weeks: get back into her exercise regime. Clipping the front door key to the special loop on the waistband of her shorts, she left.

Although it was after six, the sun remained fierce, reminding her that she had forgotten her shades and sun visor. She never slackened her stride. Perhaps the run would clear her head. She needed to know what to do. The kiss had told her that the next time they were alone, Vincent wouldn't want to stop until they'd made love. Could she give him what he wanted?

Passing neighbors cutting the lawn, walking dogs, or out jogging like herself, she waved. She'd made a place for herself in the quiet residential neighborhood since she moved there three years ago.

At that time, she'd already been maid of honor twice and, although there was no one special in her life, she had believed that surely her time would soon come. With the rising cost of housing and knowing single men seldom if ever purchased a house, she'd asked her father's help in finding a house in hopes that she'd share it with a husband and family one day. Now, she had to face reality. That day might never come. If Vincent wasn't the one, she wasn't sure she'd ever want anyone again like she wanted him.

She'd never been a whimsical woman. She devoted her all to whatever held her interest. Her family, her friends, her church, her party. Now that included Vincent. She couldn't imagine loving anyone else so completely, nor did she want to.

She barely noticed the sound of a honking horn. It was common for teenagers to blow at the women joggers. She didn't realize it was Vincent until he pulled a half block in front of her and got out of his car.

Her stride shortened until she was walking. She wanted nothing more than to run into his arms. The thought scared her. Each time she saw him, the need for him grew. When he walked out of her life, and he would, she'd be torn to pieces.

"Hello, Vincent."

Hands on his hips, he studied the weariness in her face. This wasn't the woman who had burned so hotly in his arms a scant two hours ago. "Hello, Charlotte."

"I'd stop, but I don't want to cramp up," she said as she passed him.

"No problem." Vincent activated the lock on his car and fell into step beside her.

She threw him a quick look. "You aren't dressed for this. You'll have a heatstroke."

He loosened the stone gray silk tie and kept walking. "You finish with your errands all right?"

Her strides lengthened. "Yes, thank you."

In Vincent's association with women, exaggerated politeness usually meant annoyance or anger. As Charlotte started up a sharp incline, he regretted again his reckless behavior at the Racquet Club.

"I'm sorry if the kiss embarrassed you."

Her smooth stride faltered. "It was just a kiss."

Vincent's eyes narrowed. Now he knew he was in trouble. Thunder rumbled. "Perhaps we should go back to the car."

"I don't mind the rain." She pulled ahead of him. "You go ahead. I'll call later."

"Hello, Charlotte."

Never slowing, she waved at the gray-haired woman wearing a straw hat who was watering her bed of begonias. "Good evening, Mrs. Allister."

"Good evening, young man."

"Good evening, Mrs. Allister," Vincent called and easily pulled alongside Charlotte.

Thunder grew closer and more ominous. "Vincent, if you get rained on, you're going to ruin your clothes."

"I have others."

Her mouth firmed, but she didn't say anything else, just kept jogging. When they turned the block onto Charlotte's street, the rain started to fall. Drops turned to a torrent in seconds.

"I told you," she stopped to yell at him.

She looked close to tears, standing there with her small fists balled, glaring at him. She was hurting. He stepped toward her. She backed up. He kept coming until he closed his arms around her. He thought she would fight, but her hands clutched the lapels of his suit jacket. He felt her body shaking and wished he knew the cause.

"Honey, don't cry, please. Just tell me what it is and I'll fix it. Please don't cry," he soothed, then realized it was ridiculous for them to stand in the rain. He picked her up and started for her house.

This time she reacted. "Put me down," she demanded, pushing against his chest.

He kept walking. "Hush. I have you and I'm not letting go."

Immediately she stilled. He looked down into her face. His heart clenched when tears streamed down her cheek. Gathering her closer, he continued to her house. "Whatever it is, I'll fix it."

Charlotte had almost pulled herself together by the time Vincent reached her house and stood her on her feet. "You can dry off, and then I'll drive you back to your car," she told him.

Vincent silently followed her down the hall. There was nothing he could do about the trail of water he left. In the guest bath, she handed him a large bath towel and a robe. "Your pants and shirt are probably ruined anyway, so the dryer can't do much worse to them. I'll be in the kitchen making coffee."

He caught her arm. "You need to get out of those wet clothes."

Her fist clenched. "I'll be fine."

"Take them off or I'll do it for you," he warned.

Because she so badly wanted to pick a fight with him and take the cowardly way out, she went to her room, changed, and blew her hair dry. She was reaching for her lipstick when she realized what she had been about to do. Make herself pretty for Vincent. Placing the tube on the vanity, she left her bedroom.

None of the women in her family would ever dream of letting a man other than their father see them without at least lipstick and mascara on. Another Southern tradition. She'd break that one, but no others. She had made her decision.

She heard the drone of the clothes dryer as she emerged from the hall. *Vincent.* Drawing a deep breath, she continued to the kitchen, steeling herself against seeing him again.

It did no good. He simply caused her heart to beat faster, the lower region of her body to pulse with need and desire. He wore the white terry-cloth robe she had given him. Underneath his skin would be warm and bare. She stuck her hands in the pockets of her slacks. "Since you've made the coffee, I'll get the cups."

He stepped in front of her as she was about to pass him. He watched her as she quickly staggered back. "What's going on, Charlotte?"

She couldn't meet his eyes. "Nothing."

"What happened between this afternoon at the racket match and now? It had to be more than the kiss."

This was it, the moment she had dreaded and couldn't avoid. "I decided that we should just be friends and forget about anything else."

Vincent's eyes stabbed into her. "You mean forget how it feels to have my hands and mouth all over your body and that—"

With a strangled cry, she pressed her hand to his lips. "Please, don't."

Strong, unrelenting hands grasped her upper forearms. "Talk to me. Tell me what it is, so I can fix it."

"The only way you can fix this is to destroy it."

He shook his head. A drop of water rolled down from his fore-head. He ignored it. "What are you talking about?"

"I've never been with a man and I don't plan to until my wed-ding night."

Vincent's mouth fell open and his hands dropped.

SIX

"You mean. . . ."

Her chin lifted. "Yes."

"But . . ." He stared at Charlotte, lush and beautiful. Even now, with her face free of makeup, she was still the most gorgeous woman he had ever met. The first time he'd seen her he'd wanted her and the wanting had only grown more intense since then. "Men follow behind you like birds following a path of bread crumbs."

"So?" The uncertainty in her eyes changed in a heartbeat to anger. "Where there's smoke there's fire?"

Vincent thought of all the fiery passion in Charlotte, but he didn't think he should point it out at the moment. A virgin. And every time he saw her, he wanted to be inside her. "I think I need to sit down." He did, eyeing her wearily. She didn't look any steadier than he did. "Maybe you'd better sit down."

"I'm fine."

His eyes narrowed a fraction. Charlotte pulled out a tub chair across from Vincent in the breakfast nook and stared out the window at the rain and the jasmine climbing up the redwood trellis of her neighbor's house.

"Is this what's been bothering you since Brian and Emma's shower?"

Surprise had her turning her head toward him. She hadn't thought he or anyone else had noticed. "No." The coffee began to drip into the carafe and she got up to get the cups.

"Charlotte, talk to me, help me to understand," he said quietly.

Since she had been all over him every chance she got, giving him every indication that she wanted what he wanted, she felt he deserved an explanation. Taking a wooden tray from the cabinet, she placed cloth napkins, spoons, cream and sugar, and the cups on top, then brought everything back to the table and sat down.

"I was raised in a loving Christian home and taught that intimacy meant a commitment. At the same time, I was taught to be a Southern lady and that meant charm, grace, femininity, and a deep responsibility to family and the community." Her hand trembled as she poured cream into her coffee and added sugar. "The men I've met in the past have never wanted what I wanted, a home and family." Her hands clutched around the delicate china cup. She lifted her gaze to his.

"I was melancholy at the shower, because Emma and Brian's wedding will be my ninth as a maid of honor. Men see the outside and are turned on, but none want me, the person that I am on the inside, enough to stay around once I say no." She lifted the cup to her lips. The liquid scalded as much as the unshed tears stinging her eyes. In the past, she'd had no trouble telling shortsighted men good-bye. Easy to understand why. She hadn't loved them.

She set the cup down, looked over Vincent's shoulder at the copper teakettle on the stove, then rose. "I have some business calls to make. I'll drive you back to your car when your clothes are dry."

She started to turn toward her office in the back near the kitchen, then realized she'd be too close to Vincent. "I'll be in my room. For Brian and Emma's sake, I hope we can remain civil toward one another."

She escaped; that was the only way to describe her hasty departure. In her bedroom, head bowed, she sat on the bed. First one, then a second teardrop splashed on the clasped hands in her lap.

Her chest hurt. No wonder Brian and Emma had been so miserable that night. It felt as if someone had ripped her heart out. But they loved each other and had made up. That wouldn't happen for her.

Vincent watched Charlotte go. He didn't know what to say or do. He hadn't expected this. His eyes closed, then opened. He was known as the "fixer" by his contemporaries. If there was a problem, call Maxwell, he'd fix it.

His hand rubbed over his face as he thought of what Charlotte had said. "The only way to fix it is to destroy it."

Pushing to his feet, he pulled off the bathrobe and went to the dryer. He was getting out of there. He had learned to control his zipper early in life. He knew how to court a woman, but in the back of his mind there was always the knowledge that eventually they'd become intimate. For Charlotte intimacy meant marriage.

He jerked the door open and pulled on his still-damp briefs. No woman's body was worth being tied down and all the resulting responsibilities. He liked his life the way it was, being able to go and come as he pleased, and take off at a moment's notice for business or pleasure.

Charlotte wouldn't be the first woman to use sex as a lever. She withheld hers, while Sybil had never said no. Whenever and wherever, she'd been willing. At the time, he hadn't known it was to help her on her climb to a vice-presidency of the company he'd worked for in Boston.

He'd had the ear of the president and CEO of the company and she'd known it. She'd used the same method in the past, but he hadn't found that out until later. Women used sex.

He wasn't going to make the same mistake again.

. . .

Charlotte woke with a headache and dried tears on her cheeks. Accepting that there would be more before she was completely over Vincent, she rolled from the bed and glanced at the clock on her bedside. 7:13. Weak light poured though the arched half window in her bedroom. The rain had stopped. Apparently, Vincent had preferred walking to his car rather than seeing her again. She hadn't looked forward to seeing him again either.

No, that was a lie. What she hadn't wanted to see was the accusation in his face. She should have told him sooner she couldn't be what he wanted. She couldn't blame him for not sticking around. She just hoped, as she had told him earlier, that they could be civil. Not for anything would she cause Emma and Brian's wedding to be less than perfect for them.

Pulling off her shirt and pants, she went to take a bath. The world didn't stop because she was miserable. She had a charity auction to attend. Children were depending on her, no matter how much her head was hurting.

Some time later, she stepped out of the oversized tub. After toweling dry, she rubbed her favorite jasmine-scented lotion over her body. Each movement an effort, she pulled on lacy purple lingerie trimmed in black, a garter belt, and sheer black stockings. Next came her makeup. By the time she'd applied her lipstick, the pounding in her head was excruciating. Rubbing her temple, she started to the kitchen for an aspirin.

Her head down, out of the corner of her eyes she saw a shadow move. She screamed.

"Charlotte, it's me," Vincent said, stepping away from the French doors to cut on the lamp on the end table.

Her heart pounding, she simply stared at him. As she had predicted, the combination of rain and the clothes dryer had shrunk his clothes a bit. He was almost comical with his high-water pants. "I—I thought you had gone."

His open mouth snapped shut. For some odd reason he seemed

to have difficulty swallowing. "I—I wanted to make sure you were all right."

Warmth she couldn't suppress filled her. If only . . . "That was nice of you."

"Charlotte, could you please put on a robe?"

Her hazel eyes widened. She gasped, glanced down, and tore back to her room.

Vincent closed his eyes, but he could still see her in the wicked lingerie, the string bikini with lace inserts that he could very well imagine investigating with his tongue. Shoving both hands over his head, he headed for the refrigerator. He grabbed the first thing he saw, bottled water, and chugged it down.

"Vincent."

He spun around. Charlotte was dressed, but she was in a long purple gown trimmed in black lace . . . just as her lingerie had been. He chugged the water again. "I want you, Charlotte."

"But do you love me?" she asked quietly.

In her expressive face he saw a mixture of misery and hope. "I don't know. I think about you more than I should and I worry about you."

Her eyes blinked rapidly as if she were battling tears. "I worry about my friends also. I'd like to have you as a friend."

His hand clenched on the plastic bottle, causing it to make a popping sound. "What I want to do to you and with you has nothing to do with friendship."

She gulped and glanced away. "You shouldn't say things like that."

Watching her, he took another swig of water. She was trembling. She was as aware of him as he was of her. "What would happen if I kissed you?"

Her eyes jumped back to him. "I—I . . . wish you wouldn't."

Placing the bottle on the counter, he walked to her, his gaze never leaving her. "I'm not other men, Charlotte. I see you. I see the charming, caring woman you are, but I've also tasted the pas-

sion on your mouth and on your skin." His fingertip grazed her
nipple. It hardened immediately. Closing his hand into a fist, he
stepped back. "How can I not want to make love to you knowing
you want me to?"

She fought hard to control her desire for Vincent and answer his
question. "Because you have honor and integrity. Because you're not
the kind of man to take advantage of a woman. Because I care for
you and I wouldn't care for a man who would use my feelings
against me."

"I wouldn't be so sure," he said tightly. "Where are you going?"

"To a charity auction."

"You're one of the items?"

She blushed. "No, I'm an auctioneer."

His hot gaze ran over her, remembering. "You'll do very well.
Good-bye." Pulling his suit jacket from the back of the chair in the
kitchen, he walked past her.

"Vincent, you can't go out looking like that," she called. "Please,
I insist on driving you."

He looked over his shoulder. "Scared I'd be picked up before I
reached my car?"

The only way she could handle this was to find humor in the
situation. "You do look pretty awful."

"And you look lovely."

"Thank you. I'll get my purse and you better be here when I get
back." Picking up her skirts, she ran past him. In her bedroom, she
snatched up her shawl, fumbled to transfer her necessary items into
an evening bag the size of her hand, then rushed back out. He was
still there, arms folded, leaning against the counter in the kitchen.

"Don't forget to set the alarm this time." Pushing away from
the counter, he walked out the door.

Charlotte activated the alarm and followed. In less than three
minutes she pulled up behind Vincent's car. A lump formed in her
throat. "Good-bye, Vincent."

"Is this a private auction or can anyone attend?"

Excitement and hope rushing through her, Charlotte opened the glove compartment and handed Vincent an invitation. "This will get you in."

He got out of the car. "I'm not making any promises."

"I know." Charlotte pulled away from the curb, unable to stop herself from glancing at her rear-view mirror. Vincent stood on the sidewalk, watching her just as she was watching him.

In the back of Vincent's mind he'd always known he wouldn't be able to stay away. The auction was being held at a billionaire's estate. The grounds and mansion were spectacular, with ten fireplaces, an indoor and outdoor pool, a lake for boating, a pond for fishing, a tennis court, two libraries, and every marvel known to man. However, to Vincent, the real marvel was standing on a small raised platform, shimmering and beautiful beneath a Waterford chandelier. Charlotte.

With charm and grace Charlotte worked her magic on the crowd, gently coaxing them to go just a little bit higher for the sake of the children's hospital. She smiled, winked, flattered, and bedazzled. Men and women lapped it up like whipped cream. But she could also be a steel magnolia, if needed.

Once she hadn't gotten the price she thought acceptable for a weekend getaway package for two at the Crescent Court Hotel, a five-star hotel in Dallas, and she had refused to let it go. Since she couldn't change the auction rules of highest bid winning, she simply took a seat, crossed her legs, and waited for the bidding to go higher.

Not wanting to see her embarrassed if no one bid, Vincent had lifted his number. The smile she sent him was more potent than hundred-proof whiskey. Other bidders jumped in. Vincent found his hand going up again and again until he won the bid. Mary Lou, who was there with Helen, had winked and nodded approvingly at him.

Vincent was rather dazed when a young woman came up to him and handed him his claim ticket. He didn't need a weekend package for two. Then he glanced at Charlotte and admitted the truth. She simply dazzled him. He'd do anything for her. It remained to be seen if that included not doing what he wanted to do *to* her.

A white-jacketed waiter passed and Vincent plucked a glass of champagne from his tray. Of all the available women in the Southwest, he had to be attracted to one with deep Southern roots and morality. He'd been celibate before, but he had never wanted a woman as much before.

Charlotte had expected Vincent to insist on following her home, but had not a clue what to expect afterward. Walking through the house from the garage, she never remembered being so nervous or filled with such anticipation. She opened the front door and he was there. Dark and dangerous and so desirable. Moonbeams draped over his broad shoulders.

Neither spoke, simply looked at the other for long endless moments.

As if coming to a decision, Vincent stepped closer until the warmth of their breaths and bodies mingled. "I can't imagine not wanting you, but neither can I imagine walking away."

Her breath and words trembled over her lips. "I feel the same way."

He took another step. Their bodies touched, breasts to chest, thigh to thigh. "I'll try, but I'm not making any promises."

"I know." She had come to her own decision. "Would you like to come in?"

He shook his head. "Too far. I need to kiss you now."

With the raw passion simmering just beneath the surface of his voice, Charlotte expected the kiss to be rough and demanding. Instead it was a gentle exploration of reassurance that gradually deepened into something rich and deep and arousing. Feeling her control slipping, Charlotte eased back and placed her head on Vincent's chest. His heart beat erratically, but his arms were locked around her as if he'd never let her go.

"I have to go out of town for a few days, but I'll be back Saturday. You want to go sailing?" he asked, his voice thick and tight.

Despite the needs clawing at her, she leaned her head back and smiled up at him. "That's certainly better than weeding the flower bed, as I'd planned."

"We can do both," he said, enjoying the feel of her in his arms as much as the quick emotions that flashed across her face.

"Somehow I can't imagine you on your hands and knees in the dirt," she told him.

"My mother has a flower garden and I used to help her." As he remembered, gardening was hard, tiring work. Good. "Eight early enough?"

"I'll fix breakfast."

"See you Saturday." Opening the door behind her, he gently pushed her inside and closed the door.

Vincent amazed Charlotte again. He'd shown up Saturday morning casually dressed in faded jeans and a melon-colored polo shirt, ready to work. The dandelions hadn't stood a chance. When she'd mentioned she wanted more flowers on the patio in pots, he'd insisted that they forgo sailing and go to the nursery. It wasn't until later in the afternoon that she realized he might have an ulterior motive for working so hard: Both of them would be too tired to think about sex.

If she hadn't been already in love with him, she would have fallen.

After they'd cleaned up, she'd grilled steaks and they'd enjoyed their meal on the patio surrounded by blooming flowers in Mexican urns, clay pots, and baskets hanging from the wrought-iron posts Vincent had installed. Only once or twice did she think of how wonderful it would be to have him as a husband and there all the time with her.

But he hadn't made any promises. He might leave today and never return. Even as the thought saddened her, she refused to give up hope.

The kiss that night was brief. They had looked at each other and realized that no matter how tired their bodies were, they still wanted each other.

The next day at church Charlotte noticed that Emma and Brian were nervous wrecks, worrying that a catastrophe was waiting for them. After services Charlotte called Vincent and asked him to meet them at Emma's house. He was there within the hour.

With his help, they had gone over every detail, reassured the anxious couple, then double-checked the checklist. Charlotte would contact the guests who had not responded, go with Emma on Monday to meet with the wedding photographer and the videographer. Vincent would go with Brian the same day to pick up the wedding rings and check the engraved inscriptions on them, and check on the entertainment.

When Emma and Brian had finally calmed and had been reassured of a wonderful wedding, Charlotte had glanced up to see Vincent watching her with a curious expression on his face. She had frowned at him, but he had shaken his head and suggested he take everyone, including Emma's and Brian's parents, sailing and then out to dinner.

Everyone accepted. They'd had a wonderful time. Sailing had soothed the frayed nerves of anxious parents and edgy children. As the evening progressed, Charlotte also felt a lessening of the tension in her own body.

When Vincent let her take the wheel of the speedboat, he stepped behind her to guide and help. She felt alive instead of nervous. With his arms around her, the wind in her hair, she tossed him a grin over her shoulder.

"Watch where you're going," he said, but he was smiling too.

Facing forward, Charlotte smiled. She was seeing another more playful side of Vincent and she heartily approved.

In the days that followed, she approved even more. She and Vincent saw each other almost daily. He said he was making sure she didn't let his plants die. She replied that she babied them shamefully. That earned her a kiss. It wasn't easy pulling back then or after the other kisses that followed, but they managed.

Two days before the wedding, Vincent had to go out of town. Since the wedding rehearsal and dinner were the next evening, and he wasn't sure how long he'd be away, he'd only told Charlotte. As much as he had been against the wedding in the beginning, he had finally realized how much Brian and Emma loved each other and he was happy for them. He had also come to realize that loving a person meant putting your needs behind what was best for them.

"First-class passengers may now board Flight 1222 for Chicago, Illinois."

Grabbing his garment bag and laptop, Vincent stood and followed the other first-class passengers onto the plane. On board, he handed the stewardess the bag and his suit jacket, and took his seat.

Instead of opening his laptop to work, he stared out the window and remembered Charlotte's smile and infectious laughter, the disappointment that she couldn't hide because he wouldn't be there tonight to go to his first political rally with her. He remembered her warm body and how good it felt curled trustingly against his on her sofa last night as they watched a comedy.

He twisted in his seat as his body again made him vividly aware of his long bout of sexual denial. He wasn't sure how much longer he could do this. A couple of times he was aware that if he pushed Charlotte just a little harder, she would have given herself to him. He hadn't wanted that. He wanted her there with him every step of the way. Besides, he'd never do anything to destroy her faith in him. So what was the answer? He honestly didn't know.

. . .

Charlotte was in a quandary. The wedding consultant, the officiating minister, Brian and Emma, and their parents had been asking where Vincent was for the past twenty minutes. They all were clustered in front of the podium with no best man. Charlotte considered confessing that he was out of town when the main doors to the sanctuary opened.

"Hello, everyone. Sorry I'm late," Vincent greeted, his long legs quickly carrying him down the aisle.

"I'm just glad you're here," Brian said, relief etched on his face as he reached out to shake the extended hand of his cousin. "Working late as usual, I see. I've already warned Emma my hours are going to get crazier at work."

Emma smiled up at her fiancé. "I'll miss you, but I understand it's important to you."

"Now that the best man is here, let's get started," said the wedding consultant as she hustled the bridesmaids and groomsmen back down the aisle of the church, Charlotte with them. She hadn't even gotten a chance to speak with Vincent.

Impatiently, Charlotte listened to the instructions she knew as well as the consultant. Her face must have said as much for the woman gave her a stern look of disapproval and said, "I know *some* of you have gone through this many times before, but others have not."

All of the other women except Emma looked at Charlotte. She'd never felt more keenly that she'd never be a bride.

"I'm sure you're right, Mrs. Phillips," Emma said in the ensuing silence. "But good manners are never out of place."

Charlotte blinked at the ready defense by Emma. Mrs. Phillips, however, lifted her pointed nose higher at the rebuke.

"Brian and I want our wedding to be absolutely perfect, Mrs. Phillips, that's why we chose you. You're the best at what you do. We know we won't be disappointed," Emma continued.

Mrs. Phillips preened. "No, you shan't. Groomsmen, line up by height as I instructed earlier."

The paired men started down the aisle, followed by each bridesmaid. Seeing Mrs. Phillips' attention elsewhere, Charlotte felt it safe to whisper to Emma, "Thanks, and very well done."

Emma's smile was impish. "After watching you all these years I should know how to get my point across."

"You learned well. My turn." Charlotte stepped out and started down the aisle and saw Vincent standing beside Brian. Love washed over her, and something close to fear. Her steps faltered, then she continued despite the pain deep in her chest. Would he ever love her?

Never a bride. Never a bride. Never Vincent's bride.

The taunting beat replayed itself over and over in her head as she walked slowly down the aisle when she wanted to run out of the church. Instead she dutifully took her place to the right of the minister, aware that she might never stand before him with the man she loved.

Vincent had never seen Charlotte look so sad or so hauntingly beautiful. Whether by accident or design, she'd worn an anklelength sleeveless white sheath. She might have been a bride herself. The thought brought him up short.

Charlotte had made it no secret that she wanted to get married, planned to get married. One day a man would come along who would win her. A mixture of jealousy and anger swept through Vincent at the thought of any man touching her, kissing her, making love to her.

"Isn't she beautiful?"

Vincent pulled his unsettling thoughts back to the present. His narrowed gaze went from Brian to Emma, on the arm of her father, slowly coming down the aisle. She was beautiful. From her radiant expression it was obvious she knew that she was loved, cherished, and wanted. Beside Vincent, Brian's face split into a wide, proud grin. He had done well for himself. He might be young, but he apparently knew what he wanted and how to get it.

Vincent on the other hand was still floundering. He craned his neck to see Charlotte and couldn't. Then, seeing the eagle-eyed consultant's attention on Emma, Vincent moved back until he saw Charlotte, her head slightly bent. His heart turned over.

She looked up and straight into his eyes. Vincent felt as though the world had dropped away from his feet. No, he quickly amended, he was looking at his world. *Charlotte.* As the realization sank in, his heart pounded, his legs felt wobbly. It couldn't be.

"Vincent, are you all right?" Brian asked.

Vincent didn't know how to answer. Somehow he finally managed to answer, "I'm fine. I shouldn't have skipped lunch."

Brian slapped him lightly on the shoulder. "When we finish here we're having the rehearsal dinner, so just hang in there."

Vincent was hanging, all right, and the rope was unraveling fast.

Charlotte was miserable. Each time she'd catch Vincent's attention at the rehearsal dinner, he'd quickly look away. To make matters worse, they were dining at Fish and one of Brian's groomsmen, a man she'd never met before, was trying to hit on her.

She'd tried ignoring him, gave him warning looks, but nothing seemed to dent his thick skull. The only thing that saved the overbearing man from a drink dumped in his lap to cool him off was the fact that he kept his hands to himself and she didn't want to ruin the evening for Brian and Emma.

By ten she was more than ready to go home. However, as maid of honor she had to wait until all the others had gone. Finally, there was only her and Vincent waiting for the valet to bring their cars.

"Charlotte, I realize you're tired, but do you mind coming back to my place? I'd like to ask your opinion about something," Vincent said.

Charlotte was about to say no when he added, "It's about the wedding. It won't take long."

Charlotte bit her lower lip as indecision and regret held her still. Vincent lived downtown in the new and chic town homes on Turtle Creek. And he had never asked her to his home before. Foolishly she wished that the first time hadn't been for the sake of someone else.

The valet pulled up with her car. Vincent's arrived seconds later. She pushed her earlier thoughts aside. This was for Brian and Emma's sake. "All right."

"Just follow me." Tipping her valet, then his, he got in his car and drove away.

Charlotte followed, determined to hear what Vincent had to say, then leave. Determined not to let one tear fall.

The residential building was as posh as the upscale address implied with a rose marble entryway, an immense flower arrangement in the center of the rotunda, curved stairway, and sparkling chandelier. As she followed him inside his home, Charlotte fleetingly noted the hardwood floor and tasteful furnishings.

"Would you like a glass of wine?"

"No, thank you." She sat on the sofa and rested her purse in her lap. She didn't plan to stay long. "What about the wedding? Is there some problem I don't know about?"

Vincent scooted the magazines and silk flower arrangement over on the coffee table, then sat facing her. "Yes."

"What?"

"I'm in love with you. Will you marry me?"

Charlotte's mouth opened, but nothing came out.

Vincent stared into her shocked face and talked fast. "I didn't expect it either. I knew I wanted you, but then I saw you walking down the aisle, and it began to sink in. I love you."

Her eyes closed and when they opened they were filled with accusation and pain. "How could you do this to me?"

"I lo—"

"Don't lie!" She came to her feet. "You want to sleep with me and you think the way to do it is to offer a fake proposal."

Vincent had risen with her. "Fake proposal! What kind of man do you think I am?"

"Obviously one I only *thought* I knew." She gripped her bag. "Good night."

She got two steps before he caught her by the forearms and pulled her toward him. "Now you listen to me. I said I love you and I darn well mean it. I never said that to another woman in my life, not even to that scheming Sybil."

Charlotte stopped struggling. Fire flashed in her eyes. "Who's Sybil?"

"An unscrupulous woman who thought to use me to advance in the company I worked for and was fired instead," he told her.

"You had an affair with her," Charlotte guessed, and although it had been in the past it still hurt. The woman had shared with Vincent what Charlotte might never have the chance to experience.

For a moment she didn't think he would answer, then he did. "Yes. Unlike you, she used her looks to get her what she wanted. When I found out about her duplicity I fired her."

"I'm sorry."

"Don't be. It taught me a lesson about sex and women." He sighed. "At least I thought it did until I met you. You're nothing like I thought and everything I could have wished for."

"I didn't expect you to stay after I told you," she said softly.

His thumb stroked her arms. "Neither did I."

"Why did you?"

"Probably a combination of a lot of things," he said, thinking as he went. "I enjoyed being with you, hearing your laughter, watching you enjoy life. Your kisses also nearly blew the top of my head off. The little sounds you used to make when you were clinging to me nearly drove me crazy. We both know I didn't have to propose to get you to sleep with me."

She gasped and he kept talking. "You know why I stopped every time? It was because I'd rather cut off my right arm than hurt you."

Since there were times she would have given in, all Charlotte could do was glare.

Vincent wasn't finished. "Do you think I wanted to fall in love with a career woman who I'll have to get on her calendar to see? I missed you like crazy while you were in Austin."

Charlotte felt herself softening, but felt compelled to point out, "A woman has just as much a right to a career as a man."

"A woman's place is in the home, caring for her family." He released her, then raked his hand over his head in frustration. "I cut Ashley some slack because of what you said, but I'm not the husband and family she's missing time with. There'll be times when you're gone almost as much as I am. I don't have any illusions that will change. I don't like that!"

"I believe in what I'm doing just as much as you do," she told him, wanting him to understand.

"I know," he said, his voice softening. "Helping people and trying to make a difference in their lives is as much a part of you as breathing. I finally figured out that's one of the reasons people are so drawn to you." Black eyes narrowed. "Men especially. I wanted to punch James in the nose tonight. I would have, if I hadn't thought it would upset you."

Charlotte felt her resistance fade a little bit more. "I can take care of myself."

"I realize that as well. You also have very strong moral principles and I trust you implicitly. I'll always be waiting for you to come back home to me." A slow, teasing smile came over his face as his hands settled on her waist. "It will be my pleasure to ensure that you can't wait to get home."

She pushed at his chest. "I'm still upset with you."

"I know, but I'm working on getting you over it." He kissed the curve of her jaw, her lips. "I brought you here so you couldn't toss me out until I convinced you how much I love you."

Her voice trembled. "Vincent, are you sure?"

His head lifted and he stared down at her with love in his eyes. "I love you more than life itself. You opened my eyes to what a real marriage is: trust, love, commitment, and sharing. I found my Southern comfort and I have no intention of letting her get away."

Her arms circled his neck. "I love you. Together we'll make it work."

He pulled her closer. "I figure if I can learn calculus, I can learn how to fix a meal and change a diaper."

Her heart glowed. "I'm sure of it."

"Then your answer is yes?"

"Yes, forever and always, my conservative scoundrel."

EPILOGUE

The bride wore white. Chantilly lace, tulle, and silk-satin were used to create an elegant gown with a sweeping train and veil for the formal December wedding. In her white-gloved hand was a cluster of calla lilies. As she made her way up the aisle on the arm of her beaming father, a hush fell over the packed, flower-filled sanctuary. She didn't notice; her gaze was locked on the man in the gray morning coat who would soon be her husband, just as his was on her.

As they had done so many times in the past six months since their engagement, they communicated with their eyes.

I'll love you always.

I'll love you right back.

Then she was standing beside him in front of the minister, her hand resting trustingly in his. There wasn't a shred of doubt in her mind that he would always be there for her, nor were there any doubts in his mind about her.

We made it.

We certainly did.

Soon.

Soon.

The ceremony proceeded with the solemn lighting of candles,

the exchange of vows and giving of rings, then the moment each had waited for. "I now pronounce you man and wife. You may kiss the bride."

The kiss was a brief brush of lips, then hand-in-hand they were rushing down the aisle to the waiting limousine that would take them to the reception at the posh Crescent Court Hotel. Exactly an hour later, the couple slipped away, leaving their best man and maid of honor to ensure that all the guests had a wonderful time.

"Hurry," she said impatiently, crowding him as he tried to unlock the door to their honeymoon suite in the Crescent Court. Neither had wanted to wait to start their honeymoon.

"The key card is—there!" The green light blinked on. Turning, he lifted her up in his arms and stepped inside, then kicked the door closed. He didn't stop until he was in the lavishly decorated bedroom of the suite. Vintage champagne, a huge fruit basket, and finger food waited. Neither noticed. All that mattered was the turned-down, king-sized bed.

"Please put me down and help me out of this dress." Lifting her cathedral crown off her head she tossed it and his coat he'd taken off in the elevator in the direction of the love seat.

He set her on her feet, then breathed a sigh of relief that there were only five satin-covered buttons. "My hands are shaking."

"My entire body is shaking," she said.

They both laughed, but it was nervous laughter. The last button slipped free. "Done."

She reached to pull the dress off her shoulders. He helped, then sucked in his breath as the dress slid down her body. She stood in yards of tulle and satin-silk wearing a white lace bustier, delicate lace bikini panties, and sheer white lace-top thigh-highs.

"You simply take my breath away." His hands spanned her tiny waist and lifted her out of the gown.

Her hands rested on his broad shoulders as she stared up into his intense black eyes. "I plan to do a lot more to you before we leave this room again."

He grinned. "Charlotte, I do love you."

"I love you too, Vincent. Thanks for giving me this," she said, her hands coming up to cup his face. "Now, it's my time to give." Her lips nipped his, then she traced the seam of his mouth with her tongue.

He shuddered. His hands tightened. His eyes narrowed to slits. "Why don't we give to each other?"

In his usual way, he didn't wait for her consent, but fastened his mouth on hers. The kiss was bold, erotic, and mind-bending. Her little moans and whimpers told him she was in complete agreement with his idea.

Vincent fell back on the bed, carrying Charlotte with him. He rolled and she was on the bottom. "Unbutton my shirt while I act out a fantasy."

She reached for the first pearl button with shaky hands. Vincent's tongue rimmed the bustier, its deep center. Her body quivered. The pleasure was unbelievably erotic. The only way she completed the task was by thinking she wanted to do the same thing to him.

Vincent found the zipper in the bustier and slowly drew it down, revealing lush breasts and pebble-hard nipples that begged for his attention. Not yet. He wanted to rush, but for Charlotte it would be the first time and, if he could keep his sanity, it would be one that she would always remember and cherish.

His hand drifted over the flesh he had uncovered, as gentle as a butterfly's wing, as thorough as a cat licking cream, and that was exactly what he planned next. The tip of his tongue stroked first one turgid brown point, then the other.

Beneath him, Charlotte twisted. A slow heat was building between her thighs. Her legs moved restlessly. "Vincent?"

"I'm here." His hand cupped her womanhood. She whimpered. Then he dipped one long finger inside her. Her hips came off the bed.

He stared into her eyes, eyes that were as hot as his. She leaned forward and curled her tongue around his nipple. Vincent couldn't hold back a moan nor did he try to. However, when her hand closed around his manhood and stroked the length of him, he gritted his teeth and gently pushed her hand away.

"I did it wrong?"

"You did it too right."

Her smile purely feminine, she went back to driving him crazy with her sweet mouth and nimble tongue, removing his clothes while he took enormous pleasure in acting out another fantasy in the way he got rid of her panties.

Flesh to flesh, heart to heart, they explored each other and loved each other on the way to the intimate bonding both had waited months to share.

Poised above her, he stared down at her and was gratified that he saw no hesitation, only love and desire. "I love you."

"I love you."

His hips moved to bring them together for the first time, then he was surrounded by her velvet heat. The fit was snug; the sensations exquisite. He loved her not only with his body, but with his heart and soul. She loved him back the same way. When her cry of fulfillment came, he was there with her, holding her as he always would.

The Southern lady had married her conservative Yankee scoundrel, and the fit was perfect.

the

Blind Date

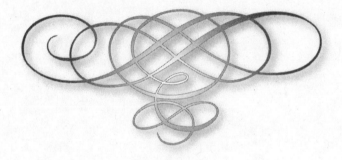

ONE

*Tanner Rafferty, one of the most sought-after bachelors in Wash-*ington, D.C., had been stood up. In his thirty-six years he could count on one hand the number of times that had happened. However, if his sister Raine had been called out of town unexpectedly on business, at least she had ensured that he'd have a wonderful dinner at Leo's.

Tanner sat back as his waitress, dressed in a slim black skirt and white blouse, cleared the remnants of his rare prime rib, cooked to perfection, while another waitress brought the coffee he'd ordered to be served after his meal.

He nodded his thanks and picked up the fine china cup. In the two weeks he'd been in town he'd heard a great deal about the popular supper club. Everyone from politicians to college students flocked in droves to Leo's to dine, unwind, and lose themselves in the ambiance. Tonight, a Thursday, taped jazz flowed through the room like a haunting melody. It seemed the accolades he'd heard about the place weren't superfluous after all.

No wonder Raine had insisted they dine here when she dropped in from Charleston that morning for an unexpected visit. A smile tugged the corners of Tanner's sensual mouth. His baby sister was checking out the competition.

Raine was beautiful, intelligent, and as competitive as they came. It wasn't a coincidence that she had chosen to have dinner at Leo's, since she had recently added a supper club in Atlanta to her growing list of restaurants. In fact, the new supper club had been the reason for her quick departure. He didn't have a doubt that whatever the problem, Raine would solve it. She'd go over, around, or through you, as tenacious as her two older brothers and father when it came to getting what she wanted. None of them believed in settling for less than the best or having their clients settle, either.

Their father, Thomas Rafferty III, had taught them never to be satisfied with the status quo, and that service was always the bottom line. As the smiling waitress approached Tanner's table to refill his half-empty coffee cup, Tanner gave Leo's additional points for an attentive staff.

He glanced appreciatively around the crowded restaurant with its elegant yet comfortable décor of Tiffany lamps on rosewood tables covered with white linen, the stained-glass, floor-to-ceiling narrow windows behind him, and the intricately patterned parquet area for dancing. Leo's had style, something else he valued.

Tanner nodded to a U.S. senator from Texas and her escort who were leaving. The table was quickly cleaned and another couple seated. Knowing Raine would want a full report, he relaxed in his chair, sipping his coffee. It was a rare moment and he planned to take advantage of it. As a hotel developer and chief operating officer of ten Rafferty Hotels dotting the coast from Florida to D.C., he usually had nonstop twelve- to sixteen-hour days.

With the scheduled opening of his newest hotel, The Rafferty Grand, six weeks away, his life was about to become even more hectic. He didn't mind. He loved what he did. There was a huge amount of responsibility but also the freedom to travel, to move from one city to the other where something new and different always waited for him. He was easily bored. His mother had often lamented that it was the reason he never stayed with one woman longer than a few weeks. In the hotel business, boredom was impossible.

In the weeks he'd been in D.C. he'd been confronted with numerous problems, from pacifying the temperamental consulting concept chef over the design of his kitchen, to the delay of the custom-made crystal chandeliers for the ballrooms, to the imported marble for the bathrooms in the suites. He'd solved each problem to his satisfaction. The opening of The Rafferty Grand would be on schedule and would be as spectacular as he had envisioned. The guests would be pampered in luxury and treated with the kind of old-fashioned southern hospitality and graciousness that he'd grown up with in Charleston.

Like Raine and their brother Adrian, who ran the Rafferty Resorts in the Virgin Islands, Tanner prided himself on service and customer satisfaction. All of his hotels were four-star. His aim was for The Rafferty Grand to be five.

He was about to put down his coffee cup and signal for his check when he looked up and saw *her*. For a long moment he just stared. In his lifetime he'd seen many beautiful women, but never one who stopped him in his tracks the way she did. Wondering why he hadn't seen her sitting there before, he finally put down the cup as he realized the four men who had been sitting at the table in front of him had been obscuring his view of her.

The men's bawdy conversation had been of easy women and tough choices in life. Tanner had tuned them out. He had excellent hearing, much to the chagrin of many of his employees. They had learned over the years that whispering was useless when he was around. Now he had no intention of ignoring the conversation of the woman in red whose skin was the color of sun-warmed honey.

A broad-shouldered man in a black raw-silk sports jacket showed a young couple to the vacant table. Tanner's frown turned into a sigh of relief when they sat next to each other, leaving an unobstructed view of the woman. She was wearing a red sleeveless top with a high collar that framed her stunning face. Seated across from her was another young woman who waved her left hand expressively in the air as she talked. A diamond ring glinted on her third finger.

From the resigned expression on her face, the woman in red wasn't thrilled with what was being said. One small, fine-boned hand, unfortunately the right, rested on the table near a half-full glass of red wine, then shoved its way impatiently though lustrous, short black curls.

Tanner absently stroked his full beard, then leaned forward and placed his arm on the table as if he were continuing to relax. He smoothed out his features and prepared to eavesdrop. He didn't consider it rude, just necessary, if he were to find out more about the woman . . . like if she was already taken.

"*Ayanna, George Collins is a* fantastic catch," Sheri said, her voice excited and rushed. "He comes from a very wealthy and influential family in Rochester. He's been here about six months. He's one of the best tax attorneys in the country. You two would have lots in common since you're the accountant for Leo's. You just *have* to go out with him Saturday night."

Ayanna Hardcastle barely kept a grimace from her face as Sheri finally wound down and stared expectantly across the table at her. Sheri had been Ayanna's best friend since high school. She agreed to meet her for dinner because she genuinely liked and admired her . . . when she wasn't trying to fix her up. At least Sheri had waited until they'd finished dinner and Sarah, their waitress, wasn't likely to return as frequently and learn that her boss couldn't get a date on her own.

"Please, Ayanna," Sheri said into the lengthening silence. "I'm sure you'll like George much better than the others I set you up with."

Which wasn't saying much, since the last three in a four-week period had been self-centered and rude. Trying to keep a smile on her face, Ayanna said, "Sheri, summer is the restaurant's busiest season. I appreciate your effort, but I really have to say no this time."

"You can't," Sheri wailed, her expressive brown eyes staring at Ayanna in alarm. "He's too good to let get away. I met him a couple of months ago at a fund-raising dinner. He's a good conversationalist and a great dancer. You know you love to dance."

Ayanna resisted draining her glass of wine and then asking Sarah to bring her a double gin and tonic. The only thing she'd accomplish would be a splitting headache in the morning, and if she drank that much Sheri would still be after her to date another total dud. "Sheri, just look around you. I have payroll, worker's comp claims, insurance, financial reports, and bills to pay. I don't have time for dating."

Sheri jerked straight in her chair, causing the multicolored scarf draped stylishly over one shoulder to slide off. "But you have to, Ayanna! How else are you going to find a man and get married? I can't imagine my life without Reginald. He's everything to me."

The double gin and tonic was looking better all the time. Sheri was a hopeless romantic, in love with Reginald since they were in the seventh grade. Four months ago, Ayanna had been Sheri's maid of honor when she'd married Reginald in a lavish garden wedding. Two hundred guests were in attendance. Sheri was happier these days than Ayanna had ever seen her and, unfortunately, even more determined that Ayanna experience the marital bliss she'd found . . . whether Ayanna wanted it or not.

"I'm happy for you and my cousins, too, but I simply don't have time for a relationship," Ayanna insisted. Now, more than ever, with her cousins and partners in Leo's taking on the added responsibility of wives, the business needed to maintain its profit margin. It didn't matter that the wives were financially solvent. Her cousins were surprisingly old-fashioned that way. Ayanna didn't plan on letting any of them down. She'd always be thankful to them for asking her to be a partner and for naming the restaurant after Leo Hardcastle.

Unfortunately Sheri's attack didn't seem to be abating anytime soon. "I love being married and I bet they do, too. Please, just one more blind date. You and George can double-date with Reginald and me to Judge Wyman's sixtieth birthday party. Like your father, George's father and the judge go way back."

The noose closed tighter around Ayanna's neck. Judge Wyman had been a friend of her father's since he'd been a cadet, fresh from the police academy, and the judge, right out of law school, had been a public defender. They'd fought bigotry and cussed meanness each day, just to do their jobs. The other police officers hadn't wanted to be a partner with her father; Wyman's clients wanted a white lawyer. Her father had gone on to become the chief of police in D.C. before he died from a stroke ten years ago. The judge sat on the U.S. Circuit Court of Appeals.

"Come on, Ayanna. You'll be there anyway," Sheri pointed out. "So will your mother."

Ayanna went into a full panic. Her mother was worse than Sheri when it came to trying to get her only child married. It was time for some straight talk. "Sheri, I couldn't love you more if you were a sister, and Reginald is a wonderful man, but you have a bit of difficulty picking out men for me." Ayanna refrained from pointing out it was probably because Sherry hadn't dated any man except her husband.

"What do you mean?" A frown worked its way across Sheri's brow.

Ayanna raised her right hand and enumerated, one finger at a time. "Blind date number one thought he should get a discount on the meal because we had dinner here." Up went another finger. "Number two wanted to know about my portfolio before we got to his car. Number three thought the evening should end in bed."

Shock broke out on Sheri's face, then it quickly cleared. "You won't have to worry about any of that with George. He's wealthy, and since we're double-dating, the three of us can pick you up last and drop you off first. It will be perfect."

Ayanna refrained from beating her head against the table. Sheri worked in the Department of Education as a reading specialist. She had to deal with enough governmental red tape not to become discouraged when something hit a snag. She simply tackled it from a different direction. Ayanna would have to do the same.

"I already have a date for Saturday night," she lied.

Sheri had already lifted her hand to brush aside any excuse by Ayanna. Her mouth gaped instead. "What? Tell me you aren't kidding."

Ayanna felt a twinge of guilt when she saw the excitement on Sheri's pretty nut-brown face, then thought of her horrendous experiences with the last three blind dates. "I'm not kidding."

Sheri's squeal garnered only a few interested looks. Ayanna wasn't surprised.

Besides being well known for its fine food and atmosphere, Leo's also had a reputation for people finding love there. It happened so often that the restaurant kept a supply of champagne on hand for these occasions. Her friend's squeal was hardly cause for a celebration. She just hoped Sheri would believe the fib she'd just told.

"I'm so happy." Sheri leaned forward and propped both arms on the table. "Details. I want all the details of how this great event came about."

Ayanna floundered, then took a sip of wine to gather her thoughts, realizing why honesty was always the best policy. Sooner or later the lie came back to nip you on the backside. She was putting together the next one in her mind when a dark-eyed man sitting two tables over caught her attention.

Men had stared at her before, but she'd never felt the need to stare back, or the slight tingling sensation that was now racing over her. She had always been attracted to men with beards. His was midnight black and neatly trimmed, just like his hair. The beard lent a roguish quality to his handsome face. The civilized trappings of a tailored gray pinstripe suit and crisp white shirt with a burgundy silk tie couldn't quite mask the untamed glint in his dark eyes. The erect set of his shoulders announced to the world that he was ready to take it on if necessary. He was a throwback, a renegade, a man who took what he wanted.

Ayanna shivered. She sensed that everything she'd read about Tanner Rafferty had been true. She'd never met him, but she recognized him from all the press he'd received since coming to D.C.

Tanner Rafferty, hotel developer, was the newest darling on the city's social scene. His family owned one of the largest conglomerates in the country. They had started out in manufacturing and then diversified. Tanner, his younger brother, and his sister Raine each headed their own successful division of the company. The well-heeled and well-connected had been doing back-flips in glee over him since his arrival. He was on everyone's "A" list, feared in the boardroom and coveted in the bedroom.

The women were welcome to him, Ayanna thought. She'd loved her father and he had loved his family, but he had been passionate about his work. Ayanna and her mother had always known that his job came first.

From what she'd read about Tanner, he felt the same way about his hotels. One article had reported that The Rafferty Grand was almost booked to capacity for its first year. No one had to tell her that his time was seldom his own. If she ever decided to dip her toe in the shark-infested waters of a relationship, she'd come first or not at all.

"Ayanna?"

She started, then looked at the frown on Sheri's face and realized she must have been trying to get her attention for some time. "What? I'm sorry."

"What were you looking at?" Sheri asked. Glancing in the same direction of Ayanna's stare, she gasped. "My goodness! It's Tanner Rafferty. What an eyeful! He's even better looking in person. I wonder if the stories I've read about him are true. He's known as

'The Renegade' because he doesn't always stick to rules of business or society. He takes what he wants."

"I believe it," Ayanna answered, her gaze unerringly returning to Tanner, her voice husky.

Sheri's attention bounced from Ayanna to Tanner. "My goodness, he's looking at you! Like—" Sheri gasped again. "It's him, isn't it? Your date. It has to be. You never pay attention to men and he's looking at you as if he wished we'd all disappear. This is absolutely fabulous!"

Ayanna attributed the sudden racing of her heart to relief that Sheri had inadvertently provided her with a way out, and not to the way she said Tanner was looking at her. Ayanna smiled knowingly and looked at her plate.

"Oh, girl, I should be upset with you for not telling me, but I'm just so happy for you!" Sheri twisted around, grinned at Tanner, then confronted Ayanna. "Introduce us."

"What?" Ayanna's head came up with a jerk. "I can't do that."

"Why?" Sheri asked, obviously perplexed.

Ayanna looked at Tanner and thought she saw an amused smile on his dark, handsome face. She twisted in her seat and took another sip of her drink. "We're keeping it a secret."

Sheri rolled her eyes. "This is D.C. Nothing stays a secret for long. Certainly not this. You're both too well known. Please," she cajoled. "I want to meet the man who's the talk of the town."

Ayanna faltered, promising herself that she'd never tell another lie if somehow she got out of this situation. Just then Tanner, lean and elegant, rose from his table. Relief swept over her. He was leaving. Everything was going to work out. She wouldn't have to admit she'd lied, or embarrass herself and upset Sheri.

"I bet he's coming over here," Sheri said in excitement, turning toward the approaching man.

Ayanna wasn't paying attention. Her mind was racing, trying to think of a way to explain why Tanner wasn't stopping without breaking the promise she had just made not to tell another lie if she got out of this mess.

"Good evening, gorgeous. I couldn't stay away a moment longer."

Ayanna went very still. Although she had never heard Tanner's voice, she instinctively knew it was him. The smooth baritone rumble made her skin prickle. She was instantly aware of the close proximity of his lean, powerfully built body, his hand that rested lightly on the back of her chair, the light pressure of his knuckles brushing against her silk dress. Heat and an unwanted something she didn't want to think about zipped though her.

She jerked her gaze up and stared straight into the deepest, most hypnotic black eyes she had ever seen. They promised to fulfill a thousand fantasies. No wonder women fought to be in his bed.

"It seems our secret is out, sweetheart, and I'm afraid I can't deny myself another second." A smile curving his sensual lips, his head descended toward her upturned face.

Instead of telling him no or, at the very least, placing a hand on his magnificant broad chest to stop him, Ayanna simply stared and waited for his kiss.

TWO

Tanner watched her eyes widen. They were deep chocolate, beau-
tiful, and alluring. If he'd seen fear in them, he would have stopped
the slow descent of his head toward the flawless perfection of her
honey-colored face. He was a man who seized opportunities where
he found them, but never without warning.

He'd heard the women's entire conversation. His relief that she
was unattached was short-lived when he heard her say she had a
date. He was stunned moments later to hear his own name.

Women had tried to trap him since he was old enough to shave.
He might have thought she had similar thoughts if he hadn't seen
the desperation in her face when she was trying to get out of the
blind date, and then the shocked look on her face when her friend
insisted on meeting him.

Now he watched her long, sooty lashes drift shut just before
his lips brushed lightly against her cheek. A jolt of awareness shot
though him. From the sudden intake of breath, she felt the same
sensation.

His eyes narrowed. He hadn't expected that to happen and apparently neither had she. He enjoyed women, but it took more than
a kiss to excite him. *Interesting.*

"Ah, hmmm." Sheri cleared her throat and grinned as Ayanna

avoided her eyes and Tanner straightened. "Mr. Rafferty, I'm Sheri Moore, Ayanna's best friend. At least, I thought I was until she kept you a secret."

Tanner straightened and flashed a smile that had been charming females since he had his first tooth. His hand remained on Ayanna's chair. He was a possessive man and made no bones about it. "Please, call me Tanner, and I hope you'll allow me to call you Sheri."

Her smile widened in pleasure. "Please do."

Tanner glanced back at the silent Ayanna. He wanted to see her reaction when he said her name for the first time. "Forgive the secrecy. My fault entirely. It was my idea, not Ayanna's."

She swallowed and licked her lips. Pleased, he said to Sheri, "I hope you and Ayanna will join me at my table."

Sheri glanced at her watch, then shook her head with regret and stood. "My husband is out of town and he's going to call me in less than thirty minutes. If I'm not at home, he'll worry."

"I understand," Tanner said graciously, aware that Ayanna remained silent. "Perhaps another time."

"That would be nice. Good night, Tanner." Sheri looked at Ayanna. "I'm calling you first thing in the morning." With those words of warning she walked off.

Tanner took the seat next to Ayanna. "I seem to have forgotten where you live and where we were going. Perhaps you can help. I certainly wouldn't want to miss our first date."

Ayanna heard the unexpected teasing note in his deep voice, and shook herself to keep from being affected by it. It was easy to see how he had gained such a notorious reputation with women. However, she didn't plan to be next on his list. A momentary lapse in judgment was one thing; going headlong into certain heartache was another.

"Mr. Raf—"

"Tanner, please."

Ayanna moistened her lips, wishing he'd move back. His body

wasn't crowding her, his overpowering presence was. "Please accept my deepest apologies for involving you. It wasn't intentional."

"I know. I heard you trying to get out of the blind date." His grin widened. "And I was your way out."

Ayanna finally stopped being embarrassed long enough to realize he must have been listening to their conversation. "You eavesdropped on a private conversation?"

"For which we both should be thankful," he said, not seeming the least disturbed by her hard stare, "since we both get what we want."

She folded her arms over her chest. Another egotistical, rude man. "And what exactly is that?"

He leaned closer until she caught a whiff of his citrus-and-spice cologne and a scent that was elementally male and dangerous. "You get out of a blind date you were dreading, and I get an introduction to you that might lead to a date." He stuck out his wide-palmed hand. "Tanner Rafferty, and you are Ayanna . . ."

It was the smile in his eyes that had her unfolding her arms and extending her hand. She'd always liked men who didn't take themselves too seriously. "Hardcastle."

His hand closed gently but firmly over hers. "Where would you like to go Saturday night, Ayanna?"

She pulled her hand free and sat back, ignoring the tingling that started in her hand and radiated all over her body. "I'm busy—"

"Sheri will be unhappy to hear that."

Ayanna made a face. "She'll get over it."

"I won't," he said, his voice drifting over her like a caress.

Ayanna felt her body heat up. He should wear a sign that said "Lethal to Females," she thought, twisting in her seat. He moved closer.

"You two at it again?" Sheri picked up her scarf from the floor. "I can never keep track of my scarves."

Ayanna tried not to look guilty. "At least you still have that one.

You'd better hurry if you're going to be home for Reginald's call."
Sheri lived twenty minutes away, near the marina.

Sheri turned to Rafferty. "Tanner, I hope to see you Saturday
night at Judge Wyman's party."

"I wouldn't miss it," he said easily.

"Good. I'll see you two then." Looping the scarf around her
neck, she turned and left again.

Ayanna waited until Sheri neared the mahogany front doors
and the hostess opened it for her to exit. "Why did you do that?"
she hissed. "I am not going anyplace with you."

This time Tanner was the one who folded his arms. "I have an
invitation to the judge's party."

She might have known. Judge Wyman's wife, Edith, was a renowned hostess. The elite of D.C.'s society vied for an invitation
from her. Sheri would want to know what happened if they weren't
together.

"She'll probably introduce you to my replacement," Tanner commented lazily, as though he'd read her mind.

Pointing out that he didn't have a replacement since she wasn't
going out with him didn't seem as important as trying to figure
out how she was going to get out of the mess she had put herself in.
As hard and as long as she thought, nothing came to mind that
didn't require her admitting she lied, which, since Sheri had introduced herself to Tanner, would embarrass her best friend as well.

"My mother will be there," Ayanna mumbled, not sure if she
wanted reassurance or to frighten Tanner off.

He gave her reassurance and a smile guaranteed to make a sane
woman act irrationally. "Mothers like me."

Ayanna resisted, but it wasn't easy. What mother wouldn't want
to see her daughter with him? He was handsome, successful, charming. She'd envision cuddling beautiful dark-haired grandchildren
who looked like him.

Ayanna blinked, berating herself for that unwanted thought.
Her body had picked a heck of a time to come out of sexual hiber-

nation. And definitely with the wrong man. She *was* telling the truth when she told Sheri she was busy. She didn't help out in the restaurant at night unless they were busy, but she did catch up on paperwork at her home office.

"I could pick you up, we could wish the judge a happy birthday, and be on our way in thirty minutes," Tanner suggested persuasively. "Sheri would be happy, and I'd have the pleasure of taking you out. It's a win-win situation."

It sounded nice and simple, but simple wasn't a word she'd associate with a renegade like Tanner. "Are you really dateless on a Saturday night or is some woman going to want my scalp?"

"Your scalp is lovely right where it is," he said, lightly brushing his fingers through her short curly hair.

"You have a date and you're just going to dump her and take another woman?" Ayanna asked, her voice incensed.

Tanner studied the outrage on Ayanna's face on behalf of a woman she didn't know. Obviously she was someone with principles, another reason not to let her get away. "I don't have a date, but I'd very much like to take you."

Resistance melted like snowflakes on a hot stove. Ayanna chalked it up to the beard and the fact that it was the only way out of a difficult situation. "We're in and out?"

"In and out," he repeated, having the good sense and manners not to gloat. "Where and what time should I pick you up?"

Ayanna gave him the information and her phone number, just in case he had to cancel.

"Not in this lifetime." He stood. "I better get back to my table and take care of the bill before my waitress thinks I'm trying to sneak off."

"Let me take care of it." Ayanna lifted her hand, then jerked as Tanner's large one closed around hers. She hoped he didn't feel her pulse skittering.

"There's no need for that," he said. "Until Saturday night." He kissed her palm.

Ayanna tried to calm herself as he paid his bill, then sent her a smile that upped the temperature in her body fifty degrees. When he left, she slumped back in her chair. What on earth had possessed her to accept a date with a renegade like Tanner Rafferty?

The tingling in her body wasn't the answer she wanted.

The phone on Ayanna's nightstand rang seconds after the six-thirty alarm went off Friday morning. She didn't have to look at her caller ID to know it was Sheri making good on her threat. With a baleful look at the phone, Ayanna debated about whether or not she should let Sheri think she had already left for her morning jog. Deciding to do just that, she bounded out of bed, but couldn't quite make herself continue to the bathroom. Sheri was a good friend.

Plopping back on the side of the bed, she picked up the phone. "How's Reginald?"

"Fine. Details," Sheri said. "And don't leave out anything."

Ayanna refused to squirm, even if her conscience was beginning to beat up on her. Sheri had been trying to help. It wasn't her fault Ayanna didn't like hurting people's feelings. "There's nothing much to tell. It just sort of happened."

"Ayanna Hardcastle, I can't believe you're not giving me anything! My best friend is going out with the yummiest man in town and you act like it's no big deal."

"It isn't. Tomorrow night will be our first date," Ayanna said slowly, glad that much was true. "It might not lead anywhere."

"If the way you two were staring at each other is any indication, I have a good idea where it's going," Sheri said frankly.

Ayanna chose to ignore that remark. Sheri had never been shy about her sex life with Reginald. They might have recently married, but they had lived together, much to the chagrin of her parents, for the past three years. "Just promise me you won't try and fix me up with any more blind dates if it doesn't?"

"I won't have to because you're too smart to let a man like Tanner Rafferty get away," Sheri said with a smile in her voice. "George is a great guy, but not many men could measure up if they were put up against Tanner."

Ayanna didn't have to meet George to know Sheri spoke the truth. "I'd better get going or else I'm going to get caught in traffic."

"That's your own fault," her friend said unsympathetically. "With your income you could get a wonderful place here instead of fighting the crazy traffic from Baltimore twice a day."

Ayanna gave her friend her usual and truthful answer. "I love living in a house with a yard and a garden that I can afford. Now let me go. I'll see you tomorrow night."

"All right. Everyone will be trying to outdo each other, so wear something that will keep Tanner's eyes on you."

"Bye." Ayanna hung up the phone and headed for the bathroom. She had no intention of dressing to impress Tanner because one date was all they were ever going to have.

Ayanna arrived at Leo's at nine sharp. Parking her Lexus in her designated spot on the side of the supper club, she grabbed her attaché case and headed inside. Her cousins' three spots were empty. Since they kept the place going until closing, they didn't come in until around two in the afternoon. In the meantime, Ayanna had the restaurant to herself, except for the security guard and the maintenance crew. Waving to the cleaning crew, she went directly to her office in the back.

Cozy was the only way to describe the converted closet, but it was functional and chic. She stepped behind her mahogany desk with ball-and-claw feet and sat down with a sigh. Across the room were mahogany file cabinets and bookshelves. On the walls were paintings by her favorite artists to add color. A six-by-three-foot mirror in a heavy ornate frame on the opposite wall added depth. She and her mother had gone searching for the office furniture soon after she'd accepted her cousins' offer to be their partner/accountant for Leo's.

Thinking of her mother brought back the present problem. Ayanna loved her, but one look at Tanner and she was going to start thinking of him as a potential son-in-law. Patricia Hardcastle was a level-headed woman. She had to be since she was an elementary school principal to over twelve hundred lucky children, but practicality went out the window when it came to the possibility of her daughter's marriage.

Ayanna leaned back in her chair, forgetting about the invoices she had planned to pay that day. Her mother had married the day after receiving her Master's in Education from Howard. Two years later, when she was twenty-four, Ayanna had been born. To her mother's and Ayanna's family's way of thinking, at thirty-three, Ayanna was getting perniciously close to being at an unsafe age for childbearing—*if* she found a husband—which it didn't look as if she would.

Perhaps things would have been different if her father had lived. The shock of his sudden death had been hard on everyone. Ayanna hadn't been dating anyone at the time and it had taken a couple of years to get back into the social swing of things. When she had, she'd found it increasingly difficult to be the same carefree woman she had once been. She didn't believe in forever so trustingly anymore.

She'd spoken to her father the morning he died. He and her mother had planned on coming to her apartment for dinner, but he never made it. It was then she discovered that the next hour wasn't promised, let alone the next day. As a result she'd guarded her emotions, perhaps too well. She hadn't dated seriously since.

Occasionally she'd feel a twinge of remorse that she wasn't married, didn't have children, but not enough to worry about it. Despite what her family thought, she had time. Tanner certainly hadn't thought she was past her prime.

Ayanna dropped her forehead into the palms of her hands. Her mother wouldn't be the only one thinking about Tanner for Ayanna. Like the gooey candy her parents had forbidden her to eat as a child because it was bad for her teeth, but which she had craved and frequently eaten anyway, Tanner was just as tempting. But he could be a lot more hazardous to her well-being.

THREE

It was nine A.M. Saturday morning and Tanner had already been up for three hours. After his routine morning workout and a two-mile swim, he'd gone to his hotel, an impressive twelve-story structure of rose marble. Many hotels were going modern with lots of black and chrome; he planned to stay with elegance and sophistication. Guests of The Rafferty Grand would be treated to the genteel refinement of the South in the most stylish setting imaginable.

Arms folded, Tanner stared across the street at his hotel. He noted the twenty-foot palms in rose-colored ceramic pots, the graceful curve of the decorative ironwork of each balcony. He could envision the uniformed doorman, the bellmen whisking luggage and harried travelers into the cool serenity of the atrium lobby.

Crystal bowls of miniature wrapped Belgian chocolate with The Rafferty Grand in gold letters would be at each check-in station. Once the guest had registered they'd receive a key to activate the oak-paneled elevator, which would take them swiftly to their floor. In their room they'd find complimentary chilled bottled water next to a mouth-watering picture of the cuisine they'd be tempted to order through room service or by dining downstairs.

Thoughts of dining brought Tanner's mind back to Ayanna. Twin lines radiated across his brow as he jaywalked across the busy street. He'd spent more time than he cared to admit thinking about her since Thursday night. Women usually didn't occupy so much of his attention.

Opening the heavy glass door, he was greeted by the sounds of workers and machinery and pushed Ayanna from his mind. After more than ten months, the outer structure was complete. Now they were putting the finishing touches on what would make The Rafferty Grand unique. He sidestepped two men rolling carpet, another three carrying one of the specially commissioned mirrors that would be hung off the main lobby, then stopped to check with the project manager before heading for the curving stairs and his office on the second floor.

On the landing he glanced back, satisfaction swelling within him. Everything was on schedule. The confirmed guest list was a who's who of the business, political, and entertainment worlds. He wanted their first impressions to be of a well-run hotel committed to excellence. He planned to start by giving them an event to remember, *and* by opening on time.

As he opened the door to his outer office he caught a flash of red out of the corner of his eye. It took only a second for him to realize that the woman coming into the hotel was a worker in a red shirt and not Ayanna. He accepted his disappointment and the undeniable fact that she wasn't going to be as easily forgotten as other women in his past. Not sure how he felt about that, he entered the office and closed the door.

Right up until thirty minutes before Tanner was due to pick her up, Ayanna had told herself she wasn't going to dress to impress. She then looked at herself in the mauve floor-length gown that had been a great buy but did nothing for her and quickly whipped it off.

With almost desperate haste she hurried to her closet and began shoving aside the padded hangers until she found what she was looking for, then quickly took out a long-sleeved black dress of clinging jersey and laid it on the bed. She exchanged the flesh-toned hose she was wearing for sheer black, took off her bra, then slipped the ankle-length gown over her head. The fit was perfect and totally provocative—the neck high and innocent, the back completely bare, stopping a scant inch above her hips. She'd bought the dress on a whim when she and Sheri were shopping for her wedding gown and had never worn it.

Looking over her shoulder at the cheval mirror in the corner of her bedroom, she admitted she'd never had the nerve. So why was she wearing it now?

The ringing doorbell was her answer. No matter how much she'd tried to deny it, she'd enjoyed Tanner's attention, enjoyed the little zip his touch caused, enjoyed being with him. He had a keen wit and he made her smile. He wasn't looking for anything long term, so there was no need for her to guard her heart. Why not just enjoy herself for the evening? In the process she'd show her family that she still had what it took to attract one of the most sought-after bachelors in the country. And she'd show Sheri she didn't need any help getting a date. Afterwards she could go back into hibernation.

Picking up a large wicker gift basket wrapped in iridescent paper with one hand, she stuck her small black beaded clutch under her arm with the other, then went to the front door and opened it. Tanner stood bathed in the soft yellow glow from the wrought-iron lantern on the porch, smiling down at her. Ayanna couldn't prevent the leap of her heart. Tanner in a black tux, bib-front white shirt, and black bow tie was even more devastating than he had been in a business suit.

"Hello, Ayanna. You look beautiful."

"Hello, and thank you," she said, pleased that her voice sounded normal.

"Let me take that for you." He lifted the basket filled with chocolate goodies and a bottle of wine. "The judge is going to be a happy man."

"He loves chocolate-covered nuts and Sweet Temptation has the best in the city." Stepping over the threshold, she turned to pull the door closed.

"Ayanna!"

She froze. There was as much reverence as admiration in the way he uttered her name. Slowly she turned to face him.

"You're beautiful," he whispered.

"I think you already said that," she said, inordinately pleased.

"Certain things bear repeating." Taking her by the elbow, he led her to the black limousine waiting by the curb. "I hope there'll be dancing tonight."

She glanced up at him. "You like to dance?"

"Sometimes." He waved the driver away and opened the door. After helping her inside, he placed the basket on the seat across from them and slid in beside Ayanna. "Do you think we might get in a few turns around the floor before we leave? I have a feeling we'd both enjoy it immensely."

Ayanna moistened her lips as the driver pulled smoothly away from the curb. She didn't have a doubt that Tanner knew just how to hold a woman, stroke her, make her burn. "I don't think we'll have time."

"Pity," he said, watching her with hooded eyes.

Ayanna felt like a baby chick in the henhouse with a sharp-toothed fox. She had forgotten one important thing: Tanner was a renegade. He made his own rules. What he wanted took precedence over the desires or plans of others. And he wanted her, a thought that both chilled and excited her. She glanced out the tinted window as the car headed up the ramp to the freeway into D.C. and tried hard not to think about how much she wanted him.

"How have things been at work?" he asked, breaking the silence.

She glanced over at him. "Routine," she said, omitting to tell him that she hadn't been able to get him off her mind. "How are things going at The Rafferty Grand?"

"We're right on schedule," he said simply. "What made you want to be an accountant?"

No man had ever asked her that before. She got the distinct impression that Tanner wasn't just being nice or needing to fill the silence; he genuinely wanted to know. "One of my father's second jobs was doing income taxes. I used to help him and found I had a skill for mathematical computations."

"What did he do?"

"He was a policeman, a very good one," she said with pride in her voice. "He'd tried to get work as an off-duty policeman in security because it would have been steadier and paid more, but very few of those jobs were given to minority police officers. Eventually the system changed and he was able to get the recognition and respect he deserved. At the time of his death he was the chief of police."

Tanner's hand closed gently over hers. "Our forefathers went through a lot, but I think it made us stronger, more resilient. You might not have known where your talent lay if not for your father's other job. Because of what he went through, he certainly understood those coming after him."

"That's what he always said."

"Sounds as if he was a wonderful man."

"He was."

"From what I've seen so far, so is his daughter."

Warmth curled though Ayanna. She forgot caution and let Tanner continue to hold her hand. A moment or two longer wouldn't hurt.

Traffic was backed up two blocks away from the Hyatt. Cars, limos, and taxis jockeyed to get to the door and drop off passengers. Tanner had attended enough social events in D.C. to expect the snarled nightmare. "I see it's business as usual tonight. Parking will be at a premium."

Ayanna smiled at Tanner. "One of the reasons I live outside of the city. Even on the one-way street in front of Leo's accidents have occurred. They've tied up traffic for hours and drastically cut into business."

"One of the requirements for the location of The Rafferty Grand was easy accessibility," he said thoughtfully. "The owners of Leo's would do well to think about the traffic situation. You never want to be vulnerable."

"I agree," she said, crossing her long legs and drawing Tanner's attention. "The building behind Leo's is for sale, but it's overpriced, even in D.C.'s inflated market."

Tanner withdrew his gaze from her trim ankle. "The owner has a problem, then."

"Owners," she corrected casually, then added, "But not an insurmountable one for us."

His brows bunched in shock. "You own part of Leo's?"

Her smile made him want to kiss her breathless. "Full partner with my other three male cousins. Leo's is named after their father."

He laughed, shaking his head. "Why am I not surprised? You continue to amaze me, Ayanna. You have quite an establishment there, but I guess you already know that."

"Yes, but it's always nice to hear it, especially from a man of your reputation," Ayanna said.

"Don't believe everything you read about me," Tanner cautioned, his knuckles brushing across her cheek.

Her breath stalled and she eased back in the seat, glancing out the window, desperately trying to calm her racing heart. "The driver may run out of gas before we get to the hotel."

Tanner allowed her escape. For now. "Pete has been my driver for six years. He knows his business."

Ayanna glanced toward the front of the limo. "You have him full time?"

"He's not a frivolous luxury. I don't have time to waste waiting for taxis, locating an address, or returning rentals. Besides, while I'm in transit, I can return phone calls or work on the laptop."

"That makes sense," she said. "You're a busy man."

"I'm going to get a lot busier when The Rafferty Grand opens. I plan for it to have five stars by the end of the first year," he told her.

"You'll get it, too," she replied with complete confidence. Few things could probably withstand the force that was Tanner Rafferty. The thought caused her a moment of unease.

"We might as well get out here, if you don't mind," he said when the car idled through another green light. "Unless you want to wait until the driver can get closer."

"This is fine."

"Let us off here, Pete. Don't bother to get out," Tanner said to the driver. "I'll call you when we're ready to be picked up."

"Yes, Mr. Rafferty," the driver said as he eased to the curb.

As soon as the car stopped, Tanner retrieved the basket, helped Ayanna out, then did what he'd wanted to do ever since he saw the enticing bare curve of her slender back. He placed his hand on that smooth, bare skin.

She jumped and whirled around. Her eyes were huge, her chest heaving with fury.

Her skin had felt like warmed silk, but if he wanted to touch it again, he knew he had better back off. He took her arm and they walked down the street toward the hotel. "Temptation is a terrible thing," he said contritely. "I had a weak moment and I'm not sure I won't have another."

Ayanna glanced up at him, no longer upset. He'd done it again. Made light of what could have been an embarrassing moment for her and, at the same time, made her aware that he thought she was desirable. "You believe in speaking your mind," she said.

"Always." He opened one of the small glass side doors to the entrance of the hotel. "Tonight is for us to have a good time. I also plan to make it a memorable one."

Ayanna didn't doubt him for a second.

· · ·

The Imperial Ballroom was a moving sea of people. The sparkle of the women's gowns and their jewelry rivaled that of the ten immense chandeliers in the vaulted ceiling. A five-piece band played Judge Wyman's favorite songs, made unforgettable by jazz legend Miles Davis. Food and drink were plentiful and people were taking full advantage of both.

Ayanna and Tanner hadn't gone five feet before the first of many guests came up to speak to him, welcome him to the city, or invite him to join a club or a business organization. Every few steps the process was repeated. With the ease of a man used to being fawned over, he thanked them and moved on without committing himself.

Ayanna would have to be blind to miss the speculative looks and outright stares she received, or the envy in many of the women's eyes. She tried to recall if Tanner's name had been linked to any woman since his arrival and drew a blank. She certainly didn't want to be the first. Having fun was one thing; being known as the first woman Tanner dumped in D.C. was quite another.

"What's the frown for?"

"Just considering how it's going to feel to be known as the first of many you dated while in D.C.," she said.

"I wouldn't worry about that if I were you," he said, handing the basket to an attendant at one of the three tables reserved for gifts. Two security guards stood nearby.

She was about to ask him why when she spotted Sheri dragging Reginald and another man toward them. Somehow she knew the slender man with the long, serious face in a tailor-made black tux was George.

"I think we're about to meet my would-be replacement." Tanner's hand moved from her arm and curved possessively around her waist. Ayanna looked up and saw the hard glint in his eyes. He was definitely staking a claim, and she wasn't quite sure how she felt about it.

Sheri, pretty in a pale blue gown, quickly made the introductions. Reginald had a wicked sense of humor and soon had all of them laughing . . . except George. He seemed more interested in letting them know of his family connections and how brilliant he was. Ayanna caught Sheri's pained look and hoped fervently that she would now stop trying to fix her up. A few minutes later Reginald saw his parents and they went off to meet them.

"We'd better find my mother and Judge Wyman," Ayanna said, trying to peer through the growing crush of people.

"Do you bare a striking resemblance to your mother?"

"Yes. Why?" she asked.

"Because, if I'm not mistaken, they've found us."

Ayanna followed the direction of his gaze. He was right. Her mother and Judge Wyman, arms linked, were heading straight for them. And both were grinning as if they'd won the lottery.

FOUR

Patricia Hardcastle, slim and lovely at fifty-six years old, had never met a stranger, Ayanna thought. Her father used to say she'd talk to a sign post. Two minutes after meeting Tanner, she was chatting with him as if they'd known each other for years. She even managed to get in a plug for her school. If Tanner ever considered being a sponsor, or if any of his staff wanted to mentor, her elementary school would be grateful.

"I'd be happy to discuss it with you when things settle down a bit," he said.

After he'd sidestepped so many requests and invitations that evening Ayanna couldn't hide her surprise. Only Tanner noticed. She had a feeling that very little got past him.

"Children need to know adults care. The earlier, the better," he said sincerely.

"Exactly," Patricia said, beaming. "Thank you, Mr. Rafferty. It would mean so much to my kids."

"Please call me Tanner," he said with urbane charm.

It would have taken a woman of stone not to melt when all that charm was directed at her. Her mother actually blushed.

Ayanna had been the recipient of that soulful voice and mesmerizing eyes, so she understood her mother's reaction. From the first she had labeled him as dangerous to the female population. Any woman who went out with him would either have to be very self-assured or so enamored of him that she didn't care that he attracted women like bees to a honey pot.

As if aware of her thoughts, Tanner smiled at her. Again heat shimmered through her. She was acutely aware of his hand on her bare skin. *Dangerous.* So what was she doing here with him, doing all this pretending, instead of being home with a good book?

"I see, as usual, you've managed to find the best," Judge Wyman said, his shrewd black eyes staring at Tanner. The judge was dressed in a black tux that fit his slender body perfectly.

"I try." Tanner smiled down at Ayanna.

She flushed and decided it was best to lighten the mood. "Judge Wyman, it's a wonderful party."

"Glad you could come." The judge looked her over and nodded his gray head approvingly. "Leo would be proud of you." He glanced at Tanner. "But he'd also be a bit concerned."

Ayanna sighed. Her ploy to keep things light hadn't worked. However, before Ayanna could speak, Tanner said, "He wouldn't have to be. I hope you and Mrs. Hardcastle won't be, either."

After a moment, the judge nodded. "You can be a ruthless SOB, Tanner, but you're a fair one."

"I trust my daughter's judgment until you show me otherwise." Patricia's eyes, the exact color of Ayanna's, narrowed. "Mess up and you'll regret it."

Ayanna flushed in embarrassment. "It's just a date, Mother. We'll probably never see each other again."

"Not if I have anything to say about it," Tanner said firmly, taking her arm. "If you'll excuse us, I'd like to have at least one dance. I promised Ayanna not to keep her out too late."

"Why so early?" her mother asked with a frown.

Tanner looked at Ayanna and she forced herself not to squirm. "I have a lot of paperwork."

"You work too hard," her mother admonished with a frown. "For once, just enjoy yourself."

"Patricia is right," the judge said. "I'd like to know that people had a good time at my party."

Everyone knew the judge's wife threw the birthday party as a social event. "I suppose we could stay a little while longer."

"Then let's dance." Tanner didn't wait for an answer.

As soon as he put his arms around her, she knew she was in trouble. Nothing in her wildest dreams could have prepared her for the erotic sensation of the feel of his hard body against hers, the arousing touch of his hand on her skin.

Warning bells went off in her head, but overriding them was the seductive pull of his body against hers. Without thought, her body softened, fitting itself against his. When the music stopped and he looked down at her, she saw reflected in his eyes her own naked desire.

"I never knew need could be this intense," he said huskily.

"Neither did I," she said without thought and watched his eyes narrow, his nostrils flair. His head started to descend. "T-Tanner."

His hand clenched in hers. He seemed to shake himself. "Would you like something to drink or eat?"

She didn't, but it was safer than another dance. "Yes."

They walked from the dance floor, their bodies brushing against the other with each step. Neither thought of moving away.

This is it, Ayanna thought as Tanner unlocked her front door. The big moment when you had to decide on the good-night kiss. With her recent dates, there hadn't been any question. She'd thanked them politely and then went inside . . . alone.

With Tanner her body had been in a humming state of arousal since they had left the party. They'd stayed about forty minutes longer, then bade everyone good night. As if both were aware their emotions were being held in check by a delicate thread, they had not returned to the dance floor, nor had Tanner touched her except on her arm.

Holding the front door open, Tanner stood aside for her to enter. The key was still in his hand. She could wait for him to give it to her, or go inside and get the kiss her body craved.

Silently she walked inside, heard the door close behind her, and turned around.

In the next second she was in his arms, his mouth devouring hers. She heard her purse land on the terrazzo floor. His hands on her burned with feverish delight. She couldn't seem to get enough of him.

He jerked his head up, his breathing harsh and deep. Ayanna's eyes flickered open and she stared into the glittering eyes of a man who ravaged and plundered to take whatever he wanted. She shivered.

He shut his eyes briefly, then drew her gently into his arms and held her. "I could kiss you forever and it still wouldn't be long enough."

Her breath shuddered over her lips. She knew exactly how he felt.

He stepped back and held her at arm's length. "I understand Leo's has brunch on Sunday. Care to join me if I can get a reservation?"

Ayanna stared up at him. He hadn't phrased the invitation as a date but more as friends meeting. He also hadn't expected preferential treatment. "I'd like that."

"After I make the reservations, I'll call." He pulled her key from his pocket and handed it to her. "Good night."

"Good night." Her hand closed around the ring of keys and felt the lingering heat.

His lips brushed so softly against her cheek it could have been her imagination. Her eyes drifted shut again. When she opened them he was gone.

. . .

Sunday morning Tanner and Ayanna arrived at Leo's shortly before their 11:30 reservation. Her cousin Noah was in front helping with seating. His astute black eyes flickered from Ayanna to Tanner, then Noah smiled. Ayanna breathed a bit easier. When it came to men, all three of her cousins tended to act as if she were operating on less than half a brain cell. Apparently marriage had mellowed her older cousin Noah. The twins, Tyrell and Tyrone, were a bit more unpredictable.

"Hi, Ayanna. Glad to have you back, Mr. Rafferty," Noah said as he stuck two menus beneath his arm.

"Hi, Noah," Ayanna greeted. It didn't surprise her that Noah greeted Tanner by name. He prided himself on remembering Leo's patrons. "Tanner, this is my cousin and one of the other owners and the manager of Leo's, Noah Hardcastle."

The handshake was firm. "This way," Noah said, leading them through the already crowded restaurant to a quiet table in the corner of the room. "Is this all right?"

"Yes," Tanner said, seating Ayanna, then taking his own seat and accepting the menu.

"Can I get either of you something to drink, perhaps a mimosa?"

"Ayanna?" Tanner said, his menu still closed.

"Tomato juice."

"I'll have the same."

"Your waitress Sarah will be with you shortly."

Tanner opened his menu as Noah left. "What's good?"

"Everything," Ayanna answered. They smiled at each other across the table.

"I'll take your word for it," he said as their waitress came up to take their orders, then left. "Do the other cousins work here as well?"

"The answer to your question is coming this way." Tyrell and Tyrone were identical twins but opposites in the way they dressed, wore their hair, in temperament, and taste. Both had made artistic triumphs in their own right, Tyrell as a master chef and Tyrone as a musical genius.

They spoke to Ayanna, nodded at Tanner, put their drink order on the table, then flanked her, each twin placing a hand on the back of her chair, and stared at Tanner. Although they were a year younger than Ayanna they had grown up protective of her. Too much so, in her opinion.

"Be good," she admonished, then made introductions.

Tanner stood and extended his hand. "Glad to see you look after her. Not that she needs it," he added when Ayanna snorted.

"No, I don't," she agreed. "Tyrell, you're probably needed in the kitchen and, Tyrone, I believe we're supposed to have live music today and I want to hear my favorite."

Both men laughed and kissed her on the cheek. "She always was bossy," Tyrone told Tanner.

"I'd better get back to the kitchen if you want your orders on time. Bye."

Tanner chuckled. "That little episode reminded me of how my sister Raine reacts to me or Adrian stepping on her independence."

Ayanna smiled across the table at him. "The newspaper reported she was going to try and duplicate her brothers' successes by acquiring restaurants across the country."

Tanner frowned. "She hates it when anyone compares her to us. Some people act as if all she has to do is ask Dad for a check. She's worked hard, just like the rest of us did to get where we are. Nothing was handed to us. We were given two years to turn a profit or go back to basics and learn why. All of us got it right the first time out."

Tanner's defense of his sister endeared him to Ayanna a little more. She'd grown up with three surrogate brothers in her cousins. "Unfortunately, some people will never look at a woman's accomplishments, her hard work and intelligence, as being equal to a man's," she commented.

His dark head tilted to one side. "I hear the voice of experience."

Sighing, she leaned back in her chair. "Although I was better qualified and had more seniority, I was passed over for promotion and then asked to train my male replacement, who didn't know a spreadsheet from a debit sheet. It galled me, but I reasoned if I showed them I was a team player, the next time it would benefit me and I would get the promotion."

She made a face. "I was so naïve and so wrong. The second time I was passed over, I handed in my resignation."

"What happened then?"

"I moped, gained ten pounds eating junk food, thought of writing to the EEOC, and then Noah, Tyrone, and Tyrell came to visit one night and offered me a chance to be an integral part of their vision." She glanced around the restaurant that had become her salvation. "I'll always be thankful to them for having enough faith in me to bring me on as a full partner, for trusting me with their money, and especially for rescuing me from a downward spiral of self-pity."

His large hand covered hers. "Everyone needs someone sometimes. I'm just glad they were there."

She wanted to ask if he had ever needed someone, but Sarah arrived with their food and she pulled her hand free.

FIVE

Ayanna grew increasingly quiet as their meal progressed. Tanner hadn't a clue as to what had caused the change in her, but he intended to find out once they were alone. He paid their bill, leaving a generous tip for their waitress, said good-bye to her cousins, then walked her to his rental. He planned to spend the day and possibly the night with her and, for reasons he hadn't yet figured out, he didn't want Pete to know.

He pulled out of the parking lot. He wasn't used to waiting for answers, but he didn't want her to be the object of the staff's gossip, or have her cousins interfering if the conversation went where he didn't want it going. There it was again, the protective instinct that kept popping up.

Stopping at a red light, his fingers tapping on the steering wheel, Tanner glanced at Ayanna. She quickly looked away. He sensed a vulnerability about her that pulled at him. Without thought, he brushed his knuckles against her cheek. Again he felt her shudder beneath his touch and he flexed his hand. The light turned green and he pulled off.

"Why so quiet?" he asked, unable to hold the questions back any longer.

"Just thinking."

Her answer told him nothing and left him with a vague sense of uneasiness that he was about to get the brush-off. That he wouldn't allow. "I've been to your place. How about coming by tomorrow to see mine?"

She was quiet for so long he guessed the answer. "That's very nice of you, but although the restaurant is closed on Mondays, I go in and work. I won't have time."

Tanner's hand gripped the steering wheel. People were practically lining up to be the first ones to see inside The Rafferty Grand. He had purposely kept the interior a secret to increase the buzz, but Ayanna had turned him down.

Shooting her a quick glance, he hit the freeway ramp with a burst of speed. Traffic into Maryland on I-95 was surprisingly heavy and he had to concentrate on driving. Finding out whatever was bothering her had to wait.

Thirty-five minutes later he pulled into her driveway. She lived in a quiet neighborhood of modest, one-story brick homes. The yards were well maintained. Scalloped tree rings filled with a profusion of flowers seemed a particular favorite of the homeowners.

He got out and went to open her door, but she got out by herself and started up the walkway. Tanner had little time to admire the graceful sway of her hips in a slim black dress that showed her long legs to perfection. He quickly caught up with her and took her arm. "Ayanna, what is it?"

"Nothing," she said, her key already out. "I had a wonderful time, Tanner."

"Do you really expect me to trot on back to the car and drive off?" he asked.

Ayanna had hoped . . . no, that was a lie, and she had lied to herself enough where Tanner was concerned. Tanner excited her as no man ever had. He stirred things in her that made her want to forget being safe, forget that caring for a man like Tanner could shatter her.

"A man like you could cause a woman a lot of trouble," she said at last.

He stepped closer. He was pure temptation dressed up in a suit.

"The same could be said of you," he said.

She tried one last time. "You have more experience at this than I do."

There was a subtle shift in his predatory posture. Something flickered in his dark eyes. "I told you not to believe everything you've read about me."

"If I hadn't read one word, I could tell." She shook her head, searching for the words. "It's in the self-assured way you carry yourself, your dogged determination to have your way in everything. Your refuse to listen to 'no' unless you're the one saying it."

His brow puckered. "You see that as bad?"

His genuine puzzlement made her want to throw up her hands. "Tanner, when has a woman ever been able to say no to you and keep saying no if you wanted a yes?"

"Do you really expect me to answer that?" he asked, his mouth tight.

She sighed. "No. Good-bye, Tanner."

"No," he said, then gritted his teeth as if remembering her comment about his refusing to listen to no unless he were saying it. "Could we please go inside and talk?"

Ayanna had lived in the quiet older neighborhood for five years and both she and her mother were acquainted with many of her neighbors. There would be enough questions from her mother as to why Tanner was no longer around without her hearing about their arguing on the front porch. Ayanna stepped aside. "I won't change my mind."

Tanner didn't say anything.

Closing the door, Ayanna waved him to a seat on the white sofa in the living room. She took a seat on the matching Queen Anne chair.

"The way I see it, my reputation has put me at an unfair disadvantage. The only way to change your mind and show you that I'm not ruthless or unconscionable is for you to spend more time with me," he reasoned.

"That's not an option."

Tanner stared at her intently. "I want to see you. What would it take for that to happen?"

Promise me you won't break my heart. She folded her hands in her lap. Life had no guarantees. She already knew that.

Tanner leaned toward her and his hand closed over hers, drawing her gaze to his. He'd moved so fast she hadn't a chance to object or evade. It probably wouldn't have done her any good, anyway, as he was not a man who yielded or backed down. And honestly would she really want to date a man who wouldn't stand up and fight for what he believed in or wanted? She glanced down at their hands, felt the heat, and experienced the fear. "I need a few days to think about this."

His hand tightened on hers, then relaxed. "You'll call me by Wednesday?"

She almost smiled at his persistence. "Yes."

He turned her hand over and pressed his lips to the inside of her wrist. With a will of its own, her other hand cupped his cheek and felt the incredible softness of his beard. In the next instant his mouth, hot and avid, was on hers, and then they were somehow on the carpeted floor.

As she'd feared and known all along, resistance never entered her mind. When in Tanner's arms, his kisses heated her blood and made her burn. She heard him moan her name, and experienced a thrill of pleasure that she wasn't the only one caught up in the madness. Then she was tumbling headlong into passion, fierce and greedy.

She moaned. Tanner was right. The need was intense.

Tanner lifted his head and stared down into Ayanna's passion-flushed face beneath him. He wanted nothing more than to strip away their clothes—if he could wait that long—and sink into her softness. He knew she wouldn't stop him.

He pulled her to him and rolled over, bringing her with him until she was on top. He muttered when his knee bumped the coffee table.

"Tanner?"

"It's all right, baby. Just give me a minute," he said, stroking her back, making sure his hand went no farther than her waist. "Nothing is going to happen."

Ayanna shifted, then stilled when she felt the rigid bulge pressed against the notch of her thighs. "You positive?"

A ragged laugh tore from him. Uncertain if he heard regret or fear in her voice, he hugged her. "I control my body. When we make love we'll both be ready."

She buried her face between his neck and shoulder. He took what little comfort he could in the fact that she didn't deny his words.

"What time do you think I could come by tomorrow?"

Slowly, very slowly, he lifted her face with his thumb and finger. "You won't regret it."

"I already know that," she said, holding his gaze.

"Not that I'm not thankful, but what changed your mind?"

Her hand stroked his chest though his white shirt. "You did. You may be ruthless, but you didn't take unfair advantage of the situation."

"I wanted to. I still want to."

Ayanna scrambled off Tanner, inadvertently rubbing against the part of him that wanted to be buried deep in her satin heat. He groaned.

"Did I hurt you?" she asked, still on her knees beside him.

He gave her a look that made her blush.

Gracefully he came to his feet, bringing her with him. "If you can make it around noon, Stephen Pointe, the consulting concept chef, has promised to serve a sampling of the Mediterranean and Asian cuisine he plans to serve in The Jade Room, which will be the largest and most formal of the two restaurants in the hotel."

"I love Asian food. We don't serve it at Leo's and when I bring take-out, Tyrell has a fit," she said.

"Then I'll see you at noon." He kissed her on the cheek and left.

Ayanna watched him get in his car and drive off. She didn't know where tomorrow might lead, but she wasn't running from it any longer. The question was no longer if she'd go to bed with Tanner, it was how soon.

Tanner was whistling when he opened the door to his leased condo. He'd chosen the location for its proximity to the hotel, but also for its view of the Potomac River. Looking out on the river always soothed and calmed him. It wasn't a coincidence that all his hotels were located near the water. Adrian was the same way. They teased Raine about being a land lover. Only one of her three restaurants was near the water.

He was in his bedroom undressing when the phone rang. He hit the speaker button and jerked off his tie. "Tanner."

"About time you made it home. I called twice."

"Hi, Ra." Raine never wasted time with small talk when she had a point to make. "Guess I forgot to turn on the machine when I left this morning."

"Problems with the hotel?" she asked, concern in her soft voice.

He slipped off his Italian loafers; his socks followed. "Things couldn't be better. I was in a rush to pick up Ayanna Hardcastle."

"Whoa, big brother. Ayanna Hardcastle? And since when have you been in a hurry to pick up any woman?"

Tanner paused in the process of zipping up a pair of jeans that seamlessly flowed over his long legs and hips. He frowned, then smiled, zipping and snapping. "I guess this is a first. How did things go in Atlanta?"

"That crooked manager I dismissed for skimming profits from the previous owner was trying to get the employees to walk out en masse." Her voice took on a hard edge. "Instead of being thankful that Holiday didn't file charges against him but let him get off with restitution, he tried to get back at me."

"Is he still in one piece?"

"Barely, but he won't pull that stunt again and neither will the staff, unless they want to find other jobs. I called a meeting, showed them a stack of applicants waiting to take their place, the same applicants who, if hired, would get a bonus proportionate to profits. They decided they didn't want to quit after all."

He chuckled. Raine was definitely a chip off the old block. Never hesitating to crush the opposition. "I'm glad you're on my team." Pulling a melon-colored polo shirt over his head, he picked up the cordless phone and walked into his home office. His long, narrow feet sank into the ecru carpet.

"That's the same thing Dad said this morning."

Their father was probably on the golf course bragging to his buddies about Raine's victory as they spoke. It was embarrassing at times, but their father always said telling the truth wasn't bragging. Tanner hit the speaker button on the office phone and deactivated the handheld one.

"We'll celebrate when you come back. I already figured out why we had reservations at Leo's." He sat at the U-shaped workstation and booted up the computer.

"So give."

Tanner gave her a full report on Leo's in glowing terms. "It's a great supper club. Ayanna and her cousins have a right to be proud."

"Any vulnerabilities?"

Tanner scrolled though his e-mail for the weekly reports from each hotel. "Nothing that you have to contend with in Atlanta or any of your locations. Leo's is on a one-way street and a couple of times accidents have tied up traffic and cut down on business. But the restaurant has been packed each time I've been there."

"So Leo's *does* have a weak spot," she mused.

Tanner's attention wavered as he read the "Urgent" e-mail from Sidney Yates, his executive manager of The Rafferty House in Charleston. Tanner reached for the second phone on his desk and keyed in the number. "Have to run, Ra. I'll call you back."

"No need. You've given me the information I wanted. Thanks."

Thinking she meant a report on how to duplicate Leo's success, he gave his full attention to the problem in Charleston. "Yates,"

Tanner said when the executive manager answered her cell phone on the second ring. "Rafferty here. What is it, why couldn't you solve it, and why didn't you call?"

Yates didn't falter as she gave Tanner the details. A guest had slipped and fallen in the gift shop because of another guest's spilled drink on the floor. The incident raised suspicion in the executive manager's mind when the young woman, although claiming to be in a lot of pain and unable to stand on her own, refused to let the hotel doctor check her. She'd left with the assistance of the man she was with to seek private care.

"I want Slaughter to do a check on everyone involved," Tanner said, referring to the head of security for the Rafferty enterprise.

"He's already on it, and he's checking the computer for similar incidents."

"Good. Now, why didn't you contact me sooner?" The episode happened when the shop opened at twelve. It was past three.

"I tried. You didn't answer at home and your cell was off."

Tanner muttered one succinct word. Not only had he forgotten to turn on his answering machine before leaving, he'd forgotten to turn his cell back on when he left Leo's. It had always aggravated him when people's cells went off in the theater or in restaurants. He'd been so concerned about Ayanna's sudden quietness, he hadn't thought about it. He had never overlooked something like that in the past.

"It won't happen again," was all he said. He didn't accept excuses or make them. "Keep me posted."

"Yes, sir."

"Yates?"

"Yes?"

"Good job."

"Thank you." There was relief in her voice.

Tanner hung up the phone, got up, and walked over to the window. Ayanna could cause him a lot of trouble and it seemed he was only beginning to realize how much.

SIX

Ayanna spotted Tanner the moment she rounded the street corner that Monday afternoon. Hands stuffed into the uncuffed pants of his double-breasted olive suit, he was pacing the sidewalk in front of his hotel. She didn't have to check her watch again to know she was ten minutes late. Since she disliked waiting on people, she hurried over to him, words of apology already running through her mind.

When she was fifteen feet away, his dark head lifted abruptly and he stared directly at her, almost as if he had sensed her presence. The impact of all that intensity directed at her caused her steps to momentarily falter, her breath to quicken. What was it about this particular man that caused her body to react so strongly?

While she was contemplating the answer to that question, his hands came out of his pockets and he started toward her. All the people on the busy street seemed to disappear; the sounds of traffic faded away.

He was a couple of feet away when she blurted, "I had trouble finding a parking spot."

His expression didn't change as he took her arm and started back. "I should have sent the car for you."

"That's not necessary," she said, still unsure of his mood. She was used to seeing a glint of humor in his eyes. Today there was none. "The laundry truck came in early and I had to check the order before I left."

He pushed opened the glass door. "Welcome to The Rafferty Grand."

Ayanna's heart experienced a little pang. His words had all the warmth of an ice cube. "Tanner, if you're busy we can do this another time."

"I invited you," he said, continuing through the lobby.

Ayanna dug in her heels on the light blue Italian stone flooring in front of the receptionist desk. "Obviously you regret it."

Tanner looked at her, his mouth tight. "There was a problem at The Rafferty House in Charleston yesterday."

Instantly contrite, Ayanna placed her hand on his chest. "Was? Does that mean it's all right now?"

"Yes." His mouth was a narrow line.

"So why are you still upset about it?" Ayanna tilted her head to one side.

He brought the full force of his gaze back to her. "Because it could have gone the other way if the executive manager hadn't been on her toes, and the head of security hadn't been able to find out the incident was a scam."

"I'm still trying to figure out why you're beating yourself over the head about it," she said. "You wouldn't have them working for you if they weren't competent enough to take care of problems."

"Because I was unreachable," he said, derision in his voice. "I have always prided myself on being available to the people who work for and with me."

Slowly Ayanna began to put everything together. "You weren't available because you were with me." It was a statement, not a question.

"I didn't turn on the answering machine when I left my place, and I failed to turn my cell back on after we left Leo's," he stated flatly.

"I can see how much that bothers you and I have the perfect solution. Good-bye, Tanner." She spun on her heels.

"No!" he said, grabbing her arm. The one word in the high-ceilinged space went through the room like a pistol shot, drawing the attention of the workers. "You can't do that."

"It was bound to end sooner than later."

"Says who?" he challenged, his eyes taking on a dangerous glint.

Ayanna was about to reply when she noticed that it had grown quiet. She glanced around and flushed at seeing they were the center of attention. Worse, a few feet behind Tanner and to the left stood a thin, middle-aged man with a neatly trimmed graying mustache wearing a chef's uniform. "I think your chef wants to speak to you."

"He can wait until we're finished." Tanner didn't even look away from her.

Ayanna's saw the chef's eyes flash. Temperamental, just like Tyrell. If Tanner wasn't careful he'd be minus a concept chef.

Sidestepping Tanner, she extended her hand to the glaring man. "Ayanna Hardcastle. Are you the wonderful concept chef Mr. Rafferty told me who is going to make my taste buds weep with joy?"

The man beamed and clasped her hand. "Stephen Pointe. Everything is ready." He looked at Tanner and his voice cooled. "If Mr. Rafferty is agreeable?"

"Of course he is," she answered for Tanner. "Why don't I walk with you and you can tell me about the delicacies you've prepared."

The chef smiled warmly at her, turning his back on Tanner. "Delighted. This way."

Ayanna walked beside the chef, a prickling sensation in her back. Tanner looked as if he could chew nails. She was trying to help, but she wouldn't put it past him to fire the chef and toss both out of his hotel.

Tanner wanted to toss the chef out the nearest window. Unfortunately, it was sealed shut. The scrawny man was fawning over Ayanna as he personally prepared her plate, all the time chatting with her as if they had known each other for years. The worse offense was when he took a seat at the table Tanner had ordered to be set with fresh cut flowers, linen, and sterling silver.

Tanner knew that his management staff was tiptoeing around him as if he were a ticking time bomb, but he couldn't seem to help it. He wasn't particularly surprised when, one by one, they quickly prepared their plates and left. If he hadn't already told them that he expected a report on the dishes served, he suspected the majority of them would have taken one look at him and left.

Ayanna certainly didn't appear concerned by the prospect of angering him, or of not seeing him again. She was sampling everything the chef put on her plate, then rhapsodizing over it as if she had never tasted anything so good. Tanner hadn't bothered to fix a plate. The one his executive secretary prepared for him sat untouched on a table several feet from Ayanna and Pointe. Tanner hadn't trusted himself to sit any closer.

"Not another bite, please." Ayanna placed her hand on her flat stomach and smiled at the chef. "You will have people begging to get a reservation. Your alliance with The Rafferty Grand will ensure that The Jade Room will create one of the most exciting dining experiences in the East." She tipped her head. "My compliments to you and Mr. Rafferty."

Pointe's thin nose tilted upward. He folded his arms. "I am in demand in my own right."

"Of course, but every star needs a stage, the right setting in which to create." She glanced around the high-ceilinged room with silk wall coverings and authentic art. "You have it here. A feast for the eyes is as important as a feast for the stomach. You and Mr. Rafferty have worked together to ensure both."

Slowly the chef's arms unfolded. "You are a wise woman." He leaned closer. "If you ever get tired of him, I'm available."

Ayanna blinked.

"That's enough," Tanner snapped, striding over to their table. "Ayanna, we need to talk."

The chef winked at Ayanna. Apparently he had wanted to get in one last jab at Tanner.

"Ayanna?" Tanner repeated, his hand on the back of her chair.

She extended her hand to the smug chef. She hoped he learned before it was too late that it wasn't wise to bait a tiger, especially when your hand was in its mouth. "Thank you again."

Pointe took her hand. "You have a standing invitation to The Jade Room. I hope to see you often." Inclining his head, he walked toward the back of the restaurant and disappeared through a swinging door.

Ayanna made herself look Tanner in the eye and prayed her voice didn't crack. "Tanner, I don't think there's anything to talk about and I need to get back to work."

His black eyes narrowed, then he turned and walked toward the open door. Ayanna bit her lip to keep from calling him back, thinking it was for the best. But instead of leaving, he closed both massive ten-foot double doors. She heard the distinct click of a lock.

"You're not leaving until we settle the issue. You're not walking out on me," he told her. He started toward her, a predator stalking its prey, a renegade who followed no rules but his own. It took all of her courage not to back up. He kept coming until he was so close she could see her reflection in his dark eyes.

"I thought nothing could bother me more than letting you come between me and my work until I was faced with the possibility of never seeing you again." His hands settled on her shoulders. "While I was trying to deal with that unthinkable possibility, Pointe was cozying up to you. I was so busy plotting his demise that I didn't realize until minutes ago that, despite my poor behavior, you were trying to pacify him to help me." He took the necessary steps until the heat of their bodies mingled. "You're an incredible woman. Tell me what I have to do to see you again."

Ayanna stared up into his face. No one had to tell her Tanner didn't ask for second chances or admit to being wrong very often. They were both dealing with emotions that were new and frightening to them. She could walk or do something she hadn't dared in a very long time. She took a deep breath and said, "I never did get a tour."

He hugged her. "Thank you," he said, as the chef reappeared, carrying a plate.

"Now that you've stopped sulking, perhaps you will taste the food I worked since dawn to prepare," Stephen said.

Tanner took the peace offering, but his arm remained around Ayanna. "Ayanna has to get back to work and I haven't shown her around."

The chef retrieved the eighteen-karat gold-trimmed plate. "Then show her. By the time you finish I will have prepared Ms. Hardcastle a few take-aways. Food should not be wasted."

"Tyrell, my cousin and the chef at Leo's, will have a fit. Please don't forget the steamed rice, the clams with black bean sauce, and the dim sum."

Both men laughed.

Ayanna had been right in her prediction of Tyrell's behavior when she came into Leo's with a shopping bag half full of food. She had sailed on past him, ignoring his protests. Tanner was coming over around seven that night to help her finish off the food. All she could think about was nibbling on him.

Grinning, she slipped the food into one of Leo's oversized refrigerators, then went to her office to work. Somehow she made herself not glance at the clock every few minutes, but it was hard. By five she was heading out the front door. After a quick stop at a corner flower shop, she was on her way home, formulating in her mind a romantic evening. She didn't know where the relationship was going, but she wasn't frightened anymore.

Arriving home, she put the food away, lit candles, then went to take her bath and get dressed. Instead of setting the dining room table, she prepared a place for them in front of the red brick fireplace, then lit fat white vanilla-scented candles on the hearth and brick mantel.

Her doorbell rang exactly at seven, and she opened the door before the musical chime had ended. Her heart skittered. "Hi," she greeted, her voice slightly husky.

"Hi," he said, closing the door behind him and taking her in his arms. His mouth unerringly found hers. It was a long, leisurely kiss that made her body hum. Lifting his head, he stared down at her. "You taste better every time I kiss you."

"So do you," she said. Watching his eyes darken, she knew if they didn't eat now they might not for a long time. "Come on, I have everything ready." Taking him by the hand, she led him into the den and gestured for him to sit on the blanket in front of a sky-blue linen tablecloth. "I thought it would be cozier this way."

"Works for me." Unbuttoning his cream-colored, lightweight sports coat, he sat on the floor and drew his long legs under him. When Ayanna started to the place across from him, he caught her hand and tugged. "You're not moving out of arm's reach."

She moistened her lips. His gaze followed and heat spiked through her. "It might be wiser."

"I'd still want to make love to you," he said bluntly, feeling her pulse leap beneath his fingertips. "But I can wait, now that I know you're willing to give us a chance. I want you close to me."

She sank down beside him. "I told you a woman couldn't say no to you."

Palming her face with hands that weren't quite steady, he turned her toward him. "When I'm with you, when I look at you, I can't remember another woman."

The words were said with such aching sincerity that tears came to her eyes. It would be so easy and so very foolish to forget this wasn't forever. "Oh, Tanner."

"If you keep looking at me like that I'm going to kiss you again, and I'm not sure if I'll be able to turn you loose until I've made you mine."

Ayanna warred within herself. She wanted to make love with Tanner, but it was too soon. She picked up his plate. "Everything is good. You're fortunate to have Stephen."

"So he keeps telling me," Tanner said without rancor as he took his plate. "I was afraid Tyrell might toss all this out."

"He wanted to." She leaned forward to pick up her plate and gave a yelp when Tanner drew her into his lap. "We only need one plate. Now, say grace, then you can tell me about your day while we eat."

She stared at Tanner. He stared back.

She could attempt to get off his lap or argue about it, but in the end she'd lose because she would be fighting against herself. There was no place else she'd rather be. She enjoyed looking at him, touching him, being with him. She even admired his relentless determination to have his way.

He'd never be an easy man. He was a renegade, but he touched a responsive cord within her no other man ever had. Bowing her head, she blessed their food.

SEVEN

Tanner and Ayanna went to a political fund-raising event on Tuesday, a gallery reception on Wednesday, and a charity function on Thursday. By Friday he was getting polite inquiries about Ayanna from business associates and acquaintances. Oddly, he wasn't pleased. He wanted to keep their relationship quiet. He was used to being in the spotlight, but he wasn't sure how Ayanna felt about it.

From the conversation he'd overheard her having with Sheri, he knew Ayanna hadn't been dating lately. He only had to look at her or recall the number of men trying to get her attention when they were out to know that it was by choice. On the other hand, the newspapers had made much of his romantic liaisons, and his past escapades were making it difficult to gain her trust. He didn't want her to think of herself as just another woman in a long line of them. She definitely wasn't. Her vulnerability and intelligence, as much as her beauty, drew him to her.

He'd never cared about what others thought of him in the past, but with Ayanna it was different. It wasn't just so they could be intimate, although if he didn't make love to her soon he might go out of his mind, it was because her opinion of him mattered. He wanted her to be proud of him when she introduced him to her family and friends.

He was doing his best to go slow and give her time to learn to have faith in him and herself, but it was interfering with his concentration and thus the opening of the hotel. He kept catching himself thinking of her instead of working, like now.

Fingers steepled beneath his chin, he leaned back in the desk chair in an office cluttered with a jumble of sample china patterns, swatches of bright fabric, and objets d'art that he'd promised the interior designer he'd have narrowed down by six that afternoon, and he knew if he didn't get his act together he wouldn't make the deadline.

He glanced at the Seth Thomas clock on his desk. Five-fifteen. It was going to be a very long two hours and forty-five minutes before he picked up Ayanna to take her to a movie. Shaking his head, he picked up the fabric swatches for the bedspreads and curtains in the suites and began flipping through them. He hadn't been to a movie in years. Maybe they could sit in the back and he could get in some serious necking.

He frowned. It was becoming harder and harder for him to pull away. In a dark theater he might lose it.

The phone rang, interrupting his troubled thoughts. Since he had asked his secretary to hold his calls, unless important, he picked it up. "Rafferty here."

"Tanner, this is George Marcel. How are you?"

Rafferty immediately placed the ring of swatches on his desk and came to attention. Marcel didn't make idle calls. He had ocean-front property on Hilton Head that Tanner had been trying to buy for three years. "Fine. I'm about to open another hotel. I hope you'll be able to attend."

"Sounds as if you're busy, but I'm hoping you can come down for a few days," he said. "I think it's time we talked again."

Slaughter had already reported that Marcel had lost heavily in the stock market, and he'd compounded the problem by borrowing money from his company, which he promptly lost to more bad investments. He was in financial quicksand.

Excitement rushed though Tanner, but his voice was cool. "What date were you looking at?"

"Tomorrow," came the quick reply. "I'll have my housekeeper prepare a room and we can play golf and discuss ways to keep both of us happy."

Tanner closed his eyes, cursed fate, and said the only thing he could: "I'll see you tomorrow."

Ayanna had just finished her bubble bath and was smoothing on lotion when she heard the phone ring in the adjoining bedroom. She ignored it as Tanner would be there soon to pick her up for their date. Humming softly, she pulled on her terry-cloth robe and went to her closet.

It was difficult to believe they'd only known each other for a short period of time. Whenever she talked with her mother and Sheri, both were quick to point out what a fabulous catch Tanner was. Ayanna always reminded them that catching him wasn't the problem, it was holding on. Many women had tried and failed.

They always laughed and disregarded her trepidations. Neither appeared to see the pitfalls of caring for a man like Tanner, a man with a love 'em and leave 'em reputation. It didn't help that he had to travel a great deal. And wherever he went, woman would be waiting. The only way Ayanna could handle the situation was to guard her heart and not think about his past or about moving on. She was taking their relationship one day at a time.

The answering machine clicked on as she drew out a long floral-print dress. Noah's voice asked the caller to leave a message.

"Please be at home, Ayanna. This is my second call. Your cousins don't know where you are. I want to see you before I leave."

Tanner. She whirled, jerking up the receiver. "I'm here. Please tell me you're joking."

"I wish I were. I'm at the front door; please let me in."

Hanging up the phone, she rushed to the front door and jerked it open. In an instant he was closing the door behind him. He gathered her in his arms, his mouth greedily devouring hers. She kissed him back with the same hunger.

"You smell good and taste better." He nibbled on her ear.

"I just got out of the tub," she said, arching her neck to give him greater access.

He groaned and tightened his hold. "Guess that's why you didn't hear the doorbell. If I didn't have to go, that robe would already be off."

She shivered. "When will you be back?"

He lifted his head. "I'm not sure. The owner of a prime piece of property is finally ready to discuss terms. I have to go. But before my plane leaves in the morning I have several loose ends to tie up."

She understood the trip was necessary. She just didn't like it very much. "You'll probably be up most of the night."

"I've already had my secretary call several of my key people to meet me in my office by seven," he told her. "I don't suppose you'd consider going with me to Hilton Head for the weekend?"

Much as she wanted to, she pushed herself out of his arms, then picked up a tapestry throw pillow from the sofa and hugged it to her chest. "I can't. I guess you have to take a lot of unexpected business trips."

"Occasionally," he said, frowning at her.

She nodded. "You'd better get going. You'll be cutting it close as it is to make it back by seven. Thanks for coming by when you could have called."

He didn't move. "Did I miss something here?"

Ayanna hugged the pillow tighter to her churning stomach. "I respect what you do, but my father was gone a great deal. His work came first. I've always promised myself that I'd never be in a relationship like that."

"I can't change who I am," he said, his expression unfathomable.

"I didn't ask you to," she said.

"Didn't you?" he said, his voice taking on a bit of an edge. "My time isn't my own, just like yours isn't with Leo's. We both do what we have to do. There's nothing I can do about that."

"Would you if you could?" she said before she could stop herself.

"Would you?" he countered, his gaze intense.

Leo's had been her salvation. Tanner's hotels were his passion. It was impossible to weigh one more heavily than the other. "No. Have a good trip."

"How can I when you're letting it come between us?" he said, his voice tight.

"I don't want it to," she whispered.

"Then don't." He took the pillow from her, tossing it back on the sofa, and took her in his arms. "If it wasn't important I wouldn't go."

How many times had she heard her father say those same words? Without another thought she repeated what her mother always said, "Be safe and hurry back."

His eyes were dark and narrowed. "I will. I'm calling you the minute I know I'm on the way back. Pointe will cook us another dinner."

She tried to smile. "I'll be waiting."

"If I kiss you again I may not let go," he said, his voice tight with suppressed longing.

"Have a safe trip," she said.

"Good-bye." Turning on his heels, he opened the door and walked to the waiting limo.

Ayanna watched the car pull away from the curb, then went to her room and sat on the side of the bed. This was not how she had planned to spend her evening. But if she continued to see Tanner she might as well get used to spending the evening alone. The phone rang, interrupting her thoughts. She planned to ignore the call until she heard her mother's cheery voice.

"Hi, sweetheart. I know you're getting dressed for your date with Tanner, but I wanted to see if you wanted to go shopping with me in the morning. It will probably be late when you get in so call—"

"Hi, Mother."

"Ayanna, I didn't expect you to pick up," her mother said, surprise in her voice.

She pulled her legs under her. "Tanner had to cancel. He's leaving in the morning on a business trip so he has to work tonight."

"I know you're disappointed, but at least he called," her mother consoled.

"He came by," Ayanna told her, no happier about the situation.

"That was very considerate of him. Your father was the same way," her mother said. "He didn't always get a chance to come home, of course, but he always called. I wasn't always happy, but I knew he was a policeman when I fell in love with him."

"Dad loved what he did."

"Yes, he did, and he was good at it. He had a very high percentage of solved cases," she said proudly. "He was dedicated, honest, and hardworking. It always amazed me when some of the other wives became upset when their husbands had to break engagements. A lot of the officers' marriages broke up needlessly because of their work. The women were upset by the same qualities in their men that had attracted them in the first place. Isn't that silly?"

Ayanna's brows knitted as she remembered her conversation with Tanner. At the time, she had thought she was being reasonable about his out-of-town trips, but now she wasn't so sure. Even if she could, she didn't want to change him. Her head fell forward. In her own selfish need to come first, she had forgotten the type of man Tanner was.

"Ayanna, are you there?"

"I was about to become one of those silly women, but you probably already guessed that," Ayanna said in a wry tone.

"The thought had crossed my mind. You hid your disappointment from your father when he couldn't make some of your school functions, but not from me."

"But he always made a point to ask me the next day how it went and take time, just for the two of us," Ayanna said softly. How had she forgotten that?

"He loved you," her mother said.

Despite his missing school events or extracurricular activities, Ayanna had never doubted her father's devotion. He wanted to make the city a safer, better place for his family and the community. His job hadn't been easy, but he had never complained or shirked his duty. He was a man of principle. Just like Tanner. "Mama, you're the best mother in the world," Ayanna said, making her way to her lingerie drawer.

Her mother chuckled. "That's nice to hear."

"I'll call you in the morning." Juggling the phone, she shimmied into her panties and snapped her bra. "Right now I have to go apologize."

"Tell Tanner to have a nice trip."

"I will." Ayanna stepped into her dress. "Bye and thanks." Hanging up the phone, she zipped up her dress, picked up her purse, and hurried out the door.

"Mr. Rafferty, the security guard says Ms. Hardcastle is downstairs requesting entrance," his secretary said, holding her slender hand over the receiver. "Would you like for me to go down and escort her up?"

Tanner couldn't keep the surprise from his face, or the unease that followed. "Thank you, Mrs. Cater, I'll take care of it." Tanner rose from the head of the conference table where seven of his top executives were seated. "Please continue. I'll be back shortly."

"Very good, sir," his secretary said, but Tanner was already heading for the door. He hit the stairs at a fast clip. If Ayanna came to break up with him, she could save her breath. He stepped off the bottom rung of the curved stairwell and started for the lobby. The instant he rounded the corner he saw her through the glass entry door. Her back was to him, and she was speaking to the security guard. The young man was grinning like a loon and standing much too close, Tanner thought with a savage twist of jealously.

He came to an abrupt halt. He had never been jealous of anyone or anything in his life. He searched his mind for another word to describe how he felt and couldn't find one. Disturbed, he stared at Ayanna's slim back, her sleek body in a soft dress that molded itself to her shapely curves with each breath of wind. Need clamored though him. He wanted her as he'd never wanted before. Ayanna was *his*.

The statement somehow smoothed the wrinkles from his forehead. He was just being his usual possessive self. He wasn't jealous. Satisfied, he started toward them again.

As if sensing him, she turned while he was still several feet away. He didn't expect the breathtaking smile on her face or her excited waving. Relief and pleasure rushed through him.

He couldn't get to her fast enough. He pushed open the heavy glass door and was hit again by how beautiful and desirable she was. "Hi, Ayanna."

"I know you're busy but I wanted to talk to you if you have the time," she said, smiling up at him.

"Come with me," he said, leading her to a little alcove off the lobby. The area was empty, the lighting low and intimate.

"I came to apologize for my poor behavior. It was selfish of me not to want you to go. After you've acquired that property, maybe you'll invite me down."

"You can count on it," he said, settling his large hands on her waist, bringing her closer. "I thought you were coming to tell me to take a hike. You surprised me."

She rested her hands on his chest and enjoyed the unsteady beat of his heart. "I don't think people do that very often."

"They don't," he muttered as if she had insulted him.

"Let's see if I can do it again." She put her mouth on his, letting her body sink against him, soften against him as she took his mouth in a kiss that drugged his senses and made him forget everything but the woman in his arms. Their tongues touched, tasted, savored, and greedily sought more.

Feeling the edges of sanity blur, Tanner fought for control and barely won. Lifting his head, he stared down at her flushed face, her slightly parted lips, wet and swollen from his mouth, and cursed Marcel once again for making the trip to Hilton Head necessary. His breathing labored, his body and loins clamoring for something he could not give, he leaned his forehead against hers. "Right now I'd like to take you to bed and forget I have eight people in my office waiting for me."

"Me too."

In her face he saw desire equal to his own. "You're certainly making it hard for me to go."

Her trembling hand cupped his jaw. "I wanted to make it easier."

"I realize that." He turned his head, kissing her palm, then drew her tightly into his arms again. "The problem is, I don't want to let you go."

She pressed closer, feeling the heat, the hardness of his arousal, and the unwavering strength of his arms around her. "They're waiting."

"In a minute." His hand made lazy circles on her back while he breathed in her unique scent, then he let his hand continue down to cup her hips against that part of him that ached to be inside of her. He moaned in sweet torture. If he didn't stop now he wouldn't until after he'd made her his.

"Is there anything I can help you with?" she asked, rubbing her cheek over the spot where his heart beat rapidly. "Do you need me to make a run for food or coffee?"

He kissed her on the side of the neck, inhaled her scent, and wished he could wallow in it, in her. His teeth closed delicately on her ear. She shivered.

"D-Does that mean you're hungry?"

His ragged laughter sent more shivers rippling through her.

"T-Tanner?"

He heard the hunger of that one word. Now wasn't the time to unleash it. He stepped back. "Go home while I have the strength to let you."

"I wish I could help so you could finish up earlier," she said.

"Thanks. We're trying to decide on vendors. . . ." His voice trailed off and he stared down at her. "Maybe you can help." Taking her by the hand he started for his office. "That place where you ordered Judge Wyman's basket, could they do customized candy?"

"Sweet Temptation can do anything with chocolate. Julia Ferrington-Braxton is the owner. She has three stores. She came up with the idea of doing the basket for lovers that we sell at Leo's." Ayanna hurried to keep up with Tanner as he climbed the curved staircase. "She met her husband Chase, a Texas Ranger, on sort of a blind date at Leo's."

About to open the door to his office, Tanner paused and stared down at Ayanna. "It's a smart man who sees what he wants and goes after it."

"What about what the woman wants?" Ayanna asked, her brow delicately arched.

He answered without hesitation. "Since a smart man would only be attracted to a smart, intelligent woman, she, of course, would see the advantage of dating him."

She shook her head. "How many years were you on the debate team?"

He chuckled. "All through high school and college."

"Figures," she said, a smile reluctantly tugging the corners of her mouth.

Still smiling, he opened the door and escorted her inside. The men in their tailored shirts stood as his secretary's eyes narrowed behind her tortoise-shell eyeglasses. Tanner had left cranky and had come back smiling. All eyes went to the stunning and happy woman by his side, then to their joined hands. Tanner didn't bring his lady friends to business meetings. Speculation ran rampant in their minds, but graciousness was their bread and butter. The executive manager immediately gave up his seat next to Tanner and moved to the end of the table.

The introductions were quickly made and the reason for Ayanna's presence explained. For the next thirty minutes she gave them the names of several reputable vendors she dealt with who met her demands for high quality and dependability. Although price wasn't an issue to Tanner, she gave the business manager facts and figures, which would be multiplied many times over for the one-hundred-forty-six-room hotel.

Tanner listened approvingly. Ayanna knew her stuff. "Any chance you might leave Leo's and come to work for me?"

She smiled at the teasing glint in his eyes. "Thanks, but no thanks."

He stood and reached for her hand. She immediately placed hers in his and came to her feet. "I'll see Ms. Hardcastle to her car."

Saying good-bye, she left, her steps slowing as they made their way to the lobby. She stopped and faced him a few feet from the door where the security guard waited. "I'll miss you."

"Not as much as I'll miss you."

He pulled her into his arms and kissed her. After a long moment he stepped away, his eyes fierce. "I'm coming over as soon as I get back."

Ayanna understood. The next time they were together they would make love. Her body burned. "I'll be waiting." Kissing him on the chin, she walked away on shaky legs.

EIGHT

Tanner had a bumpy flight and a miserable night. By the time his plane landed, he was in a foul mood. None of his irritation showed when Marcel greeted him, however. Nor did it later that afternoon when Tanner kept missing putts on the golf course. The higher his score, the more amicable his host became. By the time they reached the eighteenth hole, they were deep into discussion. Winning apparently put Marcel in a good frame of mind, but he was no pushover.

Tanner, his disposition unimproved, retired to his room that night, judging it would take at least a couple of days longer to cinch the deal. Deciding that calling Ayanna would make him miss her more and thus worsen his irritability, he woke his secretary from a sound sleep and gave her three specific requests. Finished, he went to take a shower. A very cold shower.

Ayanna couldn't believe it. After three very long days and tortuous nights, Tanner had gotten the property and returned. Rushing into her bedroom after taking a quick bath, she threw a glance at the clock on the bedside table. 4:48 A.M. He'd be there in less than twenty-five minutes.

Quickly she slipped on the new peach-colored silk charmeuse pajama bottoms, then the dyed-to-match lace bed jacket over a mesh sleeveless baby tee with lattice edging. She'd debated a long time over the lingerie, wanting to appear alluring without being too eager, then groaned. She had passed eager days ago. She'd probably rip his clothes off.

Shaking her head, she picked up her comb. She had just completed her first sweep through her curly hair when the doorbell rang. *Tanner.* The comb fell from her hand. Her heart thudded. She didn't think about how her hair was tangled and in disarray, that she wore no makeup, that he was earlier than she expected, that the intimate setting with candles and soft music was not ready. She just ran to the front door and jerked it open.

In his white shirt and jeans he looked good enough to gulp down whole.

They reached for each other at the same time. Their greeting was a long, hot kiss that left both shaking and eager for more.

"I missed you," she said, her arms still around his neck.

"I didn't think it possible, but you're more beautiful than ever," he said softly.

Beautiful. Her eyes rounded as she suddenly recalled her condition. Her nose probably outshone Rudolph's. She pushed away his arms and took another backward step. "Please have a seat. I'll be right back." Without waiting for a reply, she tore off.

In her bedroom, she saw the rumpled sheets from another restless night of thinking about Tanner and decided to straighten them up first. Smoothing out the wrinkles in the pale blue Egyptian cotton sheets, she lamented that she hadn't had time to put on the new ones or spray the sheets with perfume.

"Why bother?"

Ayanna jerked around. Tanner stood in the bedroom door. Slow and purposeful, he started toward her.

"You got my flowers, I see."

"Thank you," she whispered. Saturday she'd received a white basket overflowing with exotic flowers. She'd put them on the marble top of her chest of drawers across from her bed. Sunday she'd been surprised to receive white roses in a heavy crystal vase. She couldn't imagine how he'd had them delivered. She went to sleep breathing in their lush scent and wishing Tanner was there. "They're beautiful."

"This is for today."

Ayanna's eyes widened and her mouth formed a silent O as Tanner lifted a large basket wrapped in iridescent cellophane from behind his back. She recognized it immediately as the one Leo's sold in partnership with Sweet Temptation. Inside were lush strawberries dipped in white and dark chocolate, vintage champagne, a corkscrew, and two flutes and monogrammed napkins with the initial *L*. She had been so intent on him that she hadn't noticed anything else.

"Should I open the champagne here, or do you want to go into the kitchen or den?" he asked.

Once again he was giving her a choice, but she had already made it. She sat on the side of the bed. "Here is fine."

"Thank goodness." Sitting beside her, he reached for the bottle of chilled champagne.

Ayanna smiled and plucked the glasses from the bed of shredded lavender paper. "Prepared, I see."

"I was afraid my hands wouldn't be steady enough," he admitted as the cork gave a loud pop.

The stems wobbled in her hands. Tanner was a strong, self-assured man. Hearing him admit she affected him in such a way touched her deeply.

He filled both glasses, set the bottle back in the basket, then stared down at her. "To no more lonely nights."

She shivered. "To no more lonely nights." Their glasses clinked, their eyes locked on each other as they drank.

Tanner took her glass and set it with his on the nightstand. Standing, he dimmed the overhead lights, casting the room in intimate shadows, then came back to sit beside her. He slipped free the first satin-covered button on her bed jacket. "What time do you have to be at work?"

Her breathing quickened as he slipped the jacket off and kissed her bare shoulder. "After you called, I phoned Noah and told them not to expect me today."

"You just saved my sanity." His hot, greedy mouth fastened on hers as they tumbled back on the queen-sized brass bed, then he rolled, taking her with him, until he was stretched out on top of her.

With a hand that refused to steady, Tanner pulled the tee over her head. Her breasts were full and high, the nipples pouting. "You're exquisite."

Ayanna pushed up his shirt to find a chest ridged with muscles. "You're gorgeous." She put her mouth to his nipple and felt him shudder, then she was on her back and he was staring down at her.

"My turn."

Ayanna felt the incredible heat and hardness of his body aligned with hers, watched in excitement and fascination as his dark head lowered. She heard him murmur her name just before his lips fastened on her aching nipple. She arched on the bed with a sharp moan of pleasure, her nails sinking into his shoulders.

He tugged on the hard peak, then the other, until she withered on the bed. When the pleasure built to a point she wanted to scream, his hand moved down her flushed body, finding the most secretive and intimate part of her. She cried out again and then again as he brought them together in a single thrust.

Nothing had ever prepared her for this moment. It was wild and glorious and frightening. She felt herself losing control, but even as her mind shied away, her hips lifted to take him in deeper and deeper.

"Come with me."

The raspy voice, strained with passion and need, lured her as much as his body. She couldn't deny either. She let go and felt herself spinning out of control, but even as she did she knew he would be there with her.

Tanner stared down at Ayanna, her face damp with perspiration, her nostrils delicately flared, her lips curved slightly upward, and realized she had surprised him once again. He hadn't thought making love to her would negate the jagged claws of need, but he did think it would lessen. He had been wrong.

His hand swept away the sheet he'd pulled over her after they had made love. She was slim, elegant, lovely. His body stirred and hardened. He wanted her with a fierceness that shook him to the core. Possessing her body wasn't enough. What would be? Her eyelashes fluttered, then lifted. The smile that had been forming on her mouth blossomed. Something tugged at him, a curious warmth. Possession might not be enough, but it would do until he figured out what was. Pulling her into his arms, he joined their bodies again.

Ayanna awoke sprawled across Tanner's muscled chest, her leg sandwiched between his. Sunlight shone though the sheer curtains in her bedroom. Closing her eyes, she sighed in contentment as she felt Tanner's hand stroke her back.

"It's almost ten. You want me to fix you breakfast?"

Her mouth curved into a winsome smile at the thought of having a renegade prepare breakfast. "Would it be edible?"

"Let's find out." In one smooth motion he had her in his arms and was striding toward the bathroom.

Tightening her arms around his neck, she kissed his chin. "If you're cooking breakfast, why am I getting up?"

He set her down in the shower stall and began adjusting the water temperature. "Because I want you near me."

Her heart melted all over again. Looking at the hard muscles of his conditioned body made her shiver. She loved him deeply, irrevocably. There was no going back.

He turned, letting the spray of water pummel his broad back. "Then, too, I have this fantasy of us in the shower." Taking scented soap from a dish, he worked up lather and began to spread it over her breasts, her stomach.

Her eyes drifted shut as his hands went to the inside of her thighs. "T-Tanner. I don't think I can take this."

"Let's see," he said, proceeding to cover every inch of her body with lather. When she was weak with longing, he put her arms around his neck, wrapped her legs around his waist, and drove into her moist heat.

Ayanna closed around him, then melted, quivered. Tanner stroked her until she was clinging to him again, taking and giving pleasure. The next time they finished together.

Breakfast was champagne, chocolate-covered strawberries, and whipped cream, French toast, bacon, and grits. Tanner had never tasted anything better. "Thanks for helping."

In jeans and a knit top, Ayanna smiled at Tanner sitting next to her at the kitchen table. "You don't know the first thing about cooking."

"But I would have tried," he said, holding out a strawberry dipped in whipped cream.

Too touched to speak, Ayanna bit into the lush fruit. She was thoroughly enjoying getting acquainted with the tender, caring side of Tanner, which was even more captivating than the renegade. It would be impossible not to love him. But could he love her back?

He frowned. "What's the matter?"

She shook her head. She wasn't going to let doubts ruin their time together. "I'm just glad you're home."

Scooting his armless side chair around, he picked her up by the waist, settled her in his lap, then tucked her head beneath his chin. "I started to call the first night, but I knew if I heard your voice it would make the loneliness worse."

She nodded. "I guessed that was why you didn't call. I'm glad you got what you went after."

"My lawyers are down there now working on the papers. I have to go back to sign, but it will be a day trip," he said.

Sitting up, she gazed at him. "I'm selfish to want you here all the time."

"No you're not, because I feel the same way." His hand tangled in her hair. "When the hotel opens in four weeks there will be a month-long celebration with various events that I'll have to attend. I want you with me."

She couldn't hide her amazement. "Are you sure?"

His eyes fierce, he brought her face closer to his. "The more I'm with you, the more I want to be. Buried deep inside you or being near you is a pleasure I've never experienced before. Does that answer your question?"

Her breath fluttered out over her lips. "Eloquently, and I'd love to go."

He kissed her, then lifted his head, his eyes dark and narrowed. "Grab the bottle of champagne, the strawberries, and the whipped cream. There were a couple of other fantasies I haven't gotten around to yet."

Her body vibrating with excitement, Ayanna grabbed the things from the table. Clutching them to her chest, she smiled and wondered how many more fantasies Tanner had. She was looking forward to fulfilling each one.

"The cab is waiting."

Tanner stared down at Ayanna and wished he could send the cab away. It was almost midnight. They had been together almost nineteen hours, never farther than a few feet apart, and yet, he didn't want to leave. Another first. He'd been with numerous women, but always made it a point to go home. A woman tended to become possessive and start thinking long term when she woke up with a man in her bed or in his.

"Come with me?" The request just slipped out, but he had no wish to withdraw the offer.

She blushed. They'd made love countless ways and she could still blush. "My mother sometimes calls in the mornings."

"Have the calls transferred," he suggested.

Her gaze drifted away from his. "I don't think I could talk to her with you there."

His body stirred. The cabbie honked, and Tanner gritted his teeth. He wasn't winning this time and was disappointed, but another part of him was glad Ayanna woke up in her own bed in the mornings . . . not that he didn't plan to change that. "Pointe is preparing us dinner at my place tomorrow night. I'll pick you up at six."

Since she'd turned down his earlier invitation and had held firm, she let him get away with telling her about dinner instead of asking her. "Isn't that early?"

"That's about as long as I can stand being away from you." He kissed her, then was out the door.

A bemused expression on her face, Ayanna watched from the window as Tanner got into the taxi. She was already counting the hours until she saw him again. By then she might have enough nerve to enact one of her own fantasies. With a grin on her face, she went to bed.

Dinner at Tanner's condo exceeded her expectations. The sea bass baked with pistachio was scrumptious, the vintage wine delicious, the setting with soft lighting romantic, and the air scented with the fragrance of jasmine intoxicating, but it was Tanner who made her burn with desire and her heart sing with joy.

"This is wonderful," she said, sipping her wine on the balcony, feeling content and happy. Music drifted out to them from inside. "Thank you for inviting me."

"My pleasure," he said, taking the glass from her hand and pulling her into his arms.

She sank against him, enjoying the hardness of his muscled body, the way they fit. He danced as he did everything, with supreme confidence and ability.

He chuckled, kissing her on top of the head. "You wouldn't go to sleep on a guy, would you?"

She smiled without lifting her head. "If I did, what would you do?"

"I'd have to wake you up." Still moving to the slow beat of the music, he tilted her face and proceeded to nibble at her mouth, the curve of her jaw, her ear.

By the time he reached her mouth again, sleep was the furthest thing from her mind. "I like your method much better than an alarm clock."

"Let's see what else about me you like." Picking her up, he headed for the bedroom.

"I already know," she said, unbuttoning his shirt.

"Such as?" he said, amusement in his voice.

"Why don't I show you?" She laughed softly when he quickened his pace.

NINE

Tanner was rushing out of his bedroom when the phone rang. He had a full day planned at the hotel, and in the evening he and Ayanna were finally getting around to that movie. They had gone out almost every night since his return from the business trip two weeks ago. His interest in her showed no signs of abating. If anything, he was becoming more fascinated.

He grinned on recalling a particular evening at her place when she'd given him a full body massage. By the time she'd finished he barely knew his name. Maybe he could talk her into staying the night and letting him give *her* a massage.

Planning to ignore the caller, he grabbed his car keys on the credenza table by the front door just as he heard Raine's excited voice on the answering machine. He picked up the receiver, as they had been playing phone tag for the past week.

"Hello, big brother. I wanted you to be the first in the family to know I'm ready to make my move against Leo's."

Tanner couldn't get to the phone fast enough. "What? What did you say?"

She laughed, a bright happy sound. "You didn't think I'd be able to pull it off this fast, did you?"

Stunned, Tanner plopped down on the arm of the chair. "Raine, please start over."

She laughed again. "Leo's is going to be the next supper club I add to my growing list. Don't act so surprised. You've known from the first that's what I planned to do. You said so."

He felt like a man who'd been sucker punched. They all had complete autonomy and the considerable resources of Rafferty Enterprises to get what they wanted. He shut his eyes. This could not be happening. "I thought you wanted to know about Leo's to check out the competition."

"Well, now you know."

"You can't do this." His hand tightened on the receiver.

"Things are already in motion and your information about the one-way street helped cinch the deal." Her voice took on a hard edge. "They can either sell to me at a profit or watch their business dwindle to nothing when I tie up traffic every evening and night on very slow renovation of a building two blocks up from Leo's."

He had given Raine the means to hurt Ayanna. His stomach churned. "I didn't tell you that for you to use against Ayanna. We've been dating for over three weeks. We're going out tonight."

"Ayanna? Tanner, usually by now you've already become bored and moved on. I've run out of fingers and toes to count the number of women you've dated in the past year."

"This is different," he said, getting up to pace. "I care about Ayanna."

"Sure you do," his sister said lightly. "That's what makes you such a fabulous guy. You're genuinely fond of the women you date. Just answer me one thing, if our situations were reversed, given both our track records, would you back out of a potentially lucrative deal because I was dating one of the owners?"

Since neither their brother in St. Thomas nor his sister were known for long-term relationships, he felt trapped by the damning truth. "Not usually, but it's different this time. You have to back off, Ra."

"No can do, Tanner. I'm flying into D.C. in a few days to push the deal through personally."

Raine was as stubborn as he was. "They won't sell. It's more than a restaurant to them, especially Ayanna."

"I don't plan to give them a choice," she said, the edge back in her voice.

"Ra, we don't do business this way," he told her, anger creeping into his voice. "We come at people from the front, not behind."

"I've sent three men down to make inquiries and Noah Hardcastle refuses to even discuss the matter."

"Then give up, find another restaurant. Have Slaughter scout another location out for you."

"I don't need Slaughter to do anything for me," she said tightly. "He was the last man I sent. He doesn't think I can pull this off, but I'll show him."

Tanner shoved his hand through his hair. Things were going from bad to worse. Raine and Slaughter had been at odds since the day they met. Having him as her bodyguard while she was dating in high school and college didn't help. Having Slaughter telling her what could and couldn't be done was like waving a red flag in front of a bull. "You've never cared for being in the same city with me or near the water. Why now?"

"Demographics counted in my decision as well. There wasn't the large percentage of African Americans I wanted in your other locations. We're both in Charleston."

Raine always did her homework. Too well it seemed. "Don't do this, Ra, please."

There was a slight pause. "If I thought you were serious about her, I'd drop my plans in a heartbeat, but none of us have been lucky like our parents. The deal is going through. Good-bye, Tanner."

Tanner closed his eyes. What was he going to do?

. . .

"*Stop whatever you're doing and* get Raine on the phone. Now," Tanner instructed his secretary the instant he came through the door. He'd already called her place and talked to her answering machine. "Buzz me as soon as you locate her."

"Yes, sir." Ms. Cater took one look at his grim face and immediately hit "save" on the computer and reached for the phone.

Tanner continued into his office. He plopped his briefcase on the desk and prowled. Somehow he'd make her understand. He had to.

The phone rang and he pounced on it. "Raine."

"I'm sorry, Mr. Rafferty. Her secretary doesn't know where she is."

Tanner cursed softly under his breath. Didn't know or wasn't telling. "Find Slaughter."

"I missed him by a few minutes. His plane just took off from San Francisco, heading back to Charleston. He plane is due to arrive at 12:15 our time," she said, already anticipating the next question.

"As soon as he lands I want him on the phone," Tanner told her.

"Yes sir," she said. "Your first appointment with the head of banquet services is in ten minutes."

Her words were a statement and a question. He rubbed the back of his neck. The food for the opening had to be perfect in every detail. "We'll keep on schedule, but interrupt me when you have Slaughter on the phone." Hanging up, Tanner sat behind his desk, his brow creased. "Ra, where the devil are you?"

"*Ayanna, please come to my* office," Noah requested over the telephone intercom.

Sitting in her office at her desk, she frowned on hearing the tightness in her cousin's voice. "Is everything all right?"

"You'll find out when you get here."

Her frown deepened as she listened to the dial tone. She quickly went down the hall to Noah's office and opened the door. Her gaze narrowed on seeing an elegantly beautiful woman in a tailored black pantsuit with a white blouse sitting in front of his desk.

"Since this concerns you on a personal level, I thought you'd like to be here," Noah said, his arms propped on his desk.

Ayanna's gaze went to Tyrone and Tyrell. Their jaws were tight and they were staring daggers at the woman who sat relaxed in the leather wing chair. "Noah, I don't understand."

"It's very simple, Ayanna," the woman said. "I want Leo's and I intend to have it. Mr. Hardcastle has turned me down three times, but this time, if you refuse my very generous offer, you'll see your business dry up to a trickle when I tie up traffic with renovations."

"Who the hell are you?" Ayanna said, her anger growing toward the poised woman who calmly threatened their dream.

"She's Tanner's sister," Noah said, biting out each word.

Ayanna pulled up short, her eyes wide. All too clearly she recalled telling Tanner about the one-way street. Pain lanced through her. She clenched her fists. "He used me."

Anger flashed in Raine's black eyes "My brother doesn't use anyone."

The door behind her abruptly opened, revealing Tanner. He took one look at the angry faces of the men, the hurt, confused face of Ayanna, and knew he was too late. He went to her and took her arms. "I didn't know about her plans until this morning."

"But you told her what happens when traffic is tied up, didn't you?"

He looked into her eyes and knew regret. "Yes."

She swallowed convulsively and looked away. "Please turn me loose."

"No."

Tyrell and Tyrone moved from behind the desk toward him. So did Noah.

"Think about my very generous offer," Raine said, drawing the men's attention back to her. She drew her sunglasses from the top of her head to her eyes. "Tanner, walk me outside."

His hands flexed, then he released Ayanna. He wasn't afraid of her cousins, but having every bone in his body broken would bring the considerable wrath of the Rafferty clan down on the Hardcastles through no fault of their own. Taking Raine by the arm, he led her out the door.

"You shouldn't have come. I know you can handle yourself, but not three against one. To spare you this, I called Jim and asked him to get the Gulf Stream ready after we got off the phone." She wrinkled her nose in annoyance. "Since I know my secretary can keep a secret, Slaughter must have blabbed. The jet doesn't move unless he knows the itinerary." She glanced longingly at the fifty-foot Rosewood bar with brass railing. "I can't wait to own this place."

Tanner stopped and faced her. "Call it off."

"We already had this discussion." She ran her slim fingers over a small Tiffany-style lamp. "I think I'll get rid of the colored oil candles."

"Ra, listen to me," he said through gritted teeth. "Do this and Ayanna will never forgive me."

Raine finally gave him her full attention. "Tanner, why do you care?"

"Because I love her."

Slowly Raine lifted the oversize designer sunshades, astonishment and disbelief in her large eyes.

"I love her," Tanner repeated, his conviction growing each second. "I'll do whatever it takes for Leo's to stay in the Hardcastle family."

"Does that include going against me and the family?"

"No!"

Tanner whirled to see Ayanna standing behind him, her face pale, her body trembling. He reached for her.

Holding up her hands, she stepped back. Tanner muttered and let his hands drop to his side.

"I won't come between you and your family." Ayanna lifted her chin and faced his sister. "I came to tell you to do your worst. Leo's is not for sale at any price. We have loyal customers. We'll survive."

"I love her, Raine," Tanner said, looking tenderly at Ayanna, willing her to believe. "I'll fight through hell to keep her safe and happy."

"You don't love me!" Ayanna cried, fighting tears and so much misery and pain.

Tanner grabbed her arms and held her when she tried to pull away. "Ayanna, please listen. I didn't know what she planned."

"I believe you, but it doesn't make any difference."

Now he was the one surprised. "How can you say that? I love you."

Tears sparkled in her brown eyes. Once she would have given anything to hear those words. "And I love my cousins. Betraying them was bad enough. I can't compound it by continuing to see you."

"You didn't betray them," Tanner said, desperate for her to believe and forgive him. "I keep telling you that I had no idea Raine was going to use that information against you."

"The point is, she did, and she wouldn't have known if I hadn't told you. That makes me responsible." When she pulled away this time, he let her go. "Good-bye, Tanner. If you care for me at all, you won't try to contact me again." She turned and walked away.

Fury pulsing though him, he went to find the person who had caused all this trouble. He caught up with Raine as she was about to get into the limo at the curb. "Wait."

She turned. "I would have called later. I wanted to give you some privacy." This time it was she who took his arm. "This is not a rash decision, Tanner. There was another reason I didn't want to go where you and Adrian were. I didn't want people to think I was trading off your names." She let her hand fall. "I've proven to myself that I can make my restaurants a success. I don't care what others think."

"Does that include me, Ra?"

Shock and regret shown on her face. "You shouldn't have to ask that."

"Back off," he ordered, his voice sharp.

"If I really thought what you felt for her was lasting, I'd call off the whole operation. You like challenges. You are easily bored with the same routine, the same city, the same woman." She tentatively touched his rigid shoulder. "I'm taking the jet back to Charleston. I'll call this weekend."

Tanner watched the car pull off, then looked back at Leo's. There could be only one winner in this—his sister or the woman he loved. All things considered, there was only one choice. He got into his car and drove off.

TEN

"You all right?"

Noah had spoken, but all of her cousins were looking at her with a mixture of concern, pity, and rage.

"I'm so sorry," Ayanna said.

Noah came around his desk and took her into his arms. "There's nothing to be sorry for. You didn't know the kind of man Tanner was, and if I hear you say you're sorry again, I'll personally turn you over my knee."

She wiped the moisture away from her eyes, refusing to give into self-pity or try to defend Tanner. "I don't think she's bluffing."

"Neither do I," Noah agreed, his expression thunderous. "Business might fall off a bit but, thanks to you, we're in good shape financially."

Ayanna refused to think that might change if Raine's renovations went on for a long period of time. "I plan for us to stay that way." She picked up a pen and sheet of paper from Noah's desk. "I suggest we adjust immediately by extending happy hour by at least thirty minutes. Perhaps have Max create a special drink."

She tapped her pen on the paper, then began to write. "It wouldn't hurt to create a few new dinners with food that is plentiful and therefore reasonable at a special price. Perhaps have a drawing for a weekly dinner for two. Bill it as a way of thanking our loyal customers and welcoming new ones by making it well worth their effort to fight snarls to get here. We could also add another night to amateur/open mike night to draw in customers. What do you think?"

"The new meals shouldn't be a problem." Tyrell nodded his head. "I'll let you know what I come up with and you can add it to the menu."

"I think it should be a special pull-out section with maybe a hard hat," Ayanna said. "I'll work up a couple of ideas and we can decide on it later."

Tyrone leaned against the desk. "I don't see a difficulty with adding Thursday to amateur/open mike night. We always have disappointed people who wanted to go on."

"I think we should plan to have everything in place by next week." She tore the sheet of paper from the notepad and replaced the pad on Noah's desk. "It might not be a bad idea to make the customers aware of what's going to happen and let them know the plans we have to keep them."

"This should work," Noah said, looking at Ayanna with admiration. "Once again, you've proven we made a good business decision by making you a full partner."

"You're the only one we thought to ask," Tyrone said.

"Yeah," Tyrell agreed. "You helped make Leo's a success. Your father is probably looking down on you, smiling."

Ayanna knew they were trying to bolster her and she felt tears sting her eyes. They didn't blame her, but she blamed herself. If it took her last penny, Leo's would survive. "I better start working on the design for the new menu." She went to the door, opened it, then turned to face them. "Until we see how things shake out I'll plan on staying at least until nine or ten each night to help with seating and PR."

Tyrell and Tyrone started to protest, but Noah, always in command, held up his hand and they quieted. He understood her need to help and to stay busy. "I'd appreciate your lending a hand."

Closing the door behind her, she swallowed the huge knot in her throat and went to her office. There would be time enough for heartache later; saving Leo's had to come first.

Three days later Raine's threat became a reality. Ayanna sat in her car behind several other vehicles as they waited for a heavy piece of machinery to move so they could pass. Fear knotted her stomach. She'd boasted to Raine they'd survive, but she knew of a number of establishments that had closed when construction made it difficult for people to reach their place of business.

Finally, after waiting over five minutes, her car and the others were waved though. Driving by, she saw at least twenty-odd men in hard hats. She cut a glance at the new hard-hat menu inserts she had just picked up from the printer. There were enough men at the work site to do the renovation of the two-story brick building if that had been Raine's intent, but it wasn't. She was intent on destroying, not building.

Ayanna's hand flexed on the steering wheel. She couldn't think of Raine without thinking of Tanner. Her heart ached for him. But they could never be together. He'd respected her wishes to not contact her, and for that, she was thankful. Seeing him or hearing his voice would have only made the ache worse.

Arriving at the restaurant a little after six, she was glad to see the cars pulling into the parking lot ahead of her and behind her. Leo's would survive, just as she would without Tanner.

A week and a half later, Ayanna gazed out at the diners scattered around the restaurant and accepted that they were in trouble. On a Friday night every table should have been occupied. The restaurant was half empty. She glanced at her watch, then at the reservations. At 8:30 it was still early. People might still be coming after the theater or other events.

"It will be all right," Noah said, coming up to drape his arm around her shoulder.

"I know," she said, praying he was right.

He stared at the dark circles beneath her eyes. "I blame Tanner more for hurting you than for anything else."

"I'm fine," she told him, adding another lie to her growing list. She'd long since stopped worrying about what would happen to her. Once her mother and Sheri had found out what had happened, they constantly asked how she was doing. Her cousins and their wives were just as bad. None of them had said one word of blame or acted any differently toward her, which made her betrayal all the more painful.

"Go home and get some sleep," Noah said with a frown. "There is no need for you to come back here every night. You've gone over the books, instigating cost-cutting maneuvers. There's nothing more you can do."

She was about to tell him she wanted to do more when the double doors opened and an attractive woman in her late fifties came in. The pale pink suit was Dior, the hair fashionably cut. Twin furrows raced across Ayanna's brow. There was something vaguely familiar about the woman.

"Welcome to Leo's," Ayanna said, stepping forward.

"Thank you," the woman said, her voice soft, the words slow and drawn out like a lazy river. "Reservations for Dawson."

Ayanna already knew it was for five people. She'd booked them. "Would you like to be seated or wait for the rest of your party?"

"We're all here," she said, beaming at Ayanna. "He's parking the car. I didn't want to wait another minute so I had him let me out at the front door."

Ayanna smiled at the woman's enthusiasm. "You must have heard about our wonderful menu. Tyrell is a master chef."

"Actually I was in a hurry to meet you," she said. "Tanner said you were beautiful and he was right as usual."

Ayanna tensed as the double mahogany doors in front of her

opened again. Tanner stood poised in the doorway. Unable to conceal her longing, her gaze clung to him. Raine and two men stepped around him. Together the family resemblance was unmistakable. No one had to tell Ayanna the younger man was his brother Adrian and the other man an older version of Tanner, his father.

Noah moved past her to block Tanner. "You're not welcome here."

"I have reservations." Tanner pulled a sheet of paper from his pocket. "My faxed confirmation."

Noah cut a sharp glance at the paper. "The name says Dawson."

"My mother's maiden name," Tanner answered, folding the paper and returning it to the inside of his dove gray tailored jacket. "We're ready to be seated."

"I don't give a—"

"Noah," Ayanna interrupted and grabbed five menus. "I'll seat them. This way." Every step shredded her heart a little bit more. The Rafferty Grand's grand opening was tomorrow night. His family must have come to town to celebrate Tanner's and Raine's success . . . and rub it in Ayanna's face. She hadn't thought he would be that cruel.

"Your table," she said, seating them, then handing them each a menu. "Enjoy your meal."

She started to leave, but Tanner caught her hand. A flash of awareness caused her body to tremble. He closed her fingers around a large brown envelope.

"I love you," he whispered.

Tears threatening to spill, she hurried away, the envelope clutched in her hand. She didn't stop until she was alone in the hallway by the ladies' room. Or so she thought.

"What did he give you?" Noah demanded, taking the envelope and opening it. "If he's trying to harass you I'm going to ram this—" He held the papers out to her. "Read them, Ayanna."

She started to shake her head, but Noah stuck them in front of her face. Her eyes widened as she began to read. The papers were deeds to Raine's property and the one directly behind them. He hadn't lied. "He does love me," she whispered, finally taking the legal papers.

"Looks like it," Noah said with a wide grin. "Leo's has struck again. This time the champagne is on me."

Ayanna ran back into the restaurant and straight into Tanner's arms. "Tanner!" she cried. "Thank you! Leo's will never be vulnerable again. Somehow I'll pay you back."

He stared down into her face. "Since you're going to marry me, it's all in the family."

Her heart threatened to beat out of her chest. "You want to marry me?"

"I *am* going to marry you. However, anytime you're ready to put me out of my misery and tell me you love me too, I'd be grateful."

She grinned up at him. "Who wouldn't love a renegade?" Then she sobered and looked at Raine. "On the other hand, I'm not so sure about you. But I'd like for us to at least try to be friends."

Raine extended her slender hand. "I hope so. Tanner made me an offer I couldn't refuse . . . management of The Ming Room and first dibs on the restaurants in his future hotels."

"Did you take it?" Ayanna asked, not moving to take Raine's hand. The deal would mean a small fortune, but it was nothing less than bribery.

Raine held Ayanna's gaze. "No. Family will always mean more than money. Besides, I make my own way or not at all. I miscalculated with Leo's and I always admit my mistakes."

Ayanna ignored the hand and hugged Raine. "I think I'm going to like you." Straightening, she looked up at Tanner. "I've been miserable without you. I love you more than words can say." Her arms went around his neck. "How soon can we get married?"

"How about tonight?" he asked, kissing her deeply.

"Tanner, you have to have a large wedding," his mother protested. "The family would be outraged."

Tanner's father affectionately patted his wife of forty years on her hand. "I have a feeling they aren't listening."

Raine looked amused; Adrian, a die-hard bachelor, stunned.

Patrons began applauding. Tyrell popped the cork on the first bottle of champagne and Tyrone opened the second while Noah called Ayanna's mother.

Sheri and Ayanna's mother arrived minutes apart. Both were crying. Both voiced their objections to a quick wedding. Tanner just smiled. He had no intention of sleeping another night without Ayanna.

Two hours later the Gulf Stream raced down the runway, then banked left, heading for Las Vegas. Another jet raced after it.

Ayanna smiled at Tanner in the bedroom of the aircraft. "I could have told both our mothers that they wouldn't win against a renegade."

"Not when it's this important." He brushed his hand across her cheek. "After Raine realized I was serious about fighting her over Leo's, she knew I loved you and sold her property to me. Then I had to obtain the lot behind Leo's, find a minister, who, by the way, is waiting at the suite at the Mandalay to marry us. The reception was the easiest part. Pointe was delighted to prepare your favorite foods.

"We'll fly back after the ceremony and go straight to The Rafferty Grand. I've given up the condo and moved us into my suite at the hotel. You have a complete wardrobe with appropriate jewelry waiting for you for the month-long grand opening celebrations."

She stared at the flawless five-karat diamond on the third finger of her left hand. She'd cried buckets when he'd given it to her in the limo ride to the airport. He said he wanted them to be alone when he gave it to her so they'd remember the moment always. Who would have thought a renegade could be sentimental?

"What if I had said no?"

He pulled her fiercely into his arms. "I would have found a way to change your mind. You're going to be Mrs. Tanner Rafferty and, in less than eighteen hours, we'll greet the guests at our hotel."

She didn't think she'd ever get used to hearing that he was hers, and she his. "Since you have the wedding party in the plane following ours, perhaps we should make the most of this time," she told him.

He grinned, following her down onto the bed. "My thoughts exactly."

"The best storyteller of the century. From the first page to the last, I fell in love with Francis Ray."

—Mary B. Morrison, *New York Times* bestselling author of *Unconditionally Single,* on *And Mistress Makes Three*

Don't miss these other Francis Ray titles:

I Know Who Holds Tomorrow
Somebody's Knocking at My Door
Trouble Don't Last Always
Like the First Time
Any Rich Man Will Do
In Another Man's Bed
Not Even If You Begged
And Mistress Makes Three

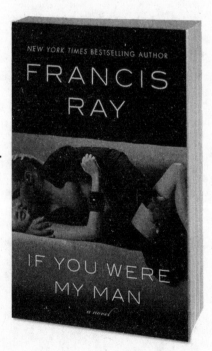

"Another solid gold hit!"

—*Romantic Times* on *Break Every Rule*

**Don't miss
these other
Francis Ray titles:**

Someone to Love Me
Until There Was You
You and No Other
Dreaming of You
Irresistible You
Only You
The Way You Love Me
Nobody But You
One Night With You
It Had to Be You
Forever Yours
Only Hers
Heart of the Falcon

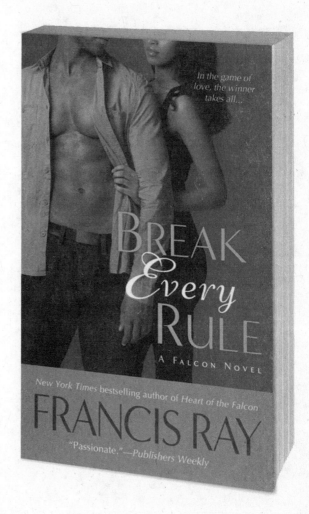

In the game of
love, the winner
takes all...

BREAK
Every
RULE

A FALCON NOVEL

New York Times bestselling author of *Heart of the Falcon*

FRANCIS RAY

"Passionate." —*Publishers Weekly*

St. Martin's Paperbacks